Wings
Against the Sky

Wings
Against the Sky

by Richard Hough

WILLIAM MORROW AND COMPANY, INC.
New York   1979

Library of Congress Cataloging in Publication Data

Hough, Richard Alexander, 1922-
  Wings against the sky.

  1. World War, 1939-1945—Fiction.   I. Title.
PZ4.H8379Wi   1979   [PR6058.O82]   823'.9'14   79-16570
ISBN 0-688-03554-X

Book Design by Michael Mauceri

Printed in the United States of America.

First U.S. Edition

1   2   3   4   5   6   7   8   9   10

Wings
Against the Sky

1

The Heinkel emerged from the cloud like a dark ghost of a machine against the slate gray of the sea, diving faster than Keith had ever seen a bomber fly. Mike was closer than he was and Keith saw him turn sharply and put down his nose in pursuit. The American boy got in one short burst at extreme range, cordite smoke streaming from his wings. The Heinkel pulled up again with remarkable agility, jinking and sliding evasively before disappearing into the cloud.

Contact! This was the moment of reckoning toward which his professional life had been directed for nearly two years, and Keith was not going to allow himself to be robbed when chance had wonderfully thrown this opportunity to him, especially on this of all days.

The speed and maneuverability of the German bomber took him by surprise. He had been warned of this, but like all his contemporaries who had conducted defense exercises against Heyfords, the bomber was synonymous with a plodding turkey of a target in stately formation, ripe for the plucking.

Mike's voice crackled, "He'll hit the deck when he comes out. You take starboard, I'll take port. O.K.?"

The cloud was scattered, low and diffuse, more like mist: North Sea mist, which had confused seamen since the beginning of time and was proving even more hazardous to airmen of the twentieth century. This cloud was too small to hold the German for more than a few seconds. Unless the pilot completed a blind 180-degree turn, one of the two Hurricane pilots was certain to spot him when he emerged.

The German held all the advantages of the hunted—the initiative and surprise, with the odds weighted progressively on his side the longer he could sustain the pursuit; while for the short-range Hurricanes, every mile from the coast and their base reduced their chances of victory.

Mike was right. The Heinkel emerged from the cloud in a steep dive, the pilot racing for the protection of the sea, and for more cloud ahead that promised concealment again. The bomber looked like one of the identification models that they had studied from every angle until their characteristics and configuration were etched into their memories for recall at the critical moment. Like now. Yet it remained difficult for Keith to believe that this was not still a Heinkel 111 of painted wood, swinging on its cotton, in the familiar warmth of the "Spy's" office back at Elgin; that this was of steel and alloy, crewed by four enemy airmen who would shortly be attempting to kill him with their 7.9-mm guns, and would probably succeed if he and Mike did not kill them first.

Mike was closing in for a classic quarter attack from the port side. He had evidently "pulled the plug" for overboost because his exhausts were streaming black smoke. Keith, closing in from the starboard quarter, decided to hold this ultimate power for later in case they were involved in a stern chase. Three minutes were all you were advised to give the Merlin engine or it could blow its gaskets.

The Heinkel was right down at wave-top height, making sighting awkward, and the pilot was kicking his rudder right —left—right—right again to confuse their deflection angle. As Keith closed in simultaneously with Mike, he remembered the instructor's warning about attacking at low level and how the swift crossing of the background over the sight tends to make for overdeflection. "And wait till there's nothing but bloody Hun in the sight before you press the button," the scarred old R.F.C. veteran had bellowed. "And watch that sodding temper of yours, Stewart. You've got to shoot cool."

Keith had already set the range bars for a Heinkel, and now as he closed in at over 300 m.p.h. in a 15-degree dive, he watched the bomber grow in size until it half filled, then three-quarters filled, the distance between the reflected white horizontal lines on his sight. He could see tracer from the upper gun arching up toward Mike, who was closer to the bomber than he was and coming in faster. Then the gunner, with his sliding transparent hood thrown back, swung the gun toward him. The tracers came up at him in a steady, white-flecked stream, tearing past his cockpit. Incredulity was his first reaction. The man was trying to *kill* him! The effrontery. Then the hot flush of anger which he promptly doused. Ordering himself firmly to ignore the fire, Keith began to pull the dot steadily through the angled silhouette of the Heinkel, his thumb on the button on his spade grip.

Mike was already making hits. Keith could see tracers hitting the port wing root and the wing of the Heinkel, and out of the corner of his eye he saw the Hurricane, still trailing black smoke, pulling up into a steep, left climbing turn for another pass.

There was no holding back now. This was it, the moment about which so many of his anxieties had been concerned for so long. The moment of killing. How many times had he asked himself, "When you've got him in your sights, that anonymous figure called an enemy, will you be able to do it?"

And now, hardly realizing what was happening, his reflexes worked with the swift efficiency of a machine-gun bolt mechanism. He allowed 30 degrees and pressed hard with his thumb. At once his Hurricane shivered under the recoil of eight Brownings, each firing 1,100 rounds a minute, and acrid cordite fumes filtered into the cockpit. His attack was more astern than Mike's, and knowing his inadequacies as a shot, he forced himself in closer until the Heinkel's wing tips were halfway along the range bars and he could identify the silhouette of the gunner still pumping out a stream of bullets at him. They were making strikes, too, these shots, which was more than he was doing. He forced himself to relax, ceased fire for a fraction of a second, and then gave a long five-second burst from no more than 5 degrees, aiming steadily at the starboard engine.

This time even he could not fail. Tracers tore into the housing and Keith pulled up sharply as white smoke and lumps of metal raced across the sky toward him like missiles. When he looked down from five hundred feet above the bomber, the smoke had increased a hundredfold in volume and had turned black. Mike was going in from dead astern this time, and it was clear that he was having to throttle back to match the crippled Heinkel's reduced speed. There was no return fire from the gunner, and spasmodic puffs of white smoke were bursting from the port engine.

Keith pushed forward his stick for a stern attack from above. He was conscious for the first time of the sweat pouring down his face and trickling under his mask. He could see the holes in the leading edge of his port wing where the gunner had hit him, but the fighting efficiency of his machine seemed unimpaired.

From above, Keith had little shooting time. He opened fire at three hundred and fifty yards, aiming for the machine's cabin, and pulled back when he saw the spray of his fire striking the sea just ahead of the Heinkel. He must have hit the pilot, for the bomber suddenly reared up onto its tail. When he had pulled around in a steep turn, he saw the Heinkel, traveling very slowly but straight and level, as if another crew member had grabbed the controls. The starboard engine was blazing, and the port engine's propeller ceased to rotate as Keith closed in alongside. Mike was on the starboard side now, formating on the German like Keith, waiting for the end.

Mike called up on the R/T, mimicking what he called "the best" R.A.F. accent, something the American boy did only when drunk or excited. "I say, ol' boy, wizard prang. Dem good shootin', Pilot Officer Stewart."

Keith was more formal. His voice shaking, he transmitted, "Hullo Red Two, I'm going aloft to give a fix. They'll be going in in a minute and the navy can send out a Walrus for prisoners."

Surely they had not killed them all! And in a moment he knew that at least one of the crew was still alive because the crippled machine prepared to land on the sea. Whoever was flying her did well, holding the nose up after the first touch and stalling onto the water into wind and along the line of the swell. The fuselage and tail plane stuck out of the water for a full thirty seconds. Just before a drift of cloud obscured the scene below, Keith saw the yellow splash of an inflatable dinghy. Two men climbed into it.

"Hullo, Shepherd," called up Keith. "Hullo, Shepherd, Sandbag Red One calling. Are you receiving me?" On the crackling confirmation, Keith continued, "Bandit in sea with survivors. Transmitting for fix. Ten, nine, eight. . . . Course for base, please. Over."

Mike came up alongside, tucking in his port wing close. He had thrown back his hood and taken off his helmet and goggles like a warrior discarding his armor and helmet after combat. His brown hair was blowing back in the slipstream. He made a mock gesture of wiping sweat from his forehead and gave the thumbs-up sign. Like all fighter squadrons, 140 had been strictly instructed to avoid unnecessary R/T chatter, as it could block the air for others and give useful information to the enemy.

In ten minutes they could see Kinnaird's Head and they flashed the letter of the day as they flew over the coast, in order to reassure any trigger-happy gunners who might be crazy enough to think single-engined German fighters could get this far north. They scudded low over the fields and patches of woods, grazing the Morayshire coast with its crinkled edging of white breakers. The familiar landscape and the reassurance of being close to base served to settle Keith's conscience, and also to remind him of the unique and fortunate nature of the fight.

Between them they had accounted for the squadron's first success in the war that had staggered on uneventfully for more than two months. What incredible luck that they had both been airborne on an exercise when the "Bandit" call had come over the R/T, followed by the course to steer! So many times the northern based squadrons had scrambled to chase enemy reconnaissance bombers from the Forth, Cromarty and Scapa Flow without making a sighting. And it had fallen to him, Keith Stewart, a comparatively new member of the squadron, and his friend Mike Browning, to make the first-ever kill. An Anglo-American kill. And, most incredible of all, on Keith's twenty-first birthday, itself the anniversary of the end of the Great War, November 11.

They celebrated by an illegal beat up and slow roll. Mike brought his Hurricane in close again, and with Keith as leader they lost height until they were skimming the tree-tops and rising and falling with the contours of the ground. They lifted to avoid the station's twin radio towers, and dipped down again so that, at the perimeter of Elgin they were "daisy-dusting." The two machines streaked across the airfield at 250 m.p.h. Keith caught a glimpse out of the corner of his eye of some fitters at the B Flight dispersal working on a Hurricane's engine, and appearing as if frozen on their stepladder, and of a taxiing Swordfish from the Fleet Air Arm squadron.

Then he lifted off, banking to the left, while Mike broke away to the right. At a thousand feet Keith put his control column over and forward and eased his machine into a climbing slow roll. As he came out at fifteen hundred feet he glanced to the right and saw to his satisfaction that Mike was just completing his roll and was at the same height. "That must have looked good," he said to himself. But at almost the same moment, Mike's voice crackled out:

"I guess I've had my engine, Red One."

Keith saw that the Hurricane was already losing height. "Try switching tanks."

"No, I'm not out of gas. I guess I picked up a Hun bullet. The engine's been running hot." His voice sounded calm, and had that merry ring in it which even a T.R.9 set could not disguise. A belly landing would be no more than a challenge—almost a welcome adventure—to the American boy.

"Pump your flaps down, then," said Keith.

"Aw, go tell your grandmother to suck eggs."

Keith could see that Mike's flaps were already 15 degrees down and were rapidly extending to their full 80 degrees. The Hurricane was down to five hundred feet and there was no chance of getting back to Elgin.

Mike chanted the opening line of a current song: "Wish me luck as you wave me good-bye." And that was all he had time for. Keith circled slowly, watching his gliding approach to a field with some cows grazing in it. The approach was not well timed, and Keith guessed that Mike's judgment was disturbed by the need to avoid the animals. He was almost halfway across before he touched down on his belly, sending up a stream of turf and soil. He had kept himself on an even keel so that neither wing touched, but he was doing over 70 m.p.h. when he hit and Keith was amazed at how far the bucking Hurricane ran. He was going to overrun the field, that was certain.

It looked like an innocent enough hedge, and Keith imagined the Hurricane would slice through it without too much trouble. But it did not work out like that. To Keith's horror the nose dug in to a deep concealed ditch, and at once the machine flipped over onto its back, lying with the roundels of the wing undersides and the big oil cooler scoop exposed. All three propeller blades had been pushed back and the tail unit was crushed beyond recognition. Worst of all there was no sign of life from the wreckage.

Keith transmitted, "Hullo Shepherd, Sandbag Red One here. Red Two has force-landed three miles due west of base. The pilot is trapped. Get a crash crew and ambulance here quick. I am circling the spot. Over."

Just to go around like this, doing nothing for his friend, was almost more than Keith could bear. At any second the Hurricane could go up in flames, or Mike might be suffocated or be losing a fatal amount of blood or . . .

The idea of landing wheels up in the same field crossed Keith's mind in his desperation, but the cool voice of the controller put an end to such a lunatic idea.

"Sandbag Red One. Return to base and pancake. We will locate Red Two. Over."

Keith took one last look at the flattened Hurricane. He was relieved to see two figures running across the field toward it. But he could not help noticing the symbolic shape of the cross the machine made against the torn grass. He headed back to Elgin. "Message received and understood," he transmitted, and, sick at heart, began the routine of landing preparation.

It was just over two years since Keith and Mike had first met. They were on what was now enemy soil, the German Black Forest, in a town called Hornberg. The Nazi Party had been in control of Germany for four years, but in spite of all the warnings both boys had heard before setting out they had seen little evidence of tyranny or hardship. Plenty of flags, plenty of uniforms, but the men looked fit and vigorous, the girls blond, nubile and happy. The villages were trim and prosperous, the towns clean and efficient. There was an air of resolution everywhere and the people walked fast, whether hiking over the hills as they were now doing, or merely going about their business.

Keith's party consisted of Eileen, Tom Mathers and Moira Singleton, all from Market Rising, all eighteen or nineteen, and all old friends. It was generally acceted that Tom and Moira would eventually marry, and that Eileen and Keith would not, being sort of half-brother and sister.

They had walked seventeen miles, up and down, that day,

and had come to drink beer and have supper before returning to the hotel for the night. The restaurant was on the main road running through the village, with a balcony extending to the pavement, and Keith felt a sense of complete contentment as he stretched out his aching legs and took a long draft of the good beer.

The others looked happy, too, he thought. Tom, small and tough and wiry, with fine hands fit for a surgeon, which was just what he was determined to be—he was going to be a first-year student at the Middlesex hospital in London in three weeks' time. He looked good for another seventeen miles as he bent, laughing, toward Moira, teasing her about the froth on her upper lip.

Moira was responding as she always did, good-naturedly but without any sharp crackle of repartee. That was not her way. Her role was that of the foil. Not the butt. Tom would not have allowed that. Keith liked the way he respected her straight simplicity and always kept his teasing within the bounds of kindness. It would have been easy to have made her look silly, but it would also have been stupid as well as unkind because her common sense was pricelessly valuable to the mercurial Tom. Moira's steadiness counterbalanced his high-strung unevenness as her tall buxomness also counterbalanced his stringy limbs and torso. In some ways they made a singular pair walking side by side, Moira three inches taller, striding with stately purpose, Tom doing seven steps to her five, gesticulating as he talked to her, sometimes raising his volume to include Eileen and Keith in his audience.

Four young men came onto the balcony. They wore leather shorts and check shirts, but even before he heard their voices, Keith singled them out as non-German, self-conscious in their new holiday clothes. After ordering four beers in a mellow twangy accent that Keith later learned was typical New England, they swung their eyes in turn toward Keith's party, and, inevitably, ended up looking with transparent admiration at Eileen.

The beers came in great mugs, to distract them momentarily, then Mike turned back and, addressing Keith in an execrable accent, asked, "Machen Sie einen Wanderlaub?"

Keith replied smartly, "Nein, wir sind Juden, die grade einen Konzentrationslager entkommen sind!"

Mike's eyes darted back to Eileen, who was starting to giggle. "Like hell you're German Jews on the run. You're Britishers, aren't you? On the walk, same as us. Mind if we join you?"

Eileen put on her cockney voice. "Well, I don't know, really. You *are* saucy," and giggled again.

The four Americans drew up their chairs, slipping them alternately between Keith's party, Mike between Eileen and Keith. They weren't brash about it, just natural and friendly and apparently eager to learn about them—their hometown, their future careers, what they thought of Germany.

Tom remained moody and reserved for a while. But one of the American boys worked on him with easy charm until he mellowed and joined in the general conversation, so that it seemed quite natural for them all to go inside and settle down for dinner at one table together when darkness fell.

Mike contrived to sit next to Eileen again, and Keith posted himself on her other side, watching protectively and listening for any sign of what, he had learned from the movies, Americans called freshness. Moira seemed to be having the time of her life with two more of the American boys, both very good looking, who sat on either side of her, while Tom had discovered that the other American was studying medicine and was deeply involved in comparing English and American practice.

At one point, as they were all busily tearing off the skin of some livid red, cold sausage, Keith heard Mike say, "Is he your guardian or something?"

Eileen said, "Don't be stupid, he's my brother. More or less."

"How more, and how less?" Mike asked, and Keith turned to intervene.

"Don't spoil a nice party," he said to the American, firmly. "Eileen and I have a special relationship—that'll do for now." Eileen put in quickly, "Where are you heading for tomorrow?"

Mike said, "O.K., Keith—no offense. We hope to make it to Schramberg tomorrow. But it's a long haul so we'll probably collapse on the way."

"We might see you on the way," said Keith. "That's our destination, too."

Eileen said quickly, "That would be nice," and Mike added, "Thank you, ma'am," with a slight bow.

Mike had ordered some wine to go with the dinner and they were all raising their glasses to toast one another when the double doors of the restaurant were thrown back violently and a party of half a dozen officers strode in and made straight for the bar behind their table. At once conversation became almost impossible. The young men were drunk and noisily aggressive, pretending to spar with one another and then turning to the restaurant as if provoking one of the diners to get up and complain. With their third beer they began singing, loudly and off key, and even started on the Horst Wessel song, linking arms as if in a paroxysm of patriotism.

Keith and Mike looked at one another, shrugging their shoulders. It was clear that a complaint to the management would have no effect and might make matters worse. Mike raised his arms as if they were wings, tilting them up and down, to indicate that they were pilots. This was proved by the Luftwaffe-style eagle and swastika above the right breast pocket on their blue tunics, and the pilot's badge low down and just above the wide leather belt.

After a while, they seemed to tire of the lack of response from the diners, and after clicking the heels of their shining boots to one another in mock farewell, they replaced their high flat-topped hats and marched out.

"Humph!" exclaimed Mike. "I hope they grow up before they go to war—for their sake."

Tom was inclined to excuse them, waving a white hand toward the swinging double doors. "Just letting off steam. The Greeks, the Roman legionaries, Cromwell's new army, Napoleon's Grand Army—they all got drunk and made a lot of noise whenever they could. And worse than that." He addressed Mike. "I bet Washington's army was swimming in alcohol the night before our little setback at Lexington."

Mike laughed, and Keith saw Eileen look at him and laugh too. Before the evening was out it had been generally agreed that they might meet up and hike together for part of the way to their next destination.

It was raining the next morning and the English party at the hotel did not bother to get up until the sun broke through. Keith and Tom woke the girls at eight-thirty and by nine o'clock they were at the same restaurant they had been at the evening before, eating hot rolls and creamy butter and the inevitable sausage, with outsize mugs of coffee. There was no sign of the Americans until later in the morning, after they had tramped for two hours uphill through the forest.

They rounded a corner, and there they were, in their very brief leather shorts and check shirts. They were stretched out on a pile of pine logs, all looking very bronzed, fit and cheerful, and sporting Tyrolean hats.

Mike got up to meet them. Keith saw that the American was quite short, no more than five feet seven or eight. He walked with a bouncy step, as if equipped with springs in his heels to emphasize his natural ebullience and eagerness to move ahead. His brown eyes were set wide apart, and Keith was amused to note the permanent anxiety lines on his forehead, which completely contradicted his transparently carefree manner.

He addressed himself three-fifths to Eileen and two-fifths to Keith. "Good morning," he greeted them in his New England accent, which Keith found attractive. "Isn't this a swell coincidence? Shall we walk together for a while? That is, if we can keep up with you English."

Eileen laughed. "That won't be difficult. Especially as I'm going to take a rest. This rucksack weighs a million tons in this damp heat."

"You must let me carry it when we get going again."

Eileen flopped to the ground with a sigh of relief, but said firmly, "Oh, no, that's breaking all the hiking rules. Anyway, think how I'd feel if we met some of those great muscular fräuleins with their hundred-pound packs."

One of the other Americans produced a bottle of fruit juice which he passed around, and after a few more minutes they arose together and began walking in earnest. They had a long climb ahead to reach their halfway point at Fohrenbühl, 2,500 feet up, where they had been told they would get wonderful views over the forest and would be able to see the Vosges in the far distance if the weather was clear.

The party arranged themselves spontaneously in loose formation with two of the Americans, called Andy and Jo, in the lead, then Tom and Moira and the American medical student, the two young men talking continuously, and finally Eileen and Mike and Keith. They all walked steadily and at about the same speed, and the arrangement was congenial to everyone throughout the rest of the morning.

In the last threesome, Mike and Keith talked of their school days, and their plans for a career, such as they were. Mike had been to St. Bernard's in New York City as a day boy, and then to Andover, which Keith gathered was an American private school in Massachusetts, like Harrow or Marlborough in England, with Georgian-style buildings set among ancient elms and well-kept playing fields. Mike had been at Bartlett Hall. His home background was obviously prosperous and privileged, with a house on Forty-fourth Street in Manhattan and a big estate on Long Island.

"Well, no, not like East Egg," Mike had protested when Keith had likened it to Gatsby's place in Scott Fitzgerald's novel. "But comfortable O.K. Yeah, a gardener or two. But sailing in the Sound. Now that's what I really enjoy. You must come and stay one day, Keith. And bring Eileen. What do you say, Eileen?"

"Very kind of you," she replied. "But I'll have to finish with Paris first. Beastly old Paris."

"But Paris is lovely."

"Not in a finishing school it isn't," Eileen said grimly. "A weekly tour of the Louvre in parties of six, no more, no less. And *that's* the fun part."

Mike said he was sorry about that. "I don't know what 'finishing' means. But if they mean polishing you up, they must be crazy. I like you as you are."

After being stalled off the previous evening, Mike was tactful enough to avoid the subject of Keith's relationship with Eileen. But it was obvious that there would be a degree of constraint between them until it was explained, and Eileen proceeded to do so when the moment seemed right.

"The thing is, Keith lives with us but isn't related at all," she began.

"I'm an orphan," Keith put in, and even as he spoke the words lightly in this glorious setting of Schonach-Tal and with the fresh scent of pine in the early autumn air, and after all these years, his mind raced back in an uncontrollable rush to that afternoon on February 21, 1931, when Sir Richard Barrett had knocked on the lodge's front door and had come in, heavy with grief and embarrassment, and told Keith that his parents were dead. They had sat side by side on the rather hard sofa, and Sir Richard had not looked at him as he spoke. Later he had said, "Would you like Eileen to come down and talk to you?" and Keith had said stiffly, "No, thank you very much. I would like to think about it by myself."

For an hour, on that cold February afternoon, he had sat quite still, saying over and over again, "I am an orphan. Keith Stewart is an orphan. I am . . ." Then he had gone out for a walk over the estate, avoiding gamekeepers and gardeners alike, concentrating his mind on small details, like the pattern of last summer's oak leaves stuck by the frost to a twig, and the ever-changing pattern of mixed snow and frost flakes on the scuffed ice of his shoes.

Now, six years and seven months later, he said to this friendly, impish but now sympathetically listening American, "It sounds rather improbable, but they were killed at a railway grade crossing. It was a small self-operated one on a track near Market Rising. The engine of the old Clyno car we had stalled in the middle of the track. My father tried to push it clear, but for some reason my mother remained in her seat. The 2:37 London train hit them. So I was an orphan at twelve. There were only unmarried aunts on my mother's side, and an eccentric bachelor uncle on my father s side. Eileen's father took me on, so to speak, which was kind of him as my father was only his estate manager and not very grand or anything. I think he felt responsible as my father was his platoon sergeant at the Front so they fought together. And I was good company for Eileen. She hasn't got any brothers or sisters, either."

"So you grew up together? That's what you meant by 'special relationship.' "

Eileen said, in an aside to Keith, "Will you shut up about grandness," and then turned to Mike. "We're practically twins. At least, he's a week younger than me. And I never let him forget it, do I?"

"Bossy," said Keith, trying to take her rebuke lightly. "Orders me about."

It was rubbish, of course. Although Eileen had gone to Wycombe Abbey for two-thirds of every year, while Keith remained, as he wished to, at Market Rising Grammar School, they had been together even more after the death of the Stewarts, for three more years as equals with similar interests, and after that still as close friends, but with Keith more in the role of older and protective brother. The lovelier she had become—fair like himself but with a touch of russet, leggy then statuesque, fresh coloring with just a scattering of freckles, and eyes the color of the lily leaves on the lake behind Rising Hall—the more alert Keith had become to his responsibilities as escort. The Barretts might, and did, have high standards for any suitor of Eileen, but they were mere pygmy by contrast with the unattainably stratospheric standards Keith had secretly laid down for her.

None of the three spoke for a minute, and they could hear Tom, a few paces ahead, saying, "But I think we ought to get down to practical medicine right away. Theory soon goes sour without *seeing* . . ."

Mike called out, "Are you two still dissecting corpses? What about Moira's appetite?"

Moira turned her happy round face to Mike. "It's healthy," she said.

"I think this is a good place to eat," Mike said. "Hey, Andy, Jo, we're going to eat. Bring out that bottle of wine."

They were at the top of the Fohrenbühl. The sun was at its meridian, and unusually hot for September. The views over the rolling forest, with the peak of the Mooswaldkopf above them and countless hills fading into the distance, made a magnificent background for a picnic.

Eileen lay flat on her back, her head on her rucksack, the top buttons of her blouse undone, showing she was as sunburned as the Americans. She was wearing shorts almost as brief as theirs, too, in rebellion against the formal standards of her finishing school in Paris.

"I think we ought to go on doing this forever," she said dreamily. "Eight of us, I mean. Very nice for Moira and me. Three of you for each of us. Just around and around and backward and forward across the Black Forest. Wine, sausage, cream, hot rolls. Then work them all off at twenty miles a day, talking philosophically or wittily, perhaps some dancing in the evening." She opened her eyes and turned to Mike. "Do you like dancing?"

"Yeah, so long as it's Cole Porter. I could dance all night to Cole Porter with you . . ."—the pause was hardly discernible—". . . and Moira."

Jo had the wine, two bottles of it, richly fruity, slightly

sweet, slightly bubbly Johannisberg wine, which they poured into their tin mugs. "Not the right glasses," the American commented. "But I guess it'll taste the same."

They were drowsily eating cheese when the bombers came. There was a roar, an assault on their ears, a rush of air like the first blast of a typhoon, and the dark shapes tore through the sky two hundred feet above them, sending the pine tops threshing. There were three, in tight V formation, and as they dipped down following the contour of the hill, three more followed, even lower, the undersurface of their wings deep blue against the blue sky, the black crosses on their fuselages and the swastika black on a white circle on their tail fins, all clearly visible. They could also see, sinister and threatening, the head and shoulders of a dark prone figure in the transparent nose of each bomber, a machine-gun barrel projecting forward like an insect's proboscis.

When the sound had faded to a distant deep hum, Mike said, "The shape of things to come."

"Don't be so depressing," Moira said sharply. "They're only practicing."

"That's what I mean."

Jo held up a half-empty bottle inquiringly. "With hang-overs like those pilots must have, they'll soon hit something. Anyone know what they were?"

"Heinkels," said Keith. "111's. They used them at Guernica last April. They can do nearly 300 m.p.h., too."

"Are you sure?" Mike asked.

Eileen said firmly, "Yes, he is. He knows as much about airplanes as your Charles Lindbergh."

They all enjoyed the remainder of the day and they reached Schramberg in time for supper. They talked hard most of the way, the sun shone, the scenery was magnificent. But the magic of the evening before, and of the morning, had slipped away as irrevocably as the bombers across the pines of the Black Forest.

2

Keith fired, swung the gun to the right and fired again. Even as he squeezed the trigger, he knew he had missed both birds. Tense and overanxious again, blast it! Was the reason guilt for killing defenseless game, or just plain anger because he was no good?

Almost at once two more shots rang out, then two more. Mike had waited until the partridges were almost directly overhead. Out of the corner of his eye, Keith saw the American with his weight nicely balanced on his right foot leaning far back and firing at the birds just before losing sight of them. They fell almost at his feet, the interval between the thuds as they struck the ground equal to the time lapse between the shots. Sheila brought them to Mike in turn, tail wagging as a hint for praise.

"A bad day for England," Barrett called out from his point nearer to the wood. So far their mixed bag comprised three hares, two shot by Mike, a brace of wild pheasant, and a woodcock, Keith's only success.

Mike said, "Typical British hospitality. You give me the best gun and all the best chances."

They stood in a group reloading. Mike was used to a

pump gun in the States but was picking up British practice with characteristic speed and efficiency. They had gone out on a rough shoot after breakfast, Keith whistling up Sheila, who had been a week without sport and was eager for the guns. Unlike Keith, she always was. They filled one pocket with grain, the other with cartridges, Barrett warning the guest that the stock was poor this winter.

"This is the most beautiful gun I've ever used, sir," Mike said, patting the lockplate of the Churchill sidelock shotgun which Barrett had lent him. "It fits me perfectly."

"That's not what Churchill would say," Barrett said with a laugh. "He'd say that it's right only for the man it was made for. But you're doing all right with it. As for you, young man," he said, turning to Keith but speaking affectionately, "you're a ruddy disgrace."

Barrett was a tall, heavily built man with thick gray hair, concealed now by a deerstalker, a gray moustache and the same startlingly green eyes as his daughter. In his shooting jacket and breeches, with his gun slung under his arm, he looked every inch the English country gentleman enjoying himself on his own shoot on a gray December day.

Keith said, "I know, sir. I'm never much good. But I'm worse than ever this year. The trouble is that they say you should only shoot partridge when you can see their eyes. But whenever we put up a covey like that, there are so many eyes I can't make up my mind in time which ones to choose."

"Just one—one only," said Barrett, affecting a world-weary voice. "Forget the rest. I don't think you *want* to hit them." He turned to Mike. "Where did you learn to shoot like that?"

"Back home, sir, on Long Island. And up in the Adirondacks. Pop used to take us all up there two or three times during the fall. In the country in America we sort of grow up with the gun. We're a gun-totin' race, sir. Every guy is his own Davy Crockett."

Barrett laughed and led them off, limping as always from the bullet that had smashed his thigh on the first day of the

Somme twenty-one years earlier. "We'll try walking up on Long Merton. It usually yields a few brace," he said. "Then it's back for lunch."

Rising Hall was a big Jacobean house, designed by Inigo Jones. It was a mile outside Market Rising on a south-facing slope overlooking the gently undulating Leicestershire countryside, surrounded on three sides by a formal garden and behind by a walled kitchen garden. Mike, on seeing it for the first time, had commented that it was just how he imagined English country gentlemen lived, and that it was always nice to see your dreams coming true. "I'm not apologizing for our place on Long Island," he said. "But at seventy years old it's regarded as historic. And Rising Hall?" He looked at Keith interrogatively.

"Rising three fifty I suppose," Keith had cracked back. "Before that some Norman baron built a castle on the site. Queen Elizabeth slept in it, of course."

Before separating at Frankfurt railway station, Keith and Eileen had offered all four Americans a standing invitation to Rising Hall if they should ever be in England. But three had gone back on board the *Berlin* to their studies in America. Only Mike had continued his restless wandering about Europe, drifting down through Austria and Italy, staying in Rome with the American ambassador, a friend of his father, two weeks in Venice with the ambassador's son, a week in Florence, and then over the frontier into the south of France. From Marseilles he had bought a passage in a Spanish Republican coaster which was taking arms to Barcelona, and by means which only nerve, initiative, influence and hard cash could achieve, he had gotten up to the fighting front and driven an ambulance for three weeks before he had had enough of the squalor and taken another ship to Gibraltar.

On December 15 he had telephoned Rising Hall from Southampton. "Tell me straight now, do you want me for Christmas or not?" he had asked Keith.

"Yes, only one condition."

"O.K., I'll have a bath first. I need one."

"No, we've got one of those. Just take it easy with Eileen."
Mike had responded quickly. "Sure. I behaved myself in
Germany, didn't I? She's only a kid. I know that. I've got
sisters, too. And morals. See you tomorrow."

Eileen's response to the news was just as Keith had expected. She was reading a magazine in the drawing room,
wrapped up in her favorite armchair. "Oh, yes," she said
without looking up.

"You don't mind?"

She went on reading for a moment. "No, why should I?
He's your friend."

Five minutes later she got up, stretched, called Sheila for
"walkies" and went out through the double glass doors onto
the terrace. "Who does she think *she's* deceiving!" Keith
asked himself, noting the flush in her cheeks that was not
caused by the blazing log fire. He liked to see her happy
with Mike, and he had every confidence that Mike would be
sensible. His adoptive father would call him "a straight
young man," and he would be right.

Mike arrived from the station with the rucksack on his
back the next afternoon. Keith saw him coming up the long
drive, walking with his characteristic slightly springy gait
which got him along surprisingly fast for his height. He
looked even harder and fitter than he had in the Black
Forest. Keith's stepmother was pruning some hybrid tea
roses in a circular bed near the fountain, and he saw Mike
deviate toward her, taking off his Tyrolean hat and greeting
her unself-consciously. Keith waited at the window long
enough to see them laughing at some joke, then he ran to
the front door to meet him.

That was two days ago. Since then they had ridden and
shot and Mike had gone out hunting with Eileen in kit borrowed from one of the gamekeepers. They had driven into
Leicester to buy Christmas presents and Keith had taken
him fishing in the lake on the far side of the estate.

At meals they listened to Mike's adventures, Eileen and
her mother exclaiming at the sufferings of the Spanish

people, the civilians as much as the fighting men. He described what it was like to be bombed in Barcelona and machine-gunned by pilots of the Condor Legion when driving his ambulance. He was as lyrical about the paintings in the Accademia in Venice as he was graphic about an advance "over the top" by the Republican troops near Salamanca. He had obviously learned the art of economy in his accounts and anecdotes from his large and highly articulate family; and was, in turn, respectfully but never ingratiatingly interested in life at Rising Hall—its history, way of life and relationship with its environment.

After dinner on the day of the rough shoot, Barrett went off to see his head gamekeeper while Constance Barrett retired to the library to prepare her speech for the Christmas meeting of the Women's Institute, of which, inevitably, she was chairwoman. Eileen, Keith and Mike relaxed over coffee in the drawing room, encouraging Stokes to build up the log fire even higher. Eileen set up the self-changing phonograph for a continuous run of Beethoven's Fifth Symphony and Keith got out the chess. Mike stretched himself on the sofa with the morning paper.

"Well, this is the good life," he said with a sigh of satisfaction. Then after a pause to read an item, "For some of us, anyway. Listen to this, from Spain. Salamanca. 'After a series of hand-to-hand clashes, the defenders succeeded not only in isolating the Republican advanced troops but also in counterattacking and pushing forward their own line.' Poor devils! That was the front I was on a couple of weeks ago." He folded away the paper. "I wonder if they got little Pedro. He said he was seventeen but I swear he wasn't above fourteen. Wounded twice. The last time I saw him he was firing like crazy at a bunch of Franco's men as if his life depended on it. And so it did. He hit them, too."

Eileen came and sat beside him. She was dressed in a long red-and-black evening dress in silk jersey with the fullness drawn to the front—striking in itself as well as striking in contrast to the hiking shorts and shirt Mike would always associate with her. "Why don't you relax and listen to this nice music? You're the most restless, anxious person I've ever known."

"Hogwash!" Mike exclaimed. "I relax without anxiety every night. Eight solid hours. Never miss it. And I did relax and listen to nice music in London. All by myself."

"At the Queen's Hall?"

"No. I wouldn't dare to trespass in the Queen's Hall. The movies. Deanna Durbin. *A Hundred Men and a Girl*. What a voice, what a face, what a figure! Beethoven's O.K. for the educated. But for ignorant saps like me. . . . Hey, Eileen, give me the record of 'It's Raining Sunbeams' for Christmas. Be nice. 'I need no sign,'" he hummed, "'I need no chart. The weather bureau in my heart, Is saying it's raining sunbeams . . .'"

Keith had laid out the board and now pushed the table toward Mike. "Let's see who's the bigger ignorant sap."

They played in silence. Eileen watched them and turned over the records halfway through the symphony and changed the needle. Mike played a predictably impulsive game, almost checkmating Keith after only nine moves. Then he made a stupid mistake, Keith caught his queen, and it was all over ten minutes later.

"That's the story of my life. Frustration and defeat," said Mike. "Let's play gin rummy."

Constance Barrett came in later, her speech completed. There was a painting of her at twenty-one by de Laszlo above the fireplace, showing the same fair-touched-with-auburn hair that Eileen had and the same slim, tall figure. Middle age had squared her off and turned her from beautiful to handsome. She spoke rapidly, with a slight stutter.

"What dreadfully v-vulgar game is this?" she asked, surveying the cards. "I hope you're not corrupting my daughter, young American."

"She's beating me hollow, ma'am," Mike said, getting up and throwing down his cards in disgust.

At half past nine, Stokes brought in tea and laid out a

tray of whiskey and soda for the men. Barrett came in, complaining of the cold and predicting snow. In two days there was going to be a big shoot with seventy guns from all over the county and twenty people for the night. The night after there was a hunt ball at a place down the river, to which they were all invited. There was beagling the next morning for anyone who wanted the exercise, and of course the hunt would be meeting, for the third time that week. . . .

"And you call us Americans a go-ahead nation!" Mike exclaimed at this program. "Don't you ever stop?"

"It's only the great English aristocracy keeping boredom at bay," Keith said, and the irony had a very slight edge to it.

"Nonsense, boy," said Barrett. "Just the traditional occupations of country gentlemen. And it keeps the weight down," he added, patting his cummerbund, which justified his claim. "Makes us sleep well, too. I'm off to bed. You boys have another whiskey and soda. We ought to have bourbon for you. I'll speak to Stokes."

Keith got up to say good night and then stood with his back to the dying fire sipping the whiskey and soda. After a while, he turned to Mike, who had begun to read the newspaper again. "What's next on your program, Mike?" he asked.

"I don't know. I feel I've grown out of college before I've even begun. The theories of politics and economics seem pretty irrelevant after you've traveled around Europe awhile seeing the reality. Or never mind about traveling. Just take this newspaper. Italy. 'Fifteen Fascist Years. From War to War. The new Imperial outlook.' China. 'Japanese bomb Nanking for third successive day. And sink the American gunboat *Panay*.' It's not raining sunbeams out there. Czechoslovakia. 'She will in no circumstances adopt a policy which might give the impression that she is wavering.' What else can she do but waver, with Hitler's tanks ready to go? And look at this, Keith. 'Queen Mary entertaining disabled ex-servicemen of the Not-forgotten Association at Buckingham

Palace.' I'll bet they're forgotten and know it. Last season's cannon fodder."

Mike turned the page, pointing at a photograph of Flight Cadets at Cranwell, smart white flash in their hats, rifles with bayonets fixed. It was a graduation inspection, with an Air Marshal taking the salute.

"Now that's the only good news in this newspaper. More of that and maybe those power-drunk dictators won't get it all their own way. Franco, Hitler, Mussolini, Stalin, Tojo and his gang of murderers in Japan—your country and mine are the only ones who can stop them."

"France?" put in Keith.

"I'm not sure about them. They haven't got a military dictatorship—yet. But they gave me the impression of being corrupt and soft."

Keith asked, "So what do we do?"

"We show our muscle and tell them it's time to stop."

"No, I mean 'we.' You and me. The new generation of cannon fodder. Future members of the next Not-forgotten Association."

Mike drained his whiskey and exclaimed, "Hell, no," and stabbed a finger at the lines of cadets. "We ought to be intrepid birdmen, too. Shoot down those goddamn bombers we saw before they blow London and Paris and then New York to smithereens."

Keith laughed. "But I can't even hit a twenty-five-mile-an-hour partridge. How could I put a bullet into a three-hundred-mile-an-hour bomber? No, after Christmas, you'll return to the States and join one of your pa's companies and wear a decent suit from Brooks Brothers and marry a pretty heiress. And I'll go out to Australia and do a twelve-month stint learning how the Barrett subsidiary in Sydney operates, and I'll be a more or less respectable businessman, considering my lowly origins. We might even do business together. For a start, shall we beagle together tomorrow?"

"Sure." Mike chuckled happily again and, rubbing his

hands with satisfaction, added, "And hunt, and shoot, and fish, and—" eyeing Keith with mock caution "—dance with Eileen at the hunt ball. It's the good life. And maybe she'll give me 'It's Raining Sunbeams' for Christmas. See she buys it, Keith."

Exactly three weeks later to the day, and a week after Mike left Rising Hall, Keith received a telegram from London. It said briefly, "I am in stop come and join stop its raining sunbeams here too stop Mike."

Keith handed it to his adoptive father at breakfast. "Can you guess what that means? It took me a minute to puzzle it out."

"What's that young man up to now? What does he want you to join?"

Eileen reached across the table for the telegram. "He's done it. He said he would, and he has."

"Done what?" demanded Barrett irritably.

"Joined the R.A.F. He said his father might be a problem. But if he could persuade him, it would be as easy as two shakes of a lamb's tail. A letter or two in the right place, a word or two in the right ear, and problems about his nationality would soon be sorted out."

Barrett reached for more toast and said, "Well, the boy's got guts. Stout fellow. I liked him. Good shot, too."

After breakfast Keith took Sheila out for a walk. He was puzzled and cross with himself at his seeming inability to lay doubts and formulate a firm personal policy. How very unlike Mike he was! One photograph in *The Times* and off he goes, changing his whole life, and perhaps losing it. Of course he was right to do what he could in time to stop the disease of fascism spreading all over the world. And of course you could not choose a more important part to play than that of a pilot —a fighter pilot.

He paused for a moment and looked up at the scattered clouds bowling across the sky on a strong northwester. That was where future wars would be won or lost—so he had read many times. And it would be fighting privately, as an individual, a short, sharp death, or sudden victory. Not endless marching, endless months in damp trenches. Barbed wire. Mustard gas. Barrages. That had been his father's and his adoptive father's war.

No one could doubt any longer that it was coming. But what Keith continued to doubt was whether he would be any good at it. The risks he would happily face. But would he be able to shoot and kill? Would the same sudden reluctance beset him up there, when it came to the firing of his guns, as on a shoot down here? When he did not want to look into the eyes of a partridge? Was his weakness as a shot, as his adoptive father hinted, because he really did not like doing it? Or, just as bad and as dangerous, would he be able to control his temper?

"I can't find out until I try," he said aloud, so that Sheila looked up at him with her head on one side. He walked fast for another three hours. When he returned, late for luncheon, the spaniel was showing weariness for the first time in her life, and Keith had made a decision of far-reaching importance.

That night, after dinner, the first round of a three-day contest with his adoptive father opened in the library at Rising Hall. The first and last lines of Barrett's defense rested on what Keith's father would have said had he been alive. "Everything we have done since that day has been governed by the single consideration—what your father and mother would have done. I knew your father longer and better than you did. He was a great man, and a great fighter. I know just what he would have said, after what we both endured in France. He would have said, 'God help us if it ever happens again. If it does, your duty will be to go. Until it does, your duty is to your career.'"

"But you said Mike had guts for joining up. Are you telling me I haven't?"

On the third evening, Keith drove one home under the belt. "But, sir, you know and I know and your lawyers know that I'm not your ward. You never legally adopted me. You just took me over, cared for me, educated me—and I'll always be in your debt for all that you have done. But I'm nineteen and you have no power to stop me from doing what I want with my life."

Keith had never seen his adoptive father look more frighteningly angry. "You dare to take advantage of the trust that existed between our families, of the trust between you and me over the past seven years, to go against my wishes and selfishly order your life according to how you want it and how your father would *not* want it—because of a legal quibble?" The big man arose from his leather armchair and limped toward the door. "I am ashamed of you, young man."

Keith got up from the table. He was trembling and knew that he had lost control. "Ashamed!" he shouted after the receding figure. "Why should you be ashamed? My father was proud to go off and fight for his country—even if he wasn't an officer. What's so bloody wrong about me wanting to fight . . . ?"

Barrett, his back to Keith, was frozen at the open door. Now he quickly closed it behind him and Keith could hear him limping across the bare oak boards of the hall.

Keith did not fall asleep that night until three o'clock, his mind in a turmoil of guilt and shame, frustration and anger. The doubts were bad enough. But having laid them, now this. Again he had laid bare both his antecedents and his temper. He remembered once, when they were much younger, Eileen had said tartly after one of Keith's bouts of anger, "It's *common* to lose your temper," as if repeating what her mother might have said; and he had felt the glow of shame spreading over his face. Oh damn, damn, damn!

At least he was determined not to succumb to the final humiliation of appearing to avoid his adoptive father the next day. So he set his alarm clock for his usual natural waking hour, and came down to breakfast girding himself for the ordeal.

Barrett was pouring out coffee from the pot on the sideboard, his back to the table.

"Good morning, sir," Keith heard himself saying.

"Ah, good morning." Barrett sat down and tucked his napkin into his collar. "I've been thinking about our discussion last night, and all things considered I think you ought to fly if that's what you want and see as your duty. Only hope the damn machines are better than in my day. Stringbags they were. Hope they teach you to shoot, too."

Keith sat down with a thump and stared at the gray-haired figure opposite, who had already propped *The Times* up in front of him and was fast working his way through two eggs, bacon and sausage. After a while, Keith was able to say, "Thank you, sir. I'm sorry about what I said last night."

"That's all right. It was a load of tommyrot anyway. Hartley and Hevershed would have made you a ward of court in twenty-four hours if I'd asked them."

Eileen said later, "Oh, good. Then you won't have to go to Australia. And you can give me a joyride. So can Mike."

3

Almost as soon as Mike had sent off the telegram from London, he realized that it was not strictly true. "Typical American exaggeration, and I'll be found out and Eileen will think I'm just another loud-mouthed Yank."

He was staying at a comfortable old-fashioned hotel off St. James's Park because his family had always stayed there, and he could be confident of credit if his money ran out. The negotiations with his father had been surprisingly swift and simple. Two long cables had done the trick. His mother had sent an anguished cable from Long Island which had pricked his conscience. His father, in New York, had been business-like and practical. Mike guessed that he had figured that it was better to let him have his head and work off his restlessness than force him to come home, resentful and uncooperative, to uncongenial work or unwanted college. At least in the R.A.F. he would be under military discipline and deprived of the opportunity of participating in any more of Europe's civil wars and disorders.

Mike also guessed that some message had been passed from the State Department in Washington to the appropriate body in London—and Mike had no idea which that might be—bypassing any formalities about citizenship and other hindrances. Anyway, his interview in Adastral House had passed off satisfactorily, and after he had waited in an anteroom for ten minutes, a messenger had passed him a memorandum ordering his presence two days hence at the Central Medical Establishment for a fitness check. Mike had scrutinized the paper with extreme care, noting and memorizing the crown of the crest, the eagle and the Latin motto *"Per Ardua ad Astra"*—"Through Hardship to the Stars." "Never mind the hardship," he told himself. "Let's get up to those stars." He had grown up with the proud knowledge that an ancestor on his mother's side—a Lindley—had fought and been wounded at Yorktown, and imagined him turning in his grave at the thought of a young descendant serving the despised British monarchy. But as it was against another threatening tyranny perhaps he would be forgiven.

He went out into the street, and into the nearest post office, to send the telegram to Keith. Provocative, and not completely true, he accepted. But no goddamn British doc could find fault with *his* health and physique. He was as good as through.

Mike was right. In the chill examination rooms of the C.M.E., with snow falling outside, he was weighed and measured, ears, lungs, heart and especially eyes put to the severest tests, in a chill, almost unfriendly, silence. "All part of the leveling experience, I guess," he comforted himself, "to make sure you don't get any heroic ideas about yourself. Damn right, too! Even if they could be easier on the testicles when they make you cough."

For two weeks, Mike dared not leave London, and haunted the baize letter board at his hotel. There were seven deliveries a day, so that occupied much of his time. In the afternoon he took in *A Hundred Men and a Girl* for the second time, and went to the theater most evenings—Priestley's *Time and the Conways,* and lightweights like Rattigan's *French Without Tears,* and Bobby Howes and Cicely Courtneidge in the musical *Hide and Seek* at the Hippodrome.

39

For the rest of the time he read restlessly, went out for long walks in St. James's and Hyde Parks, and looked up one or two acquaintances of his father's.

On the morning of February 15 when he came down to breakfast there was a buff envelope on the board. It was addressed, unbelievably, to Acting Pilot Officer Michael Browning R.A.F., and inside was a letter from an officer "commanded by the Air Council" to order him to proceed on February 17 to Royal Air Force Depot, Uxbridge, for initial ground training. A first-class railway ticket for the journey was enclosed.

"Wow! Just look at that!" Mike had so far failed to arouse more than a formal but polite response from the hall porter, but the letter thrust before his eyes by this wildly dancing American boy forced him to unbend, marginally. "I'm very glad to 'ear it, sir. We need young airmen like you, from all accounts. That 'itler!"

Even the telephone call to Eileen failed to dampen his spirits. He telephoned Rising Hall after breakfast to invite himself for the night, "just to say good-bye before I fly *ad astra*—never to be seen again."

"Oh Mike, I'm so sorry, really I am. Of course you can come, but no one'll be here. Mummy and Daddy are staying with some friends, and I'm joining them today, and Keith's leaving, too. Come and see us on your first leave," she had ended, and her invitation was so warm that he hardly felt any jolt of disappointment.

He sat alone in his compartment in the train to Uxbridge, the speculations darting about his mind. Fighters it had to be. He was going to be a defender of freedom, not a destroyer of cities. How long did it take to become a fully trained fighter pilot? Would the discipline be as strict as at West Point? Strict discipline would be a new experience for him. Andover had been easy on it in his last year at Bartlett Hall, and since then he had done what he liked and wandered the world like a rich nomad.

But at the back of his mind he knew that he was better equipped than most Americans to face up to the rigors of what might lie ahead. His family's wealth and privileged position, its long lineage by American standards, the style of his friends and their private education, all contributed to the self-assurance which made him at ease at a banquet in the American Embassy in Rome one week, and sharing a billycan of coffee on the banks of the River Segre with incoming shells splitting the air above, twelve days later.

Mike was accustomed to being liked, and he had no doubts that he could cope with anything fate and the R.A.F. might have in store for him.

When he got out onto the platform at Uxbridge he saw that he was not, after all, a lone cadet. From other compartments there jumped down a dozen or more men of around his age, identifiable by their cases of varying size and quality, most dressed in suede shoes, flannel pants and sports jackets. They looked, one and all, as if they might own fast cars, but Mike had seen the note prohibiting cars at initial training.

A last figure dropped down from his compartment, and like the others, made his way ahead of Mike toward the barrier. He was tall and fair, walking with a relaxed loping gait that was at once recognizable.

So Keith *had* taken the hint! Mike ran to catch up with him and slapped an arm across his shoulder. "Well, my intrepid birdman," he greeted him, affecting an exaggerated English accent, "this is top hole. *So* glad you could come."

Keith's interview was longer and a great deal more difficult than Mike's. There were five men, of obvious military bearing but in dark blue suits, sitting at a long table. The chairman in the center gave him a perfunctory smile of welcome and indicated a tall chair of the kind found in tailors' shops for weary customers.

"Well, Mr. Stewart, what makes you think you could be taught to fly, and why do you want to become an officer?"

Keith took his time. "Watch for the trick question, and don't let them hustle you," his adoptive father had warned him.

"I am quite good at games, sir. I have a good eye for a ball. And I want to be a pilot because I think the Royal Air Force wants men of my type." That sounded a bit pompous, he thought, and hoped that they wouldn't ask him if he was a good shot.

"Can you decarbonize a motorcar engine?" asked another of his inquisitors.

"I've not done so, sir. But I could learn." He paused, undecided, and then judged that it might sound the right note to add, "I don't have a motorcar, sir. I have a bicycle and have taken my Sturmey Archer gear to pieces and reassembled it."

It went over all right. "Damn sight more difficult." And there was a ripple of laughter.

The gray-haired man on the left asked more gently, "I see you're adopted. Would you like to tell us about your parentage, if you know?"

He did so, speaking more crisply, for there could be no trickery here. "After that, Sir Richard Barrett took me over, so to speak. He has been very good to me. And Lady Barrett, of course. They fought together, he and my father." Keith paused momentarily, and then put in for no good reason, he realized later, "My father was his sergeant." He added, "They were both wounded on the Somme, sir."

"Ah, soldiers," said the chairman in a neutral voice. "Would your father have preferred you to go into the army, Mr. Stewart, do you think?"

"Well, sir, it is difficult to speak for someone who has been dead for seven years. But I don't think he would disapprove of my choice."

This hint of a rebuke seemed to be accepted by all the men. He sensed a sympathy and warmth among them and their questions now came more freely. But Keith would not be persuaded to answer precipitately. He responded to each only after a brief pause for consideration.

At last the chairman rose and offered his hand. "Thank you, Mr. Stewart, that is all. Please be good enough to wait outside."

Keith's medical had followed that afternoon. He experienced a moment of anxiety when it came to his eye examination. Would his seeming inability to hit a moving target show up on the exhaustive and complicated tests, as it certainly should do? But all was well, for only a few days later the buff envelope arrived at Rising Hall, a token of the R.A.F.'s rapid expansion and recruitment.

"What does 'A.P.O.' stand for?" Eileen asked at breakfast. "Are they decorating you for gallantry already?"

"You'll have to address me as Pilot Officer from now on," Keith replied, assuming a mock superior expression.

"I'll do no such thing. You haven't even *seen* an airplane yet. And I'll bet 'A' stands for 'Acting,' and that's just what you're doing."

Keith had wanted to send the news to Mike, but Eileen thought it would be more fun to keep it as a surprise. Five minutes later the telephone rang in the hall and Eileen went to answer it. Barrett, who had no use for the wretched things, consigned the machine to the darkest recesses under the stairs, from which Eileen emerged laughing sympathetically.

"Poor Mike. He wanted to come here for the night to say good-bye. He's going to Uxbridge on the same day as you. So give him my love and tell him I'm longing to see him, especially when he's no longer acting and has got his wings."

In the bar of the officers' mess at Uxbridge, the new group of cadets in their mufti looked like civilians who had gained illegal entry on their way back from watching a football match. But the stewards in their white jackets called them "sir," and when the gong sent them in to dinner the real officers in regulation service uniforms treated them with fatherly consideration.

Keith heard an elderly squadron leader opposite inform

Mike that religion, women, politics and "shop" were all taboo subjects in the mess. No "shop" at all after tea. Keith saw Mike's quizzical expression turn to acute anxiety. "We find it more comfortable that way. Tomorrow you'll be given a manual called *Etiquette in the Service*. You'll find it handy, old boy."

"I guess I will, sir," Mike replied with feeling.

After coffee from silver trays in the anteroom, they left the luxury of deep armchairs and made their way to their sleeping quarters.

"From the sublime to the ridiculous," commented a dark young man called "Buffer" Davies, who had sat next to Keith at dinner, had a pencil-thin moustache, and had told Keith that his sport was motor racing—"I got the name because asses are always runnin' into me at Brooklands," he explained, naming England's most famous track.

The cadets surveyed their quarters with dismay or laughter, according to temperament. There were twelve iron cots down each side of the barrack block. At the end of each was a geometrically arranged stack of folded gray blankets on three square "biscuits," which together formed an unyielding mattress. The corporal who had escorted them from the mess through a maze of red brick buildings to their quarters explained that the bunks must be made up with the same precision, "hupon rising." "Being future hofficers and gentlemen, you will observe, gentlemen, that you are issued with sheets, a luxury not henjoyed by the other ranks."

"Big deal!" muttered Mike, making for the nearest cot and converting it deftly into some likeness to a bed.

There were twenty-four of them in the group, and as the days of lectures, physical training, marching and testing passed, more of the cadets became identifiable by speech or appearance from the gray-and-brown-clad crowd who had spilled without order from Uxbridge station on that first morning.

Mike made a buddy of a small leathery Rhodesian called

Sammy Crow, who talked fast and wise-crackingly in the characteristic "sweet" accent of that colony. His father had a huge farm forty miles from Salisbury, and had taught Sammy to fly his Puss Moth at sixteen.

Donald Avery looked set to follow his father into Lloyds Bank on the 8:32 to London Bridge instead of tearing about the sky in a Gauntlet. He was the only one who arrived wearing a suit, appearing solemn and stiffly above them all. He had a flourishing black moustache, which Keith guessed had been recently grown because he was constantly stroking it, and slicked-down black hair like William Powell's. Keith could not make up his mind whether he remained aloof from the rest of the group out of shyness or a sense of superiority. He was usually seen off duty either alone or with the station's hierarchy, who, for some reason, appeared to encourage his attentions.

In complete contrast was "Polo" Satterthwaite, who came from north Yorkshire and showed it proudly in his accent. He was not a large man and he had turned up wearing a huge, and not recently cleaned, polo neck sweater. Until they got their uniforms, he stood out for this reason alone. He was the type who would always attract the hostility of disciplinarians, and Keith wondered if he would last out the course. He smoked an evil pipe whenever he could and often when he should not. On their second morning when he was quite aware of the rules he walked across the spacious and sacred empty parade ground, pausing to light his pipe and tossing away the match. He was spotted by an ancient flight sergeant with a voice that carried far, put on a charge, and had four hours extra drill with full pack for a week, which did not appear to bother him. Polo's misdemeanor was described, in R.A.F. slang, either as "a boob" or "putting up a bad show," according to which side of authority you were on.

By design, Mike and Keith talked and drank with as many of their fellow cadets as they could. But when they were all given a twelve-hour pass and a fifty-pound voucher to buy their uniform in London, they traveled in the train together and, at Keith's suggestion, went to Sir Richard Barrett's tailor, Smithers, in Cork Street instead of Moss Bros. or Gieves. Here they were fitted with an acceptable readymade while their own dress blue and regulation uniforms were cut, and left in long overcoat, service dress hat and gloves. Mike's suggestion of carrying away the rest of the gear in a box had been received by Mr. Smithers with a hurt expression. "I don't think that would quite do, sir, for an officer."

"This feels more like it," Keith said as they went into Stewart's for tea. "Do I look O.K.?"

"Swell. Fit to break a deb's heart."

"What now?" Keith asked over the cucumber sandwiches.

"I want to hear that girl of mine singing 'It's Raining Sunbeams' for the last time."

"You're crazy."

"Crazily in love—that's all. And it's off to war soon."

They all called their posting to Eldergrove "the war." Here they were to learn to fly, be thrown out of training, or be killed.

The station warrant officer at Uxbridge commented on parade the next morning, "I pity those poor sods at Elder-grove trying to make sodding pilots out of you lot of gentlemen what can't even march properly."

Implicitly, and often explicitly, they were regarded as the lowest form of animal life at Uxbridge, even if their world-weary, gravel-voiced N.C.O. instructors called them "sir," and they passed around the port with the ferocious-looking station commander after their four-course dinner. When they acquired their smart blue uniforms—buttons to be polished, belt to be blancoed, boots to be polished, twice daily —their status seemed to improve marginally, and when a new group of cadets arrived, as lost and scruffy-looking as they had felt three weeks before, Mike and Keith agreed that they were no longer actually subhuman.

* * *

Mike said, "I once spent a month in the Mojave Desert in southern California. It was a paradise of ever-varying color and luxuriance compared with this."

"Eldergrove's a bit of a misnomer, I'll admit," Keith said. They were standing on the wooden platform of a railway stop called prosaically "R.A.F. Eldergrove" in heavy rain driven nearly horizontal by a northeast wind whipping off the North Sea, which was only ten miles away. What they could see of the landscape was entirely flat with ill-kempt hedges separating one dreary field from another. To the west there was no evidence of human life except, distantly, a single horse, driven by a single hunched figure, drawing a harrow. "He's nuts," Mike remarked pitilessly. "Nothing grows here."

To the east a huddle of gray buildings, a monstrous gray water tower, slablike gray hangars with girder wings for their sliding doors and saw-edge roofs, stood like some northern Mecca beckoning too late to gray men who had lost all hope. Before it stretched a field that might once have been green when there was color in this land.

"Nothing flies here, either," said Keith, "apparently."

"It's all a goddamn fake."

But there was life, of a sort. A driver, in dripping flat cap and cape, informed the disconsolate party on the platform that he had transport. They trooped out with their luggage and scrambled in. Mike and Keith were last and had to stand. The driver started the Denis bus and ground his way through the gears, pointing the stubby nose in the rough direction of the R.A.F. station.

There was little talk in the bus. "We might be a bunch of convicts off to Sing-Sing," Mike said to Keith. "I thought the driver looked like Peter Lorre in disguise."

There was nothing for Mike to see except the heads of his fellow officer cadets and the discarded newspaper immediately below. It was the morning's *Times*, folded back wetly to the middle page. For that newspaper, the headlines were large. "Austria Surrenders to Force, German Troops Across the

Frontier." He had already read it in the train, his thoughts turning back to those sunny, happy-seeming villages in the Black Forest, the girls always laughing, the men looking so bronzed and fit. How close they had seemed to himself, his friends at home and at Andover, in spite of the language barrier!

"Storm Troops were marching," he read again, "each man with his armband, and an indescribable tumult composed of thousands of voices shouting 'Heil Hitler! Heil Victory!' and 'One people, one Reich!'"

Could you imagine Americans, or the British, marching like storm troopers into a neighboring country—Canada, say —and taking it over by force?

And he remembered, too, those arrogant, overbearing Luftwaffe pilots, flaunting their power in that restaurant, then streaking low in their bombers over the countryside. No doubt they had played their part in the threatening flights over Vienna before the storm troopers marched in.

Next to that story, another voice screamed out its evil to the world. Vishinsky: "The traitors and spies who have sold our country to the enemy . . . shoot them like unclean dogs . . . forward with Communism . . ."

What could all this mean but war? Soon. And this little island, America's outpost of sanity and freedom, would be the first in the front line.

The bus turned sharply and halted. Mike leaned down to see out of the window. Steel gates were being opened. A guard with fixed bayonet stood stiffly to attention, saluting them. Beyond, at the head of the parade ground, the R.A.F. flag with its red, white and blue roundel stuck out stiffly in the wind.

As the bus moved forward, Mike was filled with a sudden consciousness that he was at the threshold of a new phase in his life, dark and dangerous perhaps, also exhilarating and important. "Off to the war," the facetious reference to their posting to Eldergrove, might, for them, be no less than the truth.

The soft days were past. The skiing in the Adirondacks, the tennis on Long Island, the fishing and sailing in the Sound, the shows on Broadway when they were in Manhattan. The easy life was gone. "This is where the action's going to be," Mike told himself. "And I'm going to be right here, bang in the middle of it."

"All out, please, gentlemen," a cockney voice called.

4

"Nose down a bit, that's it, a shade more, easy now, don't overcook it."

Mike glanced down at the A.S.I., trying to keep the glide approach steady. "Ease off now, back," came his instructor's calm voice through the Gosport tube. Then firmly, "Right, I have her." And Mike, with a renewed thrust of disappointment, released his firm—too firm—grip on the stick, and felt the authoritative yet sensitive movements of the control column as, once again, Flying Officer Oliphant, instead of his pupil, three-point-landed the Tutor.

The voice continued, steady, friendly, encouraging, as the instructor taxied in the machine. "You nearly had it right then. Better than yesterday, not so good as the day before. Don't worry, you're improving. I remember when I was at this stage in '17. Just when I thought I had got it right, the Chief Flying Instructor introduced a new rule: only dead-engine landings and no ground-crew assistance. That meant timing your touchdown in front of the open hangar doors with just the right momentum to carry you up the incline and into the shed. It was no good making a mark on the grass because the correct landing point varied with the wind speed. Taught us precision."

A couple of ground crew reached for the Tutor's wing tips, and with the instructor gunning the engine, the machine was soon in a straight line with the others when the engine was killed.

Mike detached the tube, raised his goggles, unstrapped himself and climbed out of the biplane trainer. "He's going to be kind and patient again, I know it," he correctly predicted. "Oily" Oliphant, as he had referred to him when he was with Keith, and had been properly rebuked. But Mike was beginning to feel that he might respond to some harsh treatment instead of this patience, which only tensed him up.

The postmortem was often the most useful part of the session and every instructor gave his student ten minutes of comment, mostly unfavorable, on the flight. Oliphant, a dark, overweight man with a face as smooth-skinned as a baby's and a demeanor as mild as his style of instruction, waited for Mike to release his harness, and then walked by his side to the flight dispersal. Their parachutes were slung over their shoulders.

"If it was just taking off and flying, we'd all solo in an hour," said Oliphant. "But the Wright brothers made the unforgivable mistake of constructing the airplane so that it had to be landed as well as taken off. They had their tiny troubles, too, Mike. And it would make my job indescribably boring if everyone learned to fly at the same speed."

"Thanks," said Mike, hoping that the facetiousness would give way to practical down-to-earthness. It did, and they were soon involved in a careful, minute-by-minute run-through of the forty-minute flight. But it only served to deepen Mike's depression and sense of inadequacy. Soon, he knew, he would be hearing those dread words, "Flight Commander's Test."

Buffer Davies caught Mike late in the afternoon at the end of the navigation lecture. "Get changed, young Yank," he said, "and let's get out of this dump. You need cheerin' up and I need beer."

Buffer, Mike had learned after three weeks at Eldergrove, affected a posh accent and a cad's manner, had a heart of gold and was constantly broke. He also possessed the fastest car on the station. He called it Garbo and it had "Greta Garbo" in flowing yellow lettering painted above the louvres of the long hood and the chrome outside exhaust. He and his racing mechanic had made it themselves from a cut-down truck chassis and a Bentley Speed Six engine. It carried two, at a pinch, but others could be accommodated on the long tail, if they were brave and tenacious.

Most student pilots used one of the two pubs in the village a mile from the station's gates. Buffer patronized the Old Coach and Horses, a flashy hostelry with much chrome and fumed oak, in Lincoln, eighteen miles away, so that, he explained, "Garbo can get into top gear and get warmed up."

They made the journey in seventeen and a half minutes, according to the stopwatch on the car's dash. Buffer put away a pint and wiped off the froth from his pencil-thin moustache before speaking.

"What are we goin' to do about you?" he asked. "You're used to bein' number one, on top, a winner, what? Not used to puttin' up a poor show, eh?"

Mike considered the beer in his pint pot. Buffer was not being patronizing, he was obviously anxious to help. And he was right. Mike could drive his father's Packard at ten, with two telephone directories on the seat, had picked up skiing first time out and was slaloming like a pro in a week, had played football for Andover against Exeter, could shoot, ride and play tennis well above average. And now, goddamn it, he couldn't fly!

He looked at Buffer, whose black eyes were ranging around the bar for a likely bird, and said with a short laugh, "National pride's at stake. I guess I've just got to get this right. What's the matter, d'you think, Buffer?"

"Tryin' too hard, maybe. When my instructor gave me

my solo test I told myself, 'Who cares? This isn t as jolly important as all that. And if they do throw me out, I can get back to Brooklands in time for the Easter Meetin' and break the lap record again. Nice to see the boys, too.' I just pretended I didn't give a damn, and it worked." He winked at the barmaid, "Same again, love."

They drank steadily and silently for a few minutes, but a new cloud of depression built up around Mike, this time with an element of uncharacteristic self-pity. "You soloed in seven and a half hours, Keith in under seven, even old Solo poloed—I mean Polo soloed at nine."

"That's good. I like that—Solo poloed. Shall we switch to the hard, ol' boy? Or hitch to the sward?" Buffer tipped back too far on the bar stool. "Whoops, nearly pranged!"

Mike called out with what he believed was absolute clarity, "Two very large scotch, please ma'am." Buffer gave each glass a half-second burst from the syphon. "Mustn't dampen it, eh? Economize on the ammo."

"Sammy Crow only did half an hour's dual, but he knew how to fly anyway," Mike continued. "Skewer Daniel soloed yesterday, Donald Avery, with extra tuition he wangled, beat the ten-hour barrier. And Michael Browning, cocky know-all citizen of the great U.S.A., has done twelve hours and can't even land the goddamn kite."

Toward closing time Buffer and Mike became maudlin and chummy. A man in plus-fours smoking du Mauriers was told by Buffer that Mike was Charles Lindbergh's nephew. "And he has the most beautiful sister, sir, with a pair of Bristols that would have your mince pies out on stalks."

Mike tried to refute this, but found his voice very elusive. So he thought about Eileen instead and almost cried remembering how lovely her hair was in the sun when they were walking through the forest. It was becoming surprisingly hot, so he put a little more soda in his next double to cool himself down, but it did not seem to make any difference.

At one point two girls came in with a young man with

the loudest check jacket Mike had ever seen. He succeeded in articulating a pun for Buffer's benefit. "Czech—o—slovak disaster." But Buffer was not listening, as one of the girls was making admiring remarks about Garbo and telling the young man she would like a car like that.

Buffer said, "Would you like a ride, dear?" And the girl, who was wearing a low-cut art silk bottle-green blouse, gave a little scream. "Oooh yes—will you?"

The young man said, "You'll do nothing of the kind. The man's incapable of standing, let alone driving."

There was a great deal of noise after that, and Mike remembered a hand under his arm and Buffer saying, "C'mon, ol' boy, we'll take our patronage to the George. Very low mob here." Mike nearly tripped over the prone figure of the young man, and welcomed the cool night air as he felt his way carefully into the passenger seat, but found himself kneeling on it instead of sitting. It did not seem to matter. And Buffer even thought it was a good idea and exclaimed in wonder that no one had ever thought before of kneeling backward to drive. "Jolly comfy, ol' boy, don't you think?"

After a minute or two of silence like this, Buffer said, "Care to drive, ol' boy? I have every trust in you. You'd be the first to go solo in Garbo—except me, of course. I have driven her before. I have driven her at 117 miles an hour. Auth-auth-authentated."

Mike thought about this proposal for a long time, and then raised his forehead from the back of the seat. "Not in the dark. It's dark now. Try it in the dark. I'll press the wopstotch." But he did not. He passed out instead, into a world that was even darker than the High Street, Lincoln.

The next thing he was aware of was a hot metallic smell. Someone was saying, "To you, from me, easy to the left." A number of helpful and relatively sober cadets were easing him out of the passenger seat. The hot smell, he learned later, was from Garbo's engine, which had driven them back to the station, if not at 117 m.p.h., then at a speed that made their survival a miracle.

Mike was very sick and after that was over, amid sounds of commiseration, he said in a slightly resentful voice that he could manage perfectly well on his own, but failed to live up to his boast. "I'm all right," he said. "O.K. as a newborn foal." He had his arms around the shoulders of two cadets, both of them taller than he was, so that only his toes scraped along the path toward their sleeping quarters. "I'm just rather tired. It's been a goddamn heavy day."

"You're sloshed. Sloshed, Yankee boy."

Mike succeeded in getting some vehemence into his voice. "Crap! That's an insult. Stone cold, you mean. Stoned cold sober. I can take my man like the next liquor. Just had something that disagreed with me. An olive. An oily olive. I have kept another oily olive for oily Oliphant."

Another voice said, "Shut up, you fool."

There was another break in the continuity of the long evening. The final installment was Keith bending over him when he was lying, partly undressed, in bed. He was smiling down at him anxiously. "Here, take this. Tomato juice and angostura and goodness knows what else. The barman brewed it up, and he should know."

Mike took a sip, supported by Keith, and almost exploded with the sudden heat in his mouth. "It'll kill me!" he exclaimed. "I'll never fly again. I'll die . . ."

"You won't fly again if you don't take it," Keith said grimly. "The Flight Commander's giving you a test at nine-fifteen tomorrow morning, and you've got to be lovely and sober for him."

Unlike Mike, Keith had at once felt at home in the Avro Tutor with the Siddeley Cheetah engine. It was a two-seat biplane with heavily stepped back lower wing, a well-braced tail assembly, simple, strong undercarriage, and good visibility all around. It was a very stable machine, easy to fly and with sensitive, but not oversensitive, controls.

At first sight it gave the impression that the airplane had advanced little since the Great War. A rigger still "rigged" the machine; the fitter was responsible for the engine.

Keith had been assigned to a very different instructor from Mike's mild and patient officer. Flight Lieutenant Randall, forty-one years old and a veteran of the days when the R.A.F. was still the Royal Flying Corps, had a lurid tongue and a short temper. The tender sensitivity with which he could touch the Tutor into a falling leaf, pulling out at two hundred feet and into a simulated forced landing in a small field, was in gross contradiction to the stream of obscenities he hurled down the Gosport tube at his pupil. He was five feet four, walked like an aging jockey and looked as if he had slept every night of his life in the bottom of a ditch. His appearance, and his contempt for authority, no doubt contributed to his failure to achieve higher rank, which did not appear to worry him. A purple scar clear across his forehead, originating from a crash in No Man's Land in an S.E.5a in 1918, as well as the early-type horizontally-striped D.F.C. ribbon under his wings, were joint badges to his courage and battle experience.

Keith was at first appalled by him, soon came to like and respect him, and rather to his surprise, progressed quickly and well with him. At school he had been above average at sports and games, but always it had taken time to work up the self-confidence to put him ahead of the competition.

It was not until the end of the second week that Mike mentioned his difficulties to Keith. They lived in adjoining rooms in the officer cadet quarters, and Mike came in late in the evening with a letter from Eileen describing a meet and the tumble she had taken over at Tuesday Meadow, and the pain she had endured trying to dance the same evening. He read it aloud to Keith, together with the postscript message that she would be writing to Keith in a few days, but thought Mike might need cheering up.

"I guess I do need some cheer," Mike said ruefully. "I think they're going to flunk me, Keith. I just can't get to grips with the thing at all. I'm O.K. on Rate Two turns and steering a steady compass course and all that. I can even get the devil into the air. After a fashion. But I get all screwed up trying to get down again."

Keith felt sorry for him, and embarrassed by his own success. He had a suspicion that things were not going right. Almost everyone had now soloed, and the presence of that second head and shoulders in Flying Officer Oliphant's Tutor when Mike was the pupil had been noticed by several people.

"If only Oily would get mad at me or something. I guess I'd be O.K. with your Randy. A bit of bad language and spitting down the tube would probably do me good."

Keith brewed up a cup of coffee on a machine he had bought in Lincoln. He found it convenient to have some basic refreshment in his sleeping quarters when he was working as hard as he was in the evenings studying for the ground examinations on guns and gunnery, navigation, Air Force history and basic engineering.

"It's rather like my shooting," said Keith to cheer him up. He laughed. "We'd make a good team for these new two-seat fighters everyone's talking about. Defiants. You can handle the guns and I'll handle the controls. Bet we'd knock up a score when the war comes."

It was two nights later when Keith saw Mike going off in Buffer Davies's "Greta Garbo." Already Buffer had gained the reputation for fast driving, fast drinking and fast womanizing, all on an ever-empty wallet, or so it seemed. Keith thought Mike might overdo it, especially as he was so depressed. But he had not expected to have to pull him back from virtual unconsciousness later that evening, nor pass on the somber news that a note had been left for him in the mess demanding his presence at Flight Dispersal at 9:15 A.M. for a Flight Commander's test. It could mean only one thing. The Great Man himself was to sit in judgment in the front seat and Mike would have to prove that he was worthy of further instruction, which his own instructor was clearly beginning to doubt.

Mike had at first been treated with reserve and even some suspicion by the rest of the cadets. Did they have another Robert Taylor in their midst and was he going to behave like a Yank at Oxford? Keith did a lot to dispel this early suspicion. Mike swept away the rest within a few days by his cheerfulness, his lightheartedness and evident modesty. When it came to be known that he was having difficulties there was a general feeling of sympathy for him. "A reet good sort, that Yank," Polo had commented. Donald Avery expressed no opinion. He had been appointed senior cadet and course commander, and had already dined out twice with the Squadron Leader Administrative and his wife. It was now evident that his stiffness—in posture and expression as well as speech—was not caused by self-consciousness. On the contrary, the young man with the full moustache was all too conscious of his superiority and certainly of his advancement. Keith felt mildly irritated that the early sympathy he had felt for this odd-man-out had been unjustified and wasted, like the friendly approaches he had made several times.

The word of Mike's imminent crisis, and his inadequate condition to deal with it, spread among the cadets, who all slept in the same block. Keith organized a morning sobering-up campaign, and at 7:30, as the batman was bringing in his tea, Mike was raised from his bed by six pairs of arms and carted off to a full-to-the-brim cold bath. He was thrust into it and held down for one minute, screaming. A quick toweling down was followed by another dose of the mixture as before, and he was then propped up on a chair and roughly shaved.

At the end of it all, he was taken back to his room, left with his clothes beside him, and ordered to dress. Looking up at them with his red-rimmed eyes he murmured, "I cannot dress, I cannot move, I sure cannot fly." He held up his hands, which were shaking like those of an octogenarian with the palsy. "I can only die." And he began to keel over sideways.

Mike was in a murderous mood when the Flight Commander stepped out of his Hillman and strode toward the Flight Dispersal. "I hate this place. I hate this officer. I hate these ships they call kites. I hate flying. And I'm going to lick the goddamn lot of them. Then quit."

With that statement to himself, Mike managed to stand and salute the Flight Commander as he came into the room.

"Good morning. Our kite is ready. I'm busy. We'll go at once. I want to see if you're going to make a pilot." The Flight Commander was handed his Irvin, helmet and goggles and the airman carried his parachute out to the Tutor.

Mike was very nearly sick climbing up onto the wing and then down into the rear cockpit, and the bitter taste of the knockout hangover cure came flooding back. The Flight Commander was evidently talking, but Mike had not secured his Gosport. The irate face turned and indicated the tube. The threatening voice flooded into Mike's ears. "A bad start, Mr. Browning."

Mike cursed back, confident in the knowledge that the engine would destroy any chance of the words reaching him. He had never been so angry in his life. "First they try to poison me. Then scare me. Then freeze me to death. Now this pompous Englishman's going to tell me I can't fly. I don't care if he does throw me out. I hate this place . . ."

"It is all yours, Mr. Browning," came the voice over the Gosport. "The green light has been flashed. Kindly take off."

Mike opened the throttle and as the Tutor gathered pace played the rudder pedals to keep her in a straight line. The tail came up and he gently eased back the stick. The machine was airborne without a bump. He climbed at the prescribed steady rate, and at a thousand feet leveled off.

"Rate Two turn to port through ninety degrees," came the order. And later, "A climbing turn to starboard, Rate One, one hundred feet per minute."

The needles remained rock steady on their dials. With grim satisfaction, Mike said, "And I'm going to land this bastard just like Lindbergh came into Le Bourget. Americans are the greatest fliers in the world." He had forgotten his pounding head, the sickness in his stomach, all the fear he would have felt on hearing the news of this test flight the evening before. Flying? Nothing to it. Nix.

"You will now do one circuit and come in to land. And please, Mr. Browning, no revving the engine. Just a clean glide approach."

"You pompous bastard! You watch this," Mike shouted into the roaring wind.

Ninety degrees to port. Ninety degrees again, coordinate stick and rudder, level off. Throttle back. A.S.I. 55. Steady there.

Mike saw nothing but the grass ahead. Completely relaxed, completely self-confident for the first time, he let the Tutor drift down to the landing point he had selected. Back, back, a shade more, steady. Deftly he held off a foot or two from the grass while the machine floated and lost the last of its flying speed. Then it stalled in to a perfect three-pointer, and Mike kept the nose steady against a distant tree until she came to a halt.

Then, with absolute aplomb, he taxied in.

The Flight Commander did not say a word until they were parked in line. And then, with the engine still running, he said, "Good. You may go off on your own now, Mr. Browning. Just one circuit."

The Flight Commander climbed out and walked toward his office without looking back. Mike stared ahead unbelievingly. The absence of head and shoulders in the cockpit in front was somewhat disconcerting for about five seconds. Then he called out, "Chocks away!"

5

They knew that the threat of war was real when they were ordered to break off the final stage of their Central Gunnery School course and fly their aged Harts in a mass formation down to Hendon to help defend London. "If you put them in a vertical dive for five thousand feet, you *might* get a Heinkel in range for a few seconds," the Chief Flying Instructor had optimistically forecast.

It was a perfect late September day in 1938, and at this time of the year, with harvest over, some of the fields already under the plow, others sown with winter crops or crisp brown with stubble, the pattern of the landscape was at its richest. A southwest wind drew stains of smoke from the villages, pungent dark streaks from Midland industrial towns, and scattered cloud shadow over this beautiful land for which Keith would gladly give his life.

Hendon appeared too crowded to take any more planes. As Keith joined the circuit, he saw Heyford heavy bombers, a pair of Ansons, some biplane Harts, Gauntlets and—the latest biplanes of all—Gladiators. And, scattered in their blastproof bays, a squadron of Hurricanes, the only machines that were faster than the threatening German bombers. Just.

The R.A.F. had little more than fifty of them, and, they had recently learned, they could not fight high because their guns froze above 15,000 feet.

After landing, Keith followed his section leader taxiing along the perimeter track past the Hurricanes. It was the first time he had seen them on the ground, and their sleekness and crouching heavy-backed menacing configuration epitomized the modern super-fast fighting machine.

The Hurricane pilots were in the officers' mess bar before luncheon. They were a professional-looking bunch sporting silk scarves, handlebar moustaches, top button of their jackets left undone, and flouting formality by wearing flying boots with maps stuffed into them. Although he and Mike and the other survivors of their course were now fully fledged pilots, Keith felt that an immense gap of experience separated them from these veterans.

In the afternoon, Keith telephoned the Barrett house in Eaton Square. To his delight, Eileen answered. "Daddy and Mummy are in Hampshire waiting for the start of the pheasant season," she told him. "So I just slipped away when I got your telegram saying you would be in London. When are you coming?"

"Right now, this instant," said Keith. He explained that they had only been delivery pilots, and that their planes had been assigned to more experienced airmen. "So we've all got twenty-four-hour passes."

Eileen hugged Keith first, then Mike. Her striking green eyes were bright with excitement. "How lovely to see you! And those gorgeous wings!" She ran her fingers over the embossed silk on Mike's chest above the left pocket of his tunic. "London'll be safe now." She spoke half flippantly, then the tone of her voice changed. "Do you really think there's going to be a war?" she asked Keith.

"Nobody knows," he said. "Not even Mr. Chamberlain. Everything seems to depend on crazy Hitler. If he wants war, then he'll get it. He always seems to get his way."

Mike said, "Well, I guess everybody's taking it damn seriously. Maybe we're going to call his bluff at last. It's about time."

They walked up the wide stairs, Eileen's arms linked with theirs. "You're right about it being serious," she said. "Do you know, just after I arrived this afternoon, a van drove slowly through Eaton Square with a voice calling out. 'Will every citizen of Westminster get their gas mask fitted as soon as possible. Your nearest station is in Elizabeth Street. Do not delay.' So I didn't. And I made the Ewhursts come too," she said, referring to the couple who ran the London house. "Poor dears, what with me turning up here unexpectedly one minute, and then being dragged along to have a funny rubber thing pushed over their faces the next, it's been a hectic day for them . . ."

She prattled on until they reached the drawing room on the first floor, which was as warmly welcoming, comfortable and decorated and furnished in the same rather old-fashioned good taste—Harrods *circa* 1923—as Rising Hall. There was a long Sheraton table under the double windows, its polish reflecting the yellowing leaves of the plane trees outside. *Country Life, The Field* and *The Shooting Times* were spread out on an occasional table between the sofas. It all seemed remote from the center of Westminster, and equally remote from the dark threat of destruction from the air.

Yet here was Mike describing their taxi ride through Hyde Park. "It was like they'd let loose a bunch of jackrabbits, hundreds of them, all burrowing away like crazy. You know what? They were digging air raid shelters—slit trenches anyhow. And they had a battery of antiaircraft guns near Marble Arch. Pretty ancient they looked, too. They were running coiled barbed wire around them, but I guess no one'd want to steal *those*."

"Oh, Mike, it isn't really a laughing matter, is it?" Eileen asked. She sat down, curling up her legs in her usual comfortable position. She was wearing a simple brown tweed suit, the skirt cut to the fashionable calf level, and country brogues as if she had just come in from taking Sheila for a walk. "What is it going to be like? What's going to happen to us? Do you think it'll be like that terrible film, *The Shape of Things to Come?*"

Mike answered for both of them. "No, not yet. Perhaps never. Meanwhile, in the best Egyptian tradition, we're going to eat and drink for tomorrow . . ."

"Tomorrow we're back at Hendon by twelve hundred hours or else."

They had leisurely baths and changed, and at six o'clock Ewhurst brought in a tray of drinks. They put on the radio to listen to Mr. Chamberlain's broadcast, which might mean the difference between war and peace, and for all three of them, life and death. Keith sprawled in an armchair sipping his whiskey and soda. They all listened to the powerful words and the striving, painfully sincere voice. ". . . Armed conflict between nations is a nightmare to me; but if I were convinced that any nation had made up its mind to dominate the world by fear of its force, I should feel that it must be resisted. Under such a domination, life for people who believe in liberty would not be worth living: but war is a fearful thing, and we must be very clear, before we embark on it, that it is really the great issues that are at stake . . ."

Keith's imagination reenacted for the thousandth time the Somme on that first terrible morning when his father and his adoptive father . . .

Mike reached toward the veneered mahogany radio and switched it off. "All bromides!" he exclaimed angrily. "What are 'the great issues'? I'll bet he'll soon be saying they're not a few slices of Czechoslovakia and backing down, like he always does."

"Oh, no," said Eileen, "Daddy says he's such a good man. 'An honorable man,' that's what he called him."

"Your pop's my favorite man," said Mike. "But I guess he's out of touch with what's really going on, even if he is a Member of Parliament."

Ewhurst brought in the evening paper. It was full of giant

crisis headlines. But there was room for a happier event up at a Clydeside shipyard. " 'The Queen launches the world's biggest ship, the *Queen Elizabeth.*' The Prime Minister launches the world's biggest blunder," Keith remarked bitterly. "We're mobilizing the fleet this evening. If we flew a Balbo, a really big one, over the Ruhr in daylight, that would scare the pants off old Hitler and stop him grabbing everything in sight."

"I think we ought to fly a Balbo up to the Caledonia, the three of us, just as a gesture of strength of course," Mike said.

"But not before one more small drink," said Keith. He did not usually drink much, and that was mostly beer. But now he felt the need to celebrate, not joyously but rather as he imagined they had celebrated in the streets of London at the outbreak of the Great War, with a mixed sense of relief that the waiting was over, the tension had snapped, and with an element of hysterical anticipation too, for what the future might hold. Their flight south, the demonstration of fighting strength it had represented, the evidence of imminent war and the contrasting normality in Eaton Square, all contributed to their certain conviction that this was a special night.

He raised his glass to Mike and Eileen, who were sitting side by side on the sofa. Mike was looking debonair in his dinner jacket, very man-of-the-world in the lively, eager-for-anything style that was very much his own; and Eileen was dressed in a long, deep-blue velvet evening dress with a single diamond pendant—a sixteenth-birthday present—around her neck. She looked like the happiest and most beautiful princess about to dance the night away.

"To war—or peace. Whichever it's to be." They drank to both, feeling half solemn and half silly, then decided to walk. It was a warm evening and they wanted the exercise.

There were a lot of people about and in Belgrave Square the embassy limousines were much in evidence, national flags fluttering from the hoods, as if the *corps diplomatique* were having one last fling before "the lights went out all over Europe" again.

Outside St. George's Hospital they paused to watch a number of young men, sleeves rolled up, filling bags from piles of sand by the light of the streetlamps. Already the sandbags rose halfway up the ground floor windows and formed a massive shelter around the doors. Keith's party in formal clothes contrasted oddly with these vigorous young volunteers and they received some hostile stares as they passed. Keith remarked on this to Eileen and Mike as they continued across Hyde Park Corner, past the great gunners' memorial to an earlier war and through Green Park toward the Ritz.

"My father used to call it 'the white feather nonsense,'" he said. "He knew a V.C. who loathed wearing uniform on leave and was given five white feathers by women between Oxford Circus and Piccadilly Circus. I suppose sanctimoniousness always goes with war."

There was not much sign of it at the Caledonia Club. It was barely 8:30 P.M., but it was already bursting with life and noise. They had a drink at the bar while waiting for a table, and Keith noticed that the faces about them seemed to reflect the abandoned feeling that he had experienced back at Eaton Square, in such sharp contrast with those patriotic sandbag fillers.

"Let's dance while we can," suggested Mike. The floor was already crowded, but they could still get in some nice long glides and chassés by dexterous steering among the other couples. The band was playing "Baby, What Else Can I Do?" in the style of Chick Webb, and Keith tapped the toes of his patent leather dancing shoes against his bar stool. "They look nice together," he thought. "Nice couple, nice music, nice nightclub." He ordered another drink and watched them do a half dozen turns as the number ended. They were about the same height and looked natural and right together. It had been a fortuitous meeting back at Hornberg, Keith was thinking, recalling their long walks through the forest a year earlier. And now Mike and he were fully trained to fight, and many of the vigorous young Germans they had seen would now be in uniform, ready to lay down their lives for the Führer.

If it really came to war, Tom might join the R.A.M.C. as soon as he had qualified, and Moira might become a nurse. And Mike and he—well, they would be unlikely to survive. Best face the reality. What did they say the average life of a scout pilot was on the Western Front in 1917? Three weeks? After the first month, your survival chances increased in ratio with the weeks you survived. A simple arithmetical calculation.

Eileen and Mike had stayed on the floor and were dancing again. Eileen would miss them when they had both gone. Keith began to feel sentimental, and he felt tears pricking the back of his eyes as he imagined Eileen attending their funerals—one, then the other. He would be the first to go. Mike had always seemed to have a strong survival capacity, and that deadliness with a gun must increase his chances. Not fair, Keith judged, a shaft of envy now piercing his maudlin mood. And not fair to dance with Eileen *all* the time.

He got up and walked onto the floor, brushing past several couples before reaching Eileen. He tapped Mike on the shoulder and the American looked up in surprise. "Mine, I think," Keith said firmly, and took Eileen away, becoming at once, and crossly, conscious that he was a less skillful dancer than Mike—certainly less skillful at avoiding the other couples.

"I think it's time we ate," Eileen said at the end of the number.

"No, I think one more."

But the question was decided for them by the band, who packed up their instruments and made off for a break.

Keith had one more drink at the table, but the others said they had had enough and wine with the meal would be all that they wanted. Keith was recalling those words of warning he had uttered in Germany. "Special relationship," was how he had described Eileen's and his mutual feelings. But he had never attempted to define more clearly, even to himself, his relationship with Eileen. They had played and romped together through adolescence, almost as brother and sister. But not quite. They had sometimes kissed, but usually only on special occasions, and cosily and comfortably, not with passion or long and lingeringly like Dorothy Lamour or Barbara Stanwyck in the movies. It had always been nice, but had never led to anything more serious.

Conveniently perhaps, their lives had diverged as they grew through their teens, with Eileen going off to boarding school and then doing her season in London. What they had done together were mostly hearty outdoor activities, especially hunting and beagling.

But all the time, even during the long periods when they were apart, Keith had been conscious of the warm knowledge of their closeness, and whenever they were together again, the glow of affection was always present. At the same time, marriage was not for serious consideration—the gaps of class and wealth were too wide for that.

Just at this moment, in the smoke and noise and heat of the Caledonia at 11:30, after a fair amount to drink and an eventful and alarming day, the tenderness was spiced with a measure of resentment. "Hold it, young Mike," he kept saying to himself. "Enough's enough."

His faint feeling of hostility to his friend caused him to abstain from the conversation toward the end of dinner, but Mike was never short of something to say, and Eileen was laughing a great deal at his anecdotes of R.A.F. life recounted with a light touch that always left Mike coming off worst.

"When's this bloody band coming back?" Keith suddenly interjected.

They both looked at him, and for a fleeting second Keith had the impression that they were regarding him critically. "Well, I guess they've got to eat like the rest of us." Mike turned to Eileen again. "Enjoy your duck?"

She nodded. "And I'm longing for Daddy to come home."
"So your heart belongs to Daddy, like the song," said
Mike. "I always suspected you had an Oedipus complex."
"Don't be rude. It's the *pheasants* he'll bring back—dozens
of brace, all for me."
Mike said, "O.K., so you're just a glutton."
Keith pushed the table away from himself a little further
than was necessary as he got up. In the lavatory he saw that
his face was shiny with sweat and his long fair hair—too
long for his flight commander—was in a state of some dis-
order. He washed slowly in cold water and got out his
comb. He was beginning to wish he had not eaten quite so
much duck. He also did not care for his face. "No wonder
she likes him better," he said aloud. At the next basin a
chinless wonder, probably a guards' officer, said, "I beg your
pardon."

"Oh, shut up," muttered Keith, and walked back into the
smoke and noisy crowd. He stood contemplating the scene
with disfavor for several minutes. He imagined a bomb
dropping into the middle of the lot of them, like that scene
in the H. G. Wells film. "No bloody loss at all," he said.
"Except Eileen. Where is she? Where's my lovely sister who
isn't?"

Through the smoke and surging bodies of waiters and
customers, he thought he could just make out their table,
and she was not at it. Nor was Mike. Keith pushed through
the crowd toward it and he saw that the table was indeed
deserted. He sat down glaring angrily about him, and
ordered a brandy. "Dancing? Of course, they must be at it
again. Enough's enough." He stood up and scanned the
small packed dance floor, studying it for a full minute
before confirming that they were not on it.

"What a bloody cheek! What does that American think
he's up to? A Yank at the Court of Queen Eileen. Well, I'm
not going to be the bloody court jester."

Keith got up again and unsteadily but thrustingly made
his way from end to end of the dark nightclub, studying

faces carefully whether standing up or sitting down, drinking or eating, or just talking. If he felt any doubt, he looked hard at the face at close range, and received some hostile looks in reply.

"After all I've done for him!" he told himself petulantly. "The swine. The seducing sod! Makes himself out as a friend, and then when your back's turned, just for a second, he's off with your sister."

Suddenly the realization of what might happen hit him like a blow and he had to sit down on the nearest empty chair. "My God, he *is* going to seduce her! That bloody swine of an American thinks he's going to get her into bed. Sex, sex, sex, that's all Americans ever think of. The lousy sod's going to seduce my Eileen!"

The enormity of it stunned his thinking until he was politely asked by an elderly man if he might have his chair back now that he had finished dancing.

Keith got to his feet and mumbled an apology. He made his way back to his own table, still deserted, intending to leave at once for Eaton Square.

"But hold it." Cunningly he reminded himself that Mike would never take her to her own house. "Oh, no! It'll be the Ritz across the road. Nothing but the best for our gallant officer. A suite no doubt. A bottle of champagne, then to bed . . ."

What was he to do? What was he to *do*? The first thing was to get out of here, out into the night air to cool down his temperature and his anger. He looked around for the waiter, realizing ruefully that he would be landed with the whole bill and would never accept repayment from Mike for the good reason that he would never speak to him again.

The waiter leaned over to speak into Keith's ear to make himself heard. "The other gentleman has paid," he said, holding out a tray. Keith put a ten shilling note on it and stuffed the folded piece of paper lying on the tray into his pocket. Now he would know the cost and at least have the doubtful satisfaction of paying *his* share. It seemed to him to be an important gesture.

He stood up and began the long struggle to reach the door. It was not yet midnight and he felt tired out and not very well, averting his eyes from the steaming plates of late diners. The band was back, playing dreamily "I'm Getting Sentimental Over You."

The steps to a higher tier of tables took Keith by surprise, and he stumbled and nearly fell. As he recovered himself he saw in the half light that there was a young woman sitting on the lower step. She looked up at him and smiled. "Why don't you sit down for a minute?" she asked.

Keith liked the sound of her voice and did so.

"You've lost your party, too, haven't you?" she said.

"How do you know?"

"Because I've been watching you, a fellow forgotten soul."

Keith looked at her more closely. She had long, wavy dark hair, dark eyes, and what he could see of her face looked agreeable. At least she was cheerful in her predicament, and that was welcome. "They couldn't have forgotten *you,*" he said.

She laughed. "Oh, yes, he did. Just like that. Never came back from the lav. But at least he paid the bill, so I suppose he's only half a cad. What happened to your girl?"

"It was the other way around for me. I came back and found them gone."

" 'Them'? You mean you had *two* girls?" She laughed. "Double-dumped. I like that."

Keith said, "No. It was a friend and my half-sister."

"*Ménages à trois* don't work. You should know that, silly. Two's company, and all that. What are you going to do now?"

"I don't know. Go out and be miserable, I suppose."

She got up briskly, smoothing out her long dress. "That's stupid. I've got a flat in Half Moon Street. Let's both cheer ourselves up with a drink."

Keith followed her to the door. He did not have much experience of London after dark. So far his life had been mainly hearty, sporty and outdoorsy, and for the past nine months, when he had given himself up to learning the skills of a pilot, monastic and celibate. Was he being picked up? he wondered. She was not his idea of a prostitute. Anyway, prostitutes did not seek custom in a place like the Caledonia.

In Piccadilly she took his arm, which he welcomed because, in aviation terms, his directional stability was not all that it should have been although he felt very much better in every way in the cool night air.

They exchanged names as they walked west. She was called Jenny Simpson and said she did modeling sometimes in a tone that vaguely hinted that she had no financial need to. He guessed she was older than he was, perhaps in her late twenties. She spoke in a deep voice, and with a slight slur as though she might be tipsy, too. But she made good sense, discussing the merits and demerits of the local night-clubs, which suggested that she was not short of escorts.

Her flat was on the third floor, approached by a small lift in which they studied one another momentarily in the full light. Yes, a nice face, thought Keith. Not beautiful, a rather thin nose, but a nice happy-looking mouth and bright eyes. And then he remembered Eileen suddenly, and Jenny, quick to detect his change of thought, said, "Yes, you do need cheering up."

The sitting room was small and low-ceilinged, comfortably furnished—very modern.

"Have you had a bad day as well as a bad evening?" she asked, throwing her fur coat onto the back of a chair.

"No, not really. I flew down to Hendon this morning. It was a nice flight—twenty-five of us including the C.O. Though I suppose that's secret with war so near."

She passed him a whiskey and soda and contemplated him closely as she leaned over to put the glass on the table. "So you're an R.A.F. pilot. How romantic! I flew once. A boy took me up at Croydon and we went around and around till I was dizzy. And then I was sick."

Keith liked her laugh and felt an increasing tingle of desire. He watched her closely as she talked, trying to assess the likely response if he should dare. Would that nice face suddenly turn hostile? Or crumple with lust? How did women's faces respond? He did not know. God, how innocent! But then, he argued, why should she go to the trouble of bringing him all the way up here if she didn't expect to be propositioned?

Suddenly he got up from his chair, timing it awkwardly when she was in the middle of a story, and strode the two steps to her, bending down and kissing her not at all accurately. She adjusted her face so that their lips met properly and he looked into her bright brown eyes that told him she would be laughing if she were not being kissed.

He decided that he liked this very much indeed and moved his hands down to her breasts. At once she drew away her head and gently pushed him back. "Well, I liked that, too," she said, "but enough's enough I think. Otherwise you might misunderstand my motives. I suggested cheering ourselves up."

She was clearly not in the least put out. He noticed that her smile was not quite even, just a little down on the left side, which he found very attractive. But he was more concerned at the moment with trying to hide the embarrassment he felt.

He said, "I'm awfully sorry."

"No need. Very few women actually *mind* being lusted after. In fact most of them rather like it." She laughed again. "But there's a time and a place for everything—or some such cliché."

Keith was surprised to see that she too was feeling embarrassed as if she might be regretting that she had picked him up so what else could she expect. He decided to put an end to the business right away and leave. But Jenny Simpson told him not to be silly and to sit down and help himself to another drink and pour one for her too.

With his back to her he gave himself a very weak whiskey and soda and her a normal measure. When he was back in his chair she said, "Tell me more about flying. What do you like best about flying?"

He tried to be brief and to make it sound interesting. At one point she asked, "Will you mind the shooting part if the war starts?"

"Why do you ask that?"

"I don't know. Silly question. Perhaps because everything's so unreal just at this moment. Anyway, forget it."

Keith fingered his glass and looked down at the light-colored drink. "Since you ask—I don't know. Not until it happens. I'm not much good at shooting game . . ."

"I rather thought so." She smiled her faintly uneven smile and then said briskly, "Of course you won't mind. Everybody else will be doing it and so will you. Very well, too. You'll be an ace with lots of pretty ribbons under your wings." She laughed and got up.

"I passed out just about bottom from the first part of gunnery school," said Keith ruefully, "so they'll probably get me first."

When he got to his feet she said, "You can kiss me again if you like."

He did so, better this time, and they stood tightly pressed together for a long time. Keith forgot everything—the imminence of war, the problems and dangers of the next day, even Mike and Eileen. He was totally consumed by the pleasure of having this woman in his arms, the softness of her body and the scent of her hair. Like this, everything was right, exactly right.

Jenny moved very gently against him and he took away his lips and put them against her right ear. "Are you *sure* this isn't the time and place?" he asked.

"No, I'm not," she answered, and a disappointing fraction of a second passed before he understood that the negative was a positive. She cleared away all misunderstanding by laughing and adding, "On reconsideration I think it is a very good time, and the place is quite near." She indicated a door and then moved away from him toward it. "Give me five minutes." She laughed and turned before opening the door. "But you must understand that I did *not* mean this to happen. Not at all."

When she had gone Keith sat down, stunned and glowing, and finished his drink. "Well, it has to happen sometime. And this seems a pleasant no-fuss way of it happening." He was filled with curiosity about what it would be like to lie beside this woman who had come so unexpectedly into his life.

In the large, comfortable double bed, with the lights out and the curtains drawn back a little to let in the street light and the murmur of late traffic, she cupped his face in her hands and said, "You have very nice hair. One of your better features. You are also very young. Not twenty-one, right? And, I suspect, a virgin. But they say there's going to be war. And virgins can't fight, you must know that. There's my handsome Keith."

Keith could see by the light of the streetlamp that it was three o'clock. He was about to slip out of the bed and dress in the living room when Jenny moved and put her hand on his face, stroking it gently.

"Don't get up for a minute. We probably won't see one another again and it would be sad after that exceptionally nice lovemaking not to know anything about each other. I mean not just come and gone with no more than a name and an orgasm."

Keith thought for a moment, feeling immensely sad at these words and deciding that he would like to stay with her forever. Then he said, "You first."

She was brief and matter-of-fact. "I'm twenty-eight, have lots of money but am not happy. I'm also rather chaste, believe it or not. I was married when I was twenty-one and it was hell almost from the start. I don't want to think about it. I managed to get a divorce last year and lost a lot of friends as one always does. I am finding life is very purposeless." She turned and kissed him lightly. "And I enjoyed making love to you."

Keith said his little piece and she made no comment until he got up and said he ought to go. Then she said, "If the world's going to blow up today as seems highly likely, thank God for letting me meet you first." She hoisted herself on an elbow. He could see her bare shoulder and her scattered hair against the little sliver of light. But not her face. "Good-bye, Keith."

It was half past seven when Keith let himself into the Eaton Square house, tired from walking around Hyde Park thinking about the night, about her, and—he decided at the end—himself. No time for introspection now. Not now that he was reminded by the gray barrels of the guns in the dawn light.

Mrs. Ewhurst was polishing the hall table. "You young people!" she said. "I thought the others were late enough, but look at you, sir."

"The others are back? What time did they get in?" he asked.

She pointed to a note on the table. "Please wake us up at 10 o'clock. Good night," it ran, in Mike's writing. "Late, I'd say. But I didn't hear them come in. Are you going to bed now, sir?"

"No. I'm changing, then I'm off," Keith said, making for the stairs.

"I'll get you some breakfast, sir."

"No, thanks, Mrs. Ewhurst. I have to get back to Hendon."

He was changed and out of the house in five minutes, and headed for Victoria tube station. "Chamberlain calls Halt" and "Nazi Ultimatum Expires Today" ran the newspaper posters. Several defensive balloons were already aloft,

76

a pathetic show of defiance against the expected onslaught of German bombers.

At the Lower Grosvenor Place entrance to Buckingham Palace, a soldier wearing a tin hat and with bayonet fixed, stood guard. A military convoy was heading south along Buckingham Palace Road. Rush hour had a note of special urgency, yet people seemed more considerate than usual as they climbed onto crowded buses, many of them carrying gas masks in cardboard boxes slung around their shoulder.

On the platform, waiting for the tube train, a small man in a bowler hat nudged Keith, saying, "Give 'em hell, airman," and then turned scarlet with embarrassment.

How rapidly things were changing, how fast events were piling up! His own life—the massed flight to London, that catastrophic evening at the Caledonia, the night spent with that kind and expert woman—seemed to match the heady unreality of the crisis building up about the nation.

At the main gates at Hendon the armed guard asked for Keith's identity card. A section of three Hurricanes was taking off in formation, their Merlin engines throbbing lustily at wide-open throttle. They were quickly off the ground, and in unison their undercarriages were tucked into their wings. Here was a new conception of a fighter plane, impressive enough to cause hardened ground crews to halt in their tracks. Turning through 180 degrees in a steep bank the three machines came back over the airfield, canopies closed now and already cruising at above the maximum speed of a Hart.

Keith walked to the officers' mess, relieved to be back in the purposeful atmosphere of the station where there were no doubts and everyone was trained to deal with the threat of hostility which the outside world was only fearing. The idea of exercising the skills which he had acquired over the past months filled him with excited anticipation. He felt more than ever a man after last night—how right that dark, laughing, heavenly scented woman had been!

As for Mike, Keith had written him off as a cad, and he would ignore him as a cad. Mike, with his pretensions to being a gentleman, with his grand private schooling and international friends! A cad and a phony. Keith did not want any explanations, he preferred not to know what had happened last night after they had deserted him. He would not say anything to anybody.

And Eileen? Poor darling Eileen. So innocent. The victim of a heel—that's what they called them in America. But how *could* she? Keith experienced a momentary sickness of heart before he thrust all thoughts of Eileen aside and went in search of a late breakfast.

There was a note for him on the baize letter board outside the dining room. It said simply: "You are reserve pilot at thirty minutes readiness with temporary "B" Squadron from 1200 hours. Report to flight dispersal."

So, if there was going to be trouble, he might be in the thick of it after all! He flattened the piece of paper on the table beside him as he ate his bacon and eggs, regarding it with the same satisfaction as a pauper contemplates a gold coin.

Waiting on readiness at flight dispersal was later to become almost a way of life in itself for Keith and all operational Fighter Command pilots. There were degrees of readiness, which could apply to sections, flights or the whole squadron. At thirty minutes readiness you could sometimes risk waiting in the mess, if it was not too distant, though some commanding officers forbade this. At five minutes readiness you certainly could not leave the dispersal area and you had to have your flying gear handy. When readiness was "immediate" you had to have half an eye on your machine and be as near to it as possible. The ground crew would be standing by, trolley-ac for quick starting plugged in, parachute laid out either on the tail or in the cockpit seat according to preference. In very cold weather the engine would be warmed up from time to time to ensure instant starting if there was a "scramble." Later there was one more stage of immediacy when the need arose, in which the pilot sat in the cockpit, strapped in, ready to press the starter on the firing of a red Very flare.

Being on readiness was the final confirmation of the saying that war is nine-tenths boredom and one-tenth terror. Keith was to fill the long hours, by day or night, improving his chess, reading, playing every conceivable card game, talking and sleeping. There were to be times of readiness when they would hunch around the coke stove in an exposed Nissen hut, lie outside their tents in the midday heat, or on chill, still, clear nights stare up at the stars and wait for the telephone to ring.

That bell ruled their lives, in times of special stress jangling their nerves, on more relaxed days sounding a note of interest to break the boredom, or when the fog crept in or the clouds began to brush the windsock, that bell could bring the single joyous word "Released"—and then the scramble was for bicycles or a truck or even a seat in the flight commander's car, and change into dress blue and down to the local pub.

For Keith at Hendon, on September 28, 1938, while Neville Chamberlain was writing a letter to Adolf Hitler telling him that he was certain the German Führer could "get all essentials without war," when reservists were hastening to their reporting stations, plans for the evacuation of schoolchildren were being prepared, when spades were out again in the parks and the People's Dispensary for Sick Animals was preparing gas-proof kennels for dogs, readiness was a solemn and important business. Even though they were only at thirty minutes, and Keith himself was only a reserve, they all sat in white overalls over their flying suits, helmet, goggles and gauntlets piled on their parachutes beside them.

There was little talk, and they all felt too tense to read much more than the headlines in the newspapers. Outside, their Harts were well dispersed but they were in the open, and it was not until the Hurricane Squadron, now with its identification marks painted out, took off in a flurry for Kenley, that they could taxi their machines into the vacated brick blast pens.

Among them all, pilots and gunners alike, there was an unspoken awareness that if German bombers made for London, they would be lucky to get near them, let alone shoot them down. In Spain, the same bombers that Keith and Mike had seen flying low over the Black Forest flew with impunity and without escort because they could comfortably outpace the fastest government fighters. They were relieved at four o'clock. The C.O.'s car, with Donald Avery sitting beside him, was first. Then came a camouflage-painted Denis bus with two dozen pilots and gunners to take over readiness until dusk, among them Buffer Davies, as lost without his Garbo as a golfer without his caddy, Sammy Crow, and—inevitably—Mike.

Keith talked to Buffer outside the door of the dispersal and ignored Mike. But Mike was not to be put off easily, and held Keith's arm as he climbed into the bus. "What's eating you? What happened to you last night, for Christ's sake?"

"I don't want to hear what happened to you," Keith said sharply and pushed his way inside. An Anson took off over their heads at that moment, drowning all other sound with its engines.

"What on earth's the matter with you?" Eileen asked crossly.

"Oh, come off it, old girl, you know as well as I do," Keith said.

"I jolly well don't, unless you're turning into a drunk. You were certainly tight as an owl at the Caledonia. Rude and drunk."

"And so you just walked out—and spent the night with Mike, I suppose. And you ask *me* what's the matter."

Eileen advanced across the study toward him threateningly, and he thought she was going to hit him. It was five years since they had fought, and this would not be the same half-playful, half-flirtatious struggle they used to indulge in sometimes. Her eyes were blazing and Keith flinched back from her angry face. "I did *what* with Mike? What did you say?"

Keith said, more lamely this time, "Well, you were getting very friendly. And why else would you suddenly stand me up like that except to get away for a bit of fun."

"And I suppose you didn't join us because you were having what you call, in your common way, 'a bit of fun'?"

"Join you? How could I join you?"

"Really, Keith. Were you too drunk even to read?" She sat down, but stiffly, not curling her feet under her. "I'll remind you of what happened. You got up to go to the lav., nearly knocking the table over incidentally. Then the Robertses came over, friends of Mike's family, and they were just leaving for a party at the Kennedys' and said we had to come, too. We waited ages for you, and then Mike scribbled you a note, saying that an embassy car would pick you up in about fifteen minutes, and gave it to the waiter. Can't you even remember getting it?"

Keith put his hand to his forehead and said slowly, and in a dead voice, "Yes, I think I did. I thought it was the receipt and the waiter wanted a tip. I stuffed it in my dinner-jacket pocket and was going to write Mike a check for half the amount. Then it passed clean out of my mind. Oh, Lord!"

Keith turned and ran from the room, ran up the stairs and opened his case, which Mrs. Stokes had not yet unpacked. The piece of paper was still in the pocket, crumpled, a memento of a strange, half ugly, half lovely evening when the world might have come to an end. "Join us soon at Kennedy's. There'll be a car for you in about fifteen minutes. Hope you're O.K." It was in Mike's unmistakable writing.

"Oh, blast, blast, blast!" Keith muttered and went downstairs to eat humble pie.

Eileen was sitting where he had left her. He could see her through the gaps between his fingers which he had spread in shame and contriteness over his face. She was still looking stiff with anger.

"Poor Mike!" he said. "Oh, I am sorry. He went off on a training assignment the next day and I've only seen him once, when I gave him the cold shoulder."

"And just remember, even if you have become just another dirty-minded airman, I do not sleep around with friends. Nor shall I. I'll go to bed with one man when I get married, which probably won't be for ages."

"I've said I'm sorry." He took away his hands and looked down at his old friend, beloved Eileen, the nearest person to a relation he had. How *could* he have thought that? He really must have a common mind.

She was unbending a little. "You'd better say sorry to Mike, too. He telephoned before you arrived. He was in London for his seventy-two-hour leave, and very miserable he sounded, too, not wanting to come here. What's more, he'd just heard that you and he are going to the same squadron when you return. And as Mike also said that "Peace in our time" was a load of hogwash and Mr. Chamberlain has been duped and there'll be a war soon anyway —then you had better get on." She looked at him with just the flicker of a smile. "Hadn't you?"

6

"Consequently this country is at war with Germany . . ."
Mike leaned back in his chair, and for a moment closed his
eyes, overwhelmed by the enormity of the hour for the
world, for Britain, for 140 Squadron, and for himself. He
was not much given to rumination, but those words, echoing in every home in the land, required consideration, especially by someone who was far from home, in the front
line and in a position of considerable danger brought about
by his own decision.

Mike's conclusion was characteristic. In essence it was:
"This is what you came for. It has come. So be it. And
you'd better be good, buddy!" Mike felt no sense of es-
trangement from his own country, nor did he feel that Britain
had adopted him. His loyalties, instinctive and ill-defined,
were to the free nations of the world, and strongly antag-
onistic toward any dictatorship that ordered the invasion
and demolition of any of these free nations.

Like most British and American people he knew almost
nothing about Poland. The fact that it was being crushed,
that it would certainly be the turn of France, Belgium, Holland, Britain and eventually the U.S.A. to be attacked, was

sufficient reason for going to war and halting what people referred to as "this evil tide." Already a few more United States citizens were signing on, and down at Middle Wallop, the first Royal Canadian Air Force fighter squadron had formed and was working up to operational status with its Hurricanes.

There was another motive. Mike Browning was highly competitive. He liked to excel. And he liked to be ahead of the game. Once having accepted that the British cause was right and that his own country would eventually be drawn into the coming conflict, Mike quickly decided that he wanted to be first in, and good at war when it came to war.

He was pleased that he had done so. There were a lot of things about the country and the people he felt impatient with—the class barriers, the arrogant assumptions of many of those who fancied themselves as the ruling class, the awful cooking and the damp climate. But there was much more that he liked about Britain. He loved flying. And he was in love with Eileen, the girl who, alone, was sufficient motive for putting the States out of his mind so that he could concentrate on fighting, winning and keeping Eileen at the end of it.

He glanced around the mess. Someone had turned off the wireless. Three pilots and 140's Engineering Officer wandered toward the billiards room, talking quietly. Others had picked up their newspapers again. A white-coated steward came in with a tray of coffee and biscuits. Ten minutes ago the nation was at peace. Now it was at war. But normality prevailed. Very British, thought Mike. Very unflappable.

Then suddenly the Tannoy spoke. From the fretwork and gauze-faced loudspeakers at both ends of the lounge a crisp voice announced, "Air raid. Air raid alert. This is an air raid alert. This is not an exercise. All nonoperational personnel to the shelters. B Flight 140 Squadron to immediate readiness."

At the same time the sirens sounded out across the station,

and Savile Farm was bursting with activity long before the last wail died and the thunder of Merlins filled the air. Mike rushed into the hall, grabbed his hat and gas mask and made for the bus waiting outside especially for this emergency. The three billiards players were hard behind him, intent on getting into the more serious game. The driver picked up five more pilots from the sergeants' mess, and then put his foot hard on the floor, hand hard on the horn, making for the B Flight dispersal on the far side of the airfield.

Everywhere blue figures were running, gas masks flapping against their backs, as they made for their shelters. The station commander's Humber was racing toward the control tower. Six Spitfires, in two untidy formations of three, were in the air before the bus reached the dispersal, and 140's A Flight—the one with Hurricanes—was taxiing fast toward the east end of the field for take-off.

"Lucky buggers!" one of the sergeants exclaimed. "They won't bother to scramble us."

140 Squadron was in the process of converting from biplane Gladiators to Hurricanes. A Flight was fully converted, and like the Spitfires of the other squadron at Savile Farm had been on immediate readiness when the air raid alert had been sounded. B Flight were due to get their Hurricanes during the next few days.

Mike recognized Keith by his height in the group of pilots standing outside the dispersal hut. He was wearing white overalls and carrying his helmet and goggles and was watching the climbing Spitfires. "He looks like that goddamn recruiting poster—'Fly with the R.A.F.,'" Mike thought.

Then they were all tumbling out of the bus and making for their lockers. If it was a mass raid on London, they would certainly be scrambled, to do as well as they could with their obsolete machines. At least the Gladiator was an improvement on the Harts they had flown down to Hendon a year ago. Now they had an armament of four machine guns, a top speed of nearly 250 m.p.h. under favorable conditions, an enclosed cockpit and the maneuverability of a seagull.

Mike had placed his parachute on the tailplane and had joined Keith and the others outside the hut when they again heard the distant sound of an air raid siren. It came from the direction of the police station of the nearby suburban town, and its note was the continuous one of the "all clear." The siren was joined by others, farther and nearer, until the station's own sirens moaned out their news that the alert was over. The troops who were not on duty emerged from the trenches behind the blast pens, and Buffer Davies was heard to drawl, "O.K., chaps, it's back to bloody boredom."

"Rot," retorted the Squadron Intelligence Officer, a crafty-looking, hard-eyed and stooping figure called Willy Williams, but always referred to as "Spy." "We're at war now. Bags of flap."

But the only other excitement on that epochal day, September 3, 1939, when half England took to the shelters for a false alarm, was the arrival of the first of B Flight's Hurricanes. After the morning scramble, both squadrons had been kept at immediate readiness, eating a cold lunch down at the dispersal, and the arrival of a single Hurricane was a welcome distraction. A Flight had had their Hurricanes for three weeks now, and they were all familiar with the purposeful configuration of the eight-gun monoplane, which made the remaining Gladiators appear so antiquated.

This one came over the center of the airfield in a shallow dive, performed an immaculate slow roll at two thousand feet, lowered undercarriage and flaps and touched down nicely fifty yards inside the boundary hedge. Then it taxied to the control tower before being diverted over to 140's dispersal.

Someone remarked a shade patronizingly, "I didn't know those delivery pilots could do more than straight and level stuff. That wasn't bad."

The pilot switched off a few yards away after giving the

Merlin a last burst to clear the plugs, and climbed out. To everyone's astonishment he was wearing a tweed plus-four suit, as if he were off for eighteen holes at the club, and instead of a helmet and goggles and all the paraphernalia with which they were equipped, he was wearing a tweed cap. He was also portly and middle-aged, which they regarded as an affront. An elderly civilian piloting a 300 m.p.h. fighter they had not yet flown themselves!

B Flight's commander, "Taffy" Jones, went out to greet him, and they heard the civilian say, "No problems. She's all right. Langley always gives them a good check." He glanced in the direction of their Gladiators and smiled grimly at the group of pilots. "A good day to get new kites. Looks as if you'll be needing them."

Later, they drew lots for the first flight. The squadron's letters RC had been painted on the fuselage, and the Hurricane's guns had been armed and synchronized and the radio adjusted for the Savile Farm and Sector wavelengths. Mike drew the right card from the pack and the announcement was greeted with mixed jeers and cheers.

Polo Satterthwaite groaned. "Eh, I can see the bloody prang already," he said. "Wheels oop in the middle of the field."

No fewer than six of the original Uxbridge intake of February 1938 had been posted to 140 Squadron, and the Yorkshire boy was one of the most popular. His crack referred to the most common mistake made by pilots who had never flown with a retractable undercarriage, in spite of the warning light and buzzer sounding out in the cockpit.

"Lucky in love, lucky in war," Keith said with a laugh.

In the past year of uneasy peace, Keith had come reluctantly to accept the love that had grown between Mike and Eileen. The adjustment had demanded patience and tact from all three of them, and there had been moments of anguish. But since that awful night during the Munich crisis, and the row that had followed, the two young pilots had become even closer friends than before. Although the engagement was unofficial and nothing had been said to Eileen's parents, Keith could now see himself, more or less cheerfully, as Mike's semi-brother-in-law.

They had all had cockpit training for the Hurricane and had watched the A Flight pilots take up the monoplane for the first time. There had been lectures on the fighter, with diagrams, and everyone had given their impressions of it. As Mike put on his gear beside his locker in the dispersal hut, he felt perfectly calm about the prospect. Since that test flight in the Tutor with the Chief Instructor at Eldergrove, when it seemed his self-confidence had at last cut in with the decisiveness of an ignition switch, he had flown a dozen types of R.A.F. machines and had two hundred and fifty hours in his logbook.

There were more things to look out for in the Hurricane, and a hundred miles an hour or so of extra speed, but it was only an airplane, a ship, a kite, a flying machine. And what better day to start, when preparation for war had turned to war itself?

Mike pretended to ignore the rest of the pilots, and they pretended not to be watching him, as he walked out to the Hurricane. Taffy Jones, who had done a dozen hours with A Flight's machines, stood on the port wing and leaned over Mike when he had settled into the cockpit.

"You know the form as well as I do," he said. "The only difference to the Glad is undercart"—and he put his hand on the lever—"flaps, and prop pitch control. If you take off in coarse, you won't. A Flight's got some kites with wooden fixed-pitch props, and one day there's going to be a nasty accident when someone forgets."

The flight commander leaned over to the right side of Mike's seat and pointed to a handle. "If your hydraulics give out that's what you pump to get your flaps and wheels down. Or up. And it's hard work. Taxi her around a bit before you go."

Mike settled himself in, adjusting the seat for his short stature, struck less by the spread of white-on-black instruments facing him than the absence of the second wing which, in the Gladiator, was almost level with the top of the windshield. The clear view ahead, uncluttered by struts and bracing wires, was wonderful when good visibility could mean the difference between life and death. The exposed feeling, a reminder not to flip over when landing, would soon disappear, he decided.

Mike unscrewed and pumped the Ki-gas a couple of times to prime the cylinders, switched on the two magnetos, called out "Contact!" to the crewman on the battery cart and pressed the starter button. The thousand-horse twelve-cylinder Merlin fired at once. He signaled away chocks, clipped the mask over his mouth, and with his hand lightly holding the brake handle on the control column, eased the Hurricane out of its bay. With the long pointed nose, visibility forward when taxiing was restricted. Constant weaving with the differential brakes was the only answer, and he dabbed the rudder pedals alternately, gradually getting the feel of the machine on the ground.

He brought the Hurricane to a halt by the windsock and at right angles to takeoff direction. With brakes locked on, he eased the throttle forward in its quadrant until the big rev counter just below and to the right of the reflector sight showed 1,000 r.p.m. Then with his left hand Mike switched off in turn the two magneto switches, watching the revs drop. No more than 50. O.K.

The cockpit procedure was spelled out and parrot-learned. Fine pitch, rad open, flaps up, fuel gauge showing full, trim, oxygen . . . Mike switched on the radio and his ears were at once filled with the crackling from the high-frequency T.R.9 set. "Hullo Nestegg, hullo Nestegg. This is Sandbag Red One," said Mike, giving the control tower the 140 Squadron call sign. "Permission to scramble, please. Over."

The voice of the flying controller came back at once. "O.K. to scramble, Red One. Out." Then as an informal postscript, "Bloody good luck."

Mike grinned to himself under his mask, pulled down his goggles, and turned the Hurricane into wind. "No arsing about," he told himself. "Let's get this over with." He opened the throttle firmly and progressively, noting at once not only the remarkable acceleration but also—in spite of full opposite tab setting—the torque pull. Then the tail came up, and in a second or two the beat of the wheels ceased, the control surfaces took a grip, and he eased back the stick. There was already over 100 m.p.h. on the clock, and the speed built up swiftly as he climbed away over the far perimeter of the airfield. Wheels up, red light confirmation on the left of the panel. Ease back the throttle, then the pitch. Radiator closed. Reach up for canopy grip, slide it shut.

The Gladiator had accustomed him to the sense of confinement created by an enclosed cockpit, and now at two thousand feet Mike felt he could relax and get the feel of this superb monoplane. Below, London's outer suburbs slipped past the trailing edge of the wing, a mosaic of little houses and gardens, larger green splashes of parks, a scattering of small factories, and ribbons of more houses following the lines of the arterial roads radiating out to the country-side beyond. The roads were busy with traffic; an electric train bound for Brighton emerged from Redhill tunnel.

Here, spread out below Mike, was a country again at war with Germany, but everything looked wonderfully normal. But would it look the same in a week's time, when perhaps Heinkels and Dorniers would have laid waste this city, and he might be in action against them in this new instrument of destruction?

Mike switched on the reflector sight, made a gentle aileron turn—rudder was scarcely necessary, so sensitive was the response—and saw himself roaring in on a stern attack against a mass formation of Junker 88's. His thumb touched the gun button, set "safe" with its guard, and he applied pressure, imagining the devastating effect of 8,000 rounds a minute—140 a second—tearing into the cockpit area of a German bomber.

Mike did some tight turns to satisfy himself that the maneuverability was all that others had claimed for it, put her into a stall, dived down to two thousand feet again, observing how rapidly the speed built up to over 300 m.p.h., and flew back over Kenley with its similar contingent of one Hurricane and one Spitfire squadron, to Savile Farm.

With permission to land given by the controller, Mike took his Hurricane downwind in full fine pitch, with rich mixture and light throttle. At 110 m.p.h. he lowered wheels, flaps, and rad, feeling at once the slight buck of resistance and further drop in speed. Then, with hood slid back, he gave all his concentration to bringing her down safely. Things happened a great deal faster than in a Gladiator, no denying that. "But don't let it fuss you," he told himself severely, "there's plenty of time. Or you can always go around again. No shame in that."

All the same, he was not going to allow it to happen. He was going to make a swell job of this—and that was for sure. There would be several hundred people watching him as he lost height toward the perimeter. Dropping his eyes frequently to his instruments and easing back the column, correcting direction with a touch of rudder to right, then to left, Mike's Hurricane swung its way over the hedge at fifty feet and leveled off with the speed dropping below 80. Back, back, steady, lift that long nose. Now sit down. And she did, with scarcely a bounce.

As soon as he was at walking speed, Mike unplugged his R/T and oxygen and pulled off his mask and helmet, exposing his face to the breeze. Boy, did he feel good! And boy, wasn't he just sweating!

A group of airmen and a corporal were sitting on their kitbags outside their barracks at Savile Farm chanting, to the tune of "Oh Come Let Us Adore Him," the song of every airman who has nothing to do but sit and hope. "Oh why are we waiting, oh why are we waiting, oh . . ."

Mike and Keith walked past on their way to the mess for lunch, and the corporal brought the airmen to their feet and saluted.

Responding to the salute, Mike said to Keith, "I still can't believe it. A year ago they brought us down to London for a false alarm. Now they're sending us to the top of Scotland when there's a genuine real live war. They're nuts."

140 Squadron had been posted away, three weeks after the declaration of war, to Elgin on the north Moray coast. Except for a handful of the squadron who lived in north Scotland, there was bitter disappointment that they were all leaving the front line station of Savile Farm in Surrey just when action was expected.

"Something to do with the navy. That's what they say," said Keith. "Got to be protected from nasty Nazis."

"The U.S. Navy looks after itself. It doesn't call in the Air Corps."

"Now, now, no nationalism," Keith rebuked him, and they both laughed, and agreed that they would at least be seeing a part of Britain they did not know. And rumor in the mess had it that the Inverness girls were really something.

Another group of airmen, awaiting trucks to take them to King's Cross for the night train, were singing lustily the Fitters' song, with the chorus:

> We are the Fitters, Fitters A.E., are we, are we,
> Armorers and Fitters D.P.
> Fitters of every kind and degree.
> We are the Fitters.

Then:

> If there is any kind of mending
> That is needed for your engine,
> All we ask is that you put in a demand (a demand)
> Gentle Sir, do not be nervous,

For behold us at your service,
At your service, Aviator, to command
(to command).

Mike and Keith passed them at this point, and belatedly and sheepishly, the men sprang to their feet and fell into silence. "That's O.K., buddies," called out Mike as he responded to the salute. "Glad to know it." The lusty voices followed them down the path to the big brick officers' mess:

If your crankshaft needs aligning,
Or your bearings need relining,
And connecting rods are creaking in their cranks
(in their cranks).

If your engine needs decoking,
If it's popping back or smoking,
We gen'rally can cure its little pranks
(little pranks).

The squadron flew up in the afternoon, dropping in at Catterick to refuel, and reaching Elgin just as dusk was falling. The North Sea was slate gray, the Cairngorms bleak and hostile, blacked-out Inverness, at the head of Loch Ness, a dark smudge to the west. When Mike climbed out of his Hurricane he was met with a chill breeze that reminded him that they were more than six hundred miles nearer the Arctic, and that winter was coming on.

There were Fleet Air Arm pilots drinking pink gins in the mess, and Mike detected an unmistakable glance of disapproval as they nodded a greeting. "I guess we're not looking our best," he told himself in mitigation as he called for a pint. They had flown up with all the luggage a Hurricane's cockpit could accommodate safely, which was one toothbrush wrapped inside a pair of pajamas, and they were all in their scruffiest uniforms.

Buffer Davies joined him at the bar, nodding toward the dark-blue-uniformed pilots. "Decent of the senior service to allow R.A.F. types into their mess, what?" he said in a loud voice that was almost but not quite provocative. The navy downed their gins and left.

"That's very ill-mannered of you, Buffer," someone remarked. "Imagine a shoal of unshaven navy types blasting into our mess."

"I'd accelerate faster than Garbo," Buffer confessed. He had threatened to resign his commission rather than be separated from his vast and fast motor car. "Where am I goin' to put all those delicious Scotch colleens?" he had demanded, and when Keith pointed out that colleens came from Ireland, he had been informed that to Buffer the name was of no consequence and that only the shape mattered.

As it turned out, such are the vagaries of war, there was more fighter action in Scotland than in southern England. In raids on Scapa Flow and the Forth, an old battleship, two modern cruisers and a destroyer were damaged, and Spitfires of 602 and 603 Squadrons shot down several of the Heinkels.

The first alarm occurred before dawn the next morning and before the ground crews and equipment and luggage had arrived on the night train. Flight Sergeant Warren, a dour veteran of twenty-eight, and two officers of A Flight were scrambled from immediate readiness in machines that had been refueled by navy mechanics. It was a false alarm, but there were a number of scrambles over the next few weeks and once the C.O. came back with his gun strips blown out, indicating that he had fired his guns. But it was only a drifting barrage balloon blown north from the Forth that he had shot down.

On the afternoon of November 11, the whole of A Flight was scrambled when Sector reported a threatened raid on the naval base of Cromarty. Mike and Keith were already airborne, however, on a navigational exercise, and the controller was able to vector them onto the bandits. Whether the Heinkel they spotted was a straggler or R.D.F. had exaggerated the size of the raid was not known at the time, although later the surviving members of the crew who were picked up by a Walrus amphibian confirmed that they were on a reconnaissance flight.

For Keith this should have been an evening of congratulation and celebration. The news that 140 had scored at last had already flashed around the station. But so had the news of Mike's crash, and he was known to be Keith's closest friend. Everyone was down at the flight dispersal, and crowded around Keith's Hurricane as soon as the propeller had stopped.

"Bloody bad luck, old boy," Buffer commiserated. "Especially after puttin' up such a good show."

Others were examining the 7.9-mm bullet holes in Keith's port wing and asking questions about the combat.

"I'm terribly sorry, I can't think straight until I hear about Mike," Keith said.

At this moment, just as the Spy was going to take him away for a proper interrogation, the C.O. arrived in his Hillman. Squadron Leader Anson had led 140 since the squadron had been formed with Gauntlets four years before. He was twenty-eight, like Flight Sergeant Warren, old for a fighter pilot, was hawk-faced with receding hair and was reserved in manner but a superb pilot and a better shot even than Mike. At this time he was angrier than anyone on 140 had ever seen him.

Anson walked straight up to Keith, who saluted and said, "Good evening, sir."

"You, Pilot Officer Stewart, are a bloody disgrace to this squadron and to the command," he began. "And I've no doubt you think you're bloody clever to shoot down a Hun and deserve a D.F.C."

"No, sir," Keith began, but was told in icy terms not to interrupt.

"Do you not know the simple rule that you don't indulge in aerobatics, or anything violent, after an action? It is not only bad manners to beat up an airfield. To roll a machine that is damaged is lunacy. And," he added bitterly, "in this case apparently suicide."

In spite of this reprimand, delivered so that all could hear it, Keith felt impelled to ask, "Is he dead, then, sir?"

"The ambulance hasn't come back yet. You both deserve to be. Except that you cost the country several thousand pounds to train and we need every fighter we've got. Report to my office at oh-nine hundred tomorrow morning."

He turned, perfunctorily responding to Keith's salute before stepping back into his car.

Keith felt like being sick. The shattering series of events were almost too much for him and he did not move for several seconds.

"That was pushing it a bit, under the circumstances," someone said quietly.

From the back of the crowd, Keith heard, "Well, it is against regulations. And very foolish. We know Americans show off, but one expects proper . . ." The voice of Donald Avery was drowned by the Spy, who took Keith by the arm and said firmly, "Come on, old boy. I've got some whiskey in my office. You can tell me all about it in your own time."

"Thanks," said Keith, and turned to Buffer. "Send along a word as soon as any news of Mike comes in."

Mike turned his head very slowly as Keith came into the room. His face was a mass of bruises and cuts, there was a bandage across his forehead and his hair had been shaved back to the crown of his head. He looked ill and his spirits were clearly at a low ebb.

Keith sat down on a chair at his bedside, trying to conceal his shocked surprise at his condition. "I won't ask you how you are," he said, "because I'm sure you're feeling rotten. Everyone sends their best, and I was commissioned to buy some nourishment for you in Inverness." He put a bowl of mixed fruit on the bedside table, and then nodded toward the pulleys holding up Mike's right leg. "How long have you got to be jacked up like that?"

"About a month. Hips can be tricky, I'm told." The fire in his voice had gone, and he spoke so slowly that Keith asked him if he wanted to talk. "No, that's O.K. They've doped me stupid, that's all. No raining goddamn sunbeams around here."

He could not, in fact, tell Keith much about the crash as he had been knocked unconscious and the two farm workers had presumed him dead. "I believe the armor plate saved me from breaking my neck. They had to lift the whole damn kite off to get me out. What about you? C.O. pleased? Gave you a nice birthday party?" He managed a smile that was twisted from a cut on his cheek.

Keith laughed. "It was an eventful twenty-first. Let's leave it at that. There was talk of a court-martial, but I think the A.O.C. quashed it. Frightened it might leak out to the papers. 'Hero on trial for shooting down enemy bomber.' Something like that. So I was severely admonished, promotion put back six months, and by the time you get back it'll all have blown over."

Keith followed the ritual of hospital visiting by eating some of Mike's grapes and peeling half a dozen for him. "I'll tell you one bit of good news. Good news for Buffer, anyway."

"I need it."

"We've got W.A.A.F.'s. Women! And they use our mess until their own's ready."

"You're kidding!" Mike exclaimed.

"Three officers, one in ops and two in admin. And a dozen aircraft women. Some pretty ones, too."

"There'll be a riot," said Mike.

A sister came in and told Keith he had to leave. "Our American is not really up to visitors yet," she said.

"You look after him, Sister. He may be a Yank but that's not his fault and he can shoot straight." Keith swung his gas mask onto his shoulder and made for the door. There he paused and turned around, grinning broadly. "Oh, there is one other bit of news. Eileen sent me a telegram saying she's coming up to see you tomorrow."

Mike raised his head off the pillow, his mouth open in

amazement. Keith closed the door behind him, thinking "If anything's going to improve his condition, that'll do the trick."

What Keith had failed to add was that one of the W.A.A.F. officers was known to him. The confrontation with Jenny in the mess at Elgin on the evening of her arrival, and only two days after his twenty-first birthday, had set tongues wagging in 140 Squadron. There were a dozen officers in the lounge when the Station Commander came in with the three newly arrived officers, all looking extremely smart in their blue uniforms. Everyone got up for the introductions, and Keith was in a corner of the room on his own so that he did not see the faces of the women until they turned with the Group Captain. "This is Pilot Officer Stewart. Section Officer Smith, Section Officer Carruthers, and Section Officer Simpson."

Keith shook the hands of the first two and then stared in disbelief at the pretty dark face and dark brown eyes. Her black hair had been cut short in accordance with regulations, and was set into a ducktail above her blue collar. She smiled and said, "All right, Keith, I'm not a ghost."

"So you two know one another," said the Group Captain. "Then you'll be able to make her welcome and look after her, Stewart."

"Yes, sir, I'll do that," said Keith with warmth.

A special effort was made on that first evening to be hospitable to the new arrivals. There was some rivalry between the navy pilots and the R.A.F. for the other two W.A.A.F. officers. Keith, in his privileged position, had Jenny to himself for the first part of the evening. He took her into the bar, followed by the amused eyes of half the squadron, and bought her a glass of sherry while he had his usual pint tankard of bitter.

"What on earth made you do anything as stupid as becoming a W.A.A.F.?" he asked. "That nice comfortable flat, theaters, nightclubs, lots of admirers . . ."

"Rubbish!" she said crisply. "I was bored stiff. Spoiled. I told you I felt life hadn't any purpose. And anyway we were all told London would be in ruins by the end of the first week. So I had a word with a friend at Air Ministry, and then I had an interview, and I was in. I am a Special Duties W.A.A.F., if you know what that means. R.D.F. Very hush-hush."

"I still can't believe it." Keith looked at her closely and remembered that face on the pillow by the light of the lamp in Half Moon Street. "What incredible luck."

"Yes, this is fun. But there'll be no time for dalliance here. Oh no, very busy and businesslike and practical. We are both holders of the King's Commission." She laughed and finished her sherry, quoting in a mocking voice the already tired admonition, "Don't you know there's a war on?"

Keith said, "Yes, but you can't stop me looking at you. After all, you were very nice that night."

"Dear Keith, and so were you. I only hope I made it clear that I'm not really a philanderer, but you looked so lost and sweet." She laughed again. "Anyway, all that was in the decadent days of peace. Now we must concentrate on marching shoulder to shoulder to victory."

Buffer arrived at their end of the bar at that point, a notable contradiction of this sentiment. He was wearing his seducing face and was full of good cheer. "You can't have this pretty lady to yourself *all* evenin', old boy. Now, what's it to be? Barman . . ."

After that, Keith saw Jenny only occasionally. She was away all day at the R.D.F. station which had plotted the Heinkel he had helped to shoot down, and was sometimes on night duty there, too. More attacks on the fleet were expected, although the main force had retreated to the west of Scotland beyond the range of German bombers, a considerable tactical victory which the Germans had so far failed to exploit.

Keith did a lot of flying, his section was scrambled twice in one week, and, as Jenny had said, they were both very busy and businesslike. But she often filled his dreams and on the rare occasions when they were alone, he had to resist sternly the urge to tell her how lovely she was. Whatever else happened, he was determined not to lose touch with her.

This was threatened when a signal arrived on December 3 instructing Pilot Officers Davies, Satterthwaite and Stewart to proceed forthwith to R.A.F. Uxbridge pending a posting to one of the squadrons with B.A.F.F., the British Air Forces in France. This caused a minor sensation in 140 Squadron. Apart from the temporary loss of Mike, the squadron had retained the same pilots for a long time now. They were used to one another, and fiercely loyal to their squadron, with its motto "Through Clouds to Glory."

The only enigma was Donald Avery. Except for his extreme right-wing political views—he was once heard to say that they all ought to have gone and fought with Franco—he seemed a very characterless and colorless fellow. He participated very little in mess talk and drinking, and never in the rough-and-tumble of mess life. His conversation was formally polite to his fellow officers and airmen alike. He was a competent pilot but unadventurous and very safety conscious, always doing his cockpit check twice and very slowly.

Avery appeared to prefer the company of senior officers, and to most people's surprise they appeared to like being cultivated by this stately, serious pilot officer. He would be seen drinking a single dry sherry with Anson or the Wing Commander Flying or even the station commander before luncheon. Or he would emerge after a long period from the C.O.'s office. "What on *earth* have they been talking about?" someone would ask.

Keith was irritated that he could not figure him out. Mike used to say, "Aw, hell, he's harmless enough. I just wouldn't want to be in a tight spot with him." But when he was suddenly promoted straight to Flight Commander of B Flight in succession to Taffy Jones, who was given a new Spitfire squadron, a shock of dismay went through them all.

Buffer's comment was brutal. "They want their soddin' heads examined at Air House." And the chorus of groans made clear the feelings of the others.

In the twenty-four hours before he had to leave, Keith managed to get over to see Mike for the last time. He was still in traction, but his face had healed up and his spirits were much improved now that he was off drugs and had seen Eileen every day for a week because she was staying with friends nearby.

"So you're going to hang out your washing on the Siegfried Line," he greeted Keith. "You really get all the luck. That's where the action is. Bags of marauding Dorniers. Get your score up, then get your gong up."

"Don't be crazy. I'll never see any medal. And I'm not sure I even want to go. I'll miss the other chaps, and you, and . . ."

He paused, and Mike said, "And who? I guess you've got yourself a little Scotch colleen, you old dog."

"Rubbish. I've got to go. Give my love to Eileen."

"Give 'em hell, boy. And watch out for the mademoiselles from Armentières."

Keith wondered if he would ever see again that cheerful face with the puckered forehead, now scarred for life. He would remember him best formating on him in a Hurricane, hood thrown back, helmet off and hair streaming in the wind, concentrating on achieving perfection.

He thought he would have to leave without even saying good-bye to Jenny. His bag was packed and his batman was taking it from the hall in the mess when the inner blackout door was opened and she came in out of the night. She looked all in, with black rings from lack of sleep under her eyes.

"I hear you're off to France," she said, slinging her gas mask onto a peg. "Dear Keith, look after yourself." And she brushed her lips lightly against his and walked on into the lounge.

7

The frames of the French railway carriage windows rattled from the vibrations of the distant guns. The train had been stationary for twenty minutes, and the boom of artillery from the Maginot Line had been continuous, the yellow muzzle flashes rippling in the distance and silhouetting trees on the skyline.

"They used to call this a 'hate' in the last lot," Keith remarked. "My God, I hope we're not going to have four more years of trench warfare."

"Not on your life," Polo Satterthwaite, ever optimistic, added. "We may not be home for Christmas. But it'll be all over by Easter, and I'll be back in Yorkshire by the summer." He applied a match to his malodorous half-smoked pipe and tossed it on the floor.

"That's what my father told me about the Great War. 'Have the boys home for Christmas.' That's what they said. But there were four more Christmases of hell and torment."

"Your pater did his bit, too, eh? Jolly good show," said Buffer.

"Wounded on the Somme. Military Medal. And invalided

out. His wounds gave him pain for the rest of his life."

Keith glanced out into the darkness again. Would the train ever move from this stretch of line? They had already been twenty-four hours on the short journey from Uxbridge to their destination in northeast France, the Air Component of the British Expeditionary Force base at Lens-La Basse.

Buffer had now fallen into a sound sleep in the far corner, the peak of his hat over his eyes. He had taken full advantage of the duty-free brandy on the cross-Channel steamer and would need some arousing. The three pilots, who had known each other since the beginning of their training and had served on the same squadron since early '39, made a disparate trio. Buffer and Keith were unusually tall at six feet two inches, Buffer's swarthiness contrasting with Keith's blond Scandinavian appearance, and Polo Satterthwaite small and chirpy and irrepressibly untidy, as always.

The windows rattled louder than ever as unusually fierce firing broke out nearer than before.

"I thought this was supposed to be a phony war," said Keith. *"La drôle de guerre."*

The train pulled into the station for Lens-La Basse at dawn—a cold, damp, misty dawn. As a late night party wearies of itself, the firing from the front had ceased and the village was stirring into life. Keith at once sensed that air of phlegmatic fatalism with which Europe's peasantry has accepted catastrophe and the threat of catastrophe since the beginning of time. The tasks had to be undertaken whether the world was about to fall apart or promise a millennium of peace and plenty.

A horse, head well down, pulled a cart with a girl and an old man on it past the station entrance. Neither horse nor humans looked up. Down the street women in black shawls were sweeping the pavement outside their houses. An ancient two-seater Citröen with a torn hood rattled past. In the forecourt a canvas-topped Albion, camouflaged and with R.A.F. number plates, was drawn up, the driver sitting on the running board, smoking. He got to his feet and ground out his cigarette as they approached. A second airman appeared and took their luggage.

Buffer answered the salutes for all of them and said, "So this is *la belle France*. How are things at Lens-La Basse? Bags of vino and mademoiselles?"

"Shambles, then a cock-up, then a shambles, sir. It's a bit better now, but we had no bleeding blankets for a week, nothing but bullybeef in the land of plenty. For real balls-ups, the R.A.F.'s got nothing on these Froggies."

Lens-La Basse was a big permanent *Armée de l'Air* base, with sturdy brick and stone buildings, steel hangars, three-floor barrack blocks, guardrooms, stores—the parachute store characterized by its extra height—and flight offices. It was very much like any R.A.F. station built between the wars, with a concrete apron outside the hangars and a macadam perimeter track, but no runways.

The adjutant met them after breakfast and made them welcome. 259 Squadron had been here as air support to the British army contingent since September, and when the generally awful weather permitted, had seen action against German reconnaissance aircraft photographing sections of the Maginot Line and the area behind for signs of military activity. They had shot down a couple of Dornier 17's, but had not yet seen the fearsome Messerschmitt fighters, the single-engined 109 and the twin-engined *Zerstörer* 110. Nobody seemed to expect much excitement before the spring.

The C.O. came into the adjutant's office while they were talking and introduced himself. He was a complete contrast to Anson. Squadron Leader Rowbotham was plump, fair, balding and a cheerful extrovert with a broken nose from some violent bout at Cranwell. He must have already seen their record sheets and turned first to Keith. "Half a Hun, and a spot of bother, I believe. You've learned your lesson. And no doubt, when the balloon goes up, you'll be able to add to your score."

Before he left he said, "The Frogs are dining in with us

tonight, so put on a good show and don't get too pissed."

Two fifty-nine shared Lens-La Basse with the *Armée de l'Air*, which had a squadron of Morane 406's on the other side of the airfield. Polo and Keith wandered over to look at them later in the day, and were impressed by the fighter's stubby, businesslike appearance. They were not so heavily armed as the Hurricane, having only two machine guns in the wings, but with a big cannon firing through the propeller which would have much greater range and hitting power than any machine gun.

They also saw one or two of the pilots. But it was not until the evening, when the blacked-out dining room was specially lit and decorated for the party, that Keith had a chance to talk to any of them at length. He found himself next to a dark, olive-skinned young man who had been at the Sorbonne a year before, and was new to the squadron. He talked in fluent English, was cheerfully extroverted, and was totally cynical about the military state of his country.

"If Marshal Joffre could see us now, he would be very very sad," said Pierre, digging into a superb duck mousse—the catering had been taken over by the French and that was one aspect of French life that was as good and efficient as ever.

"But you have a great army," Keith protested. "Fine tanks, gallant infantry, the Maginot Line . . ."

"We have great inventiveness, fine armaments, but the spirit is dead—all dead. It died at Verdun, monsieur, with the cream of our nation. Look at our *escadrille*. The pilots— O.K., as the Americans say. Our *mécaniques* are ninety percent pro-Soviet. Our Moranes, very fine design. Not as fast as your Hurricanes, but good. But badly made by workers who are nearly all communist or have no interest in their work. Sabotage sometimes. Then we have almost no spare parts. The Hispano people who make our engine—strikes, sabotage. We have no armor plate. No radio even. And if the Boche comes, we can take off perhaps five machines . . ."

Later, the evening became more informal, and the champagne seemed to revive some of the spirit of those historic and alcoholic parties of the Great War when French *aviateurs* and R.F.C. pilots had gotten together, often ending by wrecking the mess.

On the first clear day, the C.O. flew with Polo, Buffer and Keith in turn to assess their ability. "In some ways it's worse than finding your way in England," Keith was warned. "The prevailing wind brings all the smoke of French industry over this way and there are fewer distinguishing points. At least in the last 'do' the trenches helped, but the Maginot and Siegfried Lines are both camouflaged and it's too damn easy to slip over into Hunland."

Two fifty-nine was still flying fixed-wooden-propeller Hurricanes, which simplified things but reduced the flexibility of performance. When Keith scrambled in loose formation with Rowbotham, they seemed to take forever to get off the muddy grass. Once in the air and at operational height, all the qualities of response and vice-free maneuverability of the Hurricane were there.

"Just hold onto my tail," ordered the C.O., and at once threw his machine into a series of violent convolutions, ending up by hurling himself into a turn which he tightened progressively until Keith felt that he must stall and fall out into a spin. But he stuck to it, almost blacked out, and had the reward of hearing over the R/T, "Not bad. Now give me five minutes, then I'm going to try to bounce you."

Rowbotham climbed steeply at full throttle, made a banking turn into cloud and disappeared. Keith flew on, making quick turns to right and left and glancing rapidly in all directions, especially astern into his rearview mirror and by turning his head to survey the area not revealed by the mirror. They were below cloud, so an attack out of the sun was no danger, but Keith kept clear of the cloud base and recalled all the rules of responsiveness he had learned.

He spotted the monoplane in good time. It came at him fast and from above, as if it had just emerged from the cloud in a dive. Keith watched it close in and when it was an estimated four hundred yards distant, he threw his Hurricane into a violent turn to starboard, opened wide his throttle and climbed, keeping his eye on the other machine as it slipped past and below him, but already turning on its ailerons for another pass.

Just before it disappeared from view, Keith caught the clearest view he had yet had of his attacker. And it was not right. Not right at all. "My God," he said aloud, "it's a Hun. It's a 109."

There was no mistaking the slim fuselage, the clipped wing tips, and the uncompromising black crosses against white on the camouflaged upper surface of the wings. So rehearsal had turned into reality. This was not a friendly dice with his C.O. It was his first fighter-to-fighter combat. And he had better be good and quick and slip off the safety catch of his gun button because—there they were, one, two, three, four more, streaking down toward him from the same direction, sleek and deadly, faster than he was, and with their cannon, well capable of outranging his Hurricane's guns.

Against these odds his only chance of survival was to hold his circle and tighten it, tighten it as closely as he had with his C.O. a few minutes earlier. His first attacker had returned and clamped himself onto Keith's tail at about three hundred yards, firing intermittently with his nose cannon and two wing-mounted machine guns. The shots came uncomfortably close to his tail, but the 109 pilot clearly could not pull in any tighter.

Above, two more of his attackers were attempting to maneuver to get in a diving pass, but the angle was very difficult and Keith knew that he was nearly safe if he could continue to out-turn them. The temptation was to dive out and head for the ground, or reverse the turn to get a bead on one of them. The 109 could outdive him comfortably, and if he followed either course, he would be dead within seconds.

So superior was the Hurricane in the turn, that he almost pulled around and got the ring of his reflector sight onto his pursuer. He tried a half-second burst. It missed, but had the effect of forcing the Messerschmitt into a steep dive away.

Then a second opportunity occurred almost immediately. A rash pilot came in close and just above, and Keith pulled up his nose and gave the German a quick passing burst with half-ring deflection. To his utter astonishment, the 109 disintegrated into a ball of fire that turned to black smoke, and the machine scattered itself in small pieces like a shrapnel shell.

There was no sign of the pilot. The object he had destroyed might as well have been an unmanned projectile, but Keith's old conscience briefly reasserted itself and a chill flash of guilt passed through him as rapidly as his own .303 bullets had ripped into the Messerschmitt.

Or had they? For, missing the falling wreckage by less than a hundred feet, a Hurricane flashed past in a dive. "That's one of the buggers," the C.O. called out. "Now where're the others?"

Keith could see no sign of the antagonist on his tail, and jinking rapidly left and right, and looking up and down, the sky appeared to be empty, except for a small puff of smoke, gray now against the dark green of the distant ground, all that was left of the demolished German fighter.

Keith tucked into loose formation alongside the Hurricane. The C.O. had his hood thrown back, and took off his mask to grin and give the thumbs-up sign to him. He clipped his mask back on again, and transmitted, "Well done, Green Two. Nice shooting."

But Keith was half-comforted, half-disappointed when he realized that it must have been Rowbotham who had shot down the 109 with his long burst from above, jumping him as successfully as he had hoped to jump Keith. Keith's own burst had been brief and haphazard.

They flew back to base at five thousand feet, weaving and alert for a second attack. They were to hear no more from those 109's. In the Great War it had been just the same, Keith had been told many times. A sudden pass, a hectic melee, and then away.

No word of the combat had reached base, and as they taxied in, there was no sign of the reception Keith had experienced up at Elgin. It was not until they had switched off and were climbing out that an alert sergeant-pilot saw through the window of the flight dispersal that the guns had been fired. Half a dozen pilots ran out to meet them, and they burst into cheers when the C.O. said, "A 109, of all kites! Yes, Stewart was on its tail, and I came down from above and gave it another squirt. Fifty-fifty—we'll share it. That'll give you one whole," he added, turning to Keith and clapping him across the shoulder.

"Beginners' luck," A-Flight Commander commented cheerfully. "Here we've been for months, most of us seeing not a bloody thing, and then along comes this type and sends one for a burton on his third day."

Keith was congratulated by everyone and plied with drinks at the bar before lunch, but felt that he had been put into a false and uncomfortable position. He was pleased enough to have evaded those attackers at odds of five to one, until the C.O. showed up. But he retained lingering doubts that he had done more than damage that 109. Not many C.O.'s would do that for one of their new young pilot officers. . . . Lucky Keith again!

Keith's letter to Rising Hall began:

> We were visited by H.M. The King yesterday. You have never seen such b———t (I'm too polite to write that in full). The airmen's Brasso ran out and our batmen lent them ours, leaving us without any so we didn't make a very shiny showing. All the kites were lined up with crews at attention, and what a target they would have made as H.M. did his inspection, though we'd put up a section in case the Hun paid us a visit. Then he came into the mess, and into the bar where we were all downing noggins in relief it was over. You should have heard the silence! But he was very un-stiff and chatted

to some of us. What a grand man he is! The C.O. introduced *me*—what do you think of that! Said we had both had a scrap the other day and the King asked me to describe it in detail. Crikey! First and last time I'll talk to a Marshal of the Royal Air Force. And didn't I get ribbed after for shooting a line to our monarch!

Eileen had written to tell him that Mike would be well enough repaired by Christmas to come to Rising Hall to stay. For an instant, as Keith read this message in her clear rounded writing, he felt a pang of homesickness and a lingering shaft of jealousy. Of course, Mike deserved the luck. And after all he had been through, he deserved the comfort and indulgence the Hall would provide—blazing log fires, Mrs. Stokes's rare, well-hung pheasant, Mumms Extra Dry on Christmas morning. . . . Yet, and yet.

With the weather clamped down for days on end, life at Lens-La Basse became dull and restricted. The surrounding towns and villages were not in any way hostile, and the bars and restaurants in the towns from which the airfield took its name always gave them a warm welcome. But it was not the same as a pub crawl at Savile Farm or Elgin where the people spoke your own language and you could drop in to the movies.

But an evening out with Buffer was always an entertainment. He was a great friend of an Australian, Range Powell, a flying officer from Sydney, who was equally strong on the women, and odds were laid on whether Buffer, defending his reputation, got his bird before Range got his sheila. But there was a limit to the number of hangovers you could build up in a week, especially when the weather could clear quickly and you might be scrambled with a splitting headache.

Keith withdrew from the many opportunities of bedding down with the local girls. Jenny's face always seemed to intervene, and like one or two married pilots on 259—and others too—he preferred to abstain. Instead, a week before Christmas, he struck up a friendship with the curé, whom he met when studying the tombs in the local village church. On several evenings when he was off duty, he went around to his house and drank coffee and Calvados, and listened to his stories of the last war, when he had been a chaplain in the French army at Verdun. This not only kept Keith away from the bars of Lens but served to brush up his French.

On Christmas eve, a damp, chill and miserable day, he spent the evening with the curé and then helped him to prepare the church for midnight mass. "You must stay," he told Keith. "It will do you good and it is beautiful. Never mind your funny northern religion!"

So Keith did, and for half an hour was caught up in the exotic ritual of the service and the passion and depth of the local peasantry's fervor. When he left, his whole body consumed by the scent of incense, a thick fog had clamped down over the French countryside, and the temperature had fallen to far below freezing point. The air was quite still, and Keith was suddenly conscious of standing in a vacuum of silence, a paralysis of human activity. It was some seconds before he realized that the guns, which had rumbled to the east and south all day, were at last silent.

The curé came up beside him and said, "Ah, the Boche is showing a little respect this time. In 'sixteen there was no pause. Good night, my friend, and God be with you."

The weeks that followed were desperately cold, and the low temperatures became a greater preoccupation than the Luftwaffe. Everything froze, and the only place where you could get warm was within ten feet of the fire in the mess lounge. All the station's plumbing froze up, they went for days without washing, and a number of airmen suffered frostbite.

Down at the flight, the starter battery carts froze up, and the mechanics strained to turn over the engines by hand, and resorted to hot bricks and blow lamps to keep the oil from freezing. Somehow or other, a section of three Hurricanes was kept at readiness, and once Keith took off alone on a rare clear day. The cold was bitter but it was worth the suffering to see northern Europe, the English Channel, and the distant Kent countryside, transformed into a white fairyland. Only a few trains were running along lines that had been ploughed clear, the roads appeared empty, and chimney smoke rose straight into the air like gray matchsticks against the white. Even the Rhine was frozen, he saw, when he ventured across the frontier, the slim barges immobilized. But nothing came up at him, as if even the German ack-ack guns were locked solid in the grip of the cold.

When it melted at last, Lens-La Basse was turned into a quagmire. On the morning of April 12, with a steady drizzle falling, a low cloud base and a temperature close to freezing, Keith was down at the dispersal as one of his Flight on immediate readiness. They had played three rubbers of bridge to help while away the time, and the N.A.A.F.I. van had just brought them half-pint mugs of sweet tea.

Keith was sipping his, staring out at the hopeless-looking scene of mud and grass and gray wet sky. The corporal at the telephone was whistling, appropriately, "Spring Will Be a Little Late This Year," when they heard the sound of a revving engine, and distantly through the mist a taxiing Morane appeared.

"Good luck to the poor bugger," remarked Sergeant "Hawkeye" Henry at Keith's side. Henry was a pilot noted for three valuable qualities in a squadron: sobriety, a generous nature, and uncanny eyesight. "Even the sparrows are staying at home this A.M."

They watched the Morane pick up speed, its propeller blasting back a mud spray in its slipstream. A deeper note from its engine, and the tail lifted. The fighter was almost airborne when its wheels touched back again for what should have been the last time. Instead, they must have hit a particularly soft spot, because the nose suddenly tipped forward, and at 80 m.p.h. thrust into the ground; the tail came up, and the Morane cartwheeled twice, landing on its back. At once, from a speeding, sturdy fighter, it had taken on the appearance of a swatted fly.

There was a second's silence inside the hut. Then the voice of "Chiefy," a veteran flight sergeant with the Mesopotamia and Northwest Frontier ribbons, growled, "Neatest base over apex I've ever seen, sir. Nor did 'e suffer nothing, poor sod."

The French squadron's Renault crash wagon was already racing across the grass, headlights blazing. The telephone rang in their hut, too, and Keith presumed, reasonably enough, that the call would be connected with the disaster.

Instead, the corporal shouted, "Scramble! Bandits approaching northwest from Metz. Angels Fifteen."

Keith was wearing his Irvin jacket. All that he had to grab from his locker were his two pairs of inner gloves, silk and wool, and his leather gauntlets. Range Powell, Sergeant Henry, another sergeant-pilot and the C.O. himself ran for the door together. "It's going to be cold all right," said Polo.

"And bloody sticky for takeoff, as we've just seen," the C.O. called as they all ran flat out for their planes. "So take it easy. Steer zero zero after takeoff, climb at full throttle and we'll form up above cloud."

Keith had a good friendly relationship with his rigger, Tim Bushwood, an eager and efficient cockney. He was standing in rubber boots and balaclava by the cockpit step on the port side of Keith's A-Ac Hurricane, holding out his parachute like a valet who knows his master is late for dinner. Keith threw his gloves on the wing, slipped on the straps, clipped the metal ends into the box over his stomach, and leaped up. Helmet, mask and goggles were neatly arranged on the control column, and as soon as he was strapped in, he had them all fixed in a couple of seconds, R/T and oxygen plugged in. Bushwood was helping him on with his gloves and Keith cursed himself for failing to stop the shaking that always seized him at an emergency scramble. In a few seconds, control of his machine brought control of his nerves—but then there was no one to see.

Keith would have been thrown out of Eldergrove if he had taken off as riskily as this. It was a matter of contact, chocks away, and then hell for leather along the perimeter, weaving right-left-right, a dozen yards behind the C.O., the only one who had been quicker.

No pause for checking magnetos, or oxygen or fuel. The only check Keith made before turning into wind was his gunsight. It shone out momentarily, then he was away, the big wooden propeller taking great bites of air. Oh, for pitch control now! Keith thought, longing for the first touch of lift. What a moment for that poor Frenchman to go in! He caught a glimpse twenty feet below of the crash crew and a gathering of pilots and ground crew struggling to raise the Morane. Then it was up with the undercarriage and belatedly setting the gyro compass as the drizzle, then the cloud, swallowed him up and he was on instruments.

The cloud belt was thin, and at two thousand feet he was out again, into a thin sun filtering through a layer of cirrocumulus high above. The C.O.'s plane was half a mile ahead and five hundred feet above, and two more Hurricanes were just below.

"Vector one-three-five," the controller's voice ordered.

Rowbotham's voice came over the air clearly. They had V.H.F. sets now, vastly superior to the old T.R.9. "Pull your fingers out, Medway. And 'Buster,'" he ordered, the code word for full emergency boost. He was turning onto the new course, and the other five planes were struggling to match his altitude, black smoke pouring from their exhausts. They formed up finally at seven thousand feet. Rowbotham had scrapped the peacetime regulation formation of *V*'s of three with a weaving tail-ender covering the rear, and himself out in front. Among other drawbacks discovered in combat was its inflexibility and the difficulties that arose when turning, with the outside pilot having to increase and the inside decrease speed. He had watched Messerschmitt 109 *Staffeln* flying in what they called *Schwarm* formation, each *Schwarm* being of two pairs of two aircraft, numbered one, two, three and four, flying very loosely like the tips of the fingers of a spread-out hand. On turns, the number two of each pair simply ducked under and came up on the other side of his number one, and one pair similarly went under the other, all done without touching the throttle.

Keith flew as a number three in the starboard *Schwarm*, with Sergeant "Hawkeye" Henry as his number four. They were at seven thousand feet, with apparently nothing in sight, when his sergeant suddenly transmitted, "Hullo Medway leader, bandits at eleven o'clock above, course north. Blue Four over . . ."

Keith looked up, shading his eyes against the sun's glare, and spotted six shapes, no more than dots that might have been fighters or bombers, friendly or enemy. They were flying due north, rock steady in their formation, seemingly unaware of the threat from below. The C.O. kept them on the same course, until the planes had passed overhead, recognizable by their deep elliptical wings as Heinkel 111's, blue-painted underneath for camouflage, and traveling fast.

"One-eighty port—go." The Flight followed, Keith crossing over so that he was on the C.O.'s port side when they were set on their northern course, throttle wide open still and climbing faster now that they were closer to their best height.

At sixteen thousand they were a thousand feet above the Heinkels and a mile behind. The bombers might have been crewed by robots. Where could they be heading above this ten-tenths cloud which prohibited all bombing in northern France?

"Watch out above," the C.O. warned. "They'll have an escort."

They were all studying the broken cumulus which could conceal fighters and, with the varying glare of the midday sun, made visibility trying.

"Medway leader—they're at nine o'clock, very high," reported Sergeant Henry. How did he do it? It was some seconds before Keith spotted them, a dozen or more tiny dark spots far above them, at well over thirty thousand feet. "The devils, the cunning devils," Keith mused, and felt the stab of anger and fear, the prelude to cold calculation, that the imminent combat was arousing in him. There was no room for any more fastidious conscience, no squeamishness, with the odds, stacked as high against them as those alert, expectant 109's.

"We've time for one quick pass. Make it good. Keep your sections and turn into them when they come," ordered the C.O. in his crisp no-nonsense voice, always confidence inspiring.

The C.O. led his section down toward the right-hand side of the Heinkels, which had stepped up the first V and closed up even tighter for mutual protection. Keith led his sergeant down on the port side in a straight astern attack, selecting the leader for himself, as they had so often practiced, and leaving the two outer port machines for the other two of Blue section.

The Heinkels might have been Heyfords over Lincolnshire when they were still at Eldergrove. Except that these Heinkels were doing well over 200 m.p.h., their rear fire was so real and accurate that the gunners must have been centrally controlled by radio, and they, the attackers, had maybe ten seconds before a large number of 109's would be mixing it with them.

The smoke-trailing tracer from three of the bombers was concentrating on Keith and he had to shout fiercely in order to restrain himself from taking evasive action. But he managed to keep the center dot of his sight steady a half ring in front of the transparent bullet-shaped nose where all the crew except the gunner were stationed. He waited for the wing tips to merge into the range bars, checked his turn-and-bank, and squeezed the button. For the next five seconds, as he closed in fast on the big bomber, he could see no effect. Anger rose like a hot blast of flame from his stomach. Why couldn't he shoot—oh Christ! The waste!

Then the Heinkel suddenly reared up, just as that other one had done over the North Sea five months earlier, so that he was almost struck by it. He hauled back on the column, pulling his Hurricane into a steep climbing turn, and saw the full panorama of air combat as he had so often dreamed of it.

The symmetrical pattern of the bombers had been destroyed. A Heinkel was losing height fast, white smoke pouring from one engine, the other engine dead, and probably the crew too. The one he had hit was spinning down out of control. A third, also trailing smoke, was diving dead vertically toward the white low cloud below. Two more were still being closely engaged. The sixth had disappeared.

From the south, with the sun behind them, the enemy fighters were very close now, traveling faster than anything Keith had ever seen.

There was a lot of chatter on the R/T—snatched words like, "Look out behind, Jock," "I got the bastard!" and "He'll never pull out." Through it came the C.O.'s voice, authoritative and insistent. "Shut up, shut up, clear the air. Here they come."

Keith could see that Rowbotham had his number two covering him while there was no sign of his own sergeant. He threw his Hurricane into a tight turn as one of the 109's showed the flash of fire from its nose. It was like being spat at in a crowd. The melee that followed lasted thirty seconds and thirty years. To get in a half-second burst was a wild and haphazard business, and Keith once found himself, to his horror, shooting inaccurately at a Hurricane's cockpit at fifty yards with full deflection.

He thought he made some hits on one of the 109's that flicked past him and dived vertically away, and then he looked about him and the sky was empty, except for one distant Hurricane losing height to the west. All the Messerschmitts, all the bombers, all but this single Hurricane had vanished.

Keith put his nose down and came alongside the Hurricane. It was K–King, Sergeant Henry's. Keith rocked his wings and transmitted, "We'll go home together, Blue Four. If we can find our way."

There was no answer and Keith ruddered in closer. The

cockpit hood was half slid back as if the pilot had been about to bail out. Instead, he had slumped forward and was lying half across his control column. The hood was stained red in streaks which streamed back over the perspex like rain on a fast-moving car's windshield. And Keith knew that there was nothing he could do for him.

He remained in formation with the Hurricane, which had now become the young sergeant's flying coffin, willing him to raise his head. Once he called out in exasperation, "Blue Four, for God's sake pull yourself together!" But it was no more than a rebuke to the dead, and he was shocked at the hopelessness and profanity of his rebuke.

After a while he pulled away, feeling sick and angry and noticing for the first time the long tears in the fabric behind the cockpit and in the fuselage beneath the cockpit. They were not 7.9 holes: these were from 20-mm explosive cannon shells. And they had killed 259's hawk-eyed spotter.

The Hurricane slipped away beneath Keith and glided into the cloud blanket as if being ceremoniously lowered into the softest of graves. . . .

As a gesture of respect for the death of Henry, the C.O. invited all members of the sergeants' mess to the officers' mess after dinner. It was the first time the two messes had mixed since Christmas, and the senior N.C.O.'s smartened themselves up so that their boots and buttons shone in the light of the bar's chandeliers. Their studied noninterest in the decor and accommodation of the mess fooled no one, and the event was totally relaxed.

After a number of noggins had been sunk, Squadron Leader Rowbotham climbed up onto a chair and shouted, "Shut up a minute." He had had a few whiskies earlier and a bottle of Beaune with dinner, so that his cheerful squashed face and balding pate shone ruddily. "First," he continued when the chatter had ceased, "there's growing evidence that there's a big show pending. The air's not the only place life's getting busier. The invasion of Norway's probably just a start. Many people think the Hun's on the move." He paused. "Now, closer to home, we're sorry about 'Hawkeye.' A good pilot and a good man. Here's to his memory. If it's any consolation to his family and friends, I saw him blow up one of the 109's before they got him. In addition, I got another . . ."

"Line—line—line!" someone called out, and the B Flight commander, who was very drunk, added, "The C.O.'s shooting an 'orrible line. Have his pants off!"

The C.O. grinned at his audience. "You can have my pants later, if you can get them off. But I haven't finished. Pilot Officers Powell and Satterthwaite claim a Heinkel between them. So does Pilot Officer Stewart, our blond hero of the North Sea war." Cheers and jeers echoed. "The remains of both have been found. Now, back to more serious business. Barman—champers all round, for those who can take it."

The party continued until three o'clock in the morning, with a great deal of rugger, some classic dogfights and the breaking of furniture. It ended with a fire extinguisher battle between the two messes. No winner was proclaimed.

Keith remained relatively sober, although heavily bruised by flying bodies and furniture. Polo and Range Powell appeared totally unaffected by their action of the morning. Keith was conscious of a mixed response to the whirlwind events. The first was a slightly solemn consideration of the number of men he had killed—there were fragments of five bodies in the crater made by his Heinkel, he had been told. And that was a long way from Sheila collecting a single partridge. Best not linger on that, not if you're playing at this game, he told himself firmly.

The second was the question of luck. "Lucky Keith" was not a common nickname, and so far it had been only self-applied in secret. But by now, he realized, he must be on the wrong side of the credit line. How long could his overdraft last?

In the privacy of his room, which was only slightly rocking like a liner's cabin in a moderate sea, he saw there were two letters for him, placed by his batman on his laid-out pajamas.

The first was from Eileen. It began:

> Darling Keith,
>
> I've decided to join the navy. What about that? We can't *all* be airmen! I'll have to salute you when you come home on leave. Daddy says the balloon must go up soon, and I feel I'm wasting my time here doing nothing but hunting and the flowers. A proper parasite. So off to the war I shall go. Mike is simply furious and threatens to write to the Admiralty and tell them I'm unfit for duty. The dear boy went back last week from his sick leave. You can hardly see his limp now and he's been getting himself disgustingly fit around the estate, out all day long . . .

While his mind was still reeling from this news, he slit open the other letter. It was postmarked Elgin, and carried the usual "Opened by Censor" label.

Mike's letter was full of racy news and gossip about 140, all of a purely nonmilitary nature. The only hint about the squadron's more serious activities was at the end. "It's probably nonsense, but rumor has it that we may soon be involved in events overseas and not a million miles from here. And that's swell as far as I'm concerned."

How that got through the censor, Keith could not imagine, because it was a clear indication that his old squadron was off to Norway. The German invasion of Denmark and Norway had recently taken place. Denmark had sunk without trace. But the newspapers told of stout Norwegian resistance, and of Allied military support.

Keith sat on his bed and read the letters again slowly, becoming increasingly aware, through the lingering fumes of alcohol and cigarette smoke, that they were at the brink of great events and life was shortly to become significantly more eventful and dangerous.

8

A few days before the day when Keith watched in anguish as the sergeant's Hurricane slipped into the cloud above the French countryside, Mike was bicycling out to the flight dispersal at Elgin with Sammy Crow. They paused on the perimeter track when they heard the sound of an engine, and dismounted. What they saw was a close parallel to the tragedy that had unfolded eighteen miles southwest of Lille.

A bulky twin-engined machine loomed out of the mist and drizzle of that chill Scottish April day. It was very low and obviously in trouble. There were large holes in its fuselage, one airscrew was feathered and smoke was streaming from the other engine. It was clearly in desperate need to land, and there were no preliminaries. It simply continued to lose height, and with wheels still up struck the grass on the far side of the airfield, bounced once to fifty feet, a second time to a lower altitude, again shredding parts of the tail, spun on the grass once through 360 degrees and was still. It looked like a stranded killer whale thrown upon the shore.

Mike and Sammy stood on the pedals of their bikes and raced across the grass toward the wreck. It was an American-built Hudson, the type the R.A.F. had recently ordered because of its sturdiness, speed and long range. This one had taken a beating. Besides the two holes in the fuselage aft of the wing roots, half the tail assembly was missing and the peppered area around the rear gun position told its own story of combat and death.

Mike smelled for the first time the shattered metal and hot oil stench which emanates from a wrecked aircraft. He dropped his bicycle on the grass and ran the last few yards toward the cockpit. The nose had been smashed in as a result of the fight or the crash landing and there was no sign of anyone in the cockpit.

Sammy ran around to the port side of the wreck. "No one here," he said. "I reckon she's a ghost that's landed herself."

In spontaneous contradiction, a head and shoulders appeared through the emergency exit. There appeared, slowly and painfully, a teddy-bearlike figure in an outsize Irvin jacket and leather leggings. He was evidently the pilot, and his face, pale with strain though it was, with a large handlebar moustache, looked like a caricature of the popular image of an R.A.F. pilot. His opening remark was characteristic, too. "Some prang!"

Mike and Sammy gave him a hand down to the ground. "What about your crew?" Sammy asked.

"All gone for the chop," said the Hudson captain. "Bad show. Lucky to get the poor sods' corpses home. And me, for that matter." He laughed bitterly as he began zipping off his leggings with shaking hands.

At that moment the ambulance and crash wagon arrived. "Not much for you to do, chaps," the pilot greeted them. "Just a one-way trip to the mortuary."

The ambulance crew began to insist that he should go to sick quarters for a check-up. "You know the rule after a crash, sir."

"My rule is bar first, doc later. Lead me to it." While the crash crew began their work on the wreck, and the ambulance men their grisly task of removing the corpses of the wireless operator-air gunner, navigator and copilot, Mike and

Sammy walked their bicycles beside him toward the officers mess.

He and the rest of his Coastal Command squadron had flown across the North Sea in the dark, to arrive over Stravanger at dawn. Their orders had been to bomb the airfield at Sola, a key Luftwaffe base in southern Norway. "Never seen such flak, old boy. They threw up everything. Twenty, forty mill. Bofors. Heavy. The lot. We pressed on regardless, but three went in. Then the sods got a bunch of 109's airborne, and that kept us busy until a squadron of Hamdens arrived on the scene, and they thought they looked juicier meat. Poor sods, so they were, and they got massacred before they even got onto target."

He went on to describe how he had put his Hudson down to wave-top height, and his gunner had fought off a dozen passes from Messerschmitts before they had given up and gone home. But by then his gunner was dead and his copilot was bleeding to death beside him. His navigator had been cut almost in half by flak.

"And that left yours truly with the rudder controls gone, no navigator, no compass, holes letting in a nasty draft, and blood and guts everywhere."

He strode briskly into the mess, with Sammy and Mike behind him, and, as Mike described it later, "vectored onto course for the bar as if by instinct. But then, anyone who can navigate across the North Sea by watching the wave formations ought to be able to home in on alcohol when he needs it like that guy needed it. And, boy, did he put it back!"

The remains of the Hudson, the funeral of its crew, which they all attended, and the brief presence in their mess of the one survivor was 140 Squadron's first tangible evidence of the ferocity of the fighting in Norway, in which they were to play such a considerable part.

For it was only twenty-four hours later when the signal arrived from Group standing down the Squadron from operational status, canceling all leave and instructing them to kit up for overseas. In the perverse way of service organization, tropical kit for the entire squadron, air crew and ground crew alike, arrived the following day, including topees reminiscent of the great days of the British Raj, and mosquito netting and tents, airmen for the use of. A few hours later an enormous Albion truck delivered a complete set of arctic gear, with fur hoods, snowshoes, fur gloves and special underwear.

"Now we really know where we're going," remarked the Spy in despair, and proceeded to issue each flight commander with four maps in sealed envelopes, marked "Most Secret. Not to Be Opened Without Authority." A Flight's commander, the worse for drink that night, slit one of his open with a penknife, unfolded a map of central Norway and spread it across the beer-soaked bar counter. "Big surprise!" he muttered ironically.

Donald Avery, reading in the anteroom, must have heard the exclamation and the comments, and was spotted by Mike marching into the bar with a vexed and anxious expression. His position under the circumstances was a difficult one because he was the junior flight lieutenant by many months. But it did not appear to give Avery any problems. He walked straight up to the bar and began to refold the map.

"I think that there is a misunderstanding," he said in the soft, unctuous tone he used to his superiors. "They must have omitted putting your maps into a 'Most Secret' envelope." He held up his own as proof. "We do have to be careful, don't we?" Then he passed his eyes over the officers present, and said solemnly, "Please, gentlemen, forget what you have just seen and do not utter a word more, even to one another."

Before he returned to his seat, the erring senior flight commander turned his head, focused his bleary eyes on Avery, and said in a slurred, hesitant voice, "Don't get bumped off in Norway, Don-don. We couldn't manage the sodding war without you."

The mystery of how they were going to get their Hurricanes the five hundred-odd miles to their operational areas in Norway was solved when they were ordered to the nearby naval base of Invergordon. It was a misty day in mid-April and the panorama of the Scottish hills and the gray waters of Cromarty Firth was typical of the dour and mysterious character of this area of northeast Scotland. Mike could liken it only to the Maine coast before the winter snows set in.

Their squadron commander led them in low over Black Isle, holding them to a tight formation. "We'll put up a good show for those naval types," he said at briefing. "And anyone who makes a cock up'll be on a charge."

As they flew in four sections of three across the narrow strip of water, Squadron Leader Anson transmitted an uncharacteristically waggish message to his pilots. Looming up ahead of them there suddenly appeared the great dark bulk of an aircraft carrier, its long, narrow deck clear of all obstructions except the single funnel abaft the sketchy bridge. "It's all right, chaps, we're not landing on *her*." A pause. "Yet."

They touched down instead at the small Fleet Air Arm field serving the Invergordon naval base, and taxied in, under the direction of efficient F.A.A. mechanics, to the dispersal bays at the north end.

That night they were the object of much ribaldry from the naval pilots, who plied them with pink gins. A bearded Skua pilot, who had once been to New York and expected Mike to know everyone he had met, mentioned mock-casually to him that there was nothing to deck landings. "You don't want to worry about not having any hooks for the arrester wire, old chap," he said, clinking glasses for the eighth time. "We only use them in a heavy seaway to stop sliding overboard."

Mike countered coolly and with a straight face. "That's always been my experience, too, in the U.S. Navy. When I was doing my three years in the *Saratoga* we never used the wires once, except for drying the wash on Sundays."

It was their last night on shore, they had been told, so there was every justification for a party, and like the Franco-British combats at Lens-La Basse, the pilots formed up into two teams and battled violently into the small hours.

"My head!" Mike exclaimed at breakfast the next morning. "Just watch it fall off from sheer insupportable weight." His leg was aching, too, from a kick above his old wound and he cursed himself for not holding back from the most determined of the scrimmages.

At 1100 hours they all assembled in the station commander's office, where Squadron Leader Anson and a naval captain addressed them in turn. Anson stood up and began:

"Gentlemen, I do not need to tell you that the war has begun at last. We've had it soft up to now. The real thing begins—today."

Mike, at the back of the room, studied his C.O. keenly. He was a hard, humorless man who gave two predominant impressions, of tenseness and authoritative self-confidence. Mike could not say that he liked him, but he certainly admired him. Now that he was going to lead them into what he called "the real thing," Mike considered that he could not follow a better leader into battle.

As for his fellow pilots, Mike had flown with them all now, with the exception of a newly arrived sergeant who was standing beside him and looked pasty and nervous, the very antithesis of Anson. Mike did not rate them all as friends, by any means, least of all what he called the "seedy sycophant" Donald Avery, but he respected them as pilots, and he confidently expected that when the time came, they would not, in that curious British phrase, "be found wanting." Hell, no, this was going to be fun. He only wished Keith was going to embark with them. That would complete the satisfaction he felt for the enterprise that lay ahead.

For a moment his mind went back to that moment at Savile Farm when the stricken voice of the Prime Minister had told them that they were at war. Except for a few moments of tense excitement, and that unpleasant occasion when he had crashed, the war so far had seemed very tame, very phony. The dangers to which his own life would now become increasingly exposed meant very little. In the split second when his Hurricane whipped over, he had been so convinced that it was all over that every day since had seemed like a bonus undeservedly acquired.

"You will be pleased to know," continued the voice of his commander, "that you will not be expected to land on the carrier anchored off Invergordon, much as the navy—" and he glanced at the captain at his side "—might enjoy watching us smash into their smart deck in turn. Our kites will be lifted by crane on board, we hope without too much damage, and (I believe this is the right nautical expression) stowed below. But when we get near the Norwegian coast, we shall have to take off, which I am told is much easier. Our carrier, the *Swiftsure*, can do thirty knots. If we have another fifteen or twenty knots of wind, we're not so far off our takeoff speed of seventy-five-odd miles per hour. So you'll have plenty of runway. But to give you an idea of what it's all about, an area the size of the carrier's flight deck has been marked out on the field, and this afternoon you'll all make one takeoff.

"Our final destination will not be revealed until we are at sea. But our function is clear, and crucially important. We're to support the army who're having a tough time of it without any air cover. Any questions?" There were none.

Captain MacAndrew was short and chunky, with a ruddy complexion and a mariner's blue eyes, as characteristic a sailor as the Hudson pilot had been a typical airman. He spoke a few clipped sentences, making them welcome and telling them that he knew they would all happily abide by naval discipline and custom while on board. "We'll do what we can to make your stay brief *and* happy. I am informed that there is unlimited gin in the wardroom. And my quack, Surgeon-Commander Matthews, has unlimited supplies of seasickness medicine. When you've tried it once, you'll go back to gin."

He sat down amid laughter and the pilots trooped out and were driven at once to the dispersal where two Hurricanes were ready for the circuits and bumps. Thanks to a strong wind, every 140 Squadron pilot succeeded in taking off from the six-hundred-feet-long simulated "flight deck" by holding on with the brakes while revving up the engine in order to obtain maximum acceleration. Most of them also tried to land in the same area, but all overshot, and they were quite happy to know that their machines were being ferried out to the *Swiftsure* on lighters.

After tea, as darkness fell, a naval bus picked up 140's pilots with their gear and drove down to the pier at Invergordon where they embarked in a launch. A brisk breeze was blowing and Mike was glad he was wearing his Irvin jacket as they chugged out into the bay.

The *Swiftsure* looked enormous in the half light, a great slab of a ship. He could just make out the little 4.7-inch guns ranged behind shields on the main deck, below the long flat flight deck.

"I guess we'd better not meet up with anything bigger than a Hun destroyer with those peashooters," he said, but his voice was lost in the sounds of coming alongside, and no one heard him.

"If the army's supposed to need us all that badly," said Mike breathlessly, "why in the name of all that's wacky are we going around in circles in the middle of the North Sea?"

But the Spy was almost beyond speech. He was a dedicated enemy of physical exercise, and the C.O.'s order that all R.A.F. personnel must trot around the *Swiftsure*'s flight deck twenty times a day had nearly led to a one-man mutiny. "Couldn't say . . . ol' boy. Perhaps . . . we've lost the army . . . very hilly place, Norway."

He was lagging behind Mike, who could have gotten himself excluded from this daily trot because of his leg but was feeling as sluggish as the rest of them. The Spy shuffled rather than trotted, and his stooping frame and the expression of distress on his foxy face made a pathetic sight.

"Come on, Spy, only one more lap," called out Mike.

The North Sea presented its usual picture of gray sea and gray sky. During the week since they had left Invergordon they had suffered two storms, but today the seas were only moderate. Their two escorting destroyers appeared, as usual, to be half submerged, but the *Swiftsure*, a stable ship, was rolling only moderately.

They leaned, panting, against the steel base of the bridge superstructure, observed with amusement by a working party of seamen, and other pilots joined them before they went to their quarters for a shower.

"What's the gen, Spy?" "Come on, spill the beans." They had been living on rumors and rumors of rumors for days now. Flying Officer Willy Williams had long ago earned the reputation of being an optimist with special inside knowledge, which usually turned out to be false. His prophecy on the day the war broke out, that before eight months of phony war there would be "bags of flap," had been used as abusive ammunition by the pilots on many occasions.

When the Spy had gotten his breath back and lit a cigarette, and coughed a good deal, he said with a crafty expression, "The C.O.'s doing a recon this afternoon. But don't let that gen go any farther."

"Oh balls!" "You're making it up!" "Clueless *and* genless," were among the astringent comments of 140's pilots.

"Time will prove me right," retorted the Spy tartly, and made off down the gangway leading to his quarters.

And, for once, it did. At seven bells, the *Swiftsure* worked up to twenty knots and turned into the wind. A Skua came up on the lift, and with the F.A.A. Commander Flying at the controls, took off effortlessly with Squadron Leader Anson in the rear cockpit. He had a single Lewis gun on a scarfe ring, as used in the Great War, and a number of caustic remarks were made on the likely outcome of a meeting with a *Staffel* of Messerschmitt 109's.

The Skua was a radial-engined dive bomber, a squadron of which had sunk a German cruiser in a Norwegian fjord the previous week—the first major warship ever to be sunk by bombing—and the *Swiftsure*'s F.A.A. pilots were very proud of the fact.

The two senior officers survived their recon trip, and three hours after departure their Skua reappeared out of the murk, circled the carrier once, and came in with full flaps down as soon as the smoke from the marker streamed clean down the flight deck and the batsman had given the all clear. The wire picked up the hook and the machine came to a halt within a few yards.

After dinner they were ordered to the briefing cabin where an enlarged and simplified replica of the maps they had been given before embarkation had been traced out in chalk on a large blackboard. It covered the Norwegian coastline from Gravvik, north of Namsos in the north, to Kristiansund southwest of Trondheim.

Anson pointed the tip of his stick at Trondheim and said, 'Here's the key to northern Norway. If we can get the Hun out of this town, the third largest port in Norway, he'll have the greatest difficulty in supplying his troops far up in the north at Narvik. Two allied landings have been made, one to the south, and one here at Namsos. The aim is to advance on Trondheim and squeeze the Germans out with a pincer movement. This can't be done without air support. The Luftwaffe has established a strong base at this airfield, Vaernes, near Trondheim."

Anson's pointer hovered over a long shaded area south of Namsos and marked Lake Rhysjhok. "There are no airfields around here, but the Norwegians have advised us that the ice is safe enough on this lake." He paused for a moment to allow the startling news to sink in that they were going to operate off ice, and Mike was not the only 140 Squadron pilot who was wondering at the strangeness of the circumstances that led a land-based fighter squadron to be ordered off a carrier and onto a lake.

"Between the devil and the deep blue sea, so to speak, sir," commented Sammy Crow.

"Nothing to it. I've just done it—or rather Commander Wilson has shown me how to do it. Our ground crews have been ashore for three days with our equipment, and with the help of the local population have cleared enough snow to make a strip for us to land on tomorrow." Again he concluded with, "Any questions?"

Everyone was too stunned to think of any, so with the order that takeoff would begin at first light, 0300 hours, the pilots were dismissed.

The gin-drinking was moderate, the mood thoughtful and the horseplay nil in the wardroom that night. Mike retired to his cabin immediately after dinner and sat down to write a letter to Eileen.

> I can't tell you where I am, except at sea and far from you. Farther still from Keith— I wonder how he's getting on in France? Things are starting in earnest at last. Just as well, too. We can't win this war without fighting it first, and the sooner it's won the sooner I can come back to you and we can get married and I can love you for the rest of my life, which is going to be long, interesting and in every way successful. What else if I'm going to be allowed to share it with you?
>
> You are crazy to try to join the navy and I have ordered the Admiralty to dismiss your request.
>
> My best to your pa and ma, and my everlasting love to you. It'll soon be raining sunbeams all the time.

With a brief speculative thought on when, if ever, the letter would get to Rising Hall, Mike sealed the envelope. He lay in his bunk, waiting for sleep to overtake him. From around him there came the now familiar sounds of this big warship at sea, the faint creaking of its complex structure, steel straining and yielding under the ever-varying pressures, the hiss of steam and water in its arterial system, the occasional slam of a hatch or door, the clatter of feet on steel gangways and stairs. These sounds all combined into an echoing chorus, a metallic rendering of the music of Bartlett Hall after lights-out, with the additional background of mighty turbines pumping out the power that sustained and propelled this 20,000-ton carrier. A long way from Andover.

In a few hours, like it or not, he would be strapped into a fighter's cockpit, and in the half light of a northern dawn he would be required to accelerate this machine down a few hundred feet of heaving deck and into the air, then fly a hundred miles to a strip of ice between snow-capped mountains and put it down again safely.

Mike stared for a moment at the blue bulb that faintly lit his cabin, and laughed quietly before closing his eyes. Yes, a long way from Andover. From the great elms, the tolling of the Cochran church bell, the football games with Exeter —"Over the field there's a Blue wave rolling . . ." A long way from all that. I may be a big boy now, but, by jiminy, I must be nuts!

9

"I say, everyone seems to be in a frightful hurry," complained Buffer Davies. His batman had failed to get him out of bed, and three of 259's pilots—Range Powell, Polo Satterthwaite and Keith—had dragged him to his feet and propped him against the wall with his clothes at his feet.

"Get into that lot, you Pommie clot," the Australian had yelled at him. "The war's started."

First light had not yet broken when the alarm had come through from H.Q. It was scarcely necessary. Anyone awake at that time would have recognized the rise in the intensity of gunfire, and only the heaviest sleepers, Buffer among them, had not been awakened by it. The attack which had been expected since early spring had come. The date was May 10, 1940.

The squadron's Renault truck, driving on sidelights only, took them down to the dispersal hut, where bowls of hot coffee and croissants awaited them. The French Army might be seething with dissidents, gun breech blocks sabotaged by Communist factory workers, the Morane squadron at Lens-La Basse might apply three times for machine-gun ammunition and still receive only reconditioned tank tracks. But the standard of catering throughout remained at *cordon bleu* level and very French.

259's ground crews were already at work, ghostly gray figures swarming over their machines, checking glycol and fuel levels, polishing windscreens and making the Hurricanes ready for immediate takeoff. Most wore rubber boots with the tops turned down and knitted balaclavas and scarves against the cool of the dawn. Cheerful obscenities and the smell of good plebeian Woodbine cigarettes drifted across to the pilots who stood in a group waiting for the C.O.

Squadron Leader Rowbotham jumped out of his car while it was still moving, and an airman followed with his flying gear. He wasted no time with preliminaries.

"The Hun's moved into Holland and Belgium. No warning or declaration, like Norway. He's moving fast, with tanks, airborne troops, a lot of air cover, and—as you can hear—a lot of artillery. The B.E.F.'s moving into Belgium to give support." He accepted with a nod the bowl of coffee someone had offered him. "And we're going to be busy. We're all on Immediate, from now. And we may have to move during the day."

He looked at them over the top of his bowl as he sipped the coffee. "It's lucky we've had some practice with the Hun —not like those poor bloody Belgies. We can expect to be bombed at any time, so keep on tiptoe. I'm taking a couple of A Flight up on standing patrol for an hour in the hope of jumping them when they come in."

Rowbotham was about to add further orders when the telephone rang out shrilly, and before anyone could answer it, its warning message was spelled out instead by the roar of aircraft engines. The sound exploded on the field as if someone had suddenly thrown open soundproof doors. There were no preliminaries. When Rowbotham was speaking, they were aware of only the familiar rumble of guns and the scarcely noticeable vibration. A second later the gray dawn sky above them was filled with the dark shapes of bombers. The noise was earsplitting, the ground shook as if suffering an earthquake.

They were Junkers 88's, bulbous-nosed, twin-engined, deadly in demeanor, and traveling very fast at no more than two hundred feet. They banked and jinked against the anti-aircraft fire, and in their turn blazed away at the parked aircraft with their machine guns.

It was all over in twenty seconds. A half minute later, the delayed action bombs began to explode. Keith was halfway to his machine and hurled himself to the ground, his arms over his head. He felt the concussions blast against him, the closest of them lifting him momentarily clear off the grass. A chunk of debris sang over him and he felt the dirt pepper his body like minute fragments of shrapnel.

He struggled to his feet as the explosions ceased, ducked as another bomb went off distantly on the French side of the field, and began to run again.

From the lip of the nearest brick blast pen, someone was screaming and he caught a glimpse of a figure spread across the top, distorted in his agony. The Hurricane inside had received a direct hit. Nothing was left of it. A deep crater marked its grave, and the graves of its crew. Scraps of metal or flesh—who could tell in this light?—were scattered about the grass that he was sprinting across.

His own machine, A-Ac, was undamaged, and his fitter and rigger were pulling themselves out of the slit trench near it when he arrived. Their faces were white, and Tim Bushwood would not notice Keith's shaking hands this time, he was trembling so badly himself as he helped Keith into his parachute harness.

"G-give them hell, sir," he said, his voice strained. "They've done for Mick an' his lot. All gone." He moaned, but his fingers had not lost their deftness as he handed Keith his helmet and plugged the bayonet clip into the oxygen supply.

Keith pressed the button without calling out. The Merlin

fired first time, and an airman tore out the plug lead and raced off with the battery cart.

Keith was not the first away. Others were already moving fast across the grass, regardless of the wind direction, and the C.O. in Q-Queen was half airborne. The French were doing the same thing from their side, and the center of Lens-La Basse was thick with evading Moranes and Hurricanes going in opposite directions. One Morane was coming straight for Keith as he gathered speed; guessing that the Frenchman would react with the rule of the road and keep right, Keith did the same, and the two fighters brushed past, wing tip to wing tip, at a combined speed of over 100 m.p.h.

The other hazard was craters. The Junkers's bombs had peppered the field with five-foot-deep holes, and a Morane had failed to avoid one and was standing up on its nose, tail perpendicular, the pilot struggling to release himself. Keith was just airborne as he skimmed over a crater, and at once grabbed for the undercarriage lever. There was a big blaze from the fuel tanks close to the road, and the yellow light illuminated the village street and its little flanking houses. He caught a glimpse of running figures, and then concentrated on getting every last ounce of power from his engine.

Keith could just make out the silhouette of the C.O.'s machine, climbing flat out and streaming smoke, and he followed it. He switched on his radio and was almost blasted out of his seat by the sound of the controller's voice at Wing: "Steer zero four zero, Medway leader. Zero four zero. Bandits reported heading northeast . . ."

"We won't catch them in a million years," broke in the C.O.'s voice. "Calling all Medway aircraft. Medway leader. Form up over Lens at Angels Five. There'll be more trade, don't worry."

Rowbotham was right not to chase the 88's. Recent reports had given it a slight edge in speed at low level over the wooden-prop Hurricanes with which all the French-based squadrons were equipped. They would never catch those low-flying bombers, which would be faster than ever now that they were relieved of their load.

It took ten minutes for all 259 Squadron to form up. Keith found his flight commander and tucked in as number two in his blue section, and Polo Satterthwaite climbed up as number three. The sun was rising from the direction of Lille to the east but it would be some minutes before it touched the dark farmland below. The fuel-tank fire at the airfield was burning as fiercely as ever, a guiding beacon for any further attackers. The only other evidence of war was the flicker of gunfire, paler now in the dawn light, from the southeast.

Somewhere over there, soon to be lit by the blood-red early summer sun, hundreds of German tanks were grinding forward, spitting shells and bullets, rumbling over bridges and up narrow village streets. French 75's and German 88's, Mausers and 25 mm anti-tank guns, old Dutch rifles, the 75 and 120 mm guns of the Belgian fortress of Eben Emael, all were dealing out death, just as earlier weapons, from slings and crossbows to the machine guns of the Great War, had killed Europeans since time immemorial. And men would be picking up the dead and wounded, from as near as their squadron's base below to as far as the distant Dutch border.

Rowbotham's voice came through on the V.H.F. "Pull your finger out, Red Three," he reproved one errant Hurricane which was still five hundred feet below. "A Flight, patrol here at Angels Ten and keep your eyes open. I'll take B Flight east and search for trade toward Lille."

They did not have to search far for the enemy that morning. The Luftwaffe was out in force, and Wing was radioing a stream of reports: "Fifty-plus bandits heading for Metz, Angels Fifteen . . . Belgian base of Schaffen-Diest being heavily bombed . . . Vassincourt under attack . . ."

Buffer Davies, wide awake at last, was the first with a sighting report. "Medway leader, Yellow Two. Bandits one o'clock above." There were twelve of them, pencil-thin Dorniers, so near that Keith wondered why they had not been spotted earlier. They were two thousand feet above, and another two thousand feet higher were a dozen Messerschmitt 110's, weaving from side to side in anticipation of an attack, and reminding Keith of James Cagney's swaggering bodyguard.

The Hurricanes were now at their best height, and at full boost the six machines had soon pulled up level with the Dorniers. Rowbotham assigned targets in a steady, confidence-inspiring voice. Keith felt no fear. He still heard faint echoes of that airman's agonized scream and saw his splayed-out tortured body. Destroyers of the innocent, destroyers of cities . . . God, how he hated German bombers, and "Dear God," he spoke into his mask, "let me shoot well and not mind!"

The *Zerstören* came pouring down on them before they could get at the bombers, and the Hurricanes' battle formation was at once broken up into a series of individual combats. "Break right, Charlie! . . . O.K., I've got him . . . Christ, let him have it! . . . Break quick, he's right behind . . ."

The ether was filled with staccato cries of warning and jubilation. The 110's packed a tremendous punch of fire-power, and were fast. But they did not begin to match the Hurricane's maneuverability, and could not take the same punishment. Keith saw one burst into flames and the gunner get out just before it spun away, a searing coffin for the pilot. Then, by kicking hard rudder and sliding to the right violently, he managed to get in a three-quarter deflection burst at another 110. His prayer was answered. In his anger he was shooting well again and was not minding. At fifty yards he fired, this time at the other engine. Both were streaming oil and as he lifted up and over his foe, the plane must have exploded because he was at once thrown out of control as if a heavy ack-ack shell had just missed him.

When he got his machine back onto an even keel, he looked behind and saw the remains of his victim floating down, just a few pieces of alloy within a fading gray cloud.

The *Zerstören* had all gone, shot down or fleeing from their attack. None of his Flight was to be seen either. Just as before, the sky had been rubbed clear like a damp cloth over a blackboard.

But not quite. Far below and hard to see in their camouflage, still in formation, the Dorniers were streaking back east in a shallow dive, mission unfulfilled. Elation in no way reduced Keith's eagerness. He had plenty of ammunition and plenty of speed with this superiority of height.

He came down on the rearmost left Dornier just as he had, made his killing approach on the Heinkel on his twenty-first birthday, lining up the bead with careful deliberation, cold at this moment of imminent destruction, whatever qualms might follow. He was about to open fire when, to his astonishment, he saw that he had no need to. A dark ball that might have been a bomb detached itself from the fuselage, then another, a third, and after a pause, a fourth.

For a moment Keith thought the Dornier was doing no more than jettisoning its bombs. But, in turn, there streamed from each shape as it fell beneath him a flash of white which grew rapidly larger, checked the fall, and held the airman, who at once began to swing in space like an ever-slowing pendulum. The whole crew had bailed out before he had fired a shot. You couldn't have a cheaper victory than that!

He left that Dornier to its own devices and closed in on the one ahead, firing a long burst at two hundred yards, and receiving back a stream of well-directed fire from the rear gunners of all the remaining formation. His bullets appeared to have little effect, and he pulled steeply up, rolled off the top, and after a careful look above and behind, came in for another pass. This time he made it a quarter attack and was astonished at how quickly he succeeded with his eight guns in cutting the Dornier to pieces, setting fire to one engine and filling the cockpit area with a fusillade of bullets.

Then he caught a glimpse of another fast-moving hunchback shape pulling up and understood why the destruction had been so swift. It was a Hurricane, K-King—Polo's. So

Keith had not been alone after all, and with a sudden spasm of fear he realized that it could as well have been a 110 and his own end.

"Hello, Blue Three, where did you come from? Over."

"And you?"

Keith transmitted: "Hullo Medway leader, Medway leader. Medway Blue Two. I am about forty miles east of Lille. Are there any other aircraft in the vicinity?"

There was a long silence, then a distant voice, barely audible, ordered him back to base. Keith and Polo were two thousand feet above the Dorniers which were traveling east still at full throttle and losing height fast.

Polo broke in. "I'm low on fuel and ammo. I'm calling it a day."

Keith saw the Yorkshireman's Hurricane make a fast banking turn through 180 degrees, and Keith followed it. They had accomplished about all they could hope for in this sortie. Best follow orders and go home. He pulled his machine in closer to Polo and saw for the first time the damage he had suffered. His hood appeared to have been blown off, probably by a 110's cannon shell, and there was a two-foot-wide hole in the after part of the fuselage, revealing the skeleton-like primary fuselage structure. Thank God for the Hurricane's toughness!

Keith's surprise was total, and blended with laughter, when he saw that Polo, as nonchalant and irrepressible as ever, had taken off his mask and stuck his half-smoked pipe in his mouth. Moreover he had got it alight and was puffing away with contentment.

Keith flipped over the transmitting switch and called out, "Comfy?"

He grinned at Keith. "Champion."

The fuel fire at Lens-La Basse had been gotten under control, and as they circled they saw that the field was swarming with figures helping to fill in the craters. There were a dozen trucks on the field, too, loaded wtih soil and rubble. The rest of 259 had evidently landed a while ago. Keith could see the Hurricanes in their pens and the ugly scar of the crater in the pen near the flight dispersal.

"Medway Blue Two and Blue Three, permission to land," Keith transmitted.

"O.K. to pancake, if you can," replied the controller ominously.

Keith made his approach carefully. The sun was fully out, visibility perfect. But there was not much room. The repairing squads jumped into the craters they were filling as the two Hurricanes approached, and he got down without too much difficulty, ending up a dozen yards from a crater in front of his own dispersal.

Three crews converged on his Hurricane the moment he switched off, the armorers leaping onto the wings and unscrewing the gun panels. Others stood ready with long snakes of linked ammunition draped in swaths over their shoulders, ready to feed into the Brownings' boxes. At the same time, the bowser came to a halt in front of his plane and one crew swung a hose toward his wing while another took a second hose to Polo's Hurricane which he had parked close to Keith's.

Tim helped Keith out. His small freckled face looked less alarmed than two hours earlier, but the young man was tight with strain. "How was it, sir?"

"Roughish," Keith replied.

"Shall I ask the painter to add anything?" he asked, referring to the black crosses already decorating Keith's Hurricane below the cockpit.

"Another two and a half," Keith said. "But you can forget the half. I think it was Pilot Officer Satterthwaite's."

The intelligence officer was holding court in his office at the back of the flight dispersal hut. The pilots had had their hour of glory. Now it was his turn, and he was taking down their reports with punctilious care.

Keith turned to a flight sergeant. "Anyone missing?" he asked.

"All O.K. Sergeant Sheridan was shot down, but he got

out and must have come down on our side. I expect we'll see him later."

Polo sauntered in, unshaven and looking even scruffier than usual. He was trying to light his pipe again, and just as it was going nicely the telephone on the I.O.'s desk rang. "Right," he said briskly. "Scramble, the lot of you. Patrol Maastricht at fifteen thou."

The pilots thundered out of the office, the C.O. again in the lead. Keith was almost last through the door, and saw Polo knocking out his pipe in the Spy's ashtray. "A fellow never gets the chance for a decent smoke," he complained.

"You can't scramble in that kite of yours," Keith told him. "You're nuts."

"You try and stop me, lad."

It was like that all day on May 10. Keith did five sorties, damaging a Heinkel again later in the afternoon, and escaping from a swarm of 109's by the skin of his teeth when B Flight, tired and hungry, was jumped. One of the sergeants in A Flight was shot down in flames, but that was 259's only casualty to set against a total of eleven German planes shot down for certain, and half a dozen more damaged or "probables." But even that was only seventeen at the most optimistic reckoning, and what was that against the armadas of bombers that had reached and destroyed their targets unmolested, and would be back again the next day, and the next?

It was almost dark when they were released from duty at last. Keith had a couple of drinks and then, weary as he was, walked down into the village to call on the curé.

In spite of the late hour, there was a restlessness in the village. Most of the houses had a cart or old car outside, and the people were dragging out their most valuable possessions and packing them. They worked by faint lantern light and spoke quietly, but with urgency, as if the German army was already near and might overhear them. Keith could smell the fear in the air.

"Have they no confidence in their army?" he asked the curé.

"They fear the worst," was the reply.

"But why—the Germans are miles away and may be thrown back."

"That was not their experience in 1914," said the curé bitterly. "And some of the older ones remember 1870, too. When the Germans come, they conquer. That is their experience."

He gave a glass of Calvados to Keith, who felt both soothed and set alight by the fiery apple alcohol. "How was it?" asked the Frenchman, eyes cast up to the heavens. "The bombs killed three in the village."

"I killed about the same number of Germans," Keith said wearily. "If that is any comfort to them. I killed in anger, monsieur. Is that less sinful than in cold blood?"

"Neither is sinful, not under these circumstances. You have been defending my weak and helpless flock. Whether it's with a pitchfork in your hand, or with your wonderful machine, it's the same thing, and we all thank you."

Keith had four hour's sleep and was violently shaken awake by his batman at three o'clock in the morning. He lay still for a few minutes, sipping the hot tea and listening to the sound of the guns. Were they louder than yesterday morning? It was impossible to judge. But the news was not good. The vital fortress of Eben Emael had been captured. General Guderian was through Luxembourg. The advance seemed inexorable.

259 Squadron was on patrol before sunrise again, and in action five times that day, losing two more pilots and four machines, leaving them with no reserves. On the last sortie of the day, Keith realized how tired he was when B Flight was bounced by a *Staffel* of 110's, and lost one pilot. It was almost ten o'clock when he landed at dusk on the repaired airfield. Like others in B Flight, he landed roughly, and was half asleep when he taxied in.

On the previous evening, the C.O. of the Component Fighter Group had reported, "I have never seen squadrons so confident of success, so insensible to fatigue and so appreciative of their own aircraft." He could not truthfully have repeated that report on the evening of May 11. Keith, by now very sensible to fatigue, was too tired to eat, and fell asleep in an armchair in the mess. Only Buffer Davies survived long enough to prop up the bar after dinner, and he too returned reluctantly to his room when he found no one to drink with, muttering, "Poor show—damn poor show."

10

The cleared strip, a narrow gray rectangle running length-wise along the side of Lake Rhysjhok, looked no bigger than the flight deck of the *Swiftsure*. But everyone else had gotten in safely. Mike, doing slow circuits above, had watched them touch down in turn and taxi away to the partial shelter of the pine woods which came down to the lake's shoreline.

Blipping his engine in short bursts, and whistling Deanna's "Frenesi" to keep up his spirits, Mike came in on a long powered approach and cut his throttle right back just before the beginning of the snow-cleared area. The Hurricane's wheels touched lightly, and with hardly a bounce he had her safely running down the center of the strip. When he applied the brakes there was no skidding, and he was able to turn off up one of the two taxiing strips long before the end.

The first thing Mike noticed when he pulled the cutout lever and his engine died was the silence. There was not a breath of wind, the sky was crystal clear, the sun shone blindingly on the snowcapped tops of the mountains that surrounded them and seemed to tuck the newly arrived R.A.F. party into their cocoon of frozen silence.

Even the normally noisy activities of the ground crews were muffled by the snow and the close-growing pines. The fuel "bowser" was a farmcat drawn by a single aged horse, led by a villainous-looking local and piled high with two-gallon tins. It came to a halt alongside Mike's starboard wing, and a party of airmen began handing a funnel and the tins up to an airman who had climbed up to sit on the wing root.

Mike eased himself out of his cockpit and called to his own mechanic, a tall, melancholy Scot called Campbell, "Where's the goddamn war, Lofty?"

"I wouldn't know, sir. The gen's nil."

It was reassuring to hear that rich, soft Scottish voice again in this remote spot.

A party of airmen were laying branches of camouflaging pine across the fuselage and wings of his Hurricane. "How was your journey?" Mike asked.

"Sick all the way, sir. Then we landed at a wee harbor down there, close by a fish-drying plant, and I was sick worse than ever from the stench. We're short on everything," he added ominously, "except fish."

The adjutant, "Sandy" Baker, had done wonders in the three days since the ground party had arrived, bribing the local villagers and fishermen to sweep clear the runway, setting up well dispersed stores of what little food and equipment they were able to bring with them. The only road transport they had brought ashore were an Albion truck and a little Commer van. Everything else was commandeered or rented from the village of Rhysjhok and the outlying farms. Mike saw a number of the local people standing in a wondering group in the forest. They were watching him in silence, the last of the strangers who had come from out of the sky into their closed world which had seen so little change over the centuries.

Mike walked up a track through the trees with Sammy Crow. "Piece of cake, that landing," said the Rhodesian. "They ought to make more airfields of ice."

Standing alone at the side of the path, as if uncertain what to do or where to go, was the pale and nervous-looking sergeant-pilot whom Mike had first seen at the Invergordon briefing. Nobody knew anything about him, except that he was with B Flight, and Mike had not seen him during the voyage. He felt a flash of sympathy for the boy, who was obviously a loner and had experienced a tough introduction to squadron life. He determined to have a word with him at the first opportunity.

The officers' mess was a small commandeered wooden hotel, once patronized by fishermen who came to Rhysjhok for the salmon. The accommodations were basic, but Mike was impressed by the Britishers' talent for ordering their lives with the minimum of change. A bar had already been sent up in the small lounge, and the head barman from Elgin, dressed in his regular white jacket, was dispensing scotch whiskey and ferocious Norwegian akevitt and beer from a barrel. Four of A Flight were playing darts.

Squadron Leader Anson, breaking with tradition, was having an akevitt and briefing his two flight commanders with a map. He called Mike over and said, "Flight Lieutenant Avery will take you on a recon at fourteen hundred hours." He ran a finger over the map south of Namsos. "The Allied line of advance is about there. Show yourself to the troops. Old one-eyed Carton de Wiart and his brigade have been bombed and strafed ever since they arrived and need a spot of encouragement."

"Where's the Luftwaffe hiding?" Mike asked.

"They'll be around soon enough," Anson said grimly, throwing back his akevitt in one gulp.

The squadron commander was right. As they were filing in to luncheon in the diminutive dining room, they heard the sound of an aircraft. They ran out onto the wooden balcony facing the lake and looked up. There, at five thousand feet, circling arrogantly and no doubt taking photographs, was a German reconnaissance machine, a Heinkel 115 floatplane.

"We'll grab him before he gets home," muttered Anson, and, calling out for Sammy and Mike, began running down the path toward the lake. Mike had still not regained his old speed since his injury, and several more of the pilots passed him before they burst out of the trees onto the snow-covered ice.

But they were not first. They all heard the sound of a starting Merlin, and by the time they reached their machines, a Hurricane was airborne and climbing at an acute angle with emergency boost.

The C.O. shouted to the Spy, who had also been sur-prisingly quick, to prohibit anyone else from taking off, and himself led out Sammy and Mike. They were all three air-borne within two minutes, and Mike, the last to get off, strove to catch up with his C.O. and keep the Heinkel in view at the same time.

They were wasting their time, and precious fuel. Five miles southwest toward the sea, the lone Hurricane had gotten within range of the floatplane. It was a short, uneven contest, and Mike calculated that within less than a minute the big, twin-engined German aircraft was spinning down, trailing a long line of smoke. No one got out of it, and when the machine hit the side of a mountain above the snowline, the thin finger of smoke, drawn in the still air with a steady hand from the point of death above to the grave below, remained as a memorial until it dissolved to nothing.

Mike seized an opportunity of talking to Sergeant Ralph Walker later in the day. For half an hour they strolled through the pines along the frozen shoreline.

"How in hell's name did you get off so quickly?" Mike asked him.

The sergeant spoke diffidently and kept his eyes on the ground. "I guessed there might be a bit of a flap after our arrival so I just hung around my kite."

"Well, it was nice going. Where're you from, sergeant?"

"I'm a Geordie, sir. Newcastle, you know. My father works

in the Elswick yard—shipbuilding that is."

"And you didn't want to follow him?"

"Well no, not really. You see, he was out of work most of the time I was growing up. So I signed on as a boy at Halton and learned a trade—armament fitter. When I was old enough I managed to switch to aircrew." There was no trace of bitterness in his voice, but Mike could imagine the hardships and privations of those depression years in a big industrial city. No doubt his short stature and pale complexion were part of the price. What a contrast with his own childhood of affluence and comfort!

Mike broke the silence. "I guess it's an odd stroke of fate, Sergeant, that has you a Geordie and me a Yank flying off ice in the middle of Norway against Germans. What you British call a rum turnup, right?"

Sergeant Walker halted and looked at Mike for the first time, a shy smile on his lips. "I suppose it is, sir, come to think of it. It's very good of you to come all this way to fight for our country. What made you do it?"

"Fun. Action—you know, bang-bang." Then Mike at once regretted making a joke of it. He looked into the keen brown eyes of the little sergeant. "No, a bit more serious than that. I guess I don't like bullies any more than you do."

They began to saunter back to the squadron. "What about your family?" Mike asked.

"Just my mother and father. A house in Judd Street near the river—we call them back-to-backs. They make for friendliness, sir."

"They'll sure be missing you. Especially your ma, right?"

"She was very good about it, sir. But Geordies don't show their feelings much. It's a habit, like. I suppose because life can be tough on the Tyne . . ."

Mike flew his delayed patrol later in the afternoon as number two to Donald Avery. It was the first time that he had been able to study the serrated coastline of this country. A high cloud sheet had now covered the sun, and the bright magical impression it made on their arrival had lost its fairy-tale appeal, leaving a harsh monotony of snow-capped crags, pine forests, and valleys that were sometimes filled with frozen lakes like Rhysjhok or fjords cutting in deep from the sea. It was no place to have engine trouble or to be shot down.

Avery rocked his wings and pointed down. They were at three thousand feet over Verdal at the head of Trondheim Fjord. Out of sight at this height and forty miles to the southeast lay the captured town. Below on a winding track leading down to the village he could just make out a thin line of figures, no more than a few hundred in all. So this was the British battalion advancing on Trondheim! Looking down from this height at the terrain they had had to traverse from Namsos, it was a wonder that they had gotten this far, especially as they had been bombed and machine-gunned for much of the way.

Avery led Mike down over the fjord, skimming the water, and then pulled up over the hillside. The men stood and waved as they flashed overhead. Then the Hurricanes climbed and patrolled up and down for half an hour to give the troops some reassurance that they had support.

"No trade for us today," Avery transmitted, but before Mike could reply a voice in contradiction to the flight commander's assertion came crackling distantly over the ether. "Calling Blue One . . . Calling Blue One . . ." The next words were inaudible. Then, ". . . attack. Under attack . . . buster, buster."

The transmission faded away, cut off by some mountain peak between Verdal and Rhysjhok. But the meaning was clear and Avery banked his Hurricane onto a northwesterly course. Mike followed him, opening his throttle wide and climbing at the same time so that he was soon both above and ahead of the other machine.

"Keep in position, Blue Two," Avery told him. "It's important that we conserve fuel."

Reluctantly Mike closed his throttle and lost height to

take up formation alongside. They had covered less than half the distance when a rising cloud of smoke made further navigation unnecessary. They could see the attack still taking place from a dozen miles away. The smoke cloud had grown larger and the sky above their base was peppered with bursting light antiaircraft fire from the guns a small party of Royal Marines had brought up to defend Rhysjhok. At least eight hostile aircraft were diving down over the cleared strip and spouts of water fifty feet high marked where their bombs burst.

Mike could see from the shell bursts that the bombers were already withdrawing in the direction of the sea. Still Avery showed no sign of opening up and gaining the height they would so desperately need if they were to pursue and successfully attack the Germans. What's the crazy guy doing? Mike asked himself. Doesn't he want to mix it with them? Christ, the whole lot are going to slip through our fingers!

Suddenly Mike made the decision, opened his throttle wide, "pulling the plug" for emergency boost, and put himself on a course to cut off the bombers—if it was not already too late.

"Keep formation, Blue Two," came Avery's voice sharply. Mike disregarded the order and pressed on as fast as his machine would take him, watching the A.S.I. build up until the needle was close to the 300 mark, and cursing at himself that he had not taken independent action earlier.

Jeepers, the bombers were moving! Mike was scarcely gaining on them, though he could now recognize them as Junkers 88's from the configuration of their tails and their retracted tail wheels. After another five minutes of pursuit, with the black smoke pouring from his exhausts, he gave the rearmost 88 a sighting burst from five hundred yards. No result. And as he watched the machine in exasperation he noticed that it was hardly growing in size at all in his sight, while the fuel in his own tanks was draining away recklessly.

Several of the 88's were firing, too. He could see their tracers arching back from the rear gun positions, and he was just about to congratulate himself that their shooting was wild when he saw a dark shape above him. It was traveling fifty miles an hour faster than Mike and was in a power dive, heading straight into the formation, which had tightened up now to give mutual protection, regardless of the odds.

Mike saw the letters RC-T on the side of the Hurricane as it passed, and realized that it was Ralph Walker proving himself again an exceptional and courageous pilot.

The Hurricane went for the leader from above. Mike saw the kill take place before his eyes as if it was a demonstration of how to make the perfect stern attack. The sergeant did not waste a round of ammunition. He opened fire at no more than a hundred fifty yards, concentrating on the cockpit area and in a single five-second burst shredding the 88's nose to pieces. The bomber dropped out of formation as if struck down by a giant lead weight, and with both engines still racing at full revs, it dived vertically and piled into the forest a thousand feet below. It exploded with a splash of fire so bright that the image remained on the retinas of Mike's eyes for several seconds.

Meanwhile the Hurricane had climbed again, rolled, and with a reduced superiority of speed was now making a diving 45-degree beam attack on one of the left 88's. The sergeant was met by a cone of concentrated vengeful fire which he sailed through without attempting evasion. Again holding his thumb off the button until he was close in, he filled the bomber's port engine with .303 bullets. A trickle of smoke turned into a sudden blaze, and the 88 at once began to lose height and fall out of formation.

Mike glanced down at his instruments and saw that he had barely enough fuel to get himself back. The oil temperature had risen, too, from the sustained full-boost pursuit. Angry and frustrated, he pulled back the throttle and turned through 180 degrees.

Height, height, height! The one-word formula to success in air fighting. And Avery had not used it. Had not *wanted* to use it? And Mike felt a chill of apprehension. It could not be true. Yet his flight commander, without a word to Mike, had already given up the chase, and was no more than a black dot in the distance.

T-Toc came alongside and they flew back toward Rhysjhok together. A last count of the disappearing Junkers came to six. There was no sign of the second machine Sergeant Walker had hit and Mike felt no doubt that it had gone in, too. A double victory for the little sergeant, and three in one day!

This achievement was something to set against the shambles into which the bombers had turned their ice-strip base. The fire was still burning. It had begun with a direct hit on one of the fuel stores and had now got a grip on the pine trees around it. There were three holes torn in the ice, luckily all at one end of their strip, but reducing their landing run still further, and there were scars of craters along the lake edge where a well-aimed string had burst among the parked aircraft.

Circling the lake with his mixture all the way back to full lean to conserve his last few gallons of fuel, Mike watched Avery come in on a good low approach. But he was still going too fast when he ran out of runway. Mike saw him spin through 360 degrees from braking too violently, and then the Hurricane lurched into the bomb hole with a splash, held from complete submersion by its wings. A party ran to his rescue from the woods, but Mike could remain airborne no longer and landed with infinite care, kicking left rudder as he ran along on the ice so that he went into the bordering bank of snow, but not so fast that he went up on his nose.

Mike saw Avery next in the mess annex. He had changed into dry clothes and was talking to the C.O. Mike heard him say, "My number two left me against my orders and prevented us from formulating a standard coordinated attack."

Mike could hardly believe his ears, and he was not going to let Avery get away with this.

"Excuse me, sir. I don't want to appear disloyal to my flight commander, but I would like the opportunity to defend myself."

Anson turned on him sharply. "Not here and not now you won't, Browning." He addressed them both in sharp uncompromising terms. "We've enough problems here without internal personality conflict. We'll write the op. off as a failure. Dismiss." With this he stomped off.

Avery was looking at Mike with undisguised fury, his face a grotesque contrast to the calm, equable demeanor he usually presented to the world. "I'd have thought you'd have picked up the rudiments of air combat by now, Browning," he said in a steely voice. "And of discipline and obedience—something you don't seem to understand in your country."

Mike looked at the tall, stiff figure in front of him without replying. What's eating this guy? Mike was as angry with himself for failing to understand the man as he was at the insults. He hated a mystery, but here was something he just couldn't unravel.

The C.O. made no further comment on the incident, as if content that it should die a natural death, but in the evening he did comment if only implicitly and negatively on his flight commander's failure. All the pilots had assembled at the officers' mess. Anson looked more fierce and hawklike than ever, and what he had to say was of a grim nature. But first he congratulated Sergeant Walker on his victory. "You showed guts and initiative and a cool head," he said. "And a talent for being in the right place at the right time."

Mike was among the many present who turned to look at the sergeant and murmur their congratulations. He stood up at this reference to himself, pale and self-deprecating, his face a white mask in the dim light of the hotel lounge. "Thank you, sir," he said without emotion.

It seemed that he had been sitting in the cockpit of his Hurricane when the 88's came in, and had taken off in a hail of gunfire and exploding bombs. At first he had ignored them in order to gain height and offset his lack of speed. He must have worked it all out carefully without telling anyone. A loner all right.

"You'll know that we're now down to seven kites," Anson continued. "And we also lost two of our four armorers in the raid. Pilots must be prepared to rearm their own machines and refuel them, too. We've enough fuel for about two patrols a day for a week. By then we hope to have fresh supplies. But until we clear another length of snow tomorrow we can't get off . . ."

At that point, the adjutant came in and spoke quietly to the C.O., who nodded and moved toward the door. "The meeting is adjourned. I'll be back," he said before disappearing.

Later the Spy came in and said confidentially to Mike and several other pilots, "I'm laying on a rather good show in a few minutes. Do you want to come and watch?"

Somebody said, "You're line-shooting or drunk, Spy."

"You'll see," he replied. "I'm laying out a new runway for you." He went to the door and returned with two Norwegians, one they recognized as a local man who had acted as an interpreter during the period of the preparation of the base. The other was small and looked like an Eskimo tramp. He had narrow slit eyes, full cheeks and a swarthy complexion that had turned faintly pink from recent heavy drinking. He wore an ancient fur cape and held a pair of snowshoes under his arm. He grinned all the time and appeared completely pleased with life.

"This is Piet," the Spy introduced him. "Please get him a drink, someone, but not too much, as he has work to do tonight. He is a Lapp. That's right, isn't it?" he asked the interpreter. "Lap up the akevitt, then, Piet."

The Norwegian confirmed that he was indeed from Lapland. The interpreter explained that Piet had three thousand reindeer a short distance away, that this was the time of the year when the Norwegian reindeer were led from their winter quarters in the valleys up into the mountains inland on their annual migration. They normally passed through the area occupied by their camp, but Piet had been disconcerted by the presence of so many strangers, and then by the bombing and machine-gunning.

The interpreter continued, "I told him it was all right. Then your officer, Mr. Williams, had the idea that if he led his pack across the lake all these many feet might help you against the German invaders. Although I do not understand how—only how with much akevitt I can persuade Piet here to divert from his usual route."

In spite of the hardships of the long day, all who could watched in the half light at eleven o'clock as the inebriated Lapp led his big white reindeer buck, the pack leader, down through the trees from the hill above and onto the lake. They made an orderly and extraordinary procession, a seemingly endless line of gray adult reindeer, their backs steaming in the frozen night air, padding silently and without hesitation out of the forest and onto the snow-covered ice. It took the pack half an hour to pass, and at one time the dark moving mass stretched from the forest beside their camp clear into the distance in an unbroken line some fifty yards wide. They beat the six-inch-deep snow into an unyieldingly hard surface fit for even a heavy bomber to take off from.

"Spy, you're a wizard," the C.O. complimented him later. "We'll be in business again at dawn."

Instead, they were frozen at dawn. Mike awoke in the unheated room he shared with four other pilots as the first light showed in the sky. The windows were thick with patterned rime and the mug of water beside his bunk had become a lump of ice. B Flight pilots piled on all the clothes they had and went out into the half light. The air hit them like a blow to the chest and Mike felt that if he stood still for a minute he would never move again. He had spent one winter in Seattle and the temperature had dropped to 35 below, but he had never before experienced anything like this.

Down at the lake the crews were struggling to get some life

and movement into the Merlins. It was impossible to wind them manually against the pressure of the frozen oil, and the trolley-acs did not have the power. The carburetors were frozen, the controls seized up. Some crews were applying hot bricks, and one had followed the simpler procedure of lighting a fire under the engine, until pounced on by the flight sergeant—"You'll blow us all up!"—and by the Spy—"You'll have the Hun homing in, you clots!" It took two hours to get three engines started and the wheels unfrozen. Then three of A Flight were ordered up on patrol.

Reindeer Avenue, as their new long runway was called, had improved even further with the overnight frost, presenting a mile-long length of hard-beaten frozen snow. The three Hurricanes took off in turn without any trouble, the rising notes of the Merlins echoing back from the mountains, and each machine casting back a light trail of powdered snow in its slipstream.

The adjutant, the C.O. and the major of marines commanding the antiaircraft party reorganized the base's defenses during the early hours of the morning, and Mike and the rest of B Flight helped the ground party maneuver two of the less damaged Hurricanes into suitable tactical positions at the edge of the forest so that their guns could be fired down the length of the runway at any strafing German machines.

As the armament officer himself admitted, the chances of hitting anything with a set of fixed Brownings was remote. "But at least it'll encourage our troops and put the buggers off their aim," he said.

They had just gotten the second Hurricane set up, with the remains of its tail secured to a tree stump, when the Germans came in again, this time with eight Heinkel 111's which flew across the lake at above Oerlikon height, dropping sticks of bombs on the old runway, but doing no further damage to the remaining intact Hurricanes or to their stores, or even injuring anyone.

The three patrolling Hurricanes got in among the

bombers as they dropped down over the mountains and came in again, low. Mike saw one spin in and explode in the forest on the north side, and then the three A Flight machines climbed up and left things to Rhysjhok's fixed defenses.

This time they were better prepared. The Oerlikons and the bigger guns had been better sited, every airman with a rifle blasted away, and Sammy Crow, who had leaped into the damaged Hurricane as the first bombs fell, let loose a stream of Browning machine-gun fire when the Heinkels bore in toward their makeshift dispersal.

Mike lay down beside the Hurricane, shouting encouragement to Sammy and watching with equal fascination the stream of spent cases pour from the underside of the Hurricane's wings, and the sharp-nosed bombers coming straight toward them, spitting fire from their single 7.9 mm in the nose.

It was like a repeat performance of that scene he had witnessed in the Black Forest two and a half years ago. The pilots may have been the same for all anyone could ever know. But this time the airman in the nose was squeezing the trigger and the bullets were screaming at him.

The last of the big machines, racing in closer to the lake than the others, was hit by a maelstrom of fire, reared up onto its tail, caught fire and began to spin down from five hundred feet. It nosedived into the center of their old runway, piercing the ice with a shattering roar, and came to rest with only its tailplane exposed. The swastika, black against the khaki camouflage of the fin and rudder, was the last defiant gesture the German bomber could offer.

A tremendous cheer went up from the R.A.F., all of whom claimed the shot that must have killed the pilot, and with the rapid fading of the bombers into the distance, they swarmed onto the ice to seize souvenirs.

Mike helped Sammy down from the cockpit. "You won't see a better prang than that," exclaimed the Rhodesian. "All my own work, too."

"Nuts," said Mike.

It was an exhilarating start to the day for everyone. The three A Flight Hurricanes returned twenty minutes later, their gunport covers torn and stained cordite black. They appeared to be undamaged, and rocked their wings encouragingly as they flew overhead and then broke into line astern for the landing.

At breakfast time on this morning, April 20, 1940, the mood of 140 Squadron was cheerful and optimistic. The ground crews were even discussing plans to cannibalize some of the damaged machines—an aileron here, an oleo leg there, a prop and spinner off one and onto a less damaged Hurricane, in order to increase their numbers of serviceable aircraft.

Mike, drinking sweet tea from a tin mug down by the shore, was not able to share this optimism, although usually he was the first to see the cheerful side. The British had been skillful and lucky on that second raid. The Germans had lost four out of eight of their Heinkels, for a 50 percent casualty rate. But the Germans' resources could withstand this rate of attrition, whereas 140 had lost half of its machines already, and they did not have the resources to keep even a single Hurricane on standing patrol through daylight hours. The Germans would be back, to exact revenge, again and again, until the R.A.F. had nothing left to fly. They were like islanders in a frail fortress, blockaded and bombarded by an enemy fleet. That was how Mike saw things.

As chance would have it, nature struck 140 its next blow. The arrival of spring, which had been heralded by the migrating reindeer, by midday threatened the runway they had so efficiently created. The temperature, far below zero at night, now rose well above it, and the sun beat down relentlessly on the frozen lake, melting the snow and causing water, inches deep, to flood onto their two runways and taxiing tracks.

A Flight tried to take off again at 1400 hours, and after

splashing out with water above their wheel fairings, and the slipstream sending a spray up behind them, were forced to return.

Mike and Sammy went down to the dispersal after tea to inspect things for themselves. Sammy stood in his rubber boots on a small knoll watching the ever-industrious ground crews working on the damaged machines under the shelter of the shoreline trees.

"Well, tickle the cattletick!" he exclaimed, his words tumbling out at their usual hectic rate. "I don't know about you, Yank, but I think these English are barmy. Maybe lovable. Certainly mad. They send fourteen Hurricanes to deal with half the German air force and give them a bit of ice to fly off in the middle of a thaw."

"You don't do them justice, Sammy," said Mike. "They also send four antiaircraft guns."

Mike could not believe that they were the only officers at Rhysjhok who recognized the reality of their position. If they were, all the others were disillusioned a few minutes later when they heard, above the sound of hammering and welding and shouting from the ground crews, a distant deep hum of engines.

Mike and Sammy splashed out into the lake and looked up into the clear blue sky. Coming up from the south and leaving telltale contrails was a formation of bombers, shining silver in the bright light. They were at over twenty thousand feet, and there could be no doubt that Rhysjhok was their target.

Mike and Sammy ran back into the forest shouting, "Air raid! Air raid! Take cover." From the direction of the airmen's camp, a klaxon groaned out its warning. A distant whistle grew to a shriek. By that time, Mike had hit the bottom of a slit trench, his arms over his head.

For fifteen minutes the bombs rained down, the ground shook, the blast waves tore through the trees, uprooting many of them, and the sound beat over and over again at

Mike's skull until he thought it would burst. The Luftwaffe was in no hurry. To and fro the bombers flew, turning through 180 degrees in immaculate formation, making leisurely practice, confident in the knowledge that nothing could harm them.

When at last it was over, Mike crawled out of his trench with the others. His head was aching and he felt too dizzy to stand. The air was thick with smoke and the stench of burning oil mixed with burning timber. With the smoke there also drifted across their devastated base the sound of voices raised in anguish or alarm or peremptory order, and the crackle of flaming wood. Sammy was standing a few yards away, swaying on his feet. When he saw Mike he walked uncertainly toward him. All he could say was, "That's bloody that."

And so it was, they soon discovered. Very little of 140's equipment and resources were left. All their oil was going up in a dense black cloud that stained the sky until far into the night, an unextinguishable furnace. Only one petrol dump was left. The commandeered hotel had been burned out, with all their belongings, and many of the tents had been torn asunder. The miracles—and every air raid has at least one miracle—were that only eighteen were killed and the same number injured. And that the ammunition store had survived. But as only a single Hurricane remained intact, and that was unserviceable, this was an academic reckoning.

Squadron Leader Anson said, "We're pulling out tonight. The signal came through an hour ago."

"I'll tell the warrant officer and get some sort of transport organized for the wounded," said Sandy Baker. No one had done more than the "Adj" to bring some sort of order to the chaos at Rhysjhok.

From the other side of the bell tent which served as the officers' mess, someone asked, "What's the form when we get to the sea, sir?"

"Swim," snapped the C.O. and went out into the rain, which had started an hour earlier, adding further to their misery.

"Ask a stupid question . . ." said Baker. "No one knows anything. No one ever does in a war. But there's a jetty at Ahrl. That's where we disembarked last week, and where no doubt we'll embark tonight. If we ever get there."

"We came, we saw, we—retreated," another voice called out from the other end of the tent.

"Oh, shut up."

The villagers behaved wonderfully to the end, helping to bury the dead, taking some of the worst wounded into their houses, and providing everything they had in the way of transport, down to bicycles and hand carts, for the journey to the fishing port at Ahrl. Not one of them showed any sign of bitterness at the sudden arrival of these strangers in blue, their brief and eruptive sojourn, the damage caused by their presence, and their precipitate departure. Some of the women were in tears, and the children pressed pathetic presents and mementos into the hands of the departing R.A.F. and marines.

It was drizzling, cold and muddy as the first of the party set out down the stone track in the dusk. Mike was about to join the procession and was wondering how his leg would stand up to the journey when Donald Avery drew him aside.

"You're not going, Browning," he said sharply, stroking his moustache.

Mike looked up at him, his eyes attempting to penetrate the mind and motives of this cold Englishman who was so different from most of his contemporaries in the service. "This isn't a time for kidding, sir," he protested.

"No, I mean it. I need a volunteer. And that's you."

"Why don't you get off my back, Avery? What's eating you?" But even as he asked, Mike knew the truth and knew that Avery knew he knew. And that Avery knew he was safe because Mike could never let it be known that he had deliberately dodged combat.

Anson came up at that moment, a brisk, hard figure for whom temporary defeat was no worse than a gladiator's first provocative sword thrust. "I hear you're the volunteer," he said. "Chiefy's got the last kite serviceable and I want you to fly it out."

"O.K., sir. Glad to help. But where in hell to?"

"Spy'll give you the form. He and Adj. are staying, too. I've got to go. Good luck, Yank."

Over mugs of coffee in the tent they were to share, the Spy explained to Mike what was happening. He had procured a child's atlas from the schoolmaster and pointed to a port far up the Norwegian coast and inside the Arctic Circle. "We're giving up trying to take Trondheim. The Hun's too strongly established, and *we* know what air power they've got."

He explained that Namsos had been flattened and that Carton de Wiart was pulling his troops out, and that the Allies were going to concentrate on recovering Narvik, where the German occupying force was virtually without air cover. Narvik was vital to the enemy because it was through this remote little port, a few miles from the frontier, that Germany obtained her Swedish iron ore. "And that's more valuable than gold to the Hun."

"140's returning to the U.K., to Scapa Flow, for reequipping and collecting new machines." The navy was sending a Walrus amphibian to pick up the adjutant, the local schoolmaster, Björn Braarvig, and himself and take them to a small military airstrip called Romstad which they believed lay just north of Narvik. They hoped to enlarge and develop it rapidly into a base with local labor.

"And where do I come into this crackpot scheme of yours, Spy?" Mike asked. "This is the most goddamn crazy war I've ever fought!"

"You're going to make sure we get there safely. You're going to fly close escort."

Mike threw out the dregs of his coffee, and stared at the intelligence officer. "I always thought you might be nuts, Spy. Now I know you're out of your tiny mind."

11

Keith stuffed the letter from Jenny into his flying boot as the C.O. approached. It had been written on May 9, the day before the German *Blitzkrieg*. It was characteristically light and teasing in its tone. "Your friends have long since gone, as I expect you have heard, and we have only the navy to keep us company," ran the last paragraph. "But they would like to believe we don't exist—air*men* on an R.N. station was bad enough, but air*women*. I mean to say. Actually, they are very courteous in a remote sort of old-fashioned way. But not quite like you lot of reprobates . . . Anyway, I'm leaving tomorrow to go about as far away from here as possible without actually falling into the sea."

And that, Keith realized anxiously, must mean an R.D.F. station on the south coast, which could soon be the front line.

Squadron Leader Rowbotham showed few signs of his old cheerfulness these days, but his energy and fighting spirit were prodigious. "Wing wants us to send a section to this bridge at Meurville on the Oise to cover some Blenheims which will be going in at twelve hundred hours," he informed Range Powell, Buffer, Keith and a veteran warrant officer pilot. "There'll probably be bags of flak so keep out of its range. Your business is to deal with any 109's who may add to the bombers' miseries. And they've got plenty."

Range said, "If the Huns are at Meurville they must be moving fast, sir."

Rowbotham agreed that things were not looking too good. "They're across the Meuse and other big rivers, too," he said. "The French and Belgians aren't blowing the bridges, which doesn't help, and that means the bomber boys have to do it, which is very expensive, in both lives and aircraft."

He turned as four Hurricanes of A Flight took off in line abreast across the fully repaired field, raising their undercarriages and forming up into two pairs. They had shot down four German bombers the day before, but it was like swatting a few wasps from a swarm. There seemed to be no limit to the numbers of aircraft the Luftwaffe could call on, although for the present they were leaving the Allied airfields alone and concentrating on bombing and strafing the retreating forces—including, it was said, civilian refugees.

Keith took off, leading a section for the first time on an operation. Green section. It was 1120 hours, and they climbed at once to twelve thousand feet. There was broken cumulus cloud below, which allowed him to map-read his way southeast over Douai toward St. Quentin. At this height the sense of detachment from the war raging below could be treacherous. Once they caught sight of a burning farmhouse, a poignant funeral pyre of someone's cherished home and possessions. The lick of flame was like a distant star, the smoke streaming east on the prevailing wind. The roads, which had carried little traffic before the German offensive, everywhere showed signs of activity, although from this height it was impossible to distinguish advancing German Panzers from the retreating French battalions and refugees.

To the east of Douai Keith spotted the flicker of heavy artillery firing, and a few minutes later heavy flak forced them to jink and weave. The shells burst just ahead of them, dense black with yellow flashes at their center, fading to dark then light gray behind them like airborne litter.

At 1150, Keith led down his section through a hole in the cloud, leveling off just below its base and checking their position. "Green section, open out and keep your eyes skinned," he transmitted.

"Three o'clock below," said Range quickly. His eyesight was almost as sharp as Sergeant Henry's had been. Keith could now see the huddle of houses with the road passing through them, the church set in the square and the modern concrete bridge over the river. It all looked wonderfully tranquil until his eye picked out the long column of trucks, well spaced, and interspersed motorcycles with sidecars, threading its way through the village and over the bridge.

The Blenheims arrived dead on time. They made a brave sight in their tight formation, and a welcome contrast to the massed waves of German bombers that had filled the sky recently. Keith turned his section 15 degrees to bring them over the top of the Blenheims as they lined up for their long, shallow, diving approach to their target, and hoped that the Hurricanes' presence would give them some feeling of security. They would need it. With the other light bombers, the Battles, the Blenheims had suffered fearful casualties in daylight attacks. Only two had survived one squadron attack.

The flak opened up on the bombers when they were still a mile from their target, and the heavy shells were joined by light gunfire as soon as they were in range. The sky about the Blenheims was soon spotted with bursts, and quick-firing 40-mm guns sent streams of tracer arching toward the oncoming machines. One of the starboard bombers was blown to pieces, its remains flown through by the Blenheim immediately behind it.

A second caught fire in its port engine and swung out of line. A third, showing no signs of being hit, suddenly dived vertically into the ground beside the road, its exploding bombs sending circles of shock waves splaying far over the field.

The survivors came on indomitably and weaving frantically until they were forced to steady up for the last run in. The fury of the defending fire reached a crescendo during the last few hundred yards of the bombers' attack, and a fourth Blenheim burst into flames and crashed, this time onto the road, scattering trucks far and wide as if in a frenzy of suicidal revenge.

"Let's go and rake the buggers," Range called up, his Australian accent intensified by the strain he was feeling.

"Stay with me," Keith ordered briskly. He, too, longed to get down among them and do what he could with his eight Brownings against the murderous gunners. But their business was up here.

As confirmation, a sudden movement to the left drew his attention and he saw a line of 109's diving down from the cloud and heading straight for the village. The timing was like a set piece in an air show, and Keith took the cue at once. As the last surviving Blenheims dropped their bombs close to the bridge, leaving it intact, but leaving the German convoy with many lost vehicles and many casualties, he called out, "Tally ho!" and threw his throttle wide open.

They had a three-thousand-feet height advantage, and they would need it all to give them superior speed over the 109's. There were six of the clipped-wing little fighters, and they were closing in on the Blenheims at almost twice their speed. They were painted very dark and to Keith they looked like rats scavenging for the remnants left by the flak. At that moment if his guns had failed he would have rammed one of these marauders.

Hardly believing his luck, he closed in to three hundred yards behind the rearmost 109. They were going to jump them! Overconfident in their arrogance, the German fighters continued to close the gap at the same pace as the Hurricanes narrowed the distance between them and their victims.

Keith's target was firing the first rounds of machine-gun and 20-mm cannon fire from its nose when he was hit by the Hurricane's full five-second burst. For a moment the

109 jinked hectically up and down, like an animal twitching in its dying moments. Then everything seemed to fall off. The sky in front of Keith's nose was crowded with metal chunks which passed below him as he jerked back his column.

The other 109's immediately broke off their attack. Keith caught a glimpse of the suddenly reprieved Blenheims streaking away at treetop height, while the rest of his section mixed it with the remaining five fighters. The Germans did not remain for long. A flash in a field a few miles to the south indicated the end of another machine, and the voices of Range and Buffer on the R/T congratulating the warrant officer, immediately afterward, reassured Keith that his section was safe.

The low-level fight had separated them and, rather than waste time on re-forming, Keith gave them an approximate course to steer for base. "I'll try and pick you up on the way," he transmitted.

Instead, he picked up something quite different. After five minutes' flying, weaving from side to side just below cloud base and constantly looking behind, he found himself over the town of Denain. To the east, smoke stains across the landscape marked the point of the German advance, while all roads west out of the town were packed solid with the traffic of fleeing refugees. It was 1914 and 1870 and every European war in history reenacted once again—the fear, the devastating loss of honor, the frantic need to escape before the military jackboot crushed them . . .

This time, however, there was a new dimension of terror, from the skies. Mushrooming smoke and rubble told their own story of dive bombing, carried out with clinical precision against the defenseless French citizens. He could see the little Stukas, the Junkers 87's, working their way systematically along the road, killing and wounding and blocking the route for the others behind them. Immediately below him, racing across the outskirts of the town at rooftop height, was a bigger target, a Dornier 215. It was machine-gunning the crowds and dropping delayed-action bombs down the length of the road, leaving behind a series of explosions at cruelly spaced-out intervals. Figures scattered like bomb debris from the machine's path, and horses, wagons, handcarts, cars and bicycles were torn asunder.

So the tales of massacred civilians that had filtered back to Lens-La Basse were true after all. The squadron had heard, too, about the destruction of the undefended center of Rotterdam by Junkers 87's on May 14. Most of the pilots had shrugged the news aside, as unconfirmed or at least exaggerated. And wasn't it war anyway? The reality, as Keith saw it now, was something quite different.

Keith put the Hurricane's nose down to cut off the Dornier. He was not going to have the same luck again. This machine had a mid-upper gunner who saw him coming long before he was in range, and in a short time was opening fire with uncomfortable accuracy. The Dornier was going to try to effect its escape "on the deck," Keith quickly realized. The pilot put it into a steep turn, which Keith followed without difficulty.

Just below his port wing as he left the line of the main road, he caught a glimpse of something that he would never forget, and which set the final hot seal on his determination to destroy these murderers. Half in the ditch was a farm cart, its back broken, the horse in the shafts on its side in a pool of blood and with its belly torn open. The contents of the cart, an iron bedstead, a baby carriage, and a bundle of clothes, had been spilled out into the field, a lifetime of privacy now exposed to the world. There may have been four bodies. Keith was not sure. The number did not matter. But there was no doubt that one of the victims was an old woman, spread-eagled grotesquely and with her black dress half over her head. And no doubt at all that beside her—her granddaughter?—was the headless corpse of a little girl.

The bomber was in the hands of an experienced pilot who kept it very low. Keith "pulled the plug" for emergency boost, feeling at once the new surge of power from his engine. But, even so, he was only holding the Dornier, which lifted up over a line of poplars and dropped down the other side as if it were a Tiger Moth instead of a big twin-engined machine. Keith saw it bank steeply, wing tip grazing the corn tips, and realized that, conforming to the old aphorism that attack is the best form of defense, it was attempting to play the role of a fighter and get its front guns to bear on his Hurricane.

Keith quickly showed that it was not a sensible tactic. He had no trouble in keeping inside the Dornier's turning circle, and got in a short burst which clipped into his twin-finned tail. The German pilot immediately reversed his turn so that his slipstream swept at the Hurricane and forced Keith to pull back his column for fear of striking the ground.

A railway line, a grade crossing, a small house flashed beneath his wing. The Dornier had gained a few hundred yards, was streaking across a green meadow, scattering scared cows, over some pollarded willows and temporarily out of sight. Gambling on the pilot turning to port, Keith cut across the meadow at a sharper angle, and saw his antagonist only two hundred yards ahead, skimming the waters of a wide, brown river.

This time Keith tried a deflection shot, giving it a quarter ring and pulling the sight through. He was making strikes again, this time on the wing root. The pilot forced the Dornier down even lower, and Keith was about to follow when a dark shape loomed very close. His attention was torn from the gunsight and a steel cantilever railway bridge rose up scarcely two hundred yards ahead. Stark terror seized him. The cunning pilot had led him into a trap. It was too late to follow the Dornier down through the narrow gap between the pillars and the water and steel girders.

Keith wrenched the stick back into his stomach, and the gallant Hurricane responded like a hunter at a fence, clearing the top of the curving main span of the bridge by a few feet. Keith pushed the column forward so that the momentarily starved carburetors cut out the engine. The

Dornier had gained more seconds. He could see the needle-thin fuselage, the crosses on its deep wings, five hundred yards down the river, smoke pouring from its exhausts, and hugging the surface so closely that the slipstream was rippling the water in its wake.

He never caught that Dornier. He had no need to. He got in one very long-range burst, which may have resulted in some lucky hits which were the indirect cause of the bomber's end. He would never know. The river entered a deep sandstone gorge, and either the pilot's judgment erred for a fraction of a second or his nerve cracked. Or perhaps he was wounded.

Keith saw the end as if in slow-motion film. The gorge turned sharply, and the Dornier was half through in a steep banking turn. Then the port wing-tip appeared to drop. Not far. Only a few feet. That was too much. There was a splash of foam, and for one moment it seemed as if the bomber wou'd recover, then the nose slammed down into the water, and it cartwheeled once in a cloud of spume and was hurled against the cliff face of the gorge.

Keith heard the explosion above the sound of his own engine, and almost followed the Dornier to its fate. Five minutes later, from a height of four thousand feet, he could still see the gray smoke from the wreck spilling across the fields toward a nearby town.

The end had been so stunning, in every sense, that Keith had been in a state of half-confused shock since he had climbed away from the river, a sitting duck for any 109. Now he pulled himself together. He had set himself a strict discipline for combat occasions. No brooding. No doubts. This is a dangerous enough business for those who relish the killing. Keep your conscience on ice until later, if you're going to let it bother you! And this is what he did now, his strong survival element solidly reinstated.

His eye played over his instrument panel, following its set pattern from oxygen supply dial on the left around to the fuel gauge, which he pressed for a reading. No fuel problem, anyway. Then he glanced at the clock and saw that he had been airborne for an hour and three-quarters, much of it at full throttle. Not possible! His eye fell to the tank selector and saw that the finger pointed to "Reserve." The gauge was registering that he was reaching the end of his reserve, not of his main tanks! At some point, he must have switched over without consciously registering it.

Keith reckoned he had five, or at the most ten minutes of flying time left. He searched the landscape below for signs of a French airfield. He was somewhere northwest of Douai, and there was no means of telling whether it was conquered or Allied soil below. He guessed that the river he had been following was the Sensée, but the pattern of fields was monotonously the same in all directions. And, within a few minutes, he must put down somewhere.

The roads were uncrowded here. He could see two main highways, one running northwest, the other due west and as straight as only the French build them. This second one was unusual in not being flanked by poplars or any other obstruction.

Then the idea suddenly struck Keith. Why land wheels up in a field? Why not wheels down on the road? It even ran obligingly dead into wind, too. Perhaps, after all, he might be able to save his Hurricane—and, my God, every one was needed now!

At full lean mixture, and at lowest economical throttle opening, Keith circled the clearest looking stretch. Only one cyclist and one farm cart were in sight.

The gauge was now registering zero, and Keith was faced with the labor of pumping down wheels and flaps. Both green lights came on as the wheels locked, then he was down to two hundred feet with full flaps lowered, cockpit hood open. He had passed over the cart, the road ahead seemed clear and just about wide enough, only one or two trees and a small building a mile or more ahead flanked by more trees.

It was not a good touchdown. The road surface was pockmarked with holes, and the Hurricane slewed from side to side and bounced heavily once. Keith held it steady and under control with difficulty, but at length he had it at fast walking pace, and by swinging the nose was able to check his direction.

He passed the cyclist at a fair pace. He was an elderly man, and had wisely taken to the ditch, his bicycle lying on the grass. Keith called out, *"Bonjour, monsieur. Pardonnez-moi. . . ."* It was all he had time for, but he did take off his helmet as an additional courtesy. The man's expression of wide-eyed terror remained unchanged.

Keith taxied on, running once onto the grass to keep his port wing-tip clear of a small tree. He planned to travel as far as the small building he had seen, if both traffic and fuel permitted. In a moment, he was glad he had made the decision to continue, for, distinctly and indisputably, the small object he had spotted, which at first he judged to be a standing figure, took on the shape of a gas pump standing clear of the trees at the roadside.

Keith locked on the brakes of his Hurricane in the shelter of the forecourt's trees. The building was little more than a hut, accommodating an oil dispenser, some shelves and a cloverleaf Citröen car. Keith reached for the cutout lever and was about to pull it when the engine coughed and died. "Not bad timing," he told himself with satisfaction, and pulled the clip of his Sutton harness and banged the box of his parachute to release himself.

It was certain that the octane rating of fuel for French agricultural machinery and Citröen cars was a good deal lower than the required rating for a Merlin. But, Keith decided, it was worth a try because anything was better than walking.

The owner of the filling station was asleep in his hut, nodding in an ancient cane chair. A Bakelite radio was tuned loudly to a light orchestra in which the concertina predominated. As Keith was about to awaken the proprietor, the music stopped, and a voice announced: *"Ici Radio Paris.*

La guerre dans l'ouest. Les armées courageuses de la France, de la Grande Bretagne et du Belge . . ."

The man opened his eyes. He was gray haired, fiftyish, and regarded Keith in flying boots and Irvin jacket curiously. "*Monsieur,*" Keith began, "*eh bien, s'il vous plaît, de l'essence . . .*"

"*Ah, oui. Je suis fatigué—c'est la guerre, vous comprenez.*"

Keith followed him out, observing his reaction to the sight of the Hurricane, as lofty and as spectacular as some being from outer space in its commonplace location tucked into the tree-sheltered forecourt of this little filling station.

The response was admirable. The man paused and then turned to Keith. "*Ah, un avion. Bon. Vous êtes aviateur. Combien de litres, monsieur?*" he asked in a matter-of-fact voice.

The man on the bicycle had emerged from the ditch, only to be confronted by another surprise. On the same stretch of road on which Keith had made his difficult landing there arrived a motorcycle and sidecar combination of an unfamiliar nature, manned by two figures in field-gray uniform, black steel helmets, goggles, black gauntlets and carrying machine-pistols across their backs and Lügers in holsters. On a swiveling mount on the fore part of the sidecar was secured a ferocious-looking heavy Mauser machine gun. The war had arrived, midway between the villages of Sélincourt and Bourville, in the guise of two of the most up-to-date machines of destruction. It was one of the ironies and coincidences of war, which the Frenchman did not appreciate until much later, that they had, both British and German, ceased to function in the same place.

One of the soldiers looked up from the engine and, noticing the Frenchman, called out peremptorily, "*He, Bauer. Wir brauchen jemanden, der uns mit diesem Motorrad hilft. Hol' uns einen Mechaniker mit Benzin von der nächsten Werkstatt.*"

The bicyclist looked at the German, eyes wide, and shook his head. "*Je ne comprends pas, monsieur.*"

But by gestures and shouting, and the drawing of a Lüger from its holster, the German made the Frenchman understand that he was to bicycle "*Schnell, schnell!*" to the garage a half mile up the road.

And so it came about that, five minutes later, as Keith was pouring in the twentieth 10-liter can of gas into the port tank of his Hurricane, the Frenchman whom Keith had earlier greeted arrived breathless at the filling station, crying "*Les Boches—les Boches!*" and pointing behind him.

Keith jumped down from the wing, can in hand, and *monsieur le propriétaire* of the filling station hastily returned the hose nozzle to the pump and joined Keith behind the trunk of the plane tree bordering the road. They could clearly see the motorcycle combination and the two figures. As they watched, a second machine arrived in a flurry of dust and halted beside it. Clearly they were the arrow tip of a Panzer thrust, one of the many which were slicing deep into France, cutting off whole brigades and causing panic everywhere among the Belgians and French.

"*Il faut que je me départ, monsieur,*" called Keith. "*J'ai besoin de temps. Aidez-moi.*"

He took from the clips in the cockpit the two emergency starting cranks, and gave one to each of the Frenchmen, indicating where they should be inserted in the engine cowling. Then he kicked a couple of bricks in front of the wheels and leaped into the cockpit without bothering with straps or helmet.

"*Tournez, s'il vous plaît,*" he called down, and the two men, one of whom must have been over seventy and the filling-station proprietor over fifty, strained at the cranks. Fortunately, the oil still being hot, the task was not quite beyond them. After two rotations of the big Watts propeller, the Merlin caught, and Keith throttled it into life.

The Frenchmen fled for cover at the sound and it was

only with difficulty that Keith persuaded them to remove the bricks from under his wheels and pass him up the cranks. Then he released the brakes and taxied quickly out onto the road. In his rearview mirror he saw that one of the motorcycle combinations was already racing down the road, and that the gap was narrowing rapidly.

Cockpit procedure suddenly became irrelevant and, kicking the Hurricane into line with the road, Keith at once opened the throttle wide.

The acceleration with the fixed-pitch screw was agonizingly slow, and the fire from the Panzer crew was biting into his tailplane and the trailing edges of his wings before he could equal their speed. With his eyes darting from mirror to road ahead, and kicking compensating rudder for the ruts and holes, Keith managed at last to lift his machine's tail.

By now the motorbike was scarcely fifty yards behind and he could see the muzzle flash from the heavy machine gun and from the driver's gun, too; he was firing with one arm and guiding his machine with the other. It was a moment when Keith could have used a rear gunner himself. Instead he had to rely on the armor plate behind his head, and on the Germans failing to rip one of the critical control cables in his fuselage and wings. By the time he lifted off at around 85 m.p.h., the enemy was fast receding behind him. He pulled up over some trees and at last felt safe.

Clutching the column between his knees, he slipped on his helmet with unsteady hands, plugged in his radio and recovered his gauntlets from the cockpit floor. It had been comfortably warm before with the hood back. But the reaction to that moment of critical danger was chilling him, and he pulled it shut as he climbed away and cruised north on full weak mixture and economical boost.

He identified no more signs of war until he approached base, when he saw that the sky was black from an oil fire even bigger than the one caused by the last raid. There were other fires burning at different points on the airfield, and one hangar was a blazing inferno. It looked as if Lens-La

Basse had been heavily raided, but as Keith got into the circuit, he was puzzled to see no sign of a single bomb crater.

There were a dozen trucks at B Flight dispersal, and more at A Flight, all being loaded with spares and equipment, and a convoy of more trucks and staff cars was passing through the main gate of the airfield.

Range Powell ran out to Keith's Hurricane as he switched off.

"What's going on?" Keith called down to him.

"A ripe bloody old flap on, cobber. You'd better get some juice in your tanks—bloody snappy, too. We're leaving."

"Leaving?" Keith asked. "Where to?"

"Leaving, quitting, doing a bloody bunk. Retreating, cobber. Abso-bloody-lutely on the run—that's what. I'm glad to see you, though," continued the Australian as Keith joined him on the grass. "Thought you'd gone for a bloody burton." He glanced at Keith's tail, which was peppered with Mauser bullet holes. "What crook Kraut did that?"

"A fellow on a motorbike actually," said Keith teasingly.

Range kicked him toward the dispersal. "Don't give me that bloody rot."

12

In the shattered remains of R.A.F. Station Rhysjhok, three officers and one Norwegian schoolmaster awaited the arrival of a small 110 m.p.h. amphibian to transport them to an airstrip that was believed to exist more than four hundred miles to the north. Their task was to create a base for offensive operations against the German Army and Air Force, which controlled virtually the whole of Norway. The importance of their task was undoubted. Its successful accomplishment, armed with one Bren gun, three Lee-Enfield rifles, three revolvers, and a damaged but supposedly flyable Hurricane fighter, was a different matter.

The whole expedition was in the best makeshift tradition of an impossible task, to be carried out under impossible conditions. Mike's irreverent comment that this was "a goddamn crazy war" seemed justified.

The R.A.F. had struck up a close relationship with the people of the little village of Rhysjhok, and the schoolmaster had become the Spy's friend and collaborator. On the evening when the R.A.F. and marines evacuated, leaving a cold silence over the lakeside, the Spy, Sandy Baker and Mike left their two tents, picked their way through the bomb craters and rubble, and climbed the hill to the schoolmaster's house. They had been invited to a fish dinner with Björn Braarvig, the pastor, and their wives. The hospitality and kindness could not have been warmer, but Mike found the atmosphere of solemnity somewhat oppressive. He glanced once or twice at the Spy, who was clearly feeling as he did.

Toward the end of the evening, when they had settled down to a bottle of akevitt around the wood-burning stove, the pastor's wife turned to Mike and asked, "Why do you, an American, come and fight our war here in Europe?"

It was a question Mike had often been asked, and answered according to circumstances, usually flippantly. As the conversation, in halting English, had been on the heavy side until now, Mike answered, "I was bored. I had nothing else to do. I'm a good shot and have shot most things—moose, deer, coyotes, grouse—though I couldn't find any deer today when I went out hunting." He shrugged his shoulders and grinned engagingly. "So I thought I'd shoot a few people for a change. It's been pretty good hunting so far, too."

There was a puzzled silence in the simple living room. The Spy came to the rescue. "It's all right, he often talks like this. It's his wild American temperament. He is in fact filled with great ideals about democracy, as wonderful as his shooting is terrible."

The laughter in the room began uneasily and then the atmosphere relaxed with conviviality. The akevitt bottle was produced again, generous shots were poured out and President Roosevelt and the memory of the great Abraham Lincoln were toasted.

Then Mike drew from his hip pocket the slim silver flask his father had given him, with many dire warnings, on his eighteenth birthday. He poured out a bourbon whiskey for everyone and offered a toast which he thought these kind Norwegians would appreciate. "From the United States of America to the great Norwegian people and to King Haakon VII. And to the destruction of the invaders."

This struck the right note, and slightly tipsily they raised their glasses and drank the raw American whiskey.

Early the next morning, Mike and the Spy were aroused in their tent by the drone of an aircraft's engine. The Walrus amphibian, looking like something put together by the Wright brothers on one of their off-days, was circling the lake at a low altitude, searching for a sign of life.

Mike, who had slept in his Irvin jacket, slipped out of his sleeping bag and ran with it down to the edge of the lake. Standing on the frozen shore beside one of the smashed Hurricanes, he waved the sleeping bag, and after a few seconds the Walrus turned in his direction, flew low overhead, banked like some ill-favored bird, then came in very slowly to land on the wheels lowered beneath its boatlike fuselage.

The Spy, who with Sandy Baker had joined Mike at the lake shore, said in mock horror, "They're not going to take us away in that! It ought to have been made obsolete at birth."

While it taxied in, they gathered some of the discarded pine camouflaging branches and began to cover the biplane as soon as the pusher engine had been switched off.

Three F.A.A. officers got out—the pilot, radio operator and navigator. "It looks as if you've been in trouble," the pilot greeted them, looking about at the cratered shoreline and the chunks of tortured metal that were scattered far among the blasted trees.

"And it looks as if we'll be in more trouble if you're going to invite us on board this contraption," said the adjutant rudely.

The F.A.A. officers defended their amphibian good-humoredly on the grounds of its versatility. "The old Shagbat may not do three hundred miles per hour, but you can't drop a Hurricane over the side of a light cruiser in the middle of the night and land it on a lake—water or ice," he said. He looked at the Hurricane beneath its branches a hundred yards away and addressed Mike. "I hear you're going to keep the Luftwaffe at bay with that."

Mike nodded and smiled at the naval officers. "If I don't run out of gas, and can keep down to your speed."

"It's going to be dodgy for both of us. I make it four hundred fifteen miles," said the Walrus's navigator. "Come and look at this."

Mike and the naval officer studied the charts, following the route that the navigator had marked out up the long fractured coastline, over Brönnöysund, Luröy and Stött, where they would turn due north out to sea to avoid the Narvik area. "If you go down into the drink we can always pick you up," said the naval officer cheerfully. "Then we follow the length of the Lofoten Islands, approaching Romstad from the southwest."

For weight reasons, the Walrus pilot refused to carry any arms, so the Spy handed them over to the pastor. "Hide them well, Padre," he said. "You may find them useful later."

The pastor looked askance at the cache of guns. Then he produced a five-pound salmon. "You may find this useful later, too," he said. *"For aa spise seg mett,* as we say when we are hungry."

The schoolmaster's wife embraced her husband. She was crying when she gave him a pathetic packet of clothes. Two weeks ago their life in this little village, where they had both lived all their lives, was contented and peaceful. Now the anxieties, distresses and uncertainties appeared as numerous as the lakes and fjords of their cold and beautiful country.

Reindeer Avenue served them well for the last time. The overnight rain had frozen hard, and Mike had a long, smooth runway to take off the Hurricane. Ten minutes later, he caught up with the Walrus and it dropped to sea level. He positioned himself a thousand feet above, throttled right back with full weak mixture, feeling as if he were wallowing along at just above stalling speed, and weaving from time to time at 190 A.S.I. to prevent himself from overshooting.

The Walrus pilot followed the coastline from one craggy headland to the next, lifting up over small desolate islands and islets. Several times Mike could see him waving to in-shore fishermen in their "putters," and to people outside their little wooden houses and on the jetties of fishing villages.

The Hurricane's fuel gauge showed only twenty gallons left in its main tanks when Mike followed the Walrus out toward the Lofoten Islands. He could not imagine a more unpleasant latitude or a more unpleasant geography for crash landing a high-speed fighter. He scanned the cold, gray sky for the thousandth time since they had left Rhysjhok, and followed the Walrus over the coast of the southernmost of the Lofotens.

One hundred miles to go. Reserve would give him twenty minutes. At about six miles per gallon at best economical speed . . . Mike's arithmetic was weak. He studied again the white numerals on the dial, knowing that his life almost certainly depended upon them. But the result of his calculations suggested that he would be out of fuel ten miles short of their destination—at least ten miles. His only chance was to steer a straight course and leave the Walrus behind. They were away from the greatest danger of German attack now. The Walrus would remain in sight behind him for fifteen minutes or so. It was a calculated risk. Mike decided it was his duty to take it.

He rocked his wings as he passed at almost twice its speed above the Walrus. The experienced crew seemed to under-stand his dilemma, and they acknowledged by flashing a green Aldis lamp at him.

With nothing better than the page torn from the school atlas on his lap, and the memory of the configuration of this coast from the chart, Mike flew the last of 140's Hurricanes 10 degrees above the Arctic Circle in search of a flat strip of ground that might, or might not, exist. He had never felt so lonely in his life.

Forty minutes later, with his gauge showing zero, he spotted a rectangle of turf, looking like a spread-out brown towel, and surrounded by snow-clad hills. There was a wooden hut on one side, and a mile away a scattering of houses by the sawtooth coastline marked yet another fishing harbor.

Mike wasted no time on a full survey of the landscape. With his engine certain to cut out at any second he put down his wheels and flaps and prepared for the most unpredictable and hazardous landing he had ever made.

Still, he had gotten there, hadn't he? What a navigator! What a crackerjack dead-eye navigator! He laughed into his mask in relief, and as he lined up his nose on the strip that looked smaller than the *Swiftsure*'s flight deck, he hummed to himself, "I need no sign, I need no chart. The weather bureau in my heart . . ."

The moment his wheels touched, Mike knew that the cleared strip had a veneer of ice. He also knew that it was nothing like long enough. He therefore made the radical and dangerous decision to lock on his brakes *now*, at some 60 m.p.h. The result would be either a ground loop or that the Hurricane would stop before the end of the strip.

Slewing from side to side, and finally completing a circle, the Hurricane miraculously came to a halt on its three wheels, half in the snow. There was nowhere to taxi. So he reached out for the cutout lever, and looked up at the gray sky and the white mountains. His mind went back to a jump he had made from a third-floor window of Bartlett Hall into a snowdrift. The snow was softer than he had judged and the shock of landing had made him limp for a month. "You're a very lucky guy," the physician had commented. He remembered, too, a fellow American team member three years ago, after Mike had a very high-speed crash on the Cresta, saying, "Boy, you've got some charmed life, Michael Browning!"

In the cold silence of this Arctic field, breathing the air that smelled like frozen nectar and relishing the silence and the miracle of being alive, Mike was inclined to agree that the guy might have been right.

Fifteen minutes later, the "Shagbat" landed without difficulty.

No one knew anything about them at Romstad, which had become a confused and frightened community. The chairman of the local council, the Ordfører, knew about the German invasion, Björn Braarvig discovered, but had learned few details beyond the fact that Oslo had capitulated. The villagers had heard the distant sounds of the naval engagements on April 10 near Narvik in which the Germans and British had lost so many destroyers and so many lives. The firing had been even more furious three days later, and rumor had it that the Germans had lost no fewer than eight heavy destroyers.

The adjutant spoke to the Ordfører through Braarvig. "We have work for you," he said ominously. "Much work. But you will be well paid."

"That is good," replied the Ordfører. "We live by our fish here. And now there is little fishing with the fighting and the mines and other dangers. My people will welcome any work, especially if it will help to drive out the Germans."

Mike wrote to Eileen at Rising Hall on the same day, May 9, that Jenny had written to Keith in France.

Darling Eileen,

We have been "somewhere in Norway" for more than three weeks now, and as we are expecting a ship soon I'm hoping it will take this letter back to you.

I've swapped trades—pilot to manual laborer. Have forgotten how to fly. Our job is to build an airfield. And now we've done it and it looks swell. But we've worked from dawn to dusk, which up here means about twenty-four hours. First we had to clear the snow, blast out a layer of ice and move it a half mile as it can thaw in the middle of the day. Then we had to dig out the frozen soil and lay drainage pipes, dig about a quarter-million sods of turf from up the valley and lay them, roll them and cover them with chicken wire and roll them again!

After that we had to construct blast-proof bays of stacked logs, living quarters, stores and a control room. So, you see we've sure been occupied! Luckily we have about three hundred locals, who work in two shifts— they're mostly fishermen who can't fish and operatives in the fish factory that has no employment because of the war.

I hope the navy hasn't claimed you yet. I've met some swell guys in the senior service—and also some good-lookers, so you watch out, because I'm going to marry you the moment the Nazi flag's pulled down from the German Chancellery!

Your ever loving
Mike

As Mike folded the letter he heard the sound of a plane and went out of the hut to scan the pure blue sky. They had so far escaped the attentions of the Luftwaffe, which still possessed no nearby base.

Mike recognized the Swordfish while it was still well out to sea. It was the weekly "wage bus," as they called it, dispatched from one of the carriers—the *Glorious, Swiftsure* or *Furious*—operating in the North Sea. The antiquated-looking biplane made one pass over the airfield, rocking its wings, then banked around the head of the valley and came in low and at just above stalling speed. Mike saw the observer lean out of his cockpit and throw a large canvas bag over the side. As it struck the runway a loud cheer went up from the Norwegians digging a deep hole to accommodate a fuel store. That evening they would get their wads of crisp kröner notes, more than twice what they normally earned.

A sealed packet marked "Most Secret" was enclosed in the bag with the Norwegians' wages. The adjutant opened it in the presence of the Spy and Mike. In the eighteen days since they had begun work on creating this air base, the three officers had formed a harmonious partnership, working shifts on the supervisory work in conjunction with the two managers of the fish factory and the Ordfører.

Sandy Baker unfolded the sheets of official paper and smoothed them out on the table. The Swordfish that had dropped the bag was from the *Swiftsure*, which had embarked fifteen Hurricanes at Scapa on May 7, together with the same number of 140 Squadron pilots. The Fleet Auxiliary ship *Steyning*, escorted by a half flotilla of destroyers, would anchor off Romstad at midnight May 10–11 and ferry ashore ground crew, administrative personnel, a party of gunners from ack-ack command with officers and guns, and stores, fuel, etc.

Guided through the mist and cloud by a single Swordfish, 140's Hurricanes arrived at midday on May 12. Mike went out to the end of the runway half an hour before they were due, and lit a fire of oily rags to give the pilots the exact wind direction. They would have the biggest party since the war that night. The only original hut on the airfield had been converted into an officers' mess, and he had arranged for a good supply of beer and locally brewed akevitt.

Looking down the length of the 800-yard runway, and at the small town of huts and blast bays they had created in less than three weeks, he felt a surge of pride. He had not slept more than five hours in twenty-four since they had arrived, but the work had been so fascinating, and the overcoming of obstacles so satisfying, that he was fit and refreshed —and as ready for action as ever before.

The sound of the squadron's Merlins reached his ears before the machines came into sight. The familiar deep boom echoing against the steep-sided mountains seemed to bring Romstad to life as an airfield. The ground crews, who had arrived thirty-six hours earlier, were down at the dispersal, the gunners were at their Bofors and Oerlikons, the cooks were preparing lunch—and now here was their *raison d'être*, fifteen new fighter aircraft.

The Swordfish came into sight first, slow but steady and reliable looking, flying low over the sea, lifting up and heading for the runway. Behind, and throttled right back to avoid overshooting its guide, came the first of the Hurricanes, satisfyingly familiar in its head-on silhouette with its thick, tapering wings and finely pointed nose. A second followed behind it—they had evidently flown in line through the dirty weather to avoid separation—then another . . .

With wheels and flaps down and hoods thrown back on the downwind leg of the circuit, Mike could even identify several of the pilots, so familiar had their height and posture become over the months of peace and war.

Anson, characteristically hunched, was leading, then came the Geordie, Ralph Walker, who was tailing him. The sight of Donald Avery, defiantly erect even when flying, caused Mike's heart to sink. He had many times considered the possibility that he had been killed, or been posted away more suitably to a training school, thus relieving the squadron of the one pilot only senior officers seemed ready to accept.

Then came two pilots he did not recognize, and Sammy Crow, with his helmet removed for landing, a practice he had picked up from Mike, to whom he now gave the thumbs-up sign . . .

Mike ran to Sammy's plane as he switched off. It was good to see that cheerful, leathery face and satisfying to know that he would soon be fighting alongside the skillful Rhodesian again.

Sammy had felt the cold badly even at Rhysjhok. He pointed at the nearest hill. "Is that the North Pole up there? Christ, Mike, it never even got dark last night on that bloody ship—just a bit of gray in the sky and the temperature fell out of the bottom of the thermometer. And this is summer!"

They walked in toward the mess together. Mike asked, "What's the news? We haven't heard a thing for a week."

"The gen is that Holland and Belgium have gone for a burton—or just about." The Rhodesian told him of the

Blitzkrieg on the western front, of the B.E.F.'s advance into Belgium to support her retreating armies, of the French in retreat.

"Keith'll be in the thick of it," Mike said as he led Sammy into the mess.

"Yeah, he'll be packing in the ops O.K. and putting up his score. Still, we haven't come here for a party, either."

Mike smiled. "Oh, yes you have. Wait until you see the beer I've got for you."

The advantage the airman holds over the soldier, Mike recognized from twelve thousand feet over Narvik, is that he can study the whole of his fighting front in one panoramic sweep. Given the right weather, of course. And May 15 had dawned crisp and clear, by contrast with the mist and miserable drizzle of the day before.

The C.O. had sent him up with Sammy Crow on a reconnaissance patrol. All the pilots had been ordered off in turn to familiarize themselves with the terrain and to keep an eye open for Heinkels and Dorniers which flew up from Trondheim from time to time to bomb the Allied positions and the supporting warships off the coast.

The coastline here was even more indented and island-strewn than at Rhysjhok, and resembled a jigsaw puzzle in which the pieces could never be fitted to make a picture. Dark, twisting lakes, still frozen but with a layer of surface water, huddled in among the jagged peaks, and where the snow had melted it revealed only cold, harsh landscape hostile to man. The town of Narvik was no more than a scattering of wooden houses across a promontory deep inside Ofotfjord, and a thin strip of houses on an opposite shoreline.

Three nondescript ships lay at anchor off the town, and a scattering of little fishing boats were moored close inshore, deprived of their work until the fate of their town was decided.

The heart of the town, and its justification in this ferocious latitude, lay in the main harbor, its jetties and warehouses. From here the vital ore from Sweden was shipped for the six months in the year when the Gulf of Bothnia was frozen. And its lifeline, winding eastward along the coast, in and out of tunnels and cuttings and over high bridges before it reached the safety of the Swedish frontier a little over twenty miles away, was the railway line, an artery which alone had been sufficient motive for Hitler's assault on the country.

Fifty miles to the northeast, and out of sight even from this height, was the town of Bardufoss, soon to be a second R.A.F. base, they had been told. In a village close by this town King Haakon lay hidden, ready to return if the German invasion was finally repulsed, or to retreat to Britain.

The Allied forces preparing for the final assault on Narvik —South Wales Borderers, Scots Guards, Irish Guards, French Chasseurs Alpins, Polish Chasseurs de Montagne—were poised on islands and peninsulas to the northwest and southwest of the town, and Mike could make out the pencil-thin shapes of destroyers, and the larger shapes of cruisers and supply ships near Skaanland. For several weeks only the specially trained Alpine troops with skis or snowshoes had been able to move at all, but now with the thaw the final attempt to snatch the town from the Germans was imminent.

The Rhodesian was rocking his wings to attract Mike's attention, and was pointing at something immediately below them. Mike at first saw nothing except the wild snow-slashed landscape. They had been ordered to keep R/T silence in the hope of delaying the Germans in locating the position of their base and they had had to revert to the manual signals they had used in their early training days.

Mike made one steep-banked 360-degree turn, and as he was pulling out of it, he spotted the smudge of the train's smoke, and then the train itself winding along a narrow gorge, and then out onto a viaduct. At the same time, the clear sky around them was splashed by the dark smudges of ack-ack fire. Mike began jinking, experiencing a sense of outrage that enemy fire always at first aroused in him. But this was not enemy fire. The muzzle flashes from below came from the Swedish side of the frontier and the firing was unpleasantly accurate.

He realized that they must have strayed over into Swedish air space, and led Sammy west again, losing height over a village marked Hundalen on their maps, and watched the train winding on the single track along the shores of the fjord leading down to Narvik.

Mike counted the rolling stock drawn by the stubby little locomotive—four passenger cars, ten canvas-covered freight cars, and at the tail end two open cars with freight that Mike could not identify until he came down below the summit of the mountain and flew low over the water while Sammy gave him cover above. Then he recognized the long gray barrels of light artillery—they might have been 8.8-cm or 3.7-cm Flak 36 guns. From this close range he could also see that the passenger cars were packed. And they were not Norwegians returning from their summer vacation, either.

Back at Romstad Mike and Sammy reported to the C.O., Donald Avery and the Spy. Sammy said, "It's a bloody outrage, sir. The Swedes call themselves neutral, then damn nearly shoot us down and let the Huns pass all the reinforcements they want through their territory."

"War's an outrage," replied the C.O. philosophically. "What you've just seen is the rule of power in the raw. The Swedes know we can't do them any harm. But the Hun could gobble them up as quickly as he swallowed Denmark—or nearly. But so long as they behave themselves and let the Hun have all the ore, steel and ball bearings he wants and are generally cooperative he'll leave them alone."

They paused while a pair of Hurricanes took off. When the din had faded, Mike said, "I guess we ought to stop it, sir. Somehow."

"We can strafe the trains, sir," said the Spy. "But that won't stop them getting through. And they'll run them in the twilight or only when the weather's clamped down."

"I think we might do better than that," said Mike, and he glanced at the Spy, confident of a fellow conspirator's interest. "What about bombing the sons of bitches?"

To Mike's surprise, it was Donald Avery who jumped most eagerly at this idea, while Sammy and the C.O. looked at Mike as if he had lost his reason.

"I'd like to be involved in this, sir, if Chiefy and Guns can extemporize some wing racks." He turned to Mike, fingering his moustache, and said, "Of course, I would choose you as my number two if you would care to volunteer?" He made it sound as if he were passing on an unwanted gift.

They discussed the matter in more detail, and when the meeting broke up Sammy said, "Of all the bloody sauce! Crafty eye on the main chance again. I guess the old crawler's after a D.F.C. now."

Mike shrugged his shoulders. He had reconciled himself to the continued irritating presence and the style of Donald Avery now. He was just one more discomfort to endure, like the cold and damp and the never-ending reindeer meat. But it was uncharacteristic of him to put himself forward for what was going to be a difficult operation.

The squadron armament officer, his flight sergeant and the rigger flight-sergeant, were in session together for most of the afternoon, spurred on by the C.O.'s demand for urgency.

The next day four of the squadron's best riggers and two of the armorers busied themselves on the construction of two makeshift bomb racks and secured them under the wings of the Hurricanes below the gun housing. A simple manual release mechanism, actuated by a bowden cable, withdrew a splitpin from a securing plate, and was operated by a bicycle brake handle fixed inside the cockpit.

Working, for safety reasons, some distance away from the camp, the armament officer and his crew were able to produce four primitive bombs of just under one hundred pounds each, made up from adapted 40-mm Bofors shells. "It's all a bit hit-and-miss," Guns told them in the evening, "and you'll have to take off with them ready-fused with five-second delay. But it should be all right," he added cheerfully.

The armorers made up some dummy smoke bombs, and with these secured under their wings, Avery took Mike up and they made practice attacks on a stretch of nearby road, finding that they could operate with considerable accuracy by using the gunsight and releasing very low just as they were pulling out of a shallow dive.

The greatest difficulty was to locate and intercept the train. The Germans, now well aware of their proximity, had set up strong flak posts around Narvik and along the eastern approaches to the town by the railway. Sergeant Walker had been badly hit on an early morning patrol, and had only just managed to get his Hurricane back, with half the tail-plane fabric ripped off.

Whenever the weather permitted, the C.O. laid on high altitude patrols, a bitterly cold business, in order to cover any bomber interference with the Allied besieging forces and to spot the crossing of the frontier by the train. If there was a train sighting, radio silence was to be broken in order to give the two Hurricanes time to get airborne and reach it before it arrived in the station at Narvik, where it was not only heavily protected by light ack-ack but was rapidly un-loaded.

It was not until the afternoon of May 24 that the sighting report came through. The whole of B Flight was down at the dispersal when the red Very flare, the prearranged signal, arched up from the control hut. Mike, who was playing craps with Sammy Crow, grabbed his helmet and gauntlets, and all the other pilots got up to see them off. He was almost outside when he heard Avery's voice. He looked back and saw that his flight commander was standing at the door of the small room at the back of the hut which served as his office. He was looking pale and had his hand over his stomach.

"You'll have to go without me, Browning. I think I've got food poisoning, and it wouldn't be fair on you."

Sammy Crow was beside him in a flash. "I'll go instead, sir?" he asked eagerly. "I know the form."

Avery nodded his head and wished them good luck, amid groans from some of the other pilots who would gladly have gone with Mike.

They were off the ground in three minutes. They were both practiced at emergency scrambles, and the Merlins of the two machines—the "Hurribombers" as they had been named—were warmed up every hour so that they could take off without delay.

Two pilots of A Flight had made the sighting, and they must have spotted the train even before it reached the frontier because it was no more than two miles inside Norwegian territory when Mike saw it on a curve. It was traveling slowly toward the head of the fjord beneath a cloud of its own smoke.

Some gunfire sprang up from a post above a tunnel mouth. Mike flinched away, conscious of his additional vulnerability with almost two hundred pounds of high explosives under his wings. The Hurricane made light of the weight and the takeoff run had been only marginally longer, but it had lost some of its responsiveness with its volatile burden.

He felt complete confidence in Sammy's ability to cope with this unexpected demand on his skills. Except for Anson, he was the most experienced pilot on the squadron, and Mike had described to him in detail the procedure of the bombing tactics they had devised.

The Rhodesian broke away east, forming up for the line of attack on which Mike had told him he and Avery had agreed. Sammy was to follow Mike's head-on attack with his own from the rear of the train. The flak was following them both with uneasy accuracy, as if the gunners had already recognized their purpose and were determined to shoot them down before they could carry it out.

Mike jinked his Hurricane more violently, dropping and lifting her and giving strong right and left rudder to confuse the gunners' aim. The train was on a straight and level stretch, ripe for the plucking, and he banked steeply to turn inside the valley and prepare to attack. A brief glance between evasive evolutions told him that there were three passenger cars and two freight cars, and he was suddenly conscious that every soldier and every piece of fighting equipment below him represented the likely death of an Allied soldier when the attack came. He felt a shaft of fear cut through him. This was not going to be easy, not "a piece of cake" as these British pilots called it. It was going to be highly dangerous. And it was the most important undertaking he had ever faced.

He kicked his Hurricane around through 90 degrees, ready to line up for his dive, when he recognized an opportunity of such effrontery that he almost stalled his machine with the violence of his turn. "Why in the name of all that's diabolical didn't we think of this before?" he asked himself, and would have paid a hundred bucks to see the expression on the Rhodesian's happy leathery face when the plan unfolded.

The ack-ack was really getting the measure of him now. Another four-barrel 2-cm Flakvierling post west down the line, and beyond the exit from the tunnel, was adding its share of the fire coning him. Mike forced his Hurricane down to the deck, skimming over the top branches of a pine forest, and for half a mile managed to throw off the shellfire because he was below the gunners' limit of depression.

When he pulled up, he was through his throttle gate, and he began slewing even before they caught him again. The 180-degree turn was the worst part, because he had to get up to a thousand feet for the dive, and he realized that he made a horribly easy target for a few scorching seconds. He knew he was hit at least once by the sudden change in the feel of the ailerons, but he had the Hurricane around, pointing in the right direction, and she was still flying.

The train had already entered the east end of the longest tunnel on the line, the 450-yards-long Sildvik tunnel, the smoke lingering over the last disappearing cars. Half a mile in front of him was the black semicircle of the exit, faced with stone, and a hundred yards nearer to him, set up on a newly constructed wooden platform, was the four-barrel 2-cm gun post, its crouching crew of seven clearly visible as they concentrated on his destruction.

Mike's right thumb moved onto the gun button, and he raised the Hurricane's nose marginally to allow for the drop at this range. Then he squeezed, and felt the reassuring shudder of the hammering recoil and caught the first whiff of cordite. Four 20-mm Mausers against his eight .303-inch Colt-Brownings, with the shells and bullets arching in their fine trajectory toward their targets.

"Well, hot shot, it sure isn't sunbeams raining around here," was the conclusion that raced through Mike's mind as he closed at 310 m.p.h. on a dead straight line, no evasion now, concentrating his eye and mind on the dark bunch of figures intent on his destruction.

He was the better shot. He had to be. Or be dead. He did not see them fall, but they must have, because at the crucial split second the ground fire ceased, and he was suddenly clear and still flying. He slightly raised the Hurricane's nose, reached for the bomb release with his left hand, and squeezed it hard.

The blackness of the tunnel stared him in the face, then disappeared beneath the Hurricane's nose when he pulled back, assisted by the sudden release of its burden, and skimmed over the pine trees above the tunnel.

"O.K., let 'em have it," he called to Sammy, hearing his own voice in the earphones as a crackle of triumphant survival. He could see the Rhodesian's Hurricane dead ahead at fifteen hundred feet in a shallow dive toward him, the twin shapes of the bombs flanking the radiator under the machine's belly. Mike had saved him from the attention of the 2-cm gun post, but the 3.7-cm above the east tunnel entrance was pumping out its shells at 160 a minute and its steady target was getting larger second by second.

Mike was momentarily distracted by the distant flash on his left quarter of his own delayed action bombs exploding. Then he swung right, and banked steeply left again to get the big gun into his sight without risking a collision with Sammy. This time he had a clear run, and he raced in, intent on knocking out the crew before they could destroy the Hurricane. The 3.7 was set in a clearing. Mike could see the white of the pines' stumps where they had recently been felled to give the gun a clear circle of fire through 360 degrees.

Again, he opened up at maximum range in the hope of getting a few lucky shots onto the target. The tracers were falling far short. He raised the Hurricane's nose and fired again, a long burst which was ended for him by the sound of hissing compressed air and the clanking of breech blocks.

He was out of ammunition, and just when he most needed it. The 3.7 crew were unhurt and undeterred. Perhaps they had not even seen him. But they had the measure of Sammy. As Mike pulled up over the gun, with its long trumpet-muzzle barrel sliding on its recoil, he saw the shells coning the Hurricane. But the bombs fell from its wings and sailed with superb accuracy straight toward the tunnel mouth. And the Rhodesian followed them on their course to annihilation.

"Pull up!" shouted Mike, "pull up, for Christ's sake, Sammy . . ."

Perhaps he was already dead. Mike would never know. Implacably the Hurricane continued on its shallow diving course, straight into the tunnel, exploding with a searing flash.

A second later the bombs went off, like a graveside volley, bringing down the stone portico and tons of earth and rock to plug the entrance as securely as Mike's own bombs had sealed the other end.

Mike was shocked to find himself laughing hysterically as he flew down the fjord, belly brushing the gray water. "Oh God, old Sammy, what a shambles! What a goddamn shambles!" It was as well for him that the German gunners—those who were still alive—seemed as shocked as he was by the sight of the twin columns of drifting smoke and dust from the railway tunnel and the sudden incarceration of the train.

Their fire at the steadily retreating target was intermittent and desultory, and Mike was soon clear and heading for Romstad over the mountains.

He landed shakily and almost ran off the runway, partly because of his aileron damage but mostly because he did not care. He did not even remember to open his hood, and observing this and the state of his machine, his ground crew ran out and climbed anxiously onto the wings, fearing that he was injured. It was not until Lofty Campbell opened the break-out panel on the right of the cockpit that Mike slid back the hood. He had taken his helmet off and his hair and face were sodden with sweat and tears. His crewman reached down and pulled the cutout lever to stop the engine.

"Mr. Crow bought it, did he, sir?" he asked in the sudden silence.

Mike nodded and slowly pulled himself out of the cockpit, the cry repeating in his head, "Another second! Just one more second's fire!" Oh, those wasted precious rounds. "Hotshot—like hell!"

"It was a pity Flight Lieutenant Avery couldn't go at the last minute, sir," said Lofty. Mike wiped his face on the sleeve of his Irvin jacket and looked up at him. "Him having done all the practice, I mean, and being so keen."

The others were crowding around Mike now and Mike could not reply. Not that there was anything to say. Flight Lieutenant Avery was alive. Pilot Officer Crow was dead. And that was that.

13

Some fifteen hundred miles closer to the equator than Romstad, Keith and the other surviving pilots of 259 Squadron were enjoying a heat wave. While the nightly frost made for a hard runway surface on the north Norwegian airstrip, the ground at the small airfield of St. Ervienne was baked hard by the early summer sunshine.

St. Ervienne was no more than a meadow belonging to a private flying club based in Troyes, a large town on the River Seine southeast of Paris. The only buildings were two wooden hangars, which had contained several precarious-looking light planes until the ground staff had thrown them peremptorily into the nearby wood, and the clubhouse control-room. This was furnished with some ancient armchairs and a sofa, and decorated with a Michelin wall map of France and drawings cut out of *La Vie Parisienne*. The well-stocked bar had elevated their spirits when they had first arrived, and the contents disappeared as quickly as the lingering fumes of Gauloises when they opened the windows.

Keith, lying out in the sun with his shirt off, remarked sleepily to Range Powell, "If we both think hard enough, I reckon we can *will* this war away."

"Nothing easier, cobber. The Germans have asked for an armistice. The French armies are everywhere advancing, far across the Rhine, deep into the heart of Nazi Germany. Overwhelming waves of Hurricanes have cleared the skies of the crook bloody Luftwaffe." The Australian savored the prospect and added dreamily. "And all the French sheilas are pouring out of their convents, cheering and throwing themselves into our arms. I can feel the warmth of their flesh now . . ."

The only sound was the distant shrill cry of a lark. Keith could see it climbing high above him and thought how nice it would be to fly without the complicating, noisy and dangerous business of doing it in a Hurricane. Softly he murmured:

"Higher still and higher
From the earth thou springest,
Like a cloud of fire;
The blue deep thou wingest,
And singing still dost soar, and soaring ever singest"

Then some mechanic started up an engine and the familiar growl of the Merlin echoed back from the wood on the other side of the field. As if that was not bad enough, a corporal ran out of the hut behind them yelling, "B Flight scramble. Patrol Chalons Angels Fifteen!"

"I knew it couldn't last," Range grumbled. "And I was just dreaming about the scented skin of my sheila in Knightsbridge."

B Flight was now reduced to four machines, piloted on this operation by the flight commander, a flight sergeant, Range and Keith. Since they had left Lens-La Basse they had lost three pilots and five Hurricanes, which made Range's fantasy picture more remote than ever. The German armies were already nearing the Channel, and the city of Reims to the north of Troyes was threatened.

Keith had experienced numerous premonitions of death since the real shooting war had begun nine days earlier.

"Lucky Keith" could not last forever, he recognized. But each time he returned safely, he secretly rebuked himself for taking any notice of his own premonitions. Apart from the statistical likelihood, he knew himself well enough to recognize the old Puritan conscience at work again, insisting with its insidious demand for truth and justice that you could not kill so many airmen without paying the price for it.

On this morning of May 20, as he glanced to the right out of his cockpit at his three companions in their much-patched fighters, and remembered again the German fighters and bombers he had made to explode or burst into a ball of flame or had just sent less dramatically to their end, the familiar premonitory feeling overcame him once again.

Was it stronger now? Or the same? He had even guiltily asked these questions of himself before, and remembered when the sensation of imminent death was like a stab of pain and he had shouted unheard into his mask, "Forget it, you fool—watch your tail or they *will* get you . . ."

Keith spotted the Junkers 88's at the same moment as Range called out, "Bandits nine o'clock high, steering east."

There were twelve of them, north of Chalons, in stepped up *V*'s of three, the familiar pattern which would tighten and bring the coordinated fire of a dozen machine guns to bear when they attacked. Above, hovering in the sun, would be a pack of 109's, poised to fall like missiles on them. With luck, they might get one or two of the bombers. But they would need all their wits about them, and a fair measure of luck, too, to get away unscathed.

B Flight's leader ordered them to attack in pairs, and Keith flew number two to Range. It was always a comfort to have the Australian with you in combat. He was a brilliant pilot and first-class shot, who already had a score of seven yet never forgot those with whom he was flying when things became hot.

The Junkers 88's were not easy to catch even at this height. But the Hurricanes had time to gain height by pulling for overboost, and Range led Keith in on a nice quarter attack from above. "Take the last," he told Keith, the order clipped by hasty switching off at this critical moment which required such concentration.

Keith glanced up at his mirror before going in and saw only bright blue sky and the glare of the sun. Then he was pulling the dot through the fin of the 88, along the length of its fuselage, to the bulge of its "greenhouse." When the dot was a quarter ring ahead of the glass nose of the bomber, he touched the button and watched the tracer. Too much deflection, and the angle was reducing. He waited until it was down to 15 degrees, and then gave another short burst, making strikes on the fuselage. But he would have to do better than this. Luckily, the gunners were leaving him a clear run and concentrating on Range, who was fifty yards ahead of Keith and had set the leading 88's starboard engine on fire.

Keith was forced to pull up before he could do more than slight damage to his target. As he did so, the unpredictable happened, and the whole formation broke, scattering in all directions, and began mixing it with the four Hurricanes in a straight dogfight.

Keith was amazed at the maneuverability of the big machines, and the way they worked in pairs, showing that they had practiced these tactics. One of them got onto his tail, and he had to work hard and pull his machine into such a tight turn that he momentarily blacked out before he could throw it off.

Then, from out of nowhere, the little 109's came in and the fight turned into a wild melee of twisting, diving, climbing machines, some large and some small, but all, it seemed, carrying the black cross of Germany on their wings and fuselage. He lost Range at once. A voice which sounded like the sergeant's suddenly called, "Christ, look out!" But that was all that was said in the thirty seconds or so that the fight lasted.

Keith got one long and effective burst into a Junkers 88, almost stalled trying to follow it farther, kicked himself into a dive, and was at once hit. He felt his Hurricane shudder with the shock, like a man-o'-war suffering a salvo. He yawed acutely, and saw nothing more. Smoke was streaming into the cockpit, blinding his vision, and the stench of glycol and oil was suffocating. The controls were as limp as if every cable had been severed at once.

There was no doubt—no doubt whatever—that it was time to leave. It was getting very hot, too, and as he wrenched free the bayonet clip of his oxygen line, and the R/T plug, as he fumbled with the pin of his harness and then tore off his right gauntlet to get a grip, and as he reached up for the hood handle, the vision danced before his eyes of the planes he had sent down like this, the flames racing back into the cockpit, the asphyxiating fumes, the . . .

So at last the premonition was justifying itself. Or was it? He was not yet dead, not yet roasted, not yet spiraling down, laying his trail of black smoke. The hood slid back—it did not always slide when it was really hot, so the story went. But it went back all right, and Keith released the break-out panel to give himself more room.

It was no use trying to get his burning, crippled machine onto its back, the easiest way of getting out. And the heat was really hitting him. In the end, perhaps a fifth of a second later, he just dragged himself up and the wind tore him free.

The cool air was like going onto deck from the boiler room in an Arctic gale, and Keith savored it as he turned over and over, thinking again and again and exclaiming at the wonder of it, "I am alive. I *will* see Jenny again—I *will*, I *will* . . .'

He did not pull the D ring at once. Time enough. Just get well clear of those 109s, he remembered, knowing that they sometimes went for those who brolly-hopped. He had even seen it happen, though the 109 had been driven off, and then shot down, to everyone's delight.

He derived enormous satisfaction from falling through a fleck of light cirrus cloud, and decided at that moment in the heavenly silence of space, that he would take up gliding as soon as he could. Below was the flat wheatland of northeast France, and just to the north, the vineyards that produced the world's most coveted drink. I will ask for *un coup* from the farmer who finds me, he decided. Surely he could not be refused under the circumstances.

Then Keith saw a village burning, the whole village it seemed, and he saw that smoke was drifting east from countless other fires. And he realized that he had been shot down much nearer to the line of German advance than he had thought. The earlier he pulled the ripcord, the farther east he would drift, but he had already delayed for longer than he intended, so he gripped the ring, pulled it hard, and prepared himself for the jerk.

It came sooner and was less violent than he had expected, and as the swinging ceased, he began to enjoy the drop and the way the pretty sun-drenched Marne countryside appeared to come up to welcome him. A flash of flame a mile to the west, and the cloud of smoke that arose from it, reminded him of his good fortune that he had been able to bail out, unlike his predecessors in the R.F.C. twenty-five years earlier, so many of whom had remained in their blazing machines or had chosen a more merciful death and thrown themselves out into space.

During the last seconds, Keith thought about his father, who had so nearly died defending this same soil. Then he arranged himself in the approved half-crouching stance for the landing. He was above a large field of wheat, standing tall and green, and he touched down in the center of it, striking the box and releasing himself from his harness.

The landing was soft, cushioned by the wheatstalks, but it had been hard enough to send a shaft of pain up his left leg. From his sitting position, he looked down at his boot and saw that it was soaked in blood and that it was torn at the back from a bullet which had passed through it. He had never liked blood, other people's or his own, and especially blood from shot game.

Gingerly, and almost overcome with a dizzy sickness, he eased off his boot and saw that his sock and trouser leg were soaked. For a moment he lay back in the wheat, telling himself that this was no time to faint, and willing himself to do something about his injury. Then he sat up, and with a sudden burst of speed and energy, pulled out his jackknife and cut away the lower part of his trouser leg, revealing a deep gash in the flesh of his calf, which was still bleeding freely.

His first-aid kit had gone with the emergency kick-out panel of his Hurricane, so he cut some lengths of silk from his parachute which he then bound tightly around his calf with his tie. He took off his flying boot and cut through it, converting it into a shoe, slipped it painfully back on again and stood up. The pain was no worse when he put weight on the leg, so he gathered up the rest of his parachute and made a tight bundle of it, which he left where he had landed, and began to walk cautiously toward the track which, he had seen from the air, skirted one side and led to a farm. If no one was going to bring him his *coup*, he would have to go to fetch it.

It was only after he had started out on his painful journey that he became aware of the sound of firing. It came in short bursts firing so fast that it was impossible to identify the individual explosions. They were broken by the louder, more percussive sound of artillery. Then, much closer, he heard motorcycle engines. He crouched down and saw, between the waving stalks, a dozen machines traveling fast along a road on the other side of the field, followed by a rumbling half-track towing a gun. The figures squatting on the top of the half-track were German soldiers. He could even smell the sharp diesel fumes, unfamiliar and indisputably hostile exhaust fumes. He had come down on the wrong side of the lines.

Keith felt tired and dizzy and sick with apprehension when he reached the farmhouse. He approached it with caution. It was a humble affair on one floor, with creepers growing over the porch and some dusty roses in bloom in front and pot geraniums on the window sills. On the right there were some outhouses and a barn. A decrepit horse was tethered to a post.

A girl came out through the front door carrying a bucket. When she caught sight of Keith leaning against an apple tree twenty-five yards away, she put the bucket down hastily and ran back inside. In a moment she reappeared with an older woman, who was stout and was wiping her hands on her apron. They stood side by side, talking quietly as they examined him. Then the older woman looked at him more closely and in a harsh voice called out, *"Vous êtes un Boche?"*

"Non, madame, je suis un aviateur Anglais. R.A.F. *Et je suis blessé,"* Keith replied.

The girl stepped forward, as if to help Keith, but the older woman held her back. *"Venez içi, monsieur,"* she said peremptorily.

Keith hobbled across the dusty yard, conscious of the two pairs of eyes on him, the girl's compassionate, the woman's suspicious.

He stood in front of them, six feet away, as if presenting his credentials. They seemed to pass. After examining him again, studying the leather helmet he held in his hand, the single gauntlet, the wings on his chest, the revolver in its holster, and finally the roughly bandaged leg above the cut boot, she stepped forward with the girl and helped him into the house.

It was cool and dark inside, smelling of carbolic soap and garlic. Keith sat in the only armchair, the father's no doubt, and sipped the generous glass of brandy he was given. *"Votre santé, madame, mademoiselle. C'est mieux que le champagne."* They nodded, without understanding the reason for the comment.

Later, the woman instructed the girl to take him across the gently sloping yard to the barn. There, lying close to the roof on the sweet-scented newly mown hay, the girl, who said her name was Marie, washed his injured leg with water and disinfectant, and produced lint and a length of bandage. Keith lay back, feeling drained of emotion yet content. The anxiety at his situation had faded with the fumes of the brandy, and he was happy just to lie here in the late afternoon, with no thought of the future, while the capable hands of the pretty girl brushed against his bare leg. She spoke to him softly from time to time, apologizing for their hesitancy when he first appeared, and telling him how brave he must be, asking him how many planes he had shot down, and did he have a beautiful girl in England.

When she had finished she said, *"Vous êtes fatigué, mon pauvre. Restez içi."*

She left quietly and Keith slept, his leg hardly troubling him now.

He was awakened by the sound of a man's voice. It was raised in protest and anger, and he guessed at once that the farmer had returned and wanted no Allied guests now that the Germans had passed by. Keith caught the word *"Boche"* several times, and recognized the voice of his wife, counter-protesting. He evidently thought that they would be shot if *"l'aviateur Anglais"* was found on the premises—which was no doubt true—and that there would be a hue and cry because many of the advancing troops must have seen the parachute falling. Didn't they have enough trouble on their hands as a conquered people without deliberately taking risks?

The girl spoke once in Keith's defense, but was dealt with summarily by her father, who ordered her into the house. Keith made his way down from the stack of hay and hobbled toward the door, determined to leave and if necessary to give himself up rather than cause this family trouble. He had reached the half open door, noting that the light was fading from the sky, when he heard the sound of an engine, revving fast, and of tires on the track leading to the house. He guessed that it was a motorcycle, but the machine that skidded to a halt outside the house was a camouflage-painted Kraftwagen, its air-cooled engine ticking over fast.

Two soldiers in S.S. uniform swung themselves out of the small canvas-topped vehicle, tough squat men with goggles raised under the brim of their helmets and armed with 7.9-mm Schmeisser MP 40 machine pistols as well as the standard S.S. dagger and 7.65 Lüger in shining leather holster. They were clearly in a hurry, and bore the unmistakable imprint of triumphant warriors pursuing a cracking enemy, ruthless, impatient and lethally dangerous.

The farmer and his wife were standing together close to the porch and the girl had reemerged and was standing behind them. The men shouted in German as they walked threateningly toward the family, their guns very much in evidence. Keith's German was not fluent like his French, but he had no doubt what they were demanding of the father: There is an Englishman, a pilot, who has landed here. You must have seen him? If you are hiding him you will be shot —now—in front of your family.

The farmer backed away and his wife stood in front of him.

"Wo verstecken sie ihn?" One of the S.S. troops walked away looking to right and left, and then advanced firmly across the yard toward the outbuildings. Keith saw him approaching, a dark, dusty, angry figure, a killer through and through and loving this war. And the fury rose in Keith's throat like bile.

"I will not be captured by these brutes," he told himself. "They will probably shoot me anyway. And they'll certainly shoot this farmer, and I shall be responsible for his death, and will not be able to live with that truth . . ."

If Keith had once felt any compunction about bringing down a beautiful pheasant or stopping a running hare, there was no lingering fragment of doubt about the need to kill this man. The enormity of what he was about to do made no impact upon him, so bound up was he in the mechanics of doing it. His right hand went to the canvas holster, there was a faint click as he pulled open the press-button catch, and another as he withdrew the Smith and Wesson. He raised the weapon slowly and held its barrel up against the crack between the half-open door and the door post.

The S.S. storm trooper was only fifteen feet away, swinging his Schmeisser and glancing to right and left. He paused and began to shout, *"Heran! Engländer—"*

Keith fired once, hitting him full in the face. The German was thrown back by the impact, for a fraction of a second remained on his feet as if frozen in death, with blood pouring off his face onto his uniform, and crumpled onto the dusty yard.

His companion reacted with the speed of a highly trained soldier, hurling himself to the ground behind his vehicle before Keith had time to take aim. But Keith's response, too, was worthy of a practiced fighter. The Kraftwagen was parked in the center of the yard, and while the soldier had seen where the shot had been fired from, he himself was trapped unless he was prepared to risk exposure. Nor could he know that Keith's weapon was only a simple, short-range revolver.

Keith made off as quickly as he could, over the stack of hay and out through the door at the back of the barn. To his relief, he had cover to the next building, a low wooden shed, an empty pigsty. From the far end he could almost see around to the other side of the Kraftwagen. A protruding booted leg confirmed that the storm trooper still lay facing the barn. The family had disappeared and was no doubt lying under cover inside their house awaiting the outcome. The horse had broken his halter and bolted.

Keith saw now that this could be a stalemate. There was no more cover to allow him to get farther around the back of the vehicle. He could make a rush for it, firing as he ran and before his enemy could turn. But the German would be watching all quarters with greater care the longer there was no further sign from the barn.

The situation was resolved by the storm trooper. Keith saw his leg disappear. Then the Kraftwagen began to move as he reached inside and released the brake. It was already aimed toward the barn, and a second later the German ran at a crouch around to the back of the vehicle and began pushing it, using it as a shield as he closed the gap to the barn door where he supposed the enemy was still concealed.

The range was about fifteen yards, too far for a .38. But it would increase with every second, and this was in any case Keith's last and only chance. Taking steady aim, with the barrel resting against the corner wooden support of the pigsty, he squeezed the trigger. A spout of dirt sprang up a yard from the crouching figure, and he fired again as the storm trooper swung around, discharging a burst from the Schmeisser in the direction of the pigsty. Keith's second shot hit the German in the leg. He twisted around and dragged himself after the Kraftwagen, which was gathering speed toward the barn, impelled by the German's earlier pushing and by the slope.

The storm trooper fired as he scrambled for its protection and this time a stream of bullets spattered the woodwork about Keith, who fired back again, twice, once striking the Kraftwagen and once hitting the German, this time in the body. He lay still, his machine pistol a yard from his hand, while the vehicle rolled farther away, slower than before because a .38 bullet had punctured a rear tire.

Keith came out from behind the building and half ran toward the wounded German. From the other side, another figure was approaching, the farmer's wife, stout and running fast, apron flying. The German was struggling to his knees and reaching out for his weapon. He had his hand almost on it when the Frenchwoman stamped on his hand and reached down for the pistol.

For a reason Keith never understood, he found himself shouting, *"Non! Non!"* at the woman, as if he dreaded what she was about to do.

What she did was to hold the long-barreled pistol in both hands, point it down at the German at her feet, and fire a long burst into him at a range of eight feet.

When Keith arrived, she gave him only a perfunctory

glance, then threw the weapon down on the riddled corpse and spat on it. *"Boche!"* she exclaimed, and walked away.

Her husband had emerged from the house, his face white, his daughter clutching him and weeping on his shoulder. Keith was thinking, "What a mess! What a bloody awful mess! What are we going to do now?"

But events now occurred with great rapidity. Keith had always admired the French for their practicality, and having partially recovered from the sight of his wife killing an S.S. storm trooper in their own yard, the farmer worked with the speed of any man struggling for the survival of his family.

It was clear that the corpses, the Kraftwagen and Keith himself must all be gone as rapidly as possible. Indicating to Keith that he should get the bodies into the back of the vehicle, he located the Kraftwagen's tools and jacked up the back. Like a mechanic at a motor race, he unbolted the spare wheel on the front of the Kraftwagen, took off the punctured wheel and replaced it.

By this time, Keith had dragged the first victim across the yard. The farmer indicated that he should get into the storm trooper's uniform. *"C'est votre seule opportunité,"* he told him. He caught his breath, and shouted, *"Vite, vite, monsieur!"*

Of course he was right. Keith must do as he was ordered, no matter whether he was breaking international law, or risking his own life, or whether he felt sick, replacing his own jacket with the blood-soaked S.S. uniform jacket. Having put this family to such appalling risk, he must do anything . . .

The wife helped him strip it off the limp body, undoing the buttons seemingly without thought for the blood. She called Marie to bring the bucket of water she had used to clean Keith's leg, and briefly soaked and rubbed the worst stained parts, and squeezed it out before throwing it to Keith. The farmer himself helped load the bodies, heavy with their leather belts, boots and equipment, into the back of the Kraftwagen. Then he threw an old blanket and Keith's jacket upside down on top, and placed the punctured wheel over the lot.

Keith swung into the driving seat and pressed the starter. The woman stood beside the open window looking solemnly at him. Her bosom was heaving from the effort she had made. *"Bon chance, Anglais,"* she said, and, smiling for the first time, handed him the two Schmeissers she had picked up for him. *"Vous en aurez peut-être besoin,"* she said. Marie was on the porch, and she waved briefly as he accelerated away. The farmer was out of sight, doubtless making preparations to conceal the bloodstains, and Keith did not delay any longer. The heavy steel helmet with its shaft lightning S.S. badge was on his head, and the damp uniform jacket clinging to his chest when he drove out of the yard, and down the track toward the main road. Dusk was closing in. Flashes of heavy gunfire splashed yellow the red sky of the sunset to the west. A reaction to the killing and the danger through which he had passed would inevitably come. But not yet, he told himself. Not yet. The dangers that lay ahead could be greater than any he had yet faced. Lucky Keith's luck had already broken once that day, and the long night stretched ahead.

There was heavy traffic on the road, personnel carriers, trucks, half-tracks, Kraftwagen like his, all traveling fast on dimmed lights. Keith filtered in between two heavy trucks. The one in front was packed with troops, standing up and holding the skeleton bars above them. They were singing some triumphant German beer-cellar song Keith had heard on his last walking tour in '37, and they waved boisterously at him as he tucked in behind.

14

The fog came down over Romstad like a heavy gray curtain at midnight on May 27–28, obscuring the flashes and dulling the sound of the naval bombardment to the southwest.

Squadron Leader Anson was on the telephone to G.H.Q., and his language was lurid. "Of course it's essential for us to provide you with air cover," he said sharply. "Yes, I know you'll get bombed to blazes. And there's bugger all we can do about it . . . I appreciate that the sky's clear where you are and that Lord Cork is displeased. But kindly tell his Lordship that visibility here is five yards and if I ordered off my squadron, not one would get into the air and I should have a dozen corpses to answer for . . ."

He slammed down the receiver and cast his bloodshot eyes around the dispersal hut, focusing on nothing. Then he got up from the table and exclaimed, "Christ, staff officers! Somebody give me a cigarette."

The attack was going in as soon as the navy had completed its bombardment, the French Foreign Legion and a battalion of Norwegians crossing to the Narvik promontory from the north, while the Poles attacked from the south. It was known that the Luftwaffe had built an advanced landing field much closer to Narvik, and that it would respond in force as soon as the attack was underway. And now the fighters from Romstad and the other R.A.F. base farther north at Bardufoss were grounded by a freak sea fog.

The pilots dozed in the makeshift chairs around the woodburning stove. The last days before the assault had been hectic. If daylight hours at Rhysjhok had seemed freakishly long, here at Romstad close to the 69th parallel and only a few weeks from midsummer, there was no real darkness, only a dimming of light for an hour or two around midnight. On the correct definition that they were day fighters, Command had therefore considered them available for patrol and counterattack for twenty-two hours out of the twenty-four.

The machines were missing their routine maintenance inspections, there were cases of engines cutting at takeoff, and the pilots were growing dull and slack. Even Mike's spirit had been dampened by lack of rest and too much flying, and he slept now, curled up like a kitten on a rug in the corner, his Irvin jacket drawn about his shoulders.

At 4:00 A.M., Anson could bear the inactivity no longer. The naval bombardment had ceased, the troops were already going in, and the ominous thuds that could be heard distantly through the fog could only be exploding bombs. He roused his pilots and told them they would have to do something about it. Outside, the fog was as thick as ever, although it appeared less dense owing to the increase in daylight above it.

Anson gave instructions for oil-filled cans to be laid along both sides of the runway, and, with the aid of a rag wick, ignited to provide a primitive flare path. The pilots helped the ground crews, and within three-quarters of an hour had reported the flare path completed. Airmen with Aldis lamps were stationed the length of the runway in order to signal the successful takeoff of a machine and report the runway clear for the next.

Then, in turn, the Hurricanes of B Flight and the C.O.'s

machine were started and, guided by their ground crews, they taxied to the end of the runway. Mike was to have been third in line until Lofty Campbell climbed up on his wing and shouted in his ear, "Flight Lieutenant Avery's having trouble starting, sir. Says will you lead in his place."

Mike shrugged his shoulders. That was the fourth tricky operation in a week Avery had been forced to miss for one reason or another.

He awaited his turn, watching the fog now agitated by the slipstream, swirling about his plane so that at one moment he could not make out his wing tips, and at the next he could see twenty yards and the second of the burning pots on the right side of the strip.

With the all-clear signal Mike taxied the last few yards, waved to Lofty Campbell, and turned 90 degrees down the runway. He tried to recall the "to hell" attitude that had gotten him through his first solo. Then he pushed the throttle through its quadrant. He never saw more than two of the flares on either side during the whole run, and at one panic-stricken point he saw nothing at all. But there was just enough light to guide his direction, and when he pulled back gently on the stick he still had plenty of runway remaining.

The fog was a few hundred feet thick and only local, and when Mike broke through it was like emerging from a tunnel into a blinding fairy-tale world of snow, mountains, lakes, fjords and the sea—the actuality of the squadron motto "Through clouds to glory." The sun was still low in the east, which accentuated the shadows and made more mysterious than ever the deep valleys. But if the setting was for a Norse legend, the dark villainy of the plot was represented by the distant puffs of antiaircraft shells exploding above the waters of Ofotfjord and the white geysers from bombs bursting among the warships off Narvik.

The C.O.'s Hurricane was climbing fast. Sergeant Walker in R-Robert came up beside Mike, and they went through the gate in an effort to form up on Anson.

"Sandbag leader," the C.O. transmitted, "they're Junkers 87's. Buster and mix it with them, all Sandbag aircraft."

The dive bombers had been having the time of their lives with nothing but weak naval gunfire to oppose them. The 87 was a slow, awkward machine, vulnerable to fighters but devastatingly accurate against pinpoint targets on land and ships at sea. A minute later Mike could see them as distant dark shapes falling almost vertically through the gunfire put up by the warships, until, very low over the water, they pulled up and climbed away from the fountain of water that their bombs had created.

This was the best moment to catch them, when they were struggling for height again. Anson was already after one, the distance between pursued and pursuer closing with dramatic speed. Mike picked another, saw that someone else was after it, too, and switched his target to one that was just beginning its dive. As he turned the safety catch to Fire he caught one last panoramic glimpse of the assault area below: the smoke pouring from the shattered town; the fires farther along the coastline; the little puffers ferrying in the assaulting forces or returning for more, their wake like pencil brushes on the smooth water; the larger white wakes of the twisting and turning warships, one of them on fire from a direct hit.

Anson had already sent down his 87 in a corkscrew of fire, and Mike's own target, jinking violently like a doomed buck before the last pounce, was almost within range, the gunner opening fire with tracer.

Mike noted the characteristic inverted gull-shaped wing, the heavily spatted fixed wheels and the big single fin and rudder, then aimed for the pilot at the front of the long greenhouse-like cockpit, and squeezed the button. The dive bomber at once began shedding pieces as if self-dismemberment was its only defense. Among them, Mike identified the somersaulting figure of the gunner. He pulled up into a steep turn and saw that there was no need for another attack. The Junkers was going down faster than in any of its dives, followed at a leisurely pace by the gunner, now hanging beneath his parachute.

Mike damaged another before Anson transmitted, "Sandbag leader—there are 110's around. Watch your tails."

He saw them coming down at twice the speed of the dive bombers. There were ten of them, fierce *Zerstören*, a more formidable proposition, but not to be feared if you kept your head and watched your rear.

The fight over Ofotfjord developed into a typical series of running combats, all at high speed, with those heart-stabbing split seconds when you are killing or are expecting to die, when time and sound and the experience of violence are distilled and then thrown into a whirlwind. Mike got into difficulties with one of the twin-engined fighters whose pilot skillfully crowded onto his tail. The German was already firing when a Hurricane came out of nowhere and filled its port engine with a burst and set the wing tank on fire. Mike caught a glimpse of the hunchback shape whipping past him, noted the letters RC R on the fuselage, and realized that his life had been saved by the little Geordie pilot, Walker.

The 110's retreated with the surviving dive bombers, and 140 Squadron could celebrate their best day ever with five victories and several more badly damaged enemy machines that were unlikely to get back to base.

The fog had mercifully lifted when they returned to Romstad. A section of A Flight were taking off to patrol the fighting area. The C.O. let a damaged machine in first, and then they touched down in turn between the still-blazing flares and taxied in.

Mike nearly fell asleep during the Spy's interrogation. Someone had produced black coffee spiked with akevitt, and he thought he had never drunk anything so warmly life enhancing.

140 Squadron flew six more patrols on that long day of assault on Narvik. By the evening, when a section of A

Flight landed for the last time, the ground crews were capable of no more, and the flight sergeant and two corporals alone had to refuel their Hurricanes. Late in the evening, the official word went around the airfield that Narvik was in Allied hands and that the surviving Germans were retreating up the railway, leaving behind many dead and nearly four hundred prisoners.

A lot of people at Romstad were asleep when the announcement was made, and did not learn about the victory until the next day. For Mike, the exultation was muted by the total fatigue he was experiencing, the slack weariness which earlier in the day had almost led to his death. But he went to sleep with a feeling of satisfaction that he had participated in a battle, that he had witnessed an action, a victory, in a war that would one day be history.

The triumph of Narvik rapidly turned into anticlimax when news was received at Romstad that the town was to be evacuated and that the Allies were leaving for Britain again. The position on the Western Front was so desperate that every man and every ship was needed for the final rearguard actions and the withdrawal of the B.E.F. from France. Their small but hard-won victory up here in the distant north had been hardly noticed and was offset a thousand times over by the disaster on the Continent.

A hardened sergeant expressed the outrage they all felt at this mute retreat. "They send us a thousand miles into the frozen north, we fight our bloody heads off, turn out the sodding Hun, and then run away with our tails between our legs. Sod 'em all!"

Mike experienced a feeling of weary futility, remembering the struggle they had had to build this airfield out of almost nothing, the risks they had taken day after day to cover the army and navy—and, most sharply poignant of all, the loss of his old friend, whose shattered remains lay in the wreckage of his plane and the tunnel mouth he had destroyed. And all, it seemed, for nothing.

The pressure on the fighters continued implacably all during the evacuation period. Two aircraft were lost due to engine failure, though the pilots bailed out safely and got back, and Chiefy refused to sign for two more Hurricanes which were no longer fit to fly. Then on the last day of the evacuation, when renewed fires burned out the last of the dock and harbor facilities at Narvik, the C.O. called together both Flights and told them that all remaining aircraft were to be destroyed, and Romstad made unusable to the Germans as a base. The runway was to be blown up, buildings and stores burnt—nothing of any value was to be left. Pilots and ground personnel were to be evacuated by sea in forty-eight hours.

"I'm sorry about this, chaps. Orders. The Gladiators at Bardufoss are flying out to the *Glorious*. They reckon they can get in with luck, without hooks and landing wire. But not the Hurricanes. Too high wing-loading to land on a carrier. Too fast . . ."

The protests arose on all sides. "But, sir, surely we can have a go . . ." "It seems a bloody waste, sir, without even trying . . ." Mike called out, "Let me have a crack, sir, to prove it."

The C.O. raised a hand and, addressing Mike, said, "I'd like to, Yank. We'd all like a go. And I'm going to make one last effort to persuade the powers-that-be . . ."

That afternoon, a Walrus landed to evacuate the adjutant, a seriously ill airman and the squadron's secret documents. It was from a cruiser, and would also transport Anson to the *Swiftsure* for consultation with the carrier's captain. At the last moment, Flight Lieutenant Avery appeared on the runway in uniform overcoat and carrying a small case. Mike saw him talking briefly to the C.O., stroking his moustache briskly, and commented, "There's one rat that's not going to hang around any sinking ship." Two minutes later, his flight commander climbed into the amphibian and the machine lumbered up into the air.

Anson returned at 11:00 P.M., as the light was beginning to dim, and the word quickly went around that the surviving nine Hurricanes would be taking off for the *Swiftsure* at 6:00 A.M.

The C.O. related how he had persuaded Captain Mac-Andrew that they should be given the chance to save their aircraft, which were so desperately needed at Dunkirk. "I said we promised not to smear his lovely deck with blood," Anson told them, "and that the responsibility was mine alone. I'll lead, and I want eight volunteers."

Every hand went up, and the C.O. ordered a blindfold for himself and told them to stand in a line, backs toward him. Mike heard the shuffle of the Squadron Leader's feet as he felt his way along the line. A triumphant voice called out, "Very good judgment, sir." Sergeant Walker said simply, "Thank you, sir."

"That's seven," said the C.O. "One more." There was a pause, and then Mike felt his hand firmly on his right shoulder, and at once engaged in a brief dance, all on his own.

"The Yank'll prang," someone who had not been selected said. "He'll smash into the sodding bridge, you see."

Mike gave him a quick jab to the chest, and then joined the others for a briefing by the C.O.

Before he allowed his mind to switch off into the black unconsciousness of long-deserved sleep, Mike wrote a short letter to Eileen. The end of it went:

> I am giving this to someone who is coming home by a more orthodox and probably quicker way than me. But don't worry. I'll soon be with you. And even if you are a naval rating, I'll hold you in my arms and run my fingers through your gorgeous hair and listen to your heavenly English voice. I can't say we've had a swell time *all* the time here. But it has been interesting . . . I love you, pretty Wren.
>
> Mike

It was raining hard the next morning. Squadron Leader Anson led them in formation out to the *Swiftsure*, guided by the same Swordfish which had brought 140 Squadron to Romstad three weeks earlier.

By a miracle of conservation, and by sticking mainly to akevitt, as an evening drink, the mess had preserved a single bottle of Gordon's Gin. Wrapped in an old towel, it was placed on the floor of the C.O.'s Hurricane. He had promised to split it between them on safe arrival. If anyone crashed, he said, he would drink the lot.

The rain had turned to sleet by the time the wallowing Swordfish flew them over one of the escorting destroyers at mast-top height, and visibility was less than half a mile. The whole operation was turning into what someone had predicted it would be, "a flap op." In the fifty minutes it had taken to rendezvous with the navy, they had been forced to fly at wave-top height in formation close enough to remain in visual touch with the next aircraft, but not so close as to risk collision in the bumpy conditions. In addition, they had to weave and keep their speed down to little above 140 m.p.h. in order not to overshoot the Swordfish, and at lean mixture in case they had trouble finding the *Swiftsure*.

Mike had one further worry. His Hurricane, which had not had its regular overhaul due to the pressure of the last few days of the evacuation, was spitting oil back onto the windshield, and occasionally missed a beat, causing his heart to miss one, too. The Arctic Norwegian Sea below looked singularly inhospitable.

The thought of landing on the *Swiftsure*'s short, rolling deck, far from being a dreaded challenge to Mike, was a welcome relief from the anxiety of nursing his poor old tired Hurricane these last ninety miles. The carrier appeared even larger than he had remembered it as its great slab side loomed out of the low cloud and sleet, rolling some 15 degrees in a moderate sea. Smoke was streaming from her single big funnel and a great bow wave swept back from her stem along her hull. The old ship, launched as a battle cruiser twenty-five years earlier and converted from the original noble lines of a man-o'-war into this boxlike floating airbase, was still able to show a good speed.

Captain MacAndrew would have ordered every revolution from the Parsons turbines to give the high wing-loading, high-landing-speed Hurricanes some sort of chance of braking to a standstill before reaching the end of the flight deck.

By prior orders, the nine fighters slipped into line astern behind the C.O., the Swordfish now moving out into a wider circle, like a schoolmaster observing his students coping with a difficult examination.

Mike was reassured by the slowness with which the first Hurricane approached the *Swiftsure*'s stern, with the carrier traveling at over 30 m.p.h. into a 25 m.p.h. wind. Anson touched the deck within twenty feet of its beginning, bounced once, slewed to port, corrected, and in a few yards the wing tips of his Hurricane were seized by a dozen pairs of hands.

When Mike's turn came he felt reassured by the safe landing of four more of 140 Squadron, although the size of the deck, foreshortened by the angle of approach, appeared absurdly small. Checking his A.S.I. with a quick glance every few seconds, he closed the gap to the rolling deck. When he was barely a quarter mile from the carrier, his engine spluttered, cut, spluttered again, and picked up. But his screen had received a massive new splash of oil, which blended with the sleet and moved in a greasy scum up the angled windshield, totally obscuring his vision.

There was only one way of dealing with this crisis, and that was to pull the pin of his straps and stand up. He dragged down his goggles and put his head out into the slipstream, and was at once like a blind man regaining his vision.

He came in on his control column, watching the batsman guiding him down the last feet to the deck. The second the paddles were crossed as a sign to cut his engine and pull back, he dropped into his seat again, hand on brake grip, feet on the rudder pedals. He came to a standstill with his port wing over the edge of the deck. The crew waited until he taxied back toward the center of the flight deck, then ran with him as he taxied fast to the bow end and came to a rest on the lift, ready to be sent down to the hangar.

Captain MacAndrew, scarlet face beaming, invited them all to his cabin before lunch. He gave a speech, a characteristically brief one, in his clipped, no-nonsense voice. "Well done. Didn't think you could do it. Nice to have you back with us. Now we're off to Blighty." He raised his glass. "Just got a signal from Air House—don't often get such a thing. It says, in effect, that Squadron Leader Anson and Sergeant Ralph Walker are commanded to an audience with H.M. the King. D.S.O. and D.F.M. I think you R.A.F. fellows call that 'a wizard show.' So it is."

A Flight's commander led them in three cheers, and with the captain's permission the two pilots were carried to the wardroom, where a special dispensation was made for the noncommissioned pilots, and a very special party began around the bar.

But first Anson produced his much-traveled bottle of Gordon's, and asked the barman to divide the contents between nine glasses. "Happy landings!" he toasted his pilots. "And preferably on dry land." That was only the beginning of the drinking. Mike awoke three hours after luncheon to the sound of creaking and the distant deep hum of the *Swiftsure*'s turbines. He got up, put his head in a basin of cold seawater, slipped on his Irvin jacket, life jacket and cap, and made his way up onto the flight deck. The weather had cleared, visibility was now up to ten miles or more, and a pale sun on their starboard quarter had succeeded in piercing the hanging mist which had replaced the cloud. Their two destroyers, to port and starboard and slightly ahead, were making light of the seas and occasionally taking the green over their slender bows.

Above, he could see figures in duffle coats moving about

the bridge, and recognized the Commander (Flying), who was holding a large pair of binoculars to his eyes. Far aft on the starboard side three sailors appeared to be attending to a net stanchion. Nobody else was in sight, and the deck was a clear length of steel stretching from bow to stern.

Mike was feeling the chill, even through his Irvin jacket, and was about to go down to the wardroom for tea, when a bugle sounded out, so near to him and so loud that he jumped. A voice shouted on the bridge above him, then there came an answering shout. The three distant sailors were running fast across the flight deck toward the open steel door at the after end of the island. The bugle call ceased and a voice replaced its sound over the tannoy. "Action stations, action stations!" Then a pause before the words were repeated.

Mike leaned against the funnel, his collar turned up, feeling the warmth. He decided to stay to watch the fun. They had not had an exercise on any scale like this promised to be on their earlier voyage. A black square suddenly presented itself in the flight deck as the lift disappeared rapidly from sight. In thirty seconds, it was coming up again, carrying a Swordfish, the crew in their cockpits, and beneath its belly the long, dark shape of a torpedo.

The *Swiftsure*'s deck was vibrating as it had when he had first gotten out of his Hurricane that morning. The carrier was increasing speed to her maximum and was heeling as she turned sharply onto a westerly course dead into the low watery sun. The Swordfish had now extended its folding wings, like some prehistoric bird off in search of prey, and its propeller had become a round blur. Another Swordfish was rising from the bowels of the carrier, and the first one accelerated down the flight deck and was airborne long before it reached the funnel.

When its sound had faded, Mike heard a voice beside him say, "That was quick work. And they'd better be quick. And aim straight."

Mike saw that the C.O. was standing beside him, also taking advantage of the warmth of the funnel. "Hullo, sir. Have you come to watch the fun, too?"

Anson said, "I don't know about fun. But it should be interesting. And I prefer to be out in the open."

"Do they always launch planes on exercises, sir?" Mike asked. "Seems kind of extravagant."

"No." He paused, turning to watch one of the destroyers racing across their stern, black smoke streaming from her funnel as if it were on fire. "No, they don't. But this is not an exercise."

Mike stared at him in disbelief. "Are you kidding . . . sir?"

"What's that?" The C.O. pointed at the destroyer and answered his own question. "That is a smokescreen, Yank." His finger moved slightly to the right and ahead of the destroyer's bows. "And that is an enemy battle cruiser. And that is another enemy battle cruiser. The *Gneisenau* and *Scharnhorst.*"

Far on the horizon, no larger than two small dark smudges against the gray of the mist, Mike could just make out the two warships. From the left-hand one there sprang out three pinpricks of light, followed by three more.

"Ah, here they come," Anson said matter-of-factly.

The smokescreen had cut the distant ships off from sight. But, as the C.O. had economically noted, the shells were on their way. The second Swordfish was on its way, too. The pilot gave the thumbs-up sign to the bridge as he passed slowly twenty feet up.

The first two salvos whooshed by like a subway train that fails to stop. Two of the shells passed over them with a scream as if the air was protesting at the violent intrusion, and exploded just ahead. The third landed simultaneously the same distance astern, its hundred-foot-high geyser spraying the deck. Two of the next trio of 11-inch shells fell in the sea wide of their starboard bow; the third struck the end of the flight deck where the seamen, soaked from the near miss, were struggling to get the third Swordfish clear of the lift. Mike saw it pierce the deck just beside them, and he crouched as it exploded deep down in the bowels of the ship, sending up a mass of unrecognizable debris, gashing the deck wide open and spreading fragments of Swordfish and sailors almost as far as the island where they were standing.

Mike followed Anson toward the scene of carnage. The first bundle was only half a man, the second near him had no legs and was uttering strange sounds. Mike bent down over a third. He was the pilot of the Swordfish, still in his Mae West and with his goggles unbroken and over his eyes. Mike could see no injury, and raised his head. To his astonishment, the officer was talking, fast and coherently. "Steady now, steady," he was saying, "a touch to port, keep her like that," as if he was on the torpedo run he might have made if he had gotten off five seconds earlier. He looked up at Mike and his eyes behind his goggles suddenly went blank.

More competent people had arrived on the scene. A dozen stretchers were being loaded. Even the fragments were being taken away. The stretcher-bearers worked silently and swiftly. But once Mike heard someone say, "There, there—take it easy now, we'll soon have you below," in a brisk tone.

The second lift had come up with another Swordfish. Someone was pulling at Mike's arm. It was the C.O. "Come on, Yank, we're in the way." They ran together toward the island, and never made it. Another half dozen shells came in. One of them struck the flight deck forward, leaving a steaming crater with a serrated lip like a coarsely opened can of hot soup, and another struck the port side amidships. This one threw them to the deck and sent them skating on their backs over the side and into the netting.

Half stunned with the noise and shock, Mike found himself being pulled down into one of the starboard sponsons. He lay without speaking, hearing the scream of more heavy shells, some churning up the sea around them, and hitting often enough to ensure the destruction of the big carrier.

Below, men's voices were crying out, "Commence, commence," then the sound of a gong, another voice shouting, "Ready!" and at last the crack of the 4.7's.

"Oh, my God," thought Mike, "peashooters. Piddling peashooters against that lot—4.7's against the *Scharnhorst* and *Gneisenau.*"

The metallic clatter of firing guns and exploding shells, the crash of torn steel against steel became unbearable, and Mike held his hands to his ears. He was not angry. He was not even frightened. He just thought, "What a pity! More waste!" And he wished he had gone in a Hurricane instead of in this alien element. And he wished he could see Eileen once more, just as she was at nineteen, with the sun on her auburn hair, laughing as she walked through the pine-scented forest . . .

He did not hear any order to abandon ship. The noise was so sustained and cacophonous that he only just heard the voice of the seaman, his mouth to Mike's ear, bawling "Come on, airman, in you go . . ."

The wreck of the carrier was only just moving. But the big Carley float which had been thrown into the sea was slipping slowly astern. The seaman was right. Mike jumped off the sponson and it seemed a long time before he hit the water. There were oil and debris and swimmers all around him when he came up. Men were pouring off the carrier like lemmings from a cliff top, and one almost hit him. There was little shouting, and Mike saw no sign of panic. Everyone seemed totally preoccupied with his own survival. Only from the comparative safety of the rafts was any thought given to others. Those on board who had the strength were heaving others out of the water, though many slipped back from weakness or because of the oil that was spreading out from the bowels of the ship. Mike caught one retching gulp of it before he found himself being dragged upward, and did his best to help by holding the ratline on the lip of the raft. He was at last bundled in like a stuffed sack and lay outstretched on the wood grid base, panting and spitting out the last of the oil-tainted seawater.

The sound of exploding shells was distant now, and someone said, "The other poor buggers are getting it." The destroyers could have gotten away after doing what they could to conceal their charge, but Mike guessed that they would be going in on a death ride, hoping to put one of their torpedoes into the battle cruisers.

Another voice said, "She's going, lads. Give 'er a cheer."

Mike pulled himself into a sitting position. There were thirty or more on the big raft, and more coming in. The *Swiftsure* was ablaze as well as shattered by shellfire. She had turned through 90 degrees and he could see her like some Wagnerian sacrifice, smoke and flames rising from her listing hull against the setting sun. Her superstructure and funnel had completely vanished and there were five more shell holes along her flight deck, from stem to stern. Someone was continuing to fire one of the 4.7's at an unseen target. The intermittent crack of its fire continued until the sea washed over the gun's sponson like the tide putting out a beach bonfire.

A minute later, the stern began to go down quickly and the sea to boil around its victim. The bows, shattered above the waterline, stained red below, stood up for a full minute, a last cheeky gesture of defiance. Then she slipped away, the calmness of her disappearance contrasting with the violence of what had gone before. A mass of debris came shooting up from the seabed, some of it catapulting high into the air.

Mike could not bring himself to join in the cheering. How could they? Surely, this was a time for prayer and lament for the waste and suffering.

It was only when there was nothing to see and only corpses to pluck from the water that he felt the first touch of chill penetrating his body. He looked around the crowded raft. Some of the men were without coats, two were in blue denim overalls, straight from the heat of the engine room and were already gray-faced and shivering. They were not going to last long, and knew it. Sergeant Walker, who by chance had gotten into the same raft, wore an Irvin jacket, like Mike. Others were better equipped to face the night, and one had jumped with two blankets, which he had wrapped around himself and his neighbor.

But no one was going to last for long, not in this sea in this northern latitude.

15

"Stiffen the snakes! Where in heck have you blown in from?" asked Range Powell. He had dragged the ancient sofa from the clubhouse onto the grass, and was lying on it with a young girl. Both looked disheveled.

The Australian sat up and stared at Keith, who stood above him in his shirtsleeves, his fair hair white with dust from the side roads he had been driving along. "I thought you were marbled yesterday."

The girl was now also sitting up, pulling down her skirt, and was about to leave when Range grabbed her, without turning, as if she were an errant child. She looked at Keith and smiled.

"I had my troubles, I'll admit," said Keith. "But they only clipped me." He pointed down at his bandaged calf. "Then I borrowed this," he said, indicating the Kraftwagen parked beside the road. "Where's everyone else?"

There was no sign of life at St. Ervienne, only the litter of a hasty departure. The skeletons of two burned-out Hurricanes were on the other side of the field, and a third lay on its belly a hundred yards away. It was P-Pip, Range's machine.

"Search me. I got lost after that scrap yesterday. So I put down at some Frog airfield. D'you know, they wouldn't give me any juice? Said the war was over. So I shot the bastard and helped myself from the bowser. Then it was too dark to find my way back here. So I sat in the cockpit with my .38 in my lap to ward off intruders, and took off when there was a bit of light. I nearly had to shoot another Frog before I could get two to wind me up."

"And your sheila?" asked Keith with a smile, his eyes switching to the girl, who was now looking very demure and proper.

Range appeared surprised by the question. He squeezed her and gave her a kiss. "Oh, Louise, she came running out to see how I was when I bellylanded because the undercart wouldn't come down. And I persuaded her to stay. Her undercart came down all right."

He reached under the sofa and produced a liter bottle of *vin du pays*. "Want a swig?"

Keith stretched out in relief on the grass and drank half a pint of the coarse wine. His leg was hurting again and he was suffering from a delayed attack of utter weariness.

"Where did you pick up that ugly beast of a vehicle?" Range asked.

Keith told him of the shooting affray in the farmyard and how he had dumped the bodies in a ditch outside Vitry le François before discarding his S.S. uniform.

"Didn't anyone try to stop you?" Range asked.

"There weren't many French about. And anyway, they were too scared. And no one challenges the S.S. in the German army except senior S.S. Navigation was the real problem . . ."

There had been other problems, but Keith was too tired to speak anymore and went to sleep on the grass in his shirt, which was still bloodstained from the dead storm trooper's jacket. A group of German motorcyclists had tried to stop him. He had sworn at them and driven on, and when they tried to follow him in the dark, he had let loose a burst of

Schmeisser bullets in their direction, switched off his lights and turned down a farm lane.

Later he was forced to drive across a wheat field, and the four-wheel drive came in handy. He had avoided towns when he could. There was no real French fighting line, and the army was so demoralized that he went unchallenged past marching platoons of fully equipped infantry. Other *poilus* had thrown away their weapons, and he suspected that many of the young men he saw were deserters in stolen civilian clothes.

France's state of collapse was symbolized by one scene Keith had chanced upon and witnessed by the light of his headlights. A group of French soldiers were sitting on the road, fully armed, watching a garage proprietor filling the petrol tank of a German half-track towing an 88 gun just as if it was a family car. The gun crew was jeering at the Frenchmen, who sat, pretending to take no notice, smoking cigarettes and passing around a bottle of cognac.

Keith was awakened by a gentle kick from the Australian. "Look, cobber, I hate to disturb you, but I think we ought to hook our bait," he said. "The Krauts'll be along soon. And anyway, my sheila's gone home."

The sun was high, and Keith's first thought was "another beautiful day in which to lose the war." His leg was throbbing and he said, "You drive, Range. Do we make for Paris?"

"There was talk of Le Havre before I took off yesterday. The Channel ports to the east are crook. All gone or going," said Range. "But I got an idea while you were snoring."

They drove the Kraftwagen to the wood behind the hangars where the civilian light planes had been dumped. "Chiefy said one of them looked as if it might go," Range said. "I think it was this Salnier." He examined the little open two-seater civil plane. The tires were flat and someone had taken the cushions out of the seats. But the canvas wings and fuselage were intact, and when Range got in the controls responded to all his movements.

"Those bloody R.A.F. vandals burned all the fuel," he

said. "But we can hose some out of my kite."

The next hour, while the sound of firing grew louder from the northeast, was spent inflating the tires and man-handling the Salnier over to Range's Hurricane. Keith tore a length of oxygen tubing from the fighter's cockpit and sucked the fuel from the wing tanks into an oil can Range found, which he, in turn, poured into the tank of the little monoplane until it was full to the brim. Then they pushed the Salnier well clear and Keith flicked a lighted match into a pool of spilled petrol under the Hurricane, which went up in a roaring mushroom of blue flames.

With his superior mechanical knowledge, Range succeeded in manipulating the wiring to obviate the need for an ignition key for the Salnier, while Keith fetched cushions from the clubhouse and the Michelin map of France pinned to the wall. He also took the farmer's old blanket out of the Kraftwagen, remembering how cold an open cockpit could be even in a heatwave.

Range took the piece of blanket which Keith had torn in half and wrapped it around his shoulders. But he refused the parachute from the Hurricane's cockpit. "Bugger that," he remarked. "We're not going high enough to bail out." He settled himself in and turned on the petrol tap. "Give the prop a turn, cobber."

Keith found a couple of stones to act as chocks, and swung the prop the wrong way to prime the air-cooled Gnôme-et-Rhône engine.

"Contact!"

"Contact!"

The little engine buzzed into cheerful life, and Range grinned from the front cockpit, thumb raised in triumph.

Keith felt like a Great War R.F.C. observer as he climbed up into the rear cockpit, his folded Michelin map and the official-issue local map from the Hurricane in one hand, one of the Schmeisser machine pistols in the other.

Range turned around to see that he was safely strapped in

and said, "It'll be some line to shoot if you stoush a Hun with that thing." He pulled down his goggles and opened the throttle. The Salnier bobbed across the grass and was airborne in two hundred yards. Range banked steeply, made one low run across the airfield, over the still smoldering remains of his Hurricane, over the head of Louise, who had come out of her house to wave to them, and then set course due west until they hit the Seine and the railway line to Paris.

Range flew at zero feet for safety, lifting up over trees and farmhouses and the occasional high tension cable. He skirted around villages and small towns to avoid alarming the citizens, but in the open country as the toiling women in black dresses and the bent-backed men stood up he would wave and rock his wings in greeting.

From time to time he dipped down over the wide muddy waters of the Seine and skimmed the decks of barges. At one point they had a race with a train, the locomotive a huge black thing belching smoke and drawing a dozen passenger cars. Their Salnier, cruising at just over 70 m.p.h., was slowly overtaken, to the delight of the waving crew on the footplate.

Keith kept a lookout above and behind, but they saw no sign of any aerial activity, and every mile they progressed reduced the chance of trouble. As they neared Paris, the roads became more congested with refugee traffic. Range, recognizing that any low-flying aircraft might cause panic after the Luftwaffe attacks of the past days, steered clear, and then Keith tapped him on the shoulder and indicated that they had reached the point when they should change course onto a due west bearing south of the capital.

Half an hour later, they picked up another railway line which they followed until the noble and distinctive shape of Chartres Cathedral loomed up ahead. Range could not resist circling the great building at low level, and they skimmed above the white upturned faces of the people in the market square clustered around the stalls. A gendarme on traffic duty halted the vehicles in both directions while he took out a notebook, no doubt to write down their identifying letters and number.

They were getting dangerously short of fuel when Keith spotted an airfield ahead near the town of Bernay; they had traveled some 240 miles in three and a half hours. It was packed with an assortment of Bloch twin-engine bombers, various Potezes and a dozen R.A.F. Blenheims and Battles. Range touched down among them and taxied to the control tower. An Armée de l'Air officer came out and began to storm at them, accusing them of breaking every regulation and threatening them with the firing squad. Keith playfully produced his Schmeisser, which silenced the fellow, and when they climbed stiffly out and he saw their uniforms under their blankets he became unctiously deferential.

Then an R.A.F. Wing Commander appeared, and while the Salnier was refueled, he asked them about their experiences. He was gray-faced, unshaven and haggard. He told them he had lost nine out of eleven Blenheims in their last daylight raid in the Ardennes. "The flak just chopped us to pieces." He indicated two battered-looking Blenheims on the tarmac in front of a hangar. "That's what's left of my squadron. And they're not fit to cross the Channel."

When Keith asked permission to fly over to England, the Wing Commander shrugged his shoulders. "It's every man for himself now," he said. "Paddle your own canoe, if you've got one. But if you do make it, go in under the R.D.F. And don't forget the gunners'll be trigger happy."

The little Salnier sang out over the French coast north of Le Havre at three o'clock in the afternoon. The countryside all the way from Bernay had looked peaceful and remote from the tumult of war. Keith found it hard to believe that the Wehrmacht would soon be marching across this landscape, and that after four years of terrible French sacrifice a quarter century ago, the Germans would soon have conquered this rich and powerful and beautiful land.

He remembered that it was from this same Norman coast

nearly a thousand years ago that the last successful invasion of England had embarked, and he wondered how long it would be now before a German invading armada would set sail. If the Luftwaffe and ground fire could almost wipe out the R.A.F. in France in a few days, what was to stop them from destroying the R.A.F. in England? And without British domination of the air, even the navy could not halt the tide . . .

Range had set a compass bearing of 325 degrees, and there was nothing for Keith to do for the next hour. He dozed for a while, and awoke with a start of fear that he had slept in his Hurricane. Then he remembered that poor old B-Beer was no more than a burned-out tangle of wreckage, half buried in some Marne field. He remembered, too, that desperate fight and momentarily found it hard to believe that he had shot that storm trooper in cold blood at point-blank range without giving him a chance—he, Keith Stewart, once so squeamish about shooting a little partridge. Then he looked down at the ugly black Schmeisser lying across his knees and recalled, too, that this weapon would have been used to shoot that blameless farmer if his wife had not been too quick for the wounded storm trooper.

But what was this killing doing to him, Keith wondered anxiously? If he survived this war, which seemed a remote likelihood, would this experience of daily violence coarsen his character for life? It would be a relief to talk about it to someone—like the curé, or best of all, Jenny, who would be crisp and realistic. How he ached to see her again!

There was a smudge of land ahead, and Range turned to point at it and then to attempt to pat himself on the back. The white cliffs at the eastern end of the Isle of Wight emerged out of the haze. Range altered course to due north, and five minutes later they could make out Selsey Bill.

Range flew low and unchallenged over the coast at East Wittering. A double-decker bus was going west along the coast road. There were bungalows below them, with long neat little gardens. Women were shopping along the main street and two boys on bicycles stopped and looked up at their plane, no doubt puzzled by its identity. The soft countryside stretched ahead, as cared for and peaceful as the Normandy countryside they had just left behind them. And yet this could only be England, and Keith was surprised at the strength of his renewed feeling of love and loyalty to this land, and his determination to prevent those terrible scenes of fire and bombing and fleeing citizens from being repeated here. His own life was nothing—absolutely nothing —to set against this island and its freedom.

The tall spire of Chichester Cathedral, as splendid in its English way as Chartres, rose up into the sky ahead. Range skirted the city and headed for the dark hangars and radio towers of Tangmere. The appearance of the Salnier clearly puzzled the duty officer in the control tower. Civil flying had been banned since the outbreak of the war, and no prior warning of their arrival had reached the station. A figure on the balcony fired off a red Very flare to prohibit their landing, but Range ignored it, rocked his wings and brought the Salnier in on the grass in front of the control tower just as a second angry flare sailed into the sky.

An armed guard closed at once on their machine, and withdrew resentfully when Range and Keith identified themselves.

"Two Fifty-nine came in here yesterday," the station I.O. told them over a cup of tea later. "Or what's left of them. Five Hurricanes, none in good shape. Squadron Leader Rowbotham sent them all off on a week's leave, and they're going to re-form somewhere up in Twelve Group."

Range left for London by train as soon as he could get a leave pass, having an urgent appointment with his sheila in Knightsbridge who, he claimed, had been brokenhearted with loneliness since he had last seen her.

Keith, too, had urgent arrangements to make, but they were less clear-cut. "I.O.'s are supposed to know everything, aren't they?" he asked.

"Naturally."

Intelligence officers were a stylish breed, Keith reflected. He liked this one's casual authoritativeness. "I want to know the whereabouts of Section Officer J. Simpson. She's in R.D.F. Somewhere in Eleven Group, I think."

"Nothing simpler. Urgent official liaison business, I take it?" The I.O. raised the telephone, gave the handle a turn and got through to Uxbridge. Keith listened to an outpouring of initials and specialized jargon remote from the simplicities of a Hurricane's cockpit. It produced the required result in three minutes.

"Your W.A.A.F.'s at Swingham. A bit east of Dungeness." He got up and indicated an official map on the board behind his desk. The R.D.F. Chain Home (C.H.) stations were marked in red—Ventnor, Poling and the rest, around the Kent coast, to Bawdsey in Suffolk where Jenny had trained and all up the east coast of England and Scotland, the secret eyes covering the sky on all but the most unlikely lines of approach to the island.

"May I make a call?"

"Quicker if I do it."

In less than a minute, Keith heard her incisive, rather husky voice. She was answering officially as duty officer and there was a pause after Keith identified himself. "Look, I can't talk here," she said, lowering her voice. "Surrounded by people. Hold on." Her voice came through on another extension. "Where are you? Are you all right?"

That's better, thought Keith. She sounds as if she really does care how I am. "I'm O.K. I've just got back from France. No, I flew. Yes, it was somewhat eventful toward the end. I've got a week's leave and you must take the train to London tonight . . ."

"Oh, Keith, you're out of your mind. Of course I can't. We're up to our eyes here. You know they've started to bring back the B.E.F. and it's ops all around the clock."

Keith thought quickly. It was not an easy place to get to,

so he would not be able to make it that night. "Look, I'm at Tangmere. You can't be working twenty-four hours a day so I'll come to you. I've *got* to see you, Jenny . . ."

Her voice broke in, distantly. She was talking to someone else, and had clearly been interrupted. When she addressed herself to him again she said formally, "Very good, sir. Yes, I understand the orders."

Keith said, "That's my girl," and hung up.

The medical officer gave him a belated shot of antitetanus and removed the bandage that Marie had wrapped around his wound so tenderly several eons in time ago. He gave him a walking stick. "You'll be off flying for a bit with that," he said cheerfully, "even if it doesn't go septic."

"I've got more important things to do than fly," Keith told him, and limped along to the station adjutant in the hope of acquiring a hat and gloves, a pair of shoes, a jacket and a few shirts to tide him over.

It took nearly the whole day to travel by train along the south coast from Tangmere to Lydd, changing frequently and waiting for hours at deserted stations. "The army've taken over, that's the trouble," stationmasters and porters complained. "They're getting ready to meet the boys from France at the ports—that's what they say."

It was early evening when he got out onto the little wooden platform at Lydd. There was never any difficulty in finding C.H. stations. Swingham, like the others, consisted of a number of great towers, four of wood, three more of lattice steel 360 feet high like overgrown grid pylons with projecting horizontal aerials. Scattered on the flat ground about them were a number of huts, some Nissen, others of concrete, sleeping quarters, a small barracks for the military guard, air-raid shelters, and bounding the whole area a high wire fence and rolled barbed wire and concealed gun posts.

Security was strict and the guard at the gate checked his identity with unusual care. "And your business, sir?"

"Liaison," Keith said in a businesslike voice and walked toward the administration building.

"Section Officer Simpson comes off watch at eighteen hundred hours," the sergeant in the adjutant's office told him. "That's in five minutes. Very convenient," said Keith. He saw Jenny emerge from between the sandbags leading down to the underground "R" hut a few minutes later. She was slipping her respirator strap over her shoulder and had not yet put on her hat. She looked thinner than Keith remembered her from nearly six months ago, and she had grown her hair so that strictly it broke regulations by being lower than her collar.

She saw him standing on the steps, his face bronzed and his fair hair bleached by the French sun of the past weeks. He had his hat in one hand, the stick in the other. She stopped and smiled up at him. "Keith, you are a fool." She did an imitation cockney of the current poster appeal, "Is your journey really necessary?" and laughed.

"Not for me it isn't." He put on a mock heroic voice: "I've done my bit."

She looked down to where the bandage drew tight the trouser leg. "What have they done to that nice leg?"

"Not bad enough to stop me walking to the nearest pub with you."

"I can't, darling. I'm on again at midnight, and I *must* have some sleep."

"Come and sleep with me then."

She looked around at the unpromising environment with a wry, tired smile on her lips, at the camouflaged Nissen huts, the steel emergency water tank, the polished bell and triangular gas alarm outside the guardroom, the austere, unlovely sleeping quarters, the concrete administration block and the stark towers reaching up high into the evening sky. It was not a place of love.

Keith laughed and said, "You've got to eat, anyway. Let me take you to a pub for a quick drink and a meal, then I'll tuck you up into bed and kiss you good night. I'll wangle some transport."

And so he did, by ruthlessly exploiting his wound. The

S.L.A. himself said, "All right, take my Hillman. But if you prang it I'll have your guts for garters."

"A very nice way of putting it, sir. Thank you very much. Section Officer Simpson will be driving."

Jenny emerged in a newly pressed uniform. Her makeup concealed the tiredness in her face, and she said in cheerful cockney again, "Well, fancy that, going out with an orficer, like . . ."

It was no surprise to Keith that she drove skillfully and fast. He looked around at the unbroken flatness of the fields and marshland, and after a while said, "We won't find anywhere to hide coyly here, so you'd better just stop."

"Certainly not."

He reached down and pulled up the hand brake hard and she swerved onto the grass. "What are you doing, Keith?"

"Kissing you," he said, and did so, long and lingeringly, returning for a second and third time to her soft open lips and murmuring, "Oh, my goodness me, this is even better than a hot bath."

"Well, that's not very flattering, I must say," she said, stroking his hair. "I was going to say something much nicer about you."

"You try five days without changing your shirt and you would know how much I was flattering you."

She cupped his face in her hands and laughed. "I'm rather glad I've got you fresh and laundered."

A mile farther on a Commer truck full of W.A.A.F. other ranks met them. Jenny had to pull off the narrow lane and for a moment they were the object of close attention.

"That'll give my lot something to talk about on night duty," Jenny said—"Oh, ma'am, what a handsome escort . . . !"

They found a pub north of New Romney that was empty of service people. It was small and unexciting, and all of the customers were local. They looked up from their pints and turned to study them with unself-conscious interest.

"Been over there, have you, sir?" asked one elderly man, nodding his head toward France.

Keith offered him a drink. The man said, "Last time we held our ground. We didn't run for it."

Keith, taken by surprise by this comment, said nothing and joined Jenny in the corner. With their training, neither needed the "Careless Talk Costs Lives" sign on the pub wall to watch their conversation. Keith asked her if she had heard any more of Mike, and she said discreetly, "No, he's still somewhere abroad." Then she said, "Has it been very rough, Keith?"

He ordered bread and cheese and pickles and another round of drinks. "Fairly. And it looks as though there's more to come." He told her of his boyhood unease about violence and how it had affected his life in the country as the adopted son of a hunting and shooting family. "I didn't know you then, which is a pity," he said. "I know it sounds soppy, especially with things as they are, but I terribly want to know whether I am being changed by all this, whether I'll ever be the same again. I really hated killing birds, which must have been why I was so bad at it. But now I'm killing *people* every day."

She put her hand over his. "They'll kill you if you don't, so keep it up, Keith Stewart." He could see she was trying not to be frivolous, and finding his question difficult, as indeed it was. "Anyway," she went on, "it's not like a pathetic, helpless bird falling at your feet. I thought you didn't really see anything when you shot a plane down. I mean, it must be a detached sort of business?"

Keith did not answer for a minute and put the tankard to his lips.

"Well, isn't it?" she repeated.

"No, not always." He lowered his voice, but desperately tried not to sound melodramatic. "A day or two ago I shot a man at point-blank range. Right in the face, Jenny. He didn't even know I was there. And then I shot another one.

Oh, I've killed so many. So damn many."

Her hand tightened over his. Then she said briskly, "Well, thank goodness for that. If more people did then we might win the war after all."

Keith stared into her face, looking deep into her brown understanding eyes. He noticed that her makeup had not quite concealed the dark rings around them. "What am I making such a fuss about?" he asked himself angrily. "Here's she working just as hard as you, and in very great danger, and all you can do is flaunt your bloody conscience as if it's some exclusive and rare possession."

Jenny said, "I don't mean to be unsympathetic, really I don't. But killing is your business at the moment and I like efficient people. Nobody much enjoys it, I suppose, but it's better than being ordered about by Nazis and spitting at the Jews and having our children join the Hitler Jugend. And anyway," she ended, "you're much too nice to be coarsened." She picked up her gas mask and hat and gloves from the next chair, and leaned over his shoulder, whispering in his ear. "You just stay alive, Keith darling. I want you so much."

They went out into the evening. It was clear and there was still light in the sky. There were Spitfires flying overhead, steering for the French coast, eight of them in two sections, in finger formation, Keith noticed. They were learning.

He hobbled into the passenger seat and watched her sit down beside him. "Not much of a dinner," he said.

"Enough," she said. "Thank you. It's one long relay of tea and cocoa and biscuits on night duty, so don't worry."

She drove half a mile and then stopped the car just off the road and said, "Kiss me good night here." She laughed. "It may be our only chance."

He pulled her around so that she was lying across his lap and ran his fingers through her hair. "This is an altogether unsatisfactory arrangement," he said. "Very frustrating. They *must* give you leave sometime."

"In a month," she replied, smiling that slightly uneven smile.

He undid the brass buttons of her tunic and struggled clumsily with her belt. "Damn badly designed uniform," he said, pressing his lips against her face.

"Very wisely designed," she said softly. Then later, "You were really a very irresistible lover all those millions of years ago."

"Thank you. Rather inexperienced, I fear. And to think we've only slept together once—in all this time."

She lay still, with his hand cupping her breast beneath her shirt, and after a minute he realized she was breathing steadily and deeply.

He sat still for half an hour while it got colder and colder in the car, accepting the fact gratefully that now they had slept together a second time, if under strangely different circumstances. He eased his legs out through the open door, and tucked her into the passenger seat without her awakening.

Then he went around to the driver's door and got behind the wheel. It did not hurt very much pressing the clutch pedal. As he drove back along the narrow, straight road the air-raid sirens from New Romney and Lydd sounded out, wailing across the flat marshland like a presentiment of doom.

16

It was a night of pain, suffering and lament. When they were still within earshot of another raft, a voice had cried out, "We'll have a song, chaps. There's nothing like a song." And they had sung naval ditties, which Mike had never heard before, and, inevitably, "We're going to hang out the washing on the Siegfried Line" and "Roll Out the Barrel." The volume had gradually diminished as more and more of the men were so overcome with the cold that they could no longer find the strength to continue. Then the other raft drifted away.

Mike squatted hunched up against the side of the raft, his knees under his chin, and pressed close against his neighbor for warmth. There was little wind and the sour smell of vomit, oil, and sweat pervaded their little world. There were frequent frustrated efforts to light sodden cigarettes with damp matches. Someone produced a lighter, but still the tobacco would not catch. It seemed the cruelest and final deprivation.

The dying began before dawn. A seaman who had coughed for most of the hours of darkness was the first to go. Later a voice said, "Charlie's gone. Oh, God!" Dead bodies were pushed into the center of the raft because no one wanted to have the chill of a corpse close against him, nor did anyone have the heart or strength to throw them overboard. By the faint predawn light, Mike saw one of the engine-room machinists turn over one of the bodies and start undoing the duffle coat with shaking hands. A voice protested and was answered roughly, "It's no bloody good to him, mate." Others followed his example, and thus the loss of a neighbor's heat was exchanged for the warmth of the clothes that had proved inadequate to keep him alive.

By dawn the raft presented a scene of grotesque horror, with fifteen pale corpses, most of them in no more than their underwear, lying like thoughtlessly tossed kitbags in the center, and the survivors hunched and shivering in tight groups around the edge. There had been groaning and cursing in the night, but it had now ceased. Mike regretted this as any sound suggested that there was still some spirit left, and the noise kept him from falling asleep. He knew that if he nodded off it would be the end.

He could see Sergeant Walker on the other side of the raft, his face chalk white, his eyes blinking very slowly. He crawled across to him, unable to avoid all the limbs of the dead that sprawled over the wooden grating. "They'll be along soon. Don't go to sleep, buddy," he said. He put an arm around his shoulders. "We can't afford to lose good pilots like you."

Walker turned his head toward him and shook it slowly from side to side, resigned to the inevitable.

Mike said, "I guess this might help." He reached for his hip pocket and brought out the flask. His fingers were too paralyzed with cold to open the screw top and he had to use his teeth. Then he put it to Walker's lips. The young airman swallowed and coughed, spitting out some of the raw whiskey, but swallowing enough to bring a faint touch of color to his cheeks. "Thank you, sir," he muttered in a husky voice.

The hand of a petty officer next to Walker reached out. "Give us a swig, sir. Go on . . . ."

Mike handed him the flask and the sailor put it clumsily to his mouth and tipped it up. Then he let it go in disgust so that it fell at his feet. "It's bloody empty," he said in disgust.

Mike thought of the bitter irony of bourbon whiskey that might have saved lives now, being drunk so thoughtlessly by them in the warmth of that room at Rhysjhok when their bellies were already full of hot food and akevitt.

Sergeant Walker died in Mike's arms in the late morning, just before a thin sun broke through. He had stopped shivering a few minutes before and had opened his eyes and looked at Mike, but had said nothing. He died silently. Mike felt the life steal out of his body. So perhaps, he thought, the going won't be too painful after all when it comes.

The petty officer said, "Can I 'ave his coat, sir?" And Mike helped him ease it off the boy's narrow shoulders, and laid the body down gently at his side. He did not look more than fifteen, and seemed to have shrunk in death. Mike looked at the blue lips and the closed eyes that had been so keen and quick in the air, and the limp hands that had briefly proved their skill in his fierce trade.

He imagined the humble home on Tyneside that would soon receive the news of the boy's death and honor at the same time. Then later the mother and father would take the train to London, wearing their Sunday best, and the King would say a few words of comfort to them before presenting them with the oval medal with "For Courage" inscribed upon it.

Mike pulled his knife from its sheath and, clumsily with his frozen hands, cut the threads securing the wings to the sergeant's tunic and put them in his pocket. In the unlikely event of his own survival, and the likely loss of the boy's body, at least his mother and father would have these golden wings to put beside his D.F.M. ribbon and medal.

The emergency water had long since been drunk, and when the sun put a narrow flame of life back into the survivors its benefit was offset by the new ordeal of thirst. Cumulus clouds built up later in the afternoon, the wind rose and for the first time the raft began taking in water. Time and again as the hours of that dreadful day ticked by, Mike felt himself slipping into unconsciousness and had to cause himself pain to bring himself back from the gray world which he knew must soon become black if he did not keep awake.

Then at five o'clock as the rain began his head fell forward and he was dimly aware that he was losing the contest. He was also just aware of a sense of surprise that he was losing. "You have always been a winner, hotshot," a voice was saying. "This is no goddamn time to be a loser, is it?"

The question was never answered. Not for a long time, anyway. Not until just after six o'clock when the French destroyer *Courageux,* with half a battalion of *Chasseurs Alpins* on board, hove to two cables off and lowered a boat.

Mike never heard the exclamations of horror when the boat came alongside the raft, nor did he witness the difficulties the sailors experienced in getting one of their number on board the raft. The wind had risen to force seven, and it seemed a hopeless task to take the big raft in tow.

The sailor went about swiftly identifying those who were still alive and disregarding all those lying half naked in the center of the raft. With the help of a second sailor who managed to jump into the raft he lifted up Mike and, when the boat was brought near and crashed hard against the side of the raft, arms reached out and lifted his limp, sodden body safely on board.

With painful slowness, the black turned dark gray, then light gray; shapes began to form, and then color. A smell was the first conscious confirmation to Mike that he was still alive after all. It was a hot smell of antiseptic and oil, a surprising compound that led to his opening his eyes. With the recognition that the antiseptic originated from the eternal smell of the destroyer's sick bay, and the oil from his clothes lying in a heap, consciousness was complete.

He saw a sailor pick up the evil pile and remove it, taking

from the cabin the bitter stench he never wanted to smell again, and he felt the agony in his feet. A voice said, *"Mon pauvre aviateur!"* A hand was laid across his brow, and he felt other hands, strong and life-giving, massaging his limbs.

Later the captain came into the sick bay. He was wearing a leather overcoat that reached almost to his feet, and carried gauntlets and his hat in one hand, and in the other a bottle of brandy which he poured out for both of them. "Well, my friend," he said in English *"votre santé.* You are a lucky pilot. Three hours ago you were dying in that raft. And now you drink cognac with us. I hope it is good?"

"Very good," said Mike. His throat was sore and his voice gravelly from the ravages of thirst and oil. "I'm sure grateful for the trouble you took, sir. I guess it wasn't an easy task."

It had been made simpler, the captain told him, shaking his head with distress, because there were only two to recover. "Alas, forty-two corpses, and you and one other alive," he said. "In spite of your frostbitten toes, you are what we call a *vainqueur!"*

In the underground cypher room at Invergordon, Wren Barrett had been sitting beside a fully qualified cypher officer for fourteen hours, with only brief breaks, observing and sometimes assisting with the coding and decoding of signals which had been pouring in since the evacuation of the Narvik forces had begun. The work of a cypher officer could be dull and uneventful for weeks on end. Eileen's training period had begun with the unprecedented naval activity connected with the evacuation not only of the British forces in Norway but also the surviving Allied armies in France. The English Channel, the North Sea and the Norwegian Sea were swarming with vessels from battleships to private yachts, all concerned directly or indirectly with the saving of these precious battalions and the frustration of the efforts of the enemy to prevent it.

Eileen already knew enough of the rudiments of cypher

work to be able to piece together the details of the Norwegian evacuation, the departure of King Haakon and his staff from Tromsö in the cruiser *Devonshire*, the movements of the four convoys of troopships, and the composition of their passengers, of General Auchinleck's troops, the careful protective close cover given by Admiral Lord Cork's light naval forces, and the heavy and more distant forces of the naval Commander-in-Chief at Scapa Flow.

The Wren officer had soon spotted Eileen's special interest in the troopship *Windsor*, whose contingent included one of the R.A.F. squadrons, and had teased her about it. "Yes, ma'am," she had to confess, "there's an American pilot called Mike Browning I'm sort of engaged to."

Then, in the early hours of the morning, there came through in rapid succession news of a threat of an enemy landing on Iceland, the dispatch of heavy units of the fleet to meet this danger, and the appearance in the North Sea of a formidable, fast and modern German squadron of warships, clearly hellbent on the destruction of the troop convoys.

Eileen watched these developments with anguished concentration, oblivious of being without sleep for almost twenty-four hours. At 5:00 A.M. the Wren officer and herself were ordered to hand over their duties and return on shift in six hours.

Eileen dozed fitfully on one of the emergency bunks for part of this period, her dreams clouded by the face of Mike and fragments of scenes of the brief happy times they had spent together. She awoke suddenly, sweating and consumed by the nightmare she had suffered, revealing Mike looking his normal cheerful self, eyes bright and eager, but with his hair standing up and moving like tide-washed seaweed.

She rushed at once into the cypher room and pleaded shamelessly for news of the *Windsor*'s convoy. The naval officer in charge regarded the pretty, auburn-haired disheveled girl with a quizzical expression. "That lot are safe now, dear." He indicated a point north of the Shetland Islands. "The Germans won't bring their precious *Gneisenau* and

Co. that near Scapa. They're great fighters, but only when their odds are ten to one. But we've got some nasty unconfirmed news from farther north."

When Eileen came on watch again, the nightmare driven from her mind by the news that 140 Squadron was safe, her officer told her of a garbled message from a British destroyer which had been received the previous evening via one of Lord Cork's cruisers. It had indicated that she was in trouble, but no more. Then at 7:00 P.M. a signal *en clair* was received at Invergordon from the French destroyer *Courageux*: "J'ai deux survivants du *Swiftsure* . . ."

It was the first news of the loss of the carrier, and the cypher room was thrown into silence by the catastrophe. Later reports indicated that the destroyer had searched for more survivors, but had found only corpses. Eileen had recalled her nightmare, and prayed for those fifteen hundred men who would now be dead in the cold waters of the ocean, their hair floating like strands of seaweed, as she had seen Mike.

The convoy containing the *Windsor* broke up and its ships made for different ports, where trains stood ready to bring the troops rapidly south for the new threat of invasion from conquered France. It was with special excitement that Eileen learned that 140 Squadron's ship was to dock at Invergordon, the nearest suitable port to Elgin, and her officer gave her special leave to enter the naval dockyard and be present when the squadron disembarked.

It was a cold early-June day with the east wind bringing in drizzle from the North Sea, when the *Windsor* tied up alongside in the naval dockyard. Eileen waited in the shelter of a quayside store, shivering from the cold and agitated with the expectation of seeing Mike's tough little bouncy figure striding down the gangway.

Some guardsmen were first off, smart and newly shaven to impress the Royal Navy, then several platoons of *Chasseurs Alpins* with skis on their backs in addition to their other luggage and equipment. There was no one to meet them except a representative from the French Consulate in Edinburgh. Then Eileen caught a glimpse of dark blue uniforms parading on deck and forming up for landing. The officers and noncommissioned pilots of 140 Squadron were first off. They looked grim and tired, and were few in number. There were only five of them with wings on the breasts of their tunics. Eileen's eyes darted from one to the other as they advanced down the gangway carrying their small suitcases or kitbags. But where was Mike?

Eileen waited for the first of the nonflying officers. He turned and looked at the anxious figure standing alone in the drizzle on the quay.

Eileen said, "Please can you tell me where Pilot Officer Browning is?"

The officer halted in his tracks and put down his case on the cobblestones. "Who are you?" he asked, firmly but not unkindly.

"My name is Eileen Barrett. I'm a friend of Mike's."

The officer was silent for a moment, and looked away. When he spoke it was with the conscious effort of sounding matter-of-fact. But it did not work. "As you can see, we haven't got many pilots left. I'm afraid your Mike went on another ship, and it has been sunk."

"But they've all arrived safely," Eileen said in despair. "I know. I'm in cypher. None of the troopships have been sunk."

The conversation had attracted the attention of the others, and a tall, stooping officer intervened. "I'm the intelligence officer," he said. "My name's Williams. I'm afraid the squadron's had a nasty blow. Are you related to any of our pilots?"

"Engaged—sort of." Her voice was a despairing whisper.

The Spy explained the position. "We wanted to save what planes we still had so the C.O. and eight others landed them on the *Swiftsure*. If you're in signals you will know what happened to her . . ."

Eileen said, "Thank you," and turned away, walking stiffly into the drizzle for the length of the quay, with the nightmare picture of Mike's face hammering in her head. Dear, brave, laughing Mike, racing about on his crutches through the Rising Hall woods, dancing jauntily in London, mocking himself in his brand new uniform, striding up the forest hills in Germany. And now the Germans had killed him, and life and laughter had ceased for her forever . . .

Her officer found her lying face downward on her bunk in the barrack block when she failed to turn up for her watch. She took her to her own room, washed her face and tucked her into her own bed.

The *Courageux* moored in the Forth, three cables east of the bridge, twenty-four hours after the *Windsor* had docked at Invergordon. A Royal Navy picket boat went out to meet her and hand over instructions about the disembarkation of the French troops on board, and learn the identity and condition of the unnamed survivors from the *Swiftsure*.

Mike was lifted down the ladder two hours later by two stout *matelots* and lowered into a launch which took him to the dockyard, where a civilian and two naval officers, one a surgeon-commander, awaited him. In the ambulance that drove him to the naval hospital, the civilian and the other officer began to ask him for details of the action and of his own experiences.

Mike insisted on sitting up in one of the bunks. "It's only my dratted toes," he insisted. "Well, see, I'll come clean with everything," he told them. "As much as I know. But on one condition. And that is that I can make a couple of phone calls, and send a cable to my parents in America."

"That's a deal," said the naval officer. "As soon as the doctor here has finished with you." He smiled down at Mike. "It's the least the navy can do for you, after our inhospitable earlier behavior."

Constance Barrett answered the telephone at Rising Hall. Her voice was the next best thing to Eileen herself. "Mike!" she exclaimed. "How w-wonderful to hear you. Where are you?"

"I don't think I'd better answer that, ma'am. But I'm O.K. I've had a swim and my feet need a little convalescence." There was an exclamation of outraged puzzlement at the other end of the crackling line. "And I wondered if I could come to you?"

When Mike learned of Eileen's posting, he added confidently, "I think there'll be two of us, Lady Barrett."

"But she's not d-due for leave for at least three months."

"You'll see," said Mike and hung up.

They had given him a wheelchair, and he backed it momentarily away from the telephone in the hospital foyer as if requiring momentum for his next assault. This required firmness, a quick mind and ruthless exploitation of his position. On the line to the Admiralty in London, he tosséd names like Chatfield, Pound and Mountbatten around to hear how they sounded, and eventually got through to the W.R.N.S. directorate switchboard where he was stalled for several minutes, and one voice asked him several times if he knew there was a war on.

But at last, as he knew he would, he was speaking to a woman who sounded so authoritative and intimidating that Mike knew he was close to the heart of the W.R.N.S. machine. He made his request crisply, even giving Eileen's service number. "I know, ma'am, I may sound like a cheeky American. But I assure you we are to be married, and this is the second time I have been injured. I shall recover and be in my Hurricane again in half the time if she nurses me back to health for a few days."

The voice at the other end mellowed, and Mike thought he heard a distant laugh. "I'll see what I can do," said this illustrious officer.

17

Keith had not seen Tom Mathers since the Savile Farm days, before the crisis of August 1939 that led to the declaration of war. Nothing but a few brief letters had passed between them, and now here he was, studying with professional authority the flesh wound in Keith's leg in the drawing room in Eaton Square.

"It's healing up very nicely," he said. "No fear of infection now. And the less you use it the sooner it'll be all right." He put on a new dressing with hands that were suited for his chosen career.

Keith thought he would choose him to remove his appendix. But he said teasingly, "You sound like Hippocrates—you must have finished your 'Basic Bedside Manners' course."

Tom tied the bandage knot especially tight in revenge. "And that's a basic tourniquet," he said. "To give you gangrene."

Moira said, "When are you going home?"

"Tomorrow, just for a few days," Keith answered. "Come with me. Come on, it'll do you good to get away from London."

"Not a chance," said Tom decisively. "I've got exams next week."

"You then, Moira?"

She shook her head and smiled. "He needs looking after, especially around exam times. Don't you, love? All nerves."

"I'll bet he's hell," Keith said.

Moira stroked Tom's hair as if he were a cat on her lap. "Terrible hell," she said. "Besides, we're not on speaking terms with our parents and it would be awkward to be at Rising Hall."

Tom and Moira were "living in sin," as they facetiously referred to their relationship, in a small bed-sitting room in Bloomsbury. Moira earned three pounds a week in a bookshop, and they were very impoverished and happy. They had decided not to get married until the war was over in order that—by Tom's odd reasoning—the survivor would not be so heartbroken if the other was killed in the bombing, now daily expected in London.

Tom said over tea, brought in by Mrs. Ewhurst, "All that sensitive compunction of yours about shooting must have gone by the board over the past few weeks?"

Besides Eileen, and Jenny the other day, these two old friends from Market Rising were the only people in whom he had confided his uneasiness and that had been some time ago.

"In a way, yes," said Keith doubtfully. "It's all rather different if you're going to be killed unless you do something—sharpish, too."

Moira was tucking her way through the sandwiches with her customary relish. "Would it help to tell us what you've been doing? I'd love to know."

Keith thought for a moment. "No, I don't think so. Not yet, anyway. If I tell you, it's rather like putting something in writing. It's a sort of record. As it is, I'm getting quite good at keeping it out of my consciousness. And that's better for next time I have to do it."

"I think they ought to let you off any more. Not just your wound, I mean," said Moira, licking her fingers vigorously. "And Mike, too, when he gets back from Norway."

"And that'll be soon, judging by the newspapers this morning," said Tom.

The telephone rang beside Keith, and he was surprised to notice that he jumped before he reached out for it.

It was Constance Barrett. "Keith, dear, I thought I might f-find you there."

"I'm looking forward to seeing you both tomorrow," said Keith. He had earlier told them he would be on the 10:15 to Leicester, and he was longing for the familiar sights, sounds and smells of Rising Hall, and being totally indulged for a few days.

But it was not to be. "Oh, Keith, I'm heartbroken. I nearly threw away the beastly t-telegram. But you've got to report back for duty. A place called Col-Coltishall. Yes, tomorrow. It says it's urgent so I suppose you'll have to go."

Oh, God, Keith thought as he thanked her, reassured her that he would get proper leave soon, and rang off. Not *so* soon. Couldn't they give him just a few days?

He regarded the other two sitting alongside one another on the sofa. Tom, ever alert, had already half guessed what the call meant. Moira looked puzzled. "What's the matter?" she asked.

When he told them, they both exploded with indignation. "It's ridiculous," said Tom. "You shouldn't really be walking. It needs a good week's complete rest."

"Flying's very good therapy," said Keith, trying not to sound rueful. "That's an old R.A.F. truism."

"Bloody untruism!" exclaimed Tom.

Keith rang the bell, and when Mrs. Ewhurst came in he asked her for some sandwiches for the journey. "The trains are so awful just now, it may take me all night."

"Are you going to Rising Hall now, sir?" she asked, puzzled, and when he told her that he was going back to his squadron the tears began to fall down her cheeks. "Oh, sir," was all she could say before she left.

"Poor dear," said Keith. "She cries nearly all the time now. This house is being closed down for the duration, and they've been offered a cottage in the grounds. It's like the end of the world for them."

"It's going to be the end of the world for all of us in London soon," said Tom grimly. "Mrs. Ewhurst doesn't know her luck."

Coltishall, a sector station in north Norfolk, was in a state of more or less organized confusion, with aircraft of many kinds landing and taking off, and the remnants of at least two Hurricane squadrons expected or already arrived from France. Personnel turned up by air, road and rail throughout the twenty-four hours. The evacuation from Dunkirk was in full swing, and fighter cover was desperately needed.

The first person Keith recognized in the crowded mess was Buffer Davies, beaming with health and high spirits, and carrying a pint of beer in each hand. He presented one to Keith. "I knew you'd turn up so I got this ready for you."

"Liar!" exclaimed Keith. "You got two to save fighting your way to the bar again."

"What's the gen, old boy?"

"I don't know," said Keith, sitting down to ease his leg. "You tell me."

"Range Powell's here, swearin' like a trooper because his telegram arrived while he was actually in bed with some popsy. And the C.O. And half a dozen others, some new sprogs straight from O.T.U., and now you. We're goin' to Manston as soon as some kites arrive." He looked down at the stick Keith was holding. "Glad you only got winged, old boy. We all thought you'd got the chop."

Keith experienced a comforting feeling of being back home with the familiar talk, the familiar surroundings, the familiar Buffer. Dear old Buffer! And how appropriate, come to think of it, was the self-styled label! Buffer. But beneath all those strangely contrived manners and jargon was the pure gold of a good sort, a patriot and a steady fighter. He would fight with you and support you to the end. And for his part Keith knew he would support this tall, willowy, slightly ridiculous figure to the death if need be. Later in the evening, the C.O. called Keith over and listened to his account of his escape from behind the lines, and from France. "How does the leg feel?" he asked.

"Not bad. Good enough to fly."

"You can take it to the quack if you like. The trouble is, he'll ground you."

Keith said, "I know. But I'd like to fly, if we ever get anything to fly with."

"Tomorrow for sure. I've just had it from the adj. And they'll have Rotol props, thank God. I gather it's dicey over the Channel right now."

Keith was amazed at how rapidly and efficiently things happened now that it was a question of life and death. The next morning, all those who had come back by sea were fully reequipped with parachutes, Mae Wests, helmets and goggles, and when Keith explained that he had returned by air but had nothing except one complete flying boot, he received all that he needed at once without question and without even having to fill in a form. Very unpeacetime!

After lunch, they took off and Rowbotham led them in the finger formation they had learned to fly in France, over Norwich and Ipswich, across the Thames estuary to the north Kent coast. At fifteen thousand feet visibility was almost unlimited. They could see the balloons over Chatham, and more distantly like unseasonal Christmas glitter in the afternoon sun, over the city of London itself.

To the left, it was a different picture. While London was steeling itself for the first blows that must follow the fall of France, the French coastline to the southeast was smudged with smoke from the burning Channel ports, and they could

258

see the distant wake lines from ships on their rescue missions to and from Dunkirk.

To come in at Manston was like landing on the edge of England. The field was packed with aircraft. But here, as at Lens-La Basse and St. Ervienne, it was all operational business, and the only aircraft were Spitfires and Hurricanes, and a few of the latest two-seater fighters, the awkward-looking Boulton and Paul Defiant, and Blenheim night fighters.

At the dispersal they were to share with a Spitfire squadron, the Wing Commander (Flying) was standing awaiting their arrival. Rowbotham at once went over to consult with him, and the others hung around watching the ground crews rapidly refueling the Hurricanes from triple-hose bowsers. The N.A.A.F.I. van arrived with its urns of sweet tea and buns, but before they could get to it they were called for a briefing.

The Wing Commander spoke to them briefly. "I don't need to tell you what's going on. The Huns are making a great effort to sever the rescue line across here to Dunkirk." He pointed on the wall map at the port on the eastern extremity of the French coast. "They know that every man we get off is going to make the invasion of this country that much harder. They sank thirty-one ships yesterday. We're doing what we can, patrolling in relays with thirty-minute gaps, but the navy and the troops who are being hammered think very strongly it's not enough. One of our chaps was beaten up when he had to bail out over the beach the other day. The trouble is they don't see us half the time when the fighting's above cloud or not immediately above them. And when they do see us, most of 'em think we're Jerries and bang away. Some of us here have been doing four sorties a day, and we're getting pretty tired." He turned to the C.O. and asked him to take over.

Before an operation, Rowbotham looked like a belligerent bull, a demeanor Keith always found encouraging. He briefed them as if he were an All Blacks forward in a vital match at Twickenham. "I want you to stick to your pair, especially you new chaps, and try to get the buggers *before* they drop their bombs. It'll be fairly low-level stuff, and remember it's not what we've been used to, with everything you see a hostile. There'll be plenty of Spits around. Takeoff in five minutes."

As confirmation of Rowbotham's warning, the Spitfires took off while they were walking out to their machines, nine of them, looking feminine and ballerina-like with their narrow section wings and close-set wheels. Keith wondered at the untidiness of their initial climb until he remembered that the pilots had to pump up their undercarriage by hand, a tedious and awkward procedure.

Keith got a couple of fitters to help him up onto the wing and dropped into the familiar cockpit. Sometimes it seemed as if he had lived half his life in this little shell, surrounded by the paraphernalia of his calling, from trim wheel to Ki-gas pump, pitch control to mag switches. The fear that his confidence might have been dented by the near roasting he had experienced had not materialized, and it was encouraging to have a new machine with variable-pitch propeller again, especially if this was to be low-level work. In spite of jumping at sudden sounds, he reckoned his nerves were as good as ever, and his leg was not hurting too much.

He gave the thumbs-up sign and a smile of encouragement to the green sergeant in the next plane who was flying number two to him, and then called out "O.K." to the crewman on the battery cart.

Considering that they had only flown together once before, the revived 259 Squadron Hurricanes formed up efficiently, and Rowbotham at once led both flights in three fours east toward the beleaguered town. Passing over the English coast, Keith glanced down, and there, two thousand feet below, were the holidaymakers swimming and lying or playing on the beach at Ramsgate, giving the impression of carefree joy and normality. Fifteen minutes later, by grotesque contrast, the thousands of little figures in the sea off the sandy beaches of Dunkirk were wading and swimming for their lives, out to the boats that would ferry them to the ships awaiting them in deeper water. And those who were stretched out on the sand were either dead or cowering from bursting shells, bombs and machine-gun fire.

Climbing up to ten thousand feet over the burning port, Keith was again conscious, as he had been earlier in the titanic struggle in France, of witnessing history in the making. The ships lying offshore awaiting the tide, from lighters, tugs and launches, to larger tramps, pleasure paddle steamers, coasters and destroyers; the long lines of men, coiled like snakes from the town's promenade, over the dunes and down to the sea; the bursting of shellfire and bombs among them; the intermittent flash of guns from the enclosing line of the besieging German armies; and over it all the black smoke from burning oil tanks, which he could smell in the cockpit even at this height—all this made up a stunning and awe-inspiring panorama of defeat which Keith knew he would never forget.

He was reminded that he was not here as a sightseer by Rowbotham's crisp voice on the R/T. "B Flight detach and vector one eight zero. Intercept the buggers as they come in."

Some heavy flak came up at them south of the town, but it did not last. For a while they saw nothing. Then, faintly against the flat green farmland close to the Belgium frontier, Keith spotted a *Staffel* of ten 109's going very fast and low toward the burning town. He reported them to the flight commander, who transmitted, "We'll leave those to the Spits. It's the bombers we're after."

They did not have to wait for long. A formation of twelve Junkers 88's appeared from the southeast at about five thousand feet below them, obscured from time to time by the broken cloud that separated them from the Hurricanes. They went down at once, and Keith experienced again that familiar sense of tingling expectation before combat.

His number two crossed over as he had been instructed when he turned and clung to his side on the fast descent, with the needle on the rev dial climbing higher and higher.. He chose the rearmost left-hand bomber, and came in dead astern, holding his fire until two hundred yards as a good example to his number two. Then they both fired together, his own Brownings hitting the starboard engine, and his number two missing until the end of his burst when he made strikes on the fuselage. Then they both had to pull up.

The 88's did not lose their nerve. They were still in tight formation and firing back with great accuracy when Keith pulled around in a circle above them, ready to make a second pass. Behind them, he saw no sign of any fighters, only a single Hurricane streaming glycol. His own 88 was smoking but had not fallen out and there was no other sign of damage from the six Hurricanes.

The 88's put themselves into a power glide during the next attack, closing in on Dunkirk, only two minutes away. Keith and his number two had difficulty in keeping up with them, in spite of their height superiority, and they had to pull for overboost to close in. He indicated that his number two should go in first, and he watched the sergeant making better shooting, steady under the return fire from the gunner, whom he killed in a long burst that sent the machine into a steeper dive. Keith followed it down, setting fire to the other engine, then he pulled up again with the intention of renewing the attack on another Junkers.

But the survivors, only nine of them now, were already racing flat out across the town in looser formation. Keith followed them, feeling the sudden turbulence from the heat of the fires as he flew low over the shunting yards and burning railway station, and then across the promenade and the dunes beyond, where flak came up from a dozen places, undiscriminating between friend and foe.

He lost the 88's in the smoke and confusion of bursting bombs, tracer flak, shellbursts in the sand and sea. He also lost his number two, but he could hardly blame the boy under these conditions on his first operation.

Keith patrolled alone for a while, searching for a target

and any more of scattered B Flight. Then, with fuel running low, he headed west for the English coast. The cloud had built up to ten-tenths over the Channel, visibility was fast deteriorating, and he flew at three thousand, just below the cloud base.

He was uncertain of his position when he saw the faint outline of the twin-engined machine ahead of him. For a second he misidentified it as a Blenheim, then saw that it was a Heinkel 111 cruising along quite slowly and giving every impression that the pilot was as lost as he was. Keith pulled back the column sharply, and flew half in the cloud, hoping by this means to approach closer without being seen. He was a bare quarter mile from the big bomber when he saw it suddenly dip its nose steeply and dive. Keith opened his throttle wide again and followed, fearful of losing it in the sea mist which suddenly confronted him.

Ahead he could just make out a flat, projecting coastline with a lighthouse on the tip, a pebble beach, and then, looming like fine skeleton skyscrapers dead ahead of the Heinkel, the towers of a C.H. station. With a sense of terror that tore at his heart, Keith saw that he had drifted far to the west, that this was Swingham, and that it was in imminent danger of annihilation.

Light flak was coming up to meet the Heinkel, but Keith was still far out of range, though he was picking up speed fast and had gone into overboost again. The bomber shallow-dived implacably toward the towers, and was already lower than their tops. He was still trailing the bomber's tail by five hundred yards when he saw the black shapes of the bombs slanting down toward the compound and the base of the two groups of towers, above which the pilot steered with unerring accuracy. Keith pulled up ahead of the towers, intending to catch the Heinkel as it regained altitude. This was a mistake. The visibility, even at a thousand feet, was appalling, and he had to watch in fury as the bomber disappeared into the sea mist and cloud ahead of him.

Keith turned back toward Swingham, which he could just

make out behind him. The delayed action bombs were beginning to explode, sending up gouts of smoke and debris half as high as the towers. Every bomb had fallen inside the compound, and he could see direct hits on several of the buildings, the shock waves fanning out like ripples. He continued to circle in helpless anguish, whispering to himself, "Jenny, my poor Jenny!" Here was the final, explosive culmination of his association with this bomber, which had first terrified him nearly three years ago among the Black Forest pines.

With the slow clearance of the dust and smoke, he could see figures moving through the wreckage, and two men from the undamaged guardroom were tearing at the rubble of one of the nearby barracks.

The need to do something, to learn the truth of Jenny's fate, was a grinding pain. He studied the fields adjoining the C.H. site. They were flat and hard from the dry hot days of May. On some of them posts to prevent enemy gliders and transports from landing had already been installed, and it looked as if stock had been removed from another field, no more than a quarter mile from the ruined site, in preparation for the workmen to move in. Keith estimated that it would give him about four hundred yards, with only a low fence at the downwind end.

He at once threw back his hood, lowered his undercarriage, flaps and radiator, and throttled right back for the approach. He cut the throttle as he skimmed the fence, his Hurricane touched down with only the smallest bounce, and Keith was using the brakes after running a hundred yards. He unstrapped himself and wrenched off his helmet the second his machine came to a halt, and began to run toward the scene of destruction, oblivious to the pain in his leg.

There was the same pungent stench, a blend of hot metal and masonry dust, which he remembered from the day Lens-La Basse had been bombed. There was still a lot of dust about, which stung his eyes as he ran through the open gates. There was shouting to be heard, but no screaming. The first person he saw was a W.A.A.F., sitting in the middle of the road, her jacket and shoes torn off. She was studying her bleeding feet and talking quietly to herself.

Keith tried to remember where the R hut was, but it was difficult to orientate himself when most of the landmarks no longer existed. He found the remains of the administration block first, where a stretcher party was bringing out a corpse without legs and a party of dusty, bleeding airmen were breaking up the asbestos roofing with picks in order to get into the smashed interior.

The R hut should have been a mere fifteen yards from here. And then Keith saw to his horror that it no longer existed. The sandbagged entrance where he had first seen Jenny, the hut beyond leading down to the underground control room, was nothing more than a crater from a heavy bomb explosion. No one could have survived.

A voice was calling, "Give us a hand, sir." Two airmen and a corporal were trying to lever a beam off a pile of rubble which had been a sleeping hut. Two W.A.A.F.'s, bruised and bewildered in their service issue pajamas, were sitting on the grass staring into space. One was holding the torn top of her pajamas across her breasts in instinctive modesty.

When they got the beam clear, other girls who had been asleep before going on night duty could be lifted out. One, who had been sleeping in her underclothes, was dead from a frightful blow on her head. Dragging feverishly at brickwork lying on another girl, Keith was telling himself in the torment of grief for Jenny, "This is not war—war's not like this. Not for women, not for these girls. No," he kept repeating. "No, no, no!"

It was the indecency, the sudden violent deprivation of privacy that was worse than the blood and shattered bodies. The crumpled lisle stocking, the garter belt, the shoe with the lace still tied, the pile of folded but dusty clothes—that was more poignant than the dead girl, who had been so neat, lying beside them.

"I'll be all right," he heard another girl's shaky voice say. "They're worse than me." That was unlikely, thought Keith, as he helped carry out this dreadfully wounded airwoman.

"There's another down here at the end." The burly warrant officer took off his jacket and rolled up his sleeves. Keith heard the sound of several ambulance bells on the road to the camp. Soon there would be plenty of help, skilled hands to care for the wounded. He clambered over rubble to reach the warrant officer. There was a leg sticking out, in a black silk stocking. The warrant officer said, "Gently does it, sir. That's right. Now you take that end . . ."

They uncovered the W.A.A.F. carefully, removing bricks and a large chunk of concrete lying on the other leg. They recognized the better-quality material of her skirt at the same time. "She's an officer, sir," said the warrant officer. She was lying on her side and they knew she was still alive because they could hear her moaning faintly.

The warrant officer said, "Well, if it's not Section Officer Simpson."

Keith was bending down over her bruised face saying, "Jenny, oh my God. Are you all right?" He brushed brick dust gently from her face, and she opened her eyes. When she recognized Keith's face, close above her, she smiled slightly. "Fancy you," she said slowly. "You're supposed to be at Manston."

Keith got his arm under her shoulders. "Does this hurt when I lift?" he asked.

The warrant officer said, "I shouldn't move her if I was you." He got to his feet and left them to help another team of rescuers.

She sat up with Keith's help, grimacing slightly. "What about the rest of you?" he asked.

"I'm not sure yet. But I must look a sight. Give me your hanky, Keith." She wiped the dust from her eyes and pushed back the hair which had fallen across her face. "This leg feels numb," she said, "otherwise it's just aches and pains."

Her voice shook when she talked and Keith could feel her shivering. "I suppose I'm lucky, really."

She looked about her for the first time, at the piled wreckage, the devastated ground, the wounded and dead and the parties toiling among the rubble. There were three white ambulances and a red fire engine parked nearby. Then she turned her head and looked up into the misty sky where the aerial wires between the transmitting towers were hanging in tatters.

"My God!" she exclaimed. "What about the R hut?"

"All gone," said Keith. "Just a hole, I'm afraid."

She looked up at him in horror. "Oh, no!" she whispered. "Oh, no!" Tears welled up in her eyes and coursed down her bruised cheeks, making streak lines in the dust.

"I guessed you were on duty, and I thought you were dead when I saw," said Keith. "I landed in a field . . ."

"But I *was* on duty, don't you understand?" She sobbed and pressed her face against his chest. "I just left for a second to get another hanky. I got a terrible cold the other night with you . . . Oh, I wish I had stayed. It isn't fair that all my girls should die. If I hadn't got that cold . . . Oh, Keith."

A man in a white overall said, "Now, young lady, how are we? Not too bad, eh?" He was bending over Jenny, studying her with professional care. "We'll soon have you out of that and tucked up nicely in Folkestone."

She tried to stand up, but they would not let her, and she winced when they touched her left leg. They eased her gently onto a stretcher. Keith bent over and kissed her sodden dusty cheek. "You'll have a nice long rest," he said. "You deserve it."

She looked up at him without smiling. "I shouldn't have left my girls," she said. "I wish I hadn't."

"I'm very glad you did," he whispered.

Then they took her away and slid the stretcher into the ambulance.

18

"There's a call from the navy for you, Keith," the duty officer called out. "The Admiralty no less."

As he got up from the seventh game of vingt-et-un with Buffer Davies that morning, his opponent drawled, "Air Marshal Stewart to personally escort the First Sea Lord to his bleedin' flagship, I suppose."

All the Immediate Readiness pilots turned to listen and guffaw as Keith spoke.

"Yes, marvelous to hear your voice," he said to Eileen over the crackling wire. "Where are you?" A long pause, with Keith frowning and waving for silence. "I can't hear a thing," he said, putting a hand over his left ear. "There're a lot of moronic children screaming."

At last he got the gist of her message. She was in Whitehall, actually at the Admiralty, and the next day she was going on a preliminary cypher course at Greenwich. Could Keith come up to see her? She so much wanted to see him, and she had some important news.

Keith said, "I can't, I'm sorry. Not London. But I'm going to see a friend in Folkestone hospital. Could you possibly come, too? I want you to meet her. I want you to see if you like her. She's badly hurt. Please come . . ."

Eileen recognized the sharpness of appeal in his voice, even over this line, and at once agreed to come.

"You are an angel." Keith rang off and for a moment was deaf to the comments, ranging from envious to caustic and crude, that filled the dispersal hut. That afternoon he would be seeing two of the people he most wanted to see, and he would see them together.

The weather had clamped down that morning and there was little possibility of flying. There was a thick fog in the Channel and even less likelihood of the Luftwaffe getting airborne from their newly acquired French bases. But Sector insisted on the flight remaining at Immediate until midday, when they were at last released, and Keith was able to get away.

Keith hardly needed a stick anymore, his leg had healed so well, but he took one along anyway, hoping it might help soften the heart of the most steelhearted ward sister. It worked like a dream. Exaggerating his limp slightly, he stumped up to the second floor of the Folkestone hospital, to be received by the flat statement from a nurse that there were no visitors until 5:00 P.M., and then any males had to be relatives.

The sister appeared in the middle of Keith's altercation. She was an elderly, motherly-looking woman, tired from overwork, the hospital having numerous wounded from the Dunkirk beaches. Keith shamelessly exploited his advantage. "No, not a relative but a very old friend . . . I've only got an hour away from my squadron—and I've only just got back from France . . ." And the clincher, "I helped to rescue her from the wreckage and I think it would do her good to see me . . ."

Jenny was in the third bed from the end, her leg in traction as Mike's had been. He walked softly up the ward to avoid waking the other patients. But Jenny was awake, staring out over the gray misty sea, a hand across her forehead.

For the second before he made himself known, Keith found he was filled with a tenderness and feeling of pity he had never experienced before, stemming from his knowledge of her unhappy past and the affection she had shown him in spite of his clumsy callowness.

He was only two steps from her when he said softly, "Jenny."

She turned her head and the infinite sadness he fleetingly caught in her expression turned to pleasure. Her mouth formed into the characteristic smile and her bright brown eyes seemed to savor his presence. "Keith darling!" Then she put her hands over her face, and between them said, "You should have told me you were coming. I'd have done something with my face." She drew her hands away again. "Not that there's much I *can* do."

The bruise marks around both eyes and on her right cheek were medium brown where once they had been black, and her eyes were puffed up too.

He drew up a chair. "Much pain?"

She shook her head. "A bit. Much boredom—that's worse. Oh Keith, it is nice to see you. How's your leg?"

"Better than yours. I don't really need this ridiculous stick. But it made a good visitor's pass."

"You're not flying?"

"Yes, of course. That's how I managed to drop in on you when other things had already dropped on you."

Jenny looked at him in silence for a few seconds, her eyes moving about his brown face from his corn-colored hair to his anxiously smiling lips. "Yes, of course," she said at last, "I'd forgotten. But I remember now, and your voice was such a long way away. It might have been speaking through a megaphone at half a mile. Now that you remind me, it *was* rather romantic, wasn't it. 'Gallant aviator rescues his love after merciless Luftwaffe bombing.' I hope *that* didn't get into the newspapers."

She turned away, her smile gone, as if remembering the girls who had not been so lucky. Keith kept silent for a moment and then said, "You've got another visitor any minute. You remember me talking about Eileen?"

She turned her bruised face back to him, "Of course I do. Your beautiful sister—or sort of. She was the one who dumped you, or so you thought, on the evening we met."

Eileen walked up the aisle between the beds as Jenny was speaking. She looked stunning in her W.R.N.S. uniform and little hat perched on her lovely head, and she walked straight up to the bed smiling lovingly at Keith and then unshyly at Jenny.

"I'm sorry we have to meet like this," Jenny said after the introductions. "Most inconvenient, especially on your precious half day off, all the way down here."

Eileen sat on the seat vacated by Keith. "Don't be silly. It's lovely to meet you and see Keith at the same time. Anyway my war service so far seems to have been mostly made up of sitting beside poor patients lying in traction."

"You mean Keith's friend Mike. How is he?"

"Keith doesn't know yet," said Eileen, turning to him. "He had an incredible escape from Norway, Keith. I'll tell you more later. But he landed on a carrier which was then sunk by the *Scharnhorst* and *Gneisenau* and practically everyone was killed except Mike."

Keith sat down gingerly on the bed, looking at her in horror. "All dead? All the pilots in his squadron?"

"Except those who came back by another ship. And his flight commander."

"That'll be Avery. Oh, yes," Keith said bitterly, "trust him to survive."

"That's what Mike said. What's the matter with the man?" Eileen asked innocently.

"Never mind for now."

Eileen turned back to Jenny. "What happened to poor you?"

Jenny explained briefly, and then they talked happily and easily together, Eileen saying that she ought to have saluted her as an officer when she came in and Jenny congratulating

271

her on her uniform and nonissue black stockings. "I bet that suit wasn't cut by His Majesty's Tailors," Jenny said with a laugh, and Eileen confessed it was Smithers of Cork Street.

"But I've also got something serious to say," Eileen went on, "and I'm going to be a coward and say it in front of you so that Keith can't misbehave."

Keith stared from one to the other, a leaden feeling of the inevitable creeping over him. Yes, this'll be it, he was thinking. I knew it would come. It had to come. And now I must behave properly . . . Oh Lord!

It did come, quickly and nervously, which softened Keith's heart. "Mike and I are engaged, Keith. Mummy and Daddy don't mind—in fact they like the idea, and I hope you do too."

Keith felt Jenny's eyes on him, and as he spoke he hoped that he would have used the same words if she had not been watching him. "I'm very glad. Really I am. Mike's going to get through this lot all right. And perhaps he'll ask me to be best man. And perhaps he'll . . ." He turned to Jenny, who responded with the crisp practicality he loved in her so much.

"Don't get all maudlin, you silly boy. If you're thinking of proposing to me, you must be mad. Women don't want proposals when they're lying like I am, looking like this. They want a bit of Ivor Novello, you must know that." She turned her face and looked out at the discouraging sea, her voice sounding tired. "Anyway I'm old enough to be your great-grandmother."

Eileen was on her feet. "Enough of this matrimonial talk. Anyway there's a war to be won first. And Jenny has had quite enough of us." She put out her hand. "It was lovely meeting you. I'm sure we'll meet again. And I'll try and get a commission so I won't have to salute you."

She left, leaving Keith alone with Jenny for a moment.

Jenny said, "I like her. What a nice person to grow up with—if you're unlucky enough to be an orphan, that is.

Now I want to meet Mike." Keith saw that her eyes were closed, and she said in a soft voice. "But not yet. When I'm better."

Keith leaned over and kissed her unbruised cheek. "Get well soon, dear Jenny."

"Open the drawer beside you," she said, "and wear it for me when you fly. It's a bit tarnished. They found it in the wreckage."

Keith took the brass cap badge from the drawer. It was very dirty and the pin was bent. He put it in his pocket and kissed her again. She was already half asleep, but she managed to say, "Good-bye, dear Keith."

Eileen was in the hall, staring out over the wet lawns of the garden and swinging her gas mask idly. She smiled when she saw Keith and said, "You don't walk so badly, now."

"Well enough to walk to the station with you."

They walked in silence for a while, watching the sea mist roll in from the Channel. There were men camouflaging newly built blockhouses, painting them to look like seaside kiosks, and rolls of barbed wire were being run out and pegged down across flower gardens already running wild. There would be no summer tourists this year and some of the "bed-and-breakfasts" along the front had been closed and boarded up for the duration. The enemy was only twenty-five miles away, and Folkestone would soon be more a fortress than a town.

"Why didn't you tell me about Jenny before?" Eileen asked.

"Why didn't you tell me you were going to get engaged, for that matter?" Keith replied more sharply than he had intended.

"You've just said you're glad so it's too late to sound cross."

Keith slashed with his stick at a pebble thrown up onto the esplanade by recent high seas. It eased the pressure fractionally. But he still had to keep a vigorous hold on his temper. And with Eileen of all people—beloved Eileen!

273

"I'm not sounding cross. And I am glad for you. But I'd be sorry if it was just another bit—another part of the muddle of this beastly war. Things get funny in wartime. People do things they wouldn't do normally. And I don't mean just killing and getting hurt like Jenny."

Eileen sounded contrite. "Yes, I know. But it's nearly three years since we met, don't forget. And there wasn't a war on then. We're being very sensible, don't worry. And I expect you and Jenny are, too."

"You do like her, don't you?" Keith asked anxiously.

"I'm sure I shall. But it's a bit early to tell, after about ten minutes, I mean. When did you meet her?"

Keith told her, leaving out the bedroom bit, and Eileen laughed. "So if we hadn't gone off to the Kennedys' you'd never have met. Wasn't that lucky!"

They were at the station and the train was due to leave in a few minutes. A group of sailors turned as they made for the barrier and whistled, and one yelled, "You leave her to us, Brylcreem Boy—she's too good for you."

Keith ignored them and said good-bye as the inspector took the ticket. Eileen kissed him and he held onto her for a moment, staring into her shining green eyes searching for the elusive truth. All those years together, yet somehow the spontaneity had gone, driven out by separation and the violence and unbalancing effects of war.

She said, "Good-bye, and don't let those horrible Germans hurt you again."

"Good luck at Greenwich."

The ticket inspector said, "Hurry now, love," and Keith walked away out of the station and back down Cheriton Gardens to the seafront. His sense of melancholy and dissatisfaction was matched by the sight of the sea again, and a light drizzle was falling. He remembered some old cliché about war destroying more things than lives and cities. But surely it could never hurt his relationship with Eileen and her family?

He could just make out the gray shape of the hospital

274

and was tempted to return to it. The sight of Jenny, lying hurt, and the sound of her voice and the touch of her hand were what he yearned for at this moment. But the bus was leaving in ten minutes and the war could not wait. His leg began to ache again as he made his way toward the bus station. The drizzle turned to a steady rain and he turned up his collar, but he could not run.

Why did she have to say it was a bit early to tell? Why couldn't she simply say, "I think she's marvelous." It wouldn't have cost her anything. And I could have remembered that over the coming months instead of "It's too early to tell." It looks as if they're going to be difficult enough months anyway.

The bus drew up alongside the little knot of wet passengers. Keith was the last to get on. The conductor, more than triple his age and with scarcely a tooth left in his mouth, leaned down and offered him his arm. "All right, sir?"

"Fine, thanks. Very kind of you." Eyes turned toward Keith as he sat down stiffly. He looked out of the dirty window at the rain. Only fairly fine actually, he told himself. Not miserable, but not altogether 100 percent O.K. And I wish to God I hadn't asked Eileen to come . . .

Then he remembered and drew the dented brass cap badge from his pocket and felt better. He decided to string it alongside his identity tags so that he would wear it always. He considered himself completely unsuperstitious, but judged that they were both going to need good luck over the coming months.

19

Mike was showing off his feet in the officers' mess at Savile Farm, claiming that he could step into Pavlova's shoes any time.

"You're welcome," someone remarked fatefully. "She's been dead for nine years."

During the first days after his return from sick leave, Mike had been regarded more as a survival miracle than a recovered pilot, let alone a ballet dancer. Neither the ground crews nor the pilots had asked him about his ordeal, recognizing that he would prefer to forget the horrors of that night of cold and death, when the C.O. and the other pilots, and all but a dozen of the crew of the *Swiftsure* and her two escorts, who were picked up by a Norwegian fishing boat, had succumbed to exposure or died in the shellfire. The loss of the ships had been announced officially, but for security reasons no mention had been made of the R.A.F. casualties.

For his part, Mike had said nothing about the action that had led to the sinking of the *Swiftsure* and her escorting destroyers, nor the ordeal of the following night and day. He prayed that never again would he have to witness death at such close quarters, in such numbers and under such agonizing circumstances. The memory of those sights and sounds on the cold ocean was tucked away in the deepest recesses of his mind. But even if he never spoke of it to anyone—and he swore he would never do so—it would always be there, as black and cruel and merciless as guilt lurking within a good man.

Perhaps later he would tell Eileen of the Walkers, stoic and solemn, as rigid as a steel member of the Tyne Bridge down the cobbled road from their house. Mike had only just managed to hobble the few yards from the taxi, and was thankful for the physical pain he suffered because it marginally distracted him from the anguish he felt in his guilt for surviving, and distracted the couple from their grief.

Over a characteristically large Geordie tea, Mike told them of their son's courage and skill, how he had saved his own life and what the C.O. had said of him. Then he gave the couple the sergeant's wings, torn at one corner from Mike's fumbling with his frozen fingers. Yes, they had been asked to come to Buckingham Palace on a day in July, and wasn't that nice, their fare would be paid . . . Then they helped him to the door and into his waiting taxi.

Dowding's staff at Fighter Command had decided to re-form 140 without delay in order not to lose the *esprit de corps* of a squadron with such a fine fighting record under Anson. Some experienced pilots and half a dozen young men straight from O.T.U. had been assigned to it, a new C.O. was daily expected, and it was hoped to work the squadron up to operational status at its peacetime base in the south in not less than two weeks. The three pilots detached to 259 Squadron in December, and all now hardened by combat with the cream of the Luftwaffe, had all been transferred back to add new steel to the battleworthiness of the squadron.

It was the third week in June. The Norwegian and Dunkirk evacuations, the first a major accomplishment, the second a miracle, had both been completed, and Winston Churchill had warned Parliament that "We must be very careful not to assign to this deliverance the attributes of a victory. Wars are not won by evacuations." He had added, "But there was a victory inside this deliverance, which should be noted. It was gained by the Air Force."

From New York, Mike's father had sent a clipping from *The Times,* which had summed up his own feelings about the raw drama in the events in Europe, and also reflected his own and Mike's mother's pride and anxieties. "So long as the English tongue survives," ran the leading article, "the word Dunkirk will be spoken with reverence. For in that harbor, in such a hell as never blazed on earth before, at the end of a lost battle, the rage and blemishes that have hidden the soul of democracy fell away. There, beaten but unconquered, in shining splendor, she faced the enemy."

After Dunkirk, a temporary lull had ensued in the struggle between Britain and the new German Empire, which stretched from the North Cape, far north of Narvik, to the Spanish frontier south of France. Benito Mussolini had now dragged Italy into the war, sniffing at what was left of the spoils, likened by Churchill to a jackal, and by the American president to a murderer who knifes his neighbor in the back. On one side of the Channel, the Germans made steady efforts to build up an invasion fleet, while the British with more urgency steeled themselves for the blow and made every possible preparation with the inadequate material and arms available.

The war in the air had changed temporarily from the German assault that marked the opening of the *Blitzkrieg* to spasmodic but fierce flare-ups. Once, London and the southeast of England had been beyond the range of German single-seat fighters. Now, with all the French airfields at their disposal, more than a thousand 109's could cross the English Channel in minutes and support their cohorts, the twin-engined *Zerstören,* in covering bomber attacks. The R.A.F. had lost almost five hundred Hurricanes and Spitfires in the French campaign and over Dunkirk. All that now stood between German conquest of the air over southeast England and the invasion that must follow were some six hundred Spitfires and Hurricanes and the men who flew them.

The newspapers told of mammoth efforts to build up the rate of fighter production, and the flying training schools were rushing pilots through their final stages. Mike had heard of other American volunteers in England already converting to Hurricanes and Spitfires. Nothing since the beginning of the war had given him greater satisfaction than this news that more of his countrymen were joining him.

Keith and Buffer Davies arrived at Savile Farm on June 22. Garbo had been dug out of her garage and Buffer had contrived to procure enough gasoline to drive the seventy miles from Manston. Mike was reading in the mess when he heard the familiar growl of the massive motorcar. He went to the window and saw his two old friends, who had survived as many brushes with death as he had.

Buffer had painted five black crosses along Garbo's bonnet. "Do you think that's a bit of a line, old boy?" he asked.

"Well, I think it's a bit ostentatious," Mike commented.

"I don't know what that means. But they'll come off after I've downed a noggin or two. It's grand to have the old bus back, but she does give you a bit of a thirst. All that open air."

"It's the dry throat of fear for me," Keith said feelingly, but Buffer failed to hear; he had already spotted a red-haired Section Officer through the window and was drifting in the direction of the door.

Mike and Keith looked at one another. They were both smiling, and holding pint mugs of beer. Mike raised his. "Well, buddy," he said, "we're alive."

Keith took a sip of the bitter. "Here's luck," he said.

"I guess we've had our ration of that, so don't be so goddamn greedy," said Mike, laughing. He quickly corrected himself. "No, there is a bit more luck. Guess what?"

"Tell."

"No Avery. No kidding—no Avery. The Spy says the Walrus from the *Devonshire* took him on board after he left us at Romstad. And he came back safe and sound with the King of Norway and his staff. How do you like that?"

"Very much his style," said Keith. "Now what about my home?"

Mike told how he had arrived at Rising Hall to find Sir Richard Barrett having the time of his life drilling Local Defence Volunteers on the terrace, armed with shotguns and pitchforks. "Hell, they looked fierce. Like Wellington said before Waterloo—'I don't know what effect these men will have upon the enemy, but, by God, they terrify me.' "

Keith laughed, and then looked quizzically at Mike. "And Eileen?"

Mike finished his pint, stalling for time. "Well," he said, wiping his mouth, "she got four days' leave. Just to help me recover, you understand. And boy, doesn't she look swell in that Wren outfit! I nearly forgave her for joining up. Sent her love to you, of course . . . I hope you don't mind, Keith. Your step-parents don't, and . . ."

"You mean you got engaged—properly," said Keith, helping him out. "Yes, she told me. You nearly deserve her, too. And you only don't because nobody does."

Mike laughed and put on his appalling English accent. "Very decent of you, ol' boy, ol' chap."

"You've never met my Jenny," said Keith matter-of-factly. "You were in hospital when she turned up at Elgin, completing an R.D.F. course. She's a grand woman—you'll like her." He told Mike of their first meeting, of their very different meeting in the rubble of Swingham, and of his visit to her in Folkestone General Hospital where she was recovering. "Eileen came too," he added, "as you'll have heard." He had succeeded in reconciling himself to Eileen's apparent lack of spontaneous enthusiasm for Jenny, ascribing the trouble to his oversensitivity or general overwroughtness at the time. It would take more than that incident for the brightness of Eileen's star to dim even slightly in his mind.

From the women they turned inevitably to their next love, their Hurricanes, and their adventures with them. They were arguing about their own most difficult landings when the Spy came in.

Mike turned to him as arbitrator. "Which is more spectacular and dangerous, Spy, to land on a frozen lake with bombs and bullets whistling around you and on the heaving deck of a carrier in a gale, or on a nice smooth French road and a field in Kent—which Keith claims demanded so much goddamn skill?"

"I give you both ten out of ten as line-shooters," said the Spy.

They gave him a drink. "You're looking even more somber than usual, Spy," Keith commented. "What's eating you?"

The Spy, bowed over his drink, said, "The news is not good." He looked up at them darkly. "The new C.O. is arriving tomorrow."

"What's his name?"

"You won't believe it. But you'll have to. It's our dear old friend, Avery. Been sucking up to the powers that be at Bentley Priory, I suppose. Great record in Norway. King Haakon gave him a medal. The natural successor after the tragic loss of that great leader of men (and I can hear his voice dropping reverently) Squadron Leader Anson. Anyway, that's it." He turned and called out to the barman. "Three whiskies, please, and make them large double doubles . . ."

Squadron Leader Avery arrived after breakfast in a Humber staff car of the larger variety, with F/11 on the rear, and an unusually attractive W.A.A.F. driver. At the meeting he soon called, he affected a grave demeanor, but there was no mistaking the satisfaction he was experiencing at his elevation and the disdain he felt for all of the old-timers who had questioned his style as a flight commander. Keith realized he might be imagining it, but there seemed to be less defiance and more steely self-confidence in his stiffness now that he had gotten what he wanted. He was a different man from that taut, uncertain figure at Uxbridge all that time ago. Or had he been uncertain? Keith would never know. He decided he liked him even less and feared and distrusted him even more. And now Avery was to lead them!

"Well, chaps, it's very good to be back." He beamed at them and stroked his moustache. "We've had a bit of a pasting and lost some wizard chums. Now we've got to build up again for the great test that still lies ahead. I'm goin' to see to it that . . ."

The clichés came rolling out "like bombs from a Heinkel's belly," as Mike later described them. Keith glanced at Mike, whose eyebrows rose perceptibly. This is a tough enough business, Mike was thinking, without having this smooth arrogant bastard with a yellow streak in him as C.O. How can 140 ever recover its old spirit with this man in the cockpit leading us?

In the afternoon, the old hands were sent up, each with a new pilot to gain experience and carry out a sector reconnaissance. Keith felt better after that. It was good to be back in this part of the country which he knew so well, and to be passing on his experience to another pilot. He, Mike and Buffer and the other old hands were regarded with some awe by the new sergeants and pilot officers fresh from O.T.U., and Keith could not help being flattered by their admiration and their inquiries.

On the following day, however, Avery took up the squadron on what he called a full battle rehearsal and cross-country. This took them to Tangmere, and to Keith's dismay Avery ordered them to fly in V's of three, which had proven so disastrously inflexible in combat, and very tightly at that. Over France in the last weeks, 140 would have been massacred. Even here, over southern England, they might easily be jumped by marauding *Zerstören*.

"Tighten up, chaps. Right up," Avery ordered as they

passed over the South Downs at two thousand feet.

This is like a Hendon Air Show demonstration, Keith thought, as he carefully watched his number two and number three bring their wing tips close to his tail, while keeping a sharp lookout behind. But Avery was evidently determined to show off his squadron's prowess, and they flew over the center of the airfield, splitting neatly on the other side for landing.

"I guess we'll get used to it," Mike said quietly at the mess bar before luncheon.

"If we live to tell the tale," Keith answered bitterly. Avery, in his best bonhomous style, and brushing his moustache with great vigor, was recounting some of 140's experiences in Norway to the Station Commander and the C.O. of one of the Hurricane squadrons based on Tangmere.

Mike signaled over two of the new pilot officers. The old-timers had agreed that they should avoid all cliquism, talk about their past experiences only in terms of improving their future fighting efficiency, and above all utter no word of criticism of the C.O.

The Spy, representing all their views, had put it like this: "He's here, we can't move him, he hasn't blundered—yet—so we'd better work with him. It's wonderful how some people improve with new-won authority," he had added hopefully, knowing that he would not be believed.

There were signs over the following days that Avery had absorbed some of the lessons of the Norwegian campaign. He nagged less, worked harder, and in his own way, showed himself determined to make 140 into a crack squadron. He also showed himself to be even closer to the Fighter Command hierarchy than they had all suspected when he succeeded in acquiring for himself for trials under combat conditions a prototype improved Mk II Hurricane, with a more powerful Mk XX Merlin engine, and four Hispano 20-mm cannon in place of eight machine guns. This put the range and killing power of its armament far ahead of the Mk I Hurricane and the Spitfire, and of anything the

Germans possessed. Avery's Q-Queen prototype was his pride and joy, and was the center of attention for any visitors to Savile Farm.

One studying this much improved Hurricane for the first time in its specially guarded pen, Mike commented, "Give that guy his due, he can sure swing things with the bosses."

Keith patted the barrel of one of the big projecting cannon. "I only wish he could swing one for all of us. Now the Hun's fitting armor plate to his big bombers, our .303's are going to be like peashooters."

On the last day of June, B Flight was scrambled, because no fully operational Squadron was available, and to Mike and Keith's surprise Avery led the flight himself, a welcome change from the old days. A Hudson crew, back from a photographing mission over France, had come down in the Channel. The position of their dinghy was reported as fifteen miles north of Alderney. One-forty was to give cover to a Walrus which was going to try to pick them up.

Avery, always a good navigator, led them to the dinghy, a small yellow oval, without any difficulty, and they patrolled in two V's of three above it at three thousand feet, awaiting the arrival of the amphibian. Ten minutes passed, then twenty minutes, and there was still no sign of the Walrus. She came into sight, low over the water, after nearly thirty minutes. At the same time, Keith's number two reported bandits to the south. A dozen 110's, whose suspicions had been aroused by the continued presence of the Hurricanes, were coming out to investigate. They were well below them, and on a course that would bring them onto the Walrus.

Keith, leading Green Section, was ordered down to attack. "We'll give you top cover," added Avery.

They would need more than three Hurricanes to save that Walrus from destruction, Keith figured as he led his section down in a steep dive. We don't want top cover. We want more guns, especially those cannon.

The fight with the big *Zerstören* at wave-top height was brief and sharp. The Hurricanes managed to break up the attack, but could only delay the end of the Walrus. Keith was busy with two of the German planes which were making passes at his tail when he caught a fleeting distant glimpse of the Walrus, its single engine on fire, diving steeply toward the sea. After that, there was no more than another thirty seconds of combat before the Messerschmitts departed and Keith could look about him. He made out four Hurricanes, which suggested that the other flight had come down to help them.

But no one was giving any orders, so, with their fuel now low, Keith transmitted, "Green Leader calling. Form up on me. I am rocking my wings . . ."

The five Hurricanes cruised back to Tangmere at economical speed, and Keith was able to assess the results of their operation. Was the disaster compounded by the apparent loss of Avery and his precious prototype machine? It was difficult to judge. That they had failed was abundantly clear, and Keith felt sick at the loss of that helpless rescue plane.

As they went around the circuit at Tangmere, tanks almost dry, Keith identified with shock Avery's Hurricane taxiing in to its dispersal. How had he managed to get back so long before they had?

The C.O. explained that in no uncertain terms in the dispersal a few minutes later. He had already had to report failure to Group and he was black with rage. "Am I the only one prepared to mix it with the Hun? This squadron's got a yellow streak in it and I'll have the lot of you out on L.M.F.* if I have any more of this skulking," he threatened.

"Luckily, I got two of the buggers after they had finished off that Walrus, on the way back to their base, while you were all arsing about."

No one asked him how he had managed to return five minutes before them when he claimed to have pursued the *Zerstören* toward their base. But Mike told Keith quietly later, before they took off back to Savile Farm. "That's hog-

* Lack of Moral Fiber

wash. He came down with us—some of the way at least. Then I lost sight of him. I guess he streaked for home when he saw it was going to be tough . . ."

The idea was so monstrous that Keith looked at Mike as if he had lost his reason. "And," Mike added, "this is not the first time."

Over the next days the air war began to heat up again, and 140 was scrambled a number of times, even though they were still not regarded as fully operational. Mike, Keith and Buffer Davies had conspired together to fix up a form of private communication for use in emergencies in order to bypass Avery. They regarded their "Channel X" not only as a form of self-preservation but as useful for the safety of the squadron as a whole. It was brought about by a quiet conversation with "Sparks," the wireless corporal, over a few drinks one evening at an out-of-the-way pub. It called for the adjustment to a special V.H.F. wavelength of one of the several spare channels on the sets of their aircraft. It had proved useful on a number of occasions already.

On the Fourth of July, when Mike had planned an elaborate party at the Black Lion, they were kept on Readiness all day, and late in the afternoon were brought up to Immediate. Avery was driven down to the dispersal at half past six and announced that something big was brewing, and ordered the two flights to have their meal in shifts.

At eight o'clock in the evening they were all weary of the sight of the hut, and of each other. They had played chess, pontoon, bridge, darts and shove-halfpenny. They had taken part in a two-hour tip-and-run cricket match against the ground crews, and lost.

"They're convertin' us to night fighters, old boy," Buffer announced facetiously. He was suffering stoically the loss of a party and "the popsy I've organized" to go with it. "They've decided there's too much birdin' and boozin', so we'll be sleepin' all day and flyin' all night. And that," he announced solemnly, shaking his head, "is very bad."

But when the Scramble call came through at 8:30, three-quarters of an hour before sunset, there was still plenty of light in the sky.

"The Hun's trying to make a nonsense of a convoy in the Channel," the Spy told them before they grabbed their gear. "He's been at it most of the afternoon." He wished them good hunting, and remained at the door as he always did, watching them with his hooded eyes until the last plane had disappeared.

Mike, who usually took it in turns with Keith, was leading Blue Section with Keith as his number three, Buffer Davies behind and to the right of the C.O. A Flight had an experienced commander who had been with Hurricanes in France, and who deplored the traditional fighting formation insisted upon by Avery as much as the old hands from 140 and 259.

The southern suburbs of London slipped away behind them as they gained height, breaking through scattered cloud at six thousand feet into a brilliant sun that was setting behind them. They went out between Rye and Hastings. The controller vectored them onto a patrol line ten miles off the coast. "Sandbag Leader, I have no trade for you. Are you in contact with Imperial?"

Avery, flying his easily identifiable Q-Queen, confirmed that they were over the convoy, a small one of twenty coasters, some of them flying protective balloons and escorted by two *Sandwich* class sloops. They could see the ships intermittently in the cloud breaks 12,000 feet below. Keith glanced across at Mike to check his position. He had his goggles up and his hood open, as he often did when things were quiet. Keith knew how impatient he was to get on with his promised Fourth of July party, and he was struck again by the strangeness of his new wartime existence, when they could be shooting unknown men into the sea early in the evening and be drinking too much in the comfort of their local pub an hour or two later.

The thirteen Hurricanes turned at the end of their patrol

line, and Keith could see that the long shadows thrown by the ships had dissolved into the sea, indicating that the sun had already set down there. In another twenty minutes they would return to Savile Farm, with the alternative of Hawkinge, just outside Folkestone, if they ran low on fuel after combat or pursuit.

The controller's voice came through crisp and clear. "Sandbag Leader, I have trade for you now. Thirty-plus bandits at Angels Fifteen thirty miles southeast of you steering northwest. Vector one-two-zero."

The Germans were coming in for one last dusk attack on the convoy, a favorite trick of theirs. If they had to fight so late in the day, Keith hoped that they would be Junkers 87's and not 88's, which were difficult enough to deal with in broad daylight.

Group was calling up another squadron from Biggin Hill to support 140, and Keith could imagine the pilots cursing as they were scrambled after sundown. Five minutes later he picked up the faint voice of the leader, airborne now and giving his call sign and acknowledging the course he should steer.

Avery put 140 into a standard straight line in *V*'s of three, with number three of the last section acting as "tail-end Charlie." They spotted the dive bombers below them, steering straight into the near-horizontal sun, which sparkled on their perspex canopies and gave the impression of a diamond-studded pendant hanging in the sky. They were 87's all right, Keith confirmed, ripe game even if there were nearer fifty than thirty of them, and seemingly unescorted, too. But there would be a snag in it. Oh, yes, he predicted with the cynical wisdom he had rapidly acquired in so many fights with the odds always against him. There would be a snag somewhere.

Their own course was dead on, indicating that Swingham was in full operation again, and Avery put them into the old single-line battle formation which had proved time and again to be so inefficient and inflexible. "Tally-ho!" he transmitted, his voice even on R/T revealing that curiously unctuous timbre, redolent with self-satisfaction. Well, we'll see whether he has reason to be pleased with himself, Keith reflected. And he turned his button onto fire and reduced the brilliance on his reflector sight in anticipation of the darker sky below. The 87's tightened up, the *Stukageschwarden* ranging themselves to give the most effective concentration of defensive fire.

Keith saw Mike, two planes ahead, break the neat line before Avery gave the order, and he followed him and their number two into the right-hand side of the formation. The 87's made a slow, fat target by contrast with the bigger twin-engined bombers, but they could put up a lot of fire and Blue Section, in the vanguard of the attack, took the brunt of it.

He saw the thin trail of cordite smoke trailing from Mike's wings as he opened fire, shooting as always with that steady, deadly precision Keith knew he could never match. His own target was firing back with a 9-mm machine gun, and the tracer came up at him, at first deceptively slowly, then raced past just above his hood. "Sitting ducks, my eye!" Keith exclaimed to himself, resisting the urge to take evasive action.

He made hits in the wing root before pulling up, still pursued by the tracer. Out of the corner of his eye he caught the image of a yellow flash, then he saw no more of the bombers until he could pull around for a second pass. A black cloud and falling debris marked the end of one of the 87's, and two more were trailing smoke and going down fast.

Before Keith could get in among them again, they were over the convoy, and the Stukas were rapidly and in turn going over on their backs, revealing the single heavy bomb under their belly and four smaller bombs under their wings. With dive brakes extended, they began falling at 75 degrees toward their targets.

The scattered Hurricanes went down after them, but the 87's made awkward targets in their steep, slow dives and Keith saw several of his squadron overshooting. The dangerous moment for the bombers was when they pulled out. It could also be the most deadly moment for the attackers. As confirmation of his fear, Keith caught sight of 109's racing toward the convoy low over the sea, like a flight of homing mallards at dusk. Yes, there was the snag.

"Bandits on the deck," he transmitted urgently, as no one else seemed to have spotted this menacing counterattack.

The sky above the convoy had suddenly become a tumultuous confusion of heavy and light flak bursts, tracer fire that was all the more vivid in the gray light, and aircraft in every position and in every attitude planes could assume. This was air fighting at its most breathtaking, most confusing and most terrifying, its backdrop the dark ships, their trailing balloons and the waterspouts of exploding bombs. The chorus of warning cries and exclamations crowded the ether. A Hurricane went straight past Keith's line of vision trailing flames that momentarily blinded him. A Stuka went into the sea with its bombs, the explosion sending the 87's fragments high into the sky like a cannon's grapeshot.

The second Hurricane squadron joined battle, adding to the congestion. Keith saw one of them blow a 109 to pieces on his left, then he saw a brief opportunity for himself and put a two-second burst into a climbing 87. Exploding shells rocked him as he was about to open fire again, and he jammed forward his column and went after another Stuka.

The impressions were as fleeting as the dogfight itself, with the dusk light adding further to the anarchy. Keith caught a glimpse of Buffer's R-Robert trying to get onto the tail of a climbing 87, and of a 109 climbing fast from sea level. His attention was momentarily distracted by an uncomfortably close burst of tracer streaking above his own cockpit. He kicked his machine through 90 degrees with the brutality that the Hurricane always forgave, so that he was behind

Buffer and his target at a range of some five hundred yards. In the second or two that had elapsed, he saw that the climbing 109 had gotten directly behind Buffer, and it was clear that he had not been seen.

Keith shouted a warning cry and fired a short burst at the 109. The range was far too great. But it looked as if the German himself had been bounced in turn, for another Hurricane, with the letters RC-Q, was right behind at a hundred yards' range, perfectly positioned to blow the 109 to pieces. Keith waited for it to open fire, knowing that he was helpless to save his friend. Instead, the Hurricane ignored the sitting target, turned aside and dived down toward the sea.

In the next nightmare second, Keith knew that Buffer was done for. He watched in helpless horror as the German fighter poured a long burst of cannon and machine-gun fire into the Hurricane's belly. The last picture of the tragedy Keith's eyes recorded was of R-Robert upside down, its belly torn open as if by a killer shark, and smoke pouring from the engine. He pushed his own Hurricane through a 180-degree climbing turn, and when he looked about him again, the sky appeared empty except for a now distant Hurricane, and another a quarter mile away on his right.

The two machines came together for comfort like survivors from a holocaust. The plane was Mike's. Thank God he was all right. The American transmitted their single code letter X, and they both switched channels. "Where in hell is everybody?" he asked. Even the convoy was lost in the murk of the dusk. What a way to celebrate the Fourth of July!

They flew out to sea side by side, straining their eyes for any sign of a stray fleeing Stuka they might pick off. After two minutes of searching Keith said, "We'd better get back."

"Like hell!" Mike exclaimed. "What about that, at one o'clock below?"

It was no Stuka. It was a fighter, hard to identify in the half light, going fast toward the French coast.

"We'll have him," said Keith.

Mike called, "You take starboard, I'll take port. O.K.?" And Keith remembered those same words Mike had spoken eight months ago when they had shared their first kill, the first of so many kills, friend and foe alike.

They split apart and climbed into the broken cloud that might allow them to stalk their prey unseen. Both were on boost override, but with Keith's machine proving marginally faster. He was five hundred yards ahead and slightly below Mike, straining to keep the racing fighter in sight in the cloud breaks and against the dark sea which almost concealed it except where the white of breaking wavetops momentarily outlined a wing, a part of the fuselage or the tail.

There was something wrong about the configuration of this 109. Its wing tips were not square clipped, and a second later he saw that the tailplane lacked the 109's characteristic understruts.

"My God!" he breathed. "It's a Hurricane. Going the wrong way." Or had *they* been going the wrong way? Was that why every other Hurricane except Mike's had disappeared so quickly? It was the easiest thing in the world to become disoriented after combat. But the last of the light was behind him. No, he and Mike were traveling southeast —he did not even have to consult his compass. Nobody could fly to France in error under these conditions.

It was Mike who guessed right. "The son of a bitch's had enough. He's doing a bunk!" he transmitted crisply.

It had been known to happen before. On both sides. Especially during the Great War when there was no chance of salvation if you caught fire, and your nerves were cracking. But it was a shock to witness it occurring, like this, before your eyes.

"Shall we talk him back?" Mike suggested.

"Hold it a moment. We'll have to be sure." Keith paused. "Oh, no we won't," he added violently. "It's Q-Queen. And he did for Buffer just now. He let him be shot down—I saw it!" Keith, with the advantage of the better light on the

Hurricane's starboard side, could just make out the letter Q, white against the dark camouflage-painted fuselage, just aft of the wing root, and the four projecting cannon barrels. The prized prototype!

There was silence between them as if the enormity of the offense and the manner in which they must deal with it were beyond words.

The sand dunes just north of Le Touquet were below them now. Mike said shrewdly, "We haven't got gas or ammo for a fight. Wait until he lands."

Some light flak came up at Avery's Hurricane below from a battery on the eastern end of the town's *plage*. The sound from his Hurricane must have drowned the roar of their own Merlins and the cloud was seven-tenths here. More flak inland helped them to relocate the Hurricane when they dropped through a break in the cloud. But the pursuit was almost over. Avery was clearly wasting no more time, and, as always, taking the least number of risks. There was a field of ripe grain running slightly downhill, but large enough many times over to take a Hurricane, wheels up.

Mike watched Avery circle once very low, flaps down, hood back. He could just make out the head and characteristic stiff shoulders of the pilot, too preoccupied with the business of getting the touchdown right to look up into the dark, cloud-stained sky.

On a sudden impulse Mike switched the channel of his radio back to sector frequency when he saw that Avery was irreversibly committed to landing.

"You've had it, you son of a bitch," he snapped at him, putting all the contempt he felt for the man into the expletive.

He knew that it was a cruel thing to do, and he regretted it later and never told Keith what he had done. He could only partly excuse himself by totting up the multiple iniquities of the man, the deaths others better than he had suffered at the price of his own safety. And this act of throwing in as a bonus to the Hun his Mark II machine. Mike knew that they were right to kill Avery, but he also knew he had been wrong to vent his spleen like that.

The result of his words, spoken loud and clear when any other transmission of this channel would be distant or inaudible, and the message they conveyed, made the Hurricane rear up as if the shock had caused Avery to jerk back his column. Mike imagined him opening the throttle wide in a desperate attempt to regain flying speed. But he had timed the message just right. This Hurricane would never fly again. The Germans would be deprived of this secret and pricelessly valuable prototype fighter, just as they would be deprived of this man as a prisoner in safety for the rest of the war.

Q-Queen touched down heavily on its belly, and beat down a great swath of the grain as it ran and turned through 180 degrees and came to rest.

Avery was out of the cockpit almost before it stopped. He looked up. Mike saw the white of his face staring momentarily at the circling Hurricanes like two birds of prey above their quarry. Then he began to run.

Mike had pressed the button to get back onto X channel, and now he said quickly, "You get him. I'll see to the kite." He was in the better position to get the grounded Hurricane into his gunsight. With the sight turned all the way down to avoid glare, Mike came in at 20 degrees. He guessed he had only a second or two's ammunition left after that hard fighting. So every bullet must count if he was to deprive the enemy of this gift.

Keith, on the west side of the field at less than a hundred feet, banked steeply and kicked his Hurricane toward the only object he could see clearly, Avery's stationary machine. As he approached it, now flying parallel with Mike and below him, he strove to catch a glimpse of the figure. He thought he saw him running toward the hedge surrounding the field, brought the dot of his sight onto it and gave a short burst.

The tracer was a handicap now, half blinding him as the bullets raced away on their trajectory. Keith was sure he had missed, and was uncertain that he had even identified his target.

"I can't see him," he called to Mike in anguish.

Mike did not reply. Keith had spoken at the split second when he was steadying the dot of his sight between the engine and wing root of Q-Queen, which now looked as helpless a victim as a wounded animal awaiting its fate. Mike pressed the button for two seconds, catching the heady reek of cordite in his nostrils, before he heard from his guns the ominous clank of empty breech blocks. But two seconds was long enough. The Hurricane burst into flames just before he flew over it very low, the heat punching up at his machine so that he had to correct quickly and steady it.

When he looked back the flames, blue at their base and turning yellow above, were higher than he had been flying and the late dusk landscape was suddenly lit up for half a mile. The exploding ammunition provided an accompanying garish display more spectacular than any Fourth of July fireworks Mike could remember.

Keith had his cockpit hood thrown back to improve visibility and was turning low over the east end of the field in a steep bank when the flames shot up. The light of the blaze brought out the detail as if Mike had dropped a flare, showing a tree in black silhouette against the golden grain, the tiles of a workman's cottage, the wooden fence on one side of the field, the hedge and ditch on the other, startled cows in the next meadow.

It was a frozen scene. The stock appeared paralyzed, the tree as if cut from board. The cottage might have been from a child's toy farm. Only one object was moving. Avery, brightly illuminated, was running frantically toward the ditch and was more than halfway there, a desperate figure, his flight toward safety impeded by the waist-high grain.

Keith hardly had to alter the bearing or the attitude of his Hurricane. He just pushed the column very slightly forward, turned up the rheostat of his sight, and steadied the dot on the figure. Gently he nursed the nose of his plane to follow his quarry's course toward the edge of the field.

He was assailed by no doubts. The balance of compassion and practical necessity no longer existed. There was no time, nor need, for questions even if he wished to pose any to himself. And he did not. Any more than he had when he had held that simpler weapon aimed at the head of the storm trooper. Now he had eight machine guns. And again no doubts. No pleasure, no satisfaction, and no doubts. Only the steadiness that now seized him when there was killing to be done and which had made him good at it.

Mike was two hundred feet above, watching the Hurricane in its shallow dive past the blazing pyre he had made of Q-Queen. He saw the sparkle of the Brownings, the annihilating Deuser bullet pattern, synchronized at 200 yards, flailing the ground.

Mike was wondering how he could have known it was going to be like this when he joined the R.A.F. so lightheartedly back in those half-playboy, half-adventuring days of his idealistic youth? He should have known, after the squalor of Spain, that this was going to be no shining crusade. Then—Sammy Crow blown to pieces, the agony of that raft, white-faced Sergeant Walker dying in his arms. And now this. Execution for treason and cowardice. How could he have predicted any of this? No splendor. No chivalry. No Rupert Brooke nobility. Just killing. Oh, Christ . . . !

Avery was hurled horizontally thirty feet by the tearing metal of Keith's burst of gunfire, crushing down the grain in his path. He had lost the definition of a human body when he came to rest as a confused collection of tissue, organs and bone.

The flames had died down to a sulking bonfire by the time Keith had gained enough altitude to turn safely. It was unthinkable that he could wish to look down closely at his killing. It was enough that it was done. But he would have seen little anyway. The darkness had closed mercifully about the savaged corpse of Squadron Leader Avery, who had dishonored his service when he was most needed.

"We'll go home now," Mike called. In its terrible way it had been a sublime performance, far from Keith's hesitant shooting that he had witnessed at Rising Hall when they were still innocent boys. But he knew Keith would prefer no comment. "My gauge registers nil gas."

A searchlight groped for them on the way out, and again some desultory flak came up from Le Touquet. Over the sea they gained altitude, and at seven thousand feet they rediscovered the last glow of the sunset, which touched their cockpit canopies deep red. If they flew toward that they would soon hit the blacked-out coast of England.

Yes, some Fourth of July! And some party! Their own Fourth of July. Independence Day. And a kind of independence had been achieved for their squadron. At a price.

Keith felt the proximity to Jenny when, ten minutes later, they flew low over Folkestone and called Hawkinge for permission to land. Tomorrow he would call in with Mike to see her before they returned to Savile Farm. Nothing would be said about this, of course. Not yet. Perhaps never. But he felt a desperate need to see her again, to experience her comfort and warmth, to listen to the voice he loved talking lighthearted sense, to look into her brown eyes that could appraise him with such candor and affection. He wanted all this before he had to face again the renewal of battle that lay ahead, which was as inevitable as the landing he must now make in the dark, lining up his Hurricane for the approach between the lights of the flare path.

Acknowledgments

The author wishes to thank the following for their generous assistance: Wing Commander Robert Stanford-Tuck, D.S.O., D.C.F.—R.A.F. (Ret'd); Lieutenant Commander John Casson, O.B.E.—R.N. (Ret'd); Captain J. G. West—R.N. (Ret'd); Mrs. Cynthia Thomson, ex-W.A.A.F.; Dr. John Tanner, M.A., Ph.D., F.R.Hist.S., Director of the Royal Air Force Museum, and the staff of his Library; the Librarian and staff of the Royal United Services Institute; and Denis Richards, M.A., an old friend and author of the official history of the R.A.F. in the Second World War.

The extracts from the song, "It's Raining Sunbeams," © 1937, were reproduced by permission of Robbins Music Corp., Ltd., 138–140 Charing Cross Road, London WC2H 0LD.

R. H.